Sign up for our newsletter to hear
about new and upcoming releases.

www.ylva-publishing.com

Other Books by Lee Winter

On the Record series
The Red Files
Under Your Skin

The Superheroine Collection
Shattered

Standalone
Sliced Ice
Hotel Queens
Changing the Script
Breaking Character
The Brutal Truth
Requiem for Immortals

a Brutal Truth world novel

the awkward truth

career climbing just took
the oddest turn

lee winter

Acknowledgments

So many people helped me on this book.

To start at the beginning, my dear friend Marija Jelavic has worked with the homeless for years, organized open days servicing their needs, and understands intimately the lives and requirements of those on the street. She is also the great dispeller of myths and will shred to pieces anyone spouting ignorant idiocy about the homeless—even her own friends at her own dinner party. Saw that one firsthand! She's been a wonderfully kind and valuable resource.

Thanks also to the awesome and patient veterinarian Kate Buffin, who, among other things, helps out homeless people's pets. From her I learned more than I expected to know about high-on-weed dogs and the grossness of impacted anal glands!

Fellow author Quinn Ivins ran my math over the abacus to see if it worked. It did! After a fashion. I thank her for correcting my percentages vs. ratios.

Ann Etter was a godsend at helping me navigate the accounting world, specifically relating to charities and Form 990s. Think of it as a boat…or not.

Gail T. Brown gave me charming and thorough insights into all things South Bronx. She also pointed out that no unattended, street-parked vet's vehicle would still have its wheels attached by the next day, so I'd better find a fix! Her love for the area was infectious, and I'm now dying to try rainbow cookies, and the entire menu at Full Moon Pizza.

Author K. D. Williamson stepped in as my sensitivity reader once more. Thanks, as always, for the insights, bluntness, and honesty. Much appreciated.

Carolyn Bylotas was my official *Brutal Truth*-expert beta reader. It's amazing how much you forget between writing books. Thank you!

Astrid Ohletz, my publisher—and an excellent beta reader, too—pointed out whenever my ice queens were just too chilly to function. Always good to know!

Alissa McGowan and Julie Klein, my content and copy editors, respectively, helped whip my rambling words into shape with their expertise.

And lastly—thank you for the outpouring of enthusiasm for this "sidequel" to *The Brutal Truth*. The excitement I felt from readers on social media really spurred me on. Among them was Shannon Luchies, who not only came up with the term "sidequel" but also the perfect, apt book title.

There are also a couple of nuts and bolts in the book I want to mention.

The facts and statistics in my story about New York dog attacks, insurance claims, weird rich-people tax abatements, and so on, are all real. The 1482 and 1483 bills mentioned are real as well and were first introduced to the New York City Council in March 2019 to "accommodate pets of homeless individuals and families" in the shelter system.

Maybe one day street homeless won't have to choose between a shelter and keeping their pets, but at the time of this writing, those two bills remain in committee, on hold and unpassed.

Sadly, no laws have been put forward to allow for homeless people seeking addiction treatment to keep their pets with them, too. That was wishful writing on my part.

Anyway, from the bottom of my heart, I thank everyone who helped me create my fictional world, and thanks also to all those who help the homeless and/or their pets in the real world.

For all the good boys and good girls—no matter where they call home.

Chapter 1
Focus: Absolute

ON NOVEMBER 23, AT 10:07 a.m., Felicity Simmons seized her boss's tea mug and hurled it against the wall, changing her life forever.

"I am not your assistant, Elena!" Felicity stood ramrod straight and glared. "I'm NOT who you pay to fetch and carry and make drinks and photocopy paperwork. I will *never* get you another fucking chai latte ever again, so don't bother asking. I'm your *chief of staff.* Do you understand that? I'm a trained lawyer, exceptional at what I do, and I deserve to be treated accordingly."

"I see." Elena's pleased little smile took all the wind out of Felicity's sails. "It took you long enough."

Then Elena promptly promoted her.

Astonishing how a career could be advanced with nine pieces of ceramic and a sticky wet spot of chai latte (nonfat milk, extra hot) on the gunmetal gray carpet. No one ever said media mogul Elena Bartell was predictable.

It was now March 10, 8:58 p.m., well over three months later, and Felicity was still trying to get her head around what had happened. She stared out her glass balcony doors at the jutting skyline from the thirty-second floor of her Manhattan apartment. Felicity might even be able to pay her mortgage off this year with the pay hike that came with going from Elena's chief of staff to deputy chief operating officer, soon to be running all of Bartell Corp as acting COO. That did not seem real. None of this did.

A noise made her start, and she peered into the darkness of her balcony, although she had a pretty good idea as to the culprit.

Her building's balconies comprised one long strip of concrete flooring on each level with a glass parapet in front. Each apartment's balcony sides were chest-high, frosted-glass dividers with funky stylish holes to let the wind through. Unfortunately, the little holes were ideal climbing aids if you had paws. As a result, Loki, her next-door neighbor's cat, hopped from balcony to balcony and liked to make herself at home in Felicity's pair of designer topiary trees.

Oh, Felicity might not have caught the creature in the act, but she'd seen plenty of leafy evidence that the beast liked to claw her way up the tree stems, bursting up into the rounded balls on top like something from *Alien*.

This was unacceptable in about fifty ways, of course, from the defiled expensive trees to enduring an animal with trespassing issues. Perhaps the worst part was the fact that it was a cat. Felicity didn't like cats anywhere near her. Dogs, either. It was a boundaries thing. As in they had none.

Felicity knew she was being watched. She rose and slunk over to the wall next to the balcony, then flicked the lock on the sliding glass door. Inching open the door, she pushed it along its track, leaving the thinnest of gaps. Thanks to twenty years of watching her diet with the diligence of an A-list actress, the thinnest of gaps was all she needed.

The rustle sounded again.

Felicity drew in a deep breath and rammed her hand blindly into the foliage.

"Ow! Shit!" She pulled back as little puncture wounds appeared on the back of her hand.

A cream-colored head suddenly burst through the ball of leaves, blue eyes connecting with Felicity's.

They both let out a startled noise before Felicity gathered her wits, lunged forward, and grabbed, a hand clamped on each tiny shoulder.

She stared down at her squirming quarry. Good lord, the thing was like a little pom-pom with eyes. A Siamese kitten! The cuteness overload made her itch.

"Shouldn't you be posing for an Instagram page instead of attacking me and mine?" she asked acidly.

The pom-pom hissed.

A shriek sounded, outraged and piercing, and Felicity turned to see her neighbor gawping at her. The aptly named Karen Henderson was an angular forty-something doctor's wife who had a righteous opinion on all things, the pettier the better. How she hadn't wound up on a Karens Hall of Shame on social media yet was something of a mystery.

"Loki!" Mrs. Henderson gasped. Her accusing gaze flicked to Felicity. "You're strangling my kitty! Put her down right now!"

Felicity supposed her hands did look suspiciously like they were around the squirming animal's throat, but that was not the case. She marched over to the barrier separating the balconies.

"Loki should be called *locust*," Felicity noted, thrusting the animal toward its owner.

The woman snatched it off her and made cooing noises as she rocked it back and forth.

Loki eyeballed Felicity over her owner's shoulder as if plotting some nasty vengeance.

Felicity scowled back. That cute act was fur deep, clearly.

Mrs. Henderson spun back to face her. "What sort of a monster attacks a beautiful, helpless kitten?"

Helpless? Felicity had puncture wounds that told another story. "What sort of an idiot fails to keep her pet indoors?" Felicity retorted. "That's an expensive pair of imported lilly pillies she keeps defiling."

"She's a kitten!" Mrs. Henderson protested. "Sometimes she gets out. Have a heart."

Felicity narrowed her eyes. "Look, lady, lock up that devil spawn. I don't want to ever see it on my balcony again or I'll bill you for my gardener's pruning fees, and FYI, they're the high-end kind that cause nose bleeds."

"Monster! Oh, I pity you. The bitter, sad, lonely lawyer with no friends."

Ouch. Felicity had no idea her dubious social life was such common knowledge. "What? I'm not bitter. I'm a dedicated professional with high career goals."

"No, Ms. Simmons, you're a sad case. I know because you hate animals." She didn't wait for an answer, instead turning and taking Loki indoors, slamming her balcony door shut.

Felicity turned to mirror the exit strategy on her side, but her nostrils twitched. She glanced down to discover her feline visitor had left a steaming, smelly calling card in her potted plant's dirt.

Lovely.

Cleanup was a job for daylight and industrial-strength gloves. Sighing, she went inside. After delousing in the bathroom—animal saliva and claw marks could carry diseases, that much she knew—Felicity poured herself a glass of wine. Dropping onto the swanky nine-thousand-dollar couch that was the highlight of her apartment, she stared outside at her now disheveled tree. Damn, Loki. Perfection ruined.

Her eyes drifted to her own image reflected in the glass.

A bitter, sad, lonely lawyer with no friends? That was quite an impressive list Mrs. Henderson had flung at her. Not even remotely true, of course.

What do I have to be bitter about? Felicity was on top of the world professionally. Her mentor, Elena, had finally recognized her worth.

Okay, it was true she hadn't made time for friends, unless you counted her local Starbucks employees, but frankly, their getting her triple-shot espresso right every morning was an absolutely beautiful relationship.

And it was equally true her bed was absent any warm companion these days. But pfft, no loss there. Hardly her fault that her new promotion meant she was now permanently based in New York after ten months in Sydney, nor that Phillip's lack of interest in a transpacific relationship had brought things to an abrupt end.

"You're not worth it," he'd said.

That still stung.

Neither are you. That's what she should have said, of course. Instead, she'd just stood there speechless like a gaping seagull, trying to think of something clever to say while he walked away.

But it was all moot. Relationships, friendships, exes. They could all go toss their emotional deadweights into the Hudson. *Finally* her career was about to hit its peak. Everything she'd ever worked for or sacrificed for was all within touch. That was all that mattered. She plucked a stray cat hair off her designer pants with determination.

No, when it came to her work, her focus would be absolute.

◆

Elena Bartell leaned back in her austere black leather chair, smug as a cat in a puddle of sun.

Felicity surreptitiously wiped her hands down her tailored navy pants. *Appropriately corporate, not too bland. Elena doesn't like bland.* God, it was hard to sit still under the Tiger Shark's scrutiny, but she'd known this was coming. It might be a Friday, but this was day one of her training to take over Elena's job so her boss could then swan off to Australia and edit her international fashion magazines from there. It was the world's most mystifying career pivot, of course, and an even stranger choice of destination, but Felicity wasn't about to look a gift horse in the mouth.

"Your replacement for chief of staff seems adequate enough," Elena said. "Perhaps don't ask Scott to fetch your tea, though. Rumor has it chiefs of staff don't take kindly to being asked to play assistant."

Felicity felt the heat of her instant blush from her collarbone to the tips of her ears. "Erm. No."

Oh, very smooth, Felicity.

Elena smirked, which just made her even more intimidating. Her black hair was slicked back, highlighting her pale skin and razor-sharp high cheekbones and bringing out her palest of blue eyes, which always gave her a lethal quality. That, paired with her pin-striped vest, matching trousers, and white silk shirt, made for an imposing impression.

The curious thing was that Elena was not tall. In fact, Felicity was taller, but next to her boss she often felt like she was shrinking—a turtle retracting its long neck back into its shell. Somehow Elena projected a greater presence than anyone Felicity had ever met.

She couldn't look at Elena's direct, amused stare, so her gaze shifted to everywhere else. It roamed to Elena's desk. Gone was the picture frame that had held a photo of her now ex-husband Richard. *Thank God. Waste of a pulmonary system, that asshole.* Her eye fell to a new frame that hadn't been there a day ago. She craned her neck just a little—subtly—to see who'd been promoted to frame-worthy status. Then she had to force herself not to jerk away.

Good God. What on earth was Elena Bartell doing with a photo of *Maddie Grey* on her desk? The blunt former night-shift reporter from Australia had somehow connected with Elena. Who'd fired her. Then rehired her. And fired her again. Honestly, it was hard to keep up.

Somehow after all that they were now…friends? How had that happened? Felicity had been in Elena's life for years longer and had never been worthy of a framed photo. And if Felicity didn't know for a fact that the twice-divorced Elena Bartell was entirely heterosexual, she'd side-eye the hell out of that photo.

Felicity swallowed back her surge of jealousy. No, she wasn't doing this again. As part of Felicity's new resolutions to be a better person, she'd promised herself to no longer fixate on all the ways Madeleine Grey kept winning at life, even though she *totally didn't deserve it* and even if she was rather engaging, if you looked past the *totally didn't deserve it* point.

The silence had dragged on far too long, and Felicity realized with a start that she was being watched as she studied the photo.

Elena's expression was neutral, but her eyes were speculative. She waited, eyebrow half-cocked, as if expecting an awkward question.

Since Felicity was in the business of making her boss's life comfortable, not the other way around, she met the look with her usual aloof lack of interest.

Finally, Elena seemed to give up waiting for a response and shuffled some papers. "All right." She took a sip of tea from a mug on her desk that Felicity had bought her to replace the shattered one. "I'm breaking it in," Elena said, "especially since my other one met its untimely demise."

"Oh. Yes. Well, I'm truly sorry about that."

"I'm not. I've been waiting for you to be the woman I knew you could be. To stand up and demand to be treated only as a chief of staff. I was curious how long you'd take, and until recently, I didn't particularly care as I had no urgent need for you to evolve. But that has changed. Your timing was useful, given my new plans."

Felicity stared. "Well" was all she could think to say. That wasn't embarrassing in the least.

Elena chuckled, a low, throaty timbre that Felicity had taught herself several years ago to never find sexy because that would just be weird.

"Felicity," Elena said in a not unkind voice, "I cannot have someone running my company in my absence who has no spine. I need someone I trust, yes, but they have to be strong, too. I've seen you stand up to intimidating and powerful people for years. You do it for me. I need to see you do it for *you*, even if you're worried I won't approve. And that's not all I want to see more of. I have a little assignment for you."

Felicity sat up straight, mentally readying herself for anything.

"But before I give it to you, I've just been on the phone with some very angry lawyers from *The Mornington Herald*. They seem to be of the opinion that you just canceled our mutually beneficial buyout deal."

"I did."

"Isn't that the paper that employs Brad Tolliver? That acerbic columnist with a reader following in the hundreds of thousands? The same columnist *you* suggested could make us a bundle in syndication rights if we acquired the paper he's contracted with?"

"Yes." Felicity paused. "I outlined what happened in my management report. I've emailed you."

"I'm still only a third of the way through my inbox. Explain."

"I terminated the deal after I couldn't get the editor to confirm that Tolliver was still under contract with them at the time of negotiations."

Elena frowned. "He has to be. Our deal specifically named his contract as an asset we wish to acquire."

"I know. So I made some discreet inquiries. Turns out two months ago, when his contract expired, Tolliver found out he was pivotal to the buyout bid with us. He's been stalling signing a new contract to get more money from his publisher."

"Surely now that the buyout deal's at risk his paper will offer him anything to get him signed on. So why wouldn't you wait for that instead of axing the deal prematurely?"

"I did the sums and looked more closely at the other assets we'd get from acquiring *The Mornington Herald*. It's not worth it. The independent engineering report showed the aging printing presses have some worsening structural issues and need an overhaul. I know we were hoping to utilize the presses for additional external printing jobs, but that's out of the question. I concluded it's more cost-effective for us to kill the deal and sign Tolliver exclusively to a Bartell Corp contract. Tolliver's syndication potential was the only unique selling point in acquiring his paper at all."

Elena leaned in. "I see. What happened next?"

"Tolliver said he'd sign exclusively with us for twice his current salary."

"Which would be far cheaper than more or less buying his masthead just for his contract. It's a bargain."

"It is. But I said no."

Elena's eyebrows lifted. She waited.

"Instead of a hundred percent salary bump, I offered him five percent more and threw in travel expenses. Capped, of course."

"He agreed?" Elena asked in surprise.

"Immediately." Felicity hid her smirk. "He wants to travel America, and he can write on our dime from wherever he roams. That's his official reason. I also observed he's an arrogant young man who wants to get laid—often. So once I explained we'd make him famous with a new national syndication column deal, he jumped at it."

Elena snorted. "That's excellent reading of your target."

"Yes. Well." Felicity fidgeted at the compliment. "I had a hunch. It paid off."

"Okay, how much did we save killing off *The Mornington Herald* deal, subtracting expenses we've invested in it so far?"

"Four point two million dollars."

Elena's smile turned wolfish. "Well now, that'll teach a publisher not to pay their bird in the hand. All right, I'll tell their lawyers we're not changing our minds and to get over it. Which Bartell Corp publication will you base Tolliver at?"

"He's a bit of a pain in the neck and believes his own hype. I've chosen Boston National News Publications. Syndications manager Michelle Masterton should keep him filing on deadline, and she's also agreed to oversee his travel budget."

Elena gave a small laugh. "Poor man. Michelle could scare the spots off a leopard. Good." Her eyes became half-lidded "*Very* good. You keep surprising me, Felicity. That's what I like to see. Which brings me to your special assignment."

Felicity straightened, pleasure burning at Elena's approval.

"Last August I heard about a charity called Living Ruff New York, which helps the pets of homeless people. This charity goes out to the streets to the homeless, supplies pet food, offers free access to animal healthcare, neutering, and so on. The story I read about them was compelling, so I decided to make an anonymous donation." Elena's blue eyes grew stormy. "A sizable one."

With a nod, Felicity waited. It was hardly the first time she'd noticed anonymous donations in Elena's private expenses. She always did take on such odd little charities, though. Like this one, it seemed.

"The charity should have been flourishing for several years on the money I gave them, but less than twelve months later, I see *this*." She spun her computer monitor around to face Felicity.

Charity for animals of the homeless facing closure

The story explained the impending closure of the charity due to lack of funds, and the attached photo showed a smiling woman with a natural tan and sandy blond hair pulled into a ponytail who was holding a huge dog. The caption read: "Dr. Sandy Cooper, a vet at Living Ruff NY, with Gladiator, the American Bulldog she is checking up for homeless veteran Martin Ruiz."

"There is no possible way Living Ruff New York could have gone through the funds I gave them in such a short time," Elena said firmly. "So I contacted the charity director, Harvey Clifford. Since my donation was anonymous, he had no idea why I'm interested. I hinted I might be considering giving to his charity, but first I wanted to ask whether the story was true. I explained that if the charity is about to call in liquidators, there's little point in me throwing good money after bad."

"What did he say?"

Elena's eyes narrowed. "He claimed the story was just a play for more donations, they're business as usual, and the charity is not about to close. He welcomed all new donations and called the news story a media beat-up. Christ, the man is a terrible liar." A look of disdain crossed her face. "He's trying to tell someone who owns half the world's newspapers what a media beat-up looks like? They *never* look like that. Sympathetic and with quotes and photos from the staff? This was a management-endorsed story."

Felicity nodded. "So the director was lying."

"Yes. I'm just not sure why. Maybe this *is* just a way to drive more donations, maybe not. But I want to know for sure. I want to know where my money went because if it's been embezzled, I'll be damned if I'll be taking that lying down."

"Understood," Felicity said, on firm ground now that she understood the problem: assess a charity's full financial status and work out where Elena's donation had gone. "We can get Thomas in accounts to—"

"Thomas has lost my faith."

"What?" Felicity blurted. The man had been with Bartell Corp for sixteen years. He was their most senior accountant.

"When I originally made my donation, I had him check that the charity's books were sound and all was aboveboard. I asked him to *personally* look into it. I found out today he'd handed that task off to an underling. When I ask someone to handle something themselves, I don't mean find someone less qualified whom I do not know or trust to…take a stab at it."

The man was a complete fool. Elena always meant what she said. "Right. Yes, I see."

"Good," Elena said, eyes tight. "Now I need someone I trust to investigate what Living Ruff does and how, and determine whether there are any irregularities. Wave around the possibility I might make a donation, should they be less than forthcoming."

"Charities by law have to disclose to the public their financial status," Felicity said with a frown. Surely Elena knew that already? "Most post their financial statements on their websites."

"Of course. And Living Ruff does that, too. It's also listed on multiple charity-accountability websites as excellent. But you know more than anyone from the deals we do how often a business hides details it doesn't want disclosed. So it's simple—go down to that little animal charity and find out where my money went. But I want discretion. I know you can barge in like Rambo to get things done. Can you do *delicate*, Felicity? Nuance? I want to know whether my new acting COO can problem-solve using a softly-softly approach while far outside her comfort zone. So let's find out. Show me who you are."

Felicity blinked. She could be subtle, for God's sake!

"I am not implying you can't do it," Elena said carefully. "I've just never given you much scope to test yourself in subtleties or come up with outside-the-box ideas. So I need the problem defined, then a solution for it, and my name kept out of all of it. My best-case scenario involves the fewest people possible aware of what you're up to and how you've addressed it."

What on earth? Since when did Elena tiptoe around anything? "Why?" she blurted out.

"Felicity," Elena said with a sigh, "if I wanted to get the police involved, I would have simply called them."

"You…want to protect the charity?" Felicity asked incredulously. "Even if they've misused your donation?"

"Of course not. But good charities can close on the merest hint of investigation. I don't want that happening if everything *is* aboveboard."

"Okay. But what if they are straight-up corrupt? Surely we'd get the police involved then?"

"We'll cross that bridge when we come to it."

Felicity sensed Elena was holding something back. Did she know someone involved in that charity or something? Or maybe she thought it would reflect badly on her if it came out that she'd dumped a lot of money on a charity that was corrupt without doing her due diligence first. Curse Thomas for putting her in that position. He was lucky he still had a job.

"It would be easier for my investigation if you would allow me to tell the charity you've already donated and have a right to know where your money went."

"No."

Felicity didn't bother pushing it. Elena had long protected her privacy on the causes she chose to donate to. It was smart; she'd be inundated by people with their hands out if they knew how generous she could be.

"So," Felicity finally said, almost afraid to ask, "how much did you donate exactly?"

"One point four million."

Holy hell! Felicity's eyes widened, and she didn't entirely manage to stop a choking noise from the back of her throat.

"Mm," Elena said, voice tight. "So now you see my concern. Get to the bottom of this. And don't take anything that director says at face value. Dealing with that man was like trying to talk to a sheepdog."

"A…sheepdog?"

"Exuberant, overfamiliar, and somehow clueless. Solve this for me, Felicity. Show me what you can do."

"Of course, Elena." Sudden pride swelled in Felicity's chest. "You can count on me. It shouldn't take more than a few hours to get to the bottom of this. I'll just—"

"Felicity," Elena said, cutting her off, "I expect you to take a lot more time than that. Take a week or weeks, if you have to. I want thoroughness, as if I were doing this investigation myself. Fine-tooth comb."

"I— Yes, of course, Elena." Wait— *Weeks?* "How can I learn to be your replacement as COO if I'm off with a charity? I can't do both."

"All in good time. And I can always extend my time with you if needed when you return."

Oh. Well. Felicity wasn't sure how to take that. "So...where exactly is this place?"

"The Bronx." A slow smile crossed her boss's face as she slid her gaze over Felicity's expensive suit. "Maybe...dress down a little when you head over there next week. I mean, if you have that in your corporate wardrobe."

Felicity's throat tightened. *The Bronx? The actual Bronx?* She wondered if she'd start hyperventilating. That did not sound safe. Or clean. Or...nice. Felicity made it her business to only swan around in safe, clean, and nice.

Elena's eyes were practically gleaming with amusement now. "Good luck." She took one last sip of her tea and placed the mug on her desk with finality. "We're done."

Chapter 2
Roller Derby Amazons

Felicity spent the weekend researching everything she could find on Living Ruff in preparation for her visit on Monday. Apparently, it wasn't a regular charity but rather a foundation set up by a wealthy, clever socialite called Rosalind Stone. Felicity knew her by reputation—a shrewd operator to be dismissed at your own peril—but hadn't ever met the woman.

Rosalind famously loved animals and threw an abundance of parties for her rich friends to raise money for Living Ruff. That explained the charity's annual donations of about $700,000, a tidy sum for such a small organization that had on staff one director, two full-time vets, several retired vets as on-call temps, a receptionist/vet tech, and a part-time cleaner.

It was still early, the sun barely risen, and Felicity hadn't quite managed to get out of her cozy mellow-gray Lunya pajamas and into something befitting a corporate weekend warrior. She hunkered deeper into the warm blanket cloaking her on her couch and poked around a few more research websites on her phone.

She had determined it was unusual for any foundation to run its own charity hands-on rather than just cut a check to whichever organization did the closest work to what they endorsed. But apparently, Ms. Stone didn't do anything by halves. Or perhaps she liked the power trip. After all, the board was headed by Rosalind and stacked entirely with her family and friends.

The director—the "sheepdog" Elena had mocked—was Rosalind's husband, Harvey Clifford, an unremarkable man on the page with a background in bookkeeping who had married far above his station. Maybe his appeal would be obvious when Felicity met him, but so far she couldn't see it. Little wonder, perhaps, that Rosalind had kept her own name after marrying the man.

A sound distracted her, and she glanced over to the balcony doors to see Loki creeping past on her way to the nearest lilly pilly.

Felicity's eyes narrowed. "Hisss!" she called out loudly, flapping her arm to shoo her away.

Loki stopped, turned, met her eyes, then sat. And bold as brass began to lick her paws as though she hadn't just been caught in the act of repeated interloping.

Picking up a cream and blue cushion, not even caring that its provenance was a French boutique...from *actual France*...Felicity hurled it at the glass, where it bounced off harmlessly.

Loki shot up the plant's stem and disappeared into the ball of green at the top only to reappear a moment later, her white pom-pom face and huge eyes all that were visible.

"Oh, come on! You couldn't even *pretend* to care I can see you?"

"Mreoow."

"You'd better not use my lilly pillies as a litter box again, or I swear..."
What? What would I actually do?

Felicity sighed. Was it seriously the worst thing in the world if she couldn't contain *every* element in her ordered life? She glanced back at the kitten. "Consider yourself lucky that I'm both solving a mystery and having an existential crisis."

Loki merely ignored her and maintained her treetop vigil.

Giving up, Felicity returned to her work with a huff of annoyance. So far she'd dug up Living Ruff's Form 990PF from last year. Charities had to supply these annual financial summaries to the Internal Revenue Service, which in turn posted the information online. With a final scan of the most recent 990 and still finding nothing obvious amiss, she called Thomas.

"Ms. Simmons?" came a disgruntled voice. "It's six on a Sunday morning."

"So it is. And if I were in Elena's bad books for dropping the ball, I'd be *very* keen to get in her good books again by helping with a question she wants solved."

That woke him up a little. "What question? What can I do?"

"Look into Living Ruff for me. *Yourself* this time." She took another deep draft of hot chocolate. Not even close to the buzz her triple-shot espressos gave her, but she was trying to break bad habits. "Find out if they're hiding anything."

"What makes you think they are?"

"Elena donated $1.4 million last September. It's only March, so too early for this year's 990 to be submitted, which would show where that money went. But it went *somewhere,* if one news article is to be believed saying the charity's about to fold. I need you to find out if they've been up to any funny business. Go back over all the 990s and anything else publicly available. You accountants know where all the figures are buried."

"Yes, of course."

"I need it COB Tuesday at the latest. Call me as soon as you know something."

"There may be nothing to know. Peter's preliminary investigation before Ms. Bartell donated found nothing irregular."

"And Peter's been in accounting for how long?"

Silence fell.

"Exactly. No wonder Elena is disappointed in you. So can I count on you, Thomas," Felicity asked, voice silky, "to help Elena?"

"Of course." Worry filled his voice at the reminder. "Always."

"Good." Felicity hung up without further ado.

"We're here, ma'am," Bartell Corp's senior driver announced.

Felicity's gaze flicked from her phone to the uninspiring washed-out two-story redbrick building in front of them. Graffiti tags littered the bottom of it. She sighed. Classy joint.

She glanced back at Amir as she gathered her things. It wouldn't be long now and he'd be taking up Elena's offer to relocate to Sydney to drive for her there. Quite the adjustment for him. Was it loyalty, Felicity wondered, or simply an opportunity for better weather that made him accept such an enormous lifestyle change?

Loyalty, probably. Elena had that effect on people.

Felicity found it hard to imagine anyone loyally dedicating themselves to her in the same way they did Elena. But honestly, as long as her staff did their jobs, she didn't care whether they loved or hated her. She didn't much think about them at all. It always shocked her that more people didn't share her supremely logical view of the world.

It was still early, and the gleam of metal caught her eye. A grubby man with unwashed hair was shuffling past, pushing a shopping cart loaded with his possessions. He was the third homeless person she'd seen in as many minutes on the drive over. She pursed her lips. Would it kill someone to fix this situation? It was a failure of the system to have the South Bronx's streets strewn with tired and miserable unfulfilled people pushing their worldly goods around. Honestly, how hard could it be to solve?

Next to the redbrick building was a vacant park, which seemed an ironic use of the word, since it had no trees or nature of any kind. Only concrete seating areas and a few square tables. What was its function? She frowned. Surely no one would willingly eat their lunch here to admire the view of—she squinted—three pawn shops, a donut establishment, and an eyewear office with a cracked window.

Illegally parked amidst all that concrete sat a white van half facing the street, marked LIVING RUFF. Well, it made sense they'd have their own vehicle, since outreach to the homeless was part of the charity's mission statement.

She glanced back at the charity's headquarters. A line of windows on the top level yielded no sign of life. The large shuttered window at the front below a worn sign that said LIVING RUFF NY also screamed "shut."

"It's supposed to be open by now," Felicity murmured to Amir, and flicked to her phone. "The website says '7:30 a.m. to late. Our doors are open to all.' Got a funny idea of open."

"Yes, Ms. Simmons," Amir said amiably. "Do you wish to wait for them to open?"

The man deserved a gold medal for sedateness. His unruffled personality was as genial as the way he drove. On that note, he'd probably never had a speeding ticket in his life.

Felicity had always thought life should be accomplished at full speed—God only knew if you'd get everything done otherwise. She never walked anywhere. No, she paced and strode and stalked. Far more efficient, if you asked her, than those who sidled about, stopping to smell the roses.

A movement caught her eye, and she swiveled to see a homeless man who had buried most of his body inside the Living Ruff van on the driver's side. The hell? Some passing hobo had just broken in and decided to rummage about looking for something to steal.

With the door blocking Felicity's view, she could only see grubby jeans-clad calves sticking out and boots that looked like they'd worn through every layer of polish and were back to raw leather.

Oh, hell no.

Amir gave her a startled look. "Ms. Simmons?"

Had she said that aloud? Whatever. Her eyes hardened on the thief. What if he were about to make off with goods purchased with Elena's donation? That made it personal, didn't it? She had an obligation here. "I'm going in," she told Amir. "Call the police if things get dicey."

Amir's eyebrows shot up in astonishment. "Ma'am?"

Felicity flung open the car door, leaped out, and headed over to the vagrant at a fast clip. He was still busy rummaging, so she tapped him hard on the back—well, poked, more like—and said, "Excuse me! Just what do you think you're doing?"

The man straightened, bumping his head on the van ceiling as he did and emitting a sharp, high-pitched yelp. He spun to face Felicity, unfurling to full impressive height.

Felicity took a startled step back. Okay, who in the ever-loving Brienne of Tarth was this?

To begin with, *he* was a *she*. And not just any she. The woman was block-out-the-sun tall and solid as a brick wall. She had powerful thighs and broad muscled shoulders that looked like she could probably toss a Shetland pony with ease.

Felicity's breath caught when her gaze slid down. Generous breasts and an unexpectedly rounded stomach softened her imposing form so that she looked a bit like a teddy bear—well, if teddy bears came in Amazon-at-the-roller-derby editions.

Felicity blinked. She'd never encountered anyone like this before. Never, ever, *ever*.

With few exceptions, the professional women in Felicity's circle of media, law, and fashion tended to fit a certain type: delicate and fine-boned TV-ready perfection draped in expensive corporate attire. They were sleek ribbons of femininity who seamlessly melted into spaces and backgrounds. They observed, played clever games from the shadows, and manipulated their worlds one high fake laugh at a time.

This woman took up the space of three such women. Her whole attitude seemed to shout, *Yeah, just try and budge me. And good luck not noticing me!* Probably followed by an amused wink.

Amused wink? Felicity's fried brain was clearly just making up nonsense now.

The woman cleared her throat.

Felicity shifted her gaze higher, skidding briefly over her rumpled shirt that bore the Living Ruff logo.

Oh.

Underneath the logo was an embroidered slogan: THINK PAW-SITIVE. Felicity's eye twitched at the awful pun. At least it wasn't about helping the less fur-tunate.

Right. So she might have made a few faulty assumptions about whether the van was being broken into. But seriously, the woman's jeans and boots were in appalling condition. Did the staff of the charity have no professionalism in their appearance whatsoever? Felicity was about to ask just that when she met startlingly intelligent eyes. Suddenly her usual indifference as to what anyone other than Elena thought of her died abruptly, along with the question.

"Who are you?" The woman asked in a throaty, irritated voice, rubbing her head where she'd hit it on the van. Her eyebrow hiked up. "And why were you jamming your finger into me like that? I'm not your voodoo doll."

"I thought you were a vagrant hunting for drug money from a charity's van." She trusted that would earn her some favor, Good Samaritan Felicity and all.

Instead, the woman frowned. "Ex-cuse me?"

Or not. "I didn't see your logo." Felicity scrambled. She tapped her own blouse to indicate the spot where the woman's Living Ruff badge was. "So I thought—"

"Yes, I heard you. A vagrant. After drug money. Because all homeless are addicts, right?" Her lips pinched.

Oh. Well, Felicity had said that, hadn't she? She resisted the urge to take another step back to get some distance. *Wait, why does she look familiar?* A memory clicked into place. Okay, they'd styled her up for the photo shoot and attempted to morph her into something safe for mainstream consumption, not to mention cropped the pic at chest level, but Felicity was pretty sure this was the vet from the article declaring the charity was closing. Dr. Sandy Cooper.

It was weird how they'd also magicked away the sheer enormity of her presence.

"Cat got your tongue?" Dr. Cooper's lips twitched. "Heh. Vet joke."

"Not a very good one," Felicity shot back without thinking. "I mean, it's a bit unoriginal."

"True enough." The woman shrugged, looking completely unfazed by the criticism. Her eyes dragged over Felicity's outfit.

It was a new season Elie Saab pantsuit. Felicity knew she looked good in it. Professional. Something the vet might want to look into.

"Shall we start again? I'm Doctor—"

"Sandy Cooper," Felicity cut in. And…weird how that had come out like an accusation.

The woman tilted her head in acknowledgment. "Everyone calls me Cooper." She shut the driver's door, locked it, and eyed Felicity. "It seems you have me at a disadvantage. And you are?"

"Felicity Simmons," she said before adding her new title, "deputy chief operating officer of Bartell Corp." Soon to be acting COO, she wanted to add but restrained herself. Felicity rose a little higher on the balls of her feet. It still didn't feel real.

"Proud of that title, I see."

"Why wouldn't I be?" Felicity snapped.

The other woman sighed. "Care to explain how you know me?"

"There was an article in the paper," Felicity began. "Living Ruff New York closing?"

"Ah." Cooper's eyes tightened as if to say *oh that*, and she headed past Felicity to the back of the van, opening its double doors wide.

Felicity stood back transfixed as the woman hauled out two enormous bags stamped *DOG FOOD 20LB* and dumped them on the ground beside her.

"Donations," Cooper said, noticing her interest. "Close to their expiration date, so I got them for free." She eyed Felicity up and down as though deciding something, then laughed. "I was about to ask for a hand getting the bags inside. Never mind."

"Yes. Well. I'm a lawyer, not a Sherpa." Felicity folded her arms. She was quite sure she wouldn't be able even to nudge a bag with her toe, let alone lift it. *That's what you hired people with muscles for.*

"Lawyer, hmm? Here to sue us or something?" Cooper's eyes grew sharp. "Because we haven't got much. Everything goes to the animals and their owners."

"Of course not. I'm here to look at what you do at Living Ruff and consider making a donation. On behalf of Bartell Corporation."

Cooper paused and squinted at Felicity. "I see." She tossed a huge bag over one shoulder. "Big media company, right?"

"The biggest."

Then as if the first bag were easy, she flung the second over the other shoulder and headed toward the building. "Get the door, can you?" she called back.

Felicity glanced back at the van, nodded, then gave the doors a firm push until they slammed shut.

"Not those doors, although thanks. I meant the office." She tilted her head toward the redbrick monstrosity.

Oh. Of course. Cheeks scalding at her stupidity, Felicity scurried ahead and went to open the door. It didn't budge. "It's locked."

"Damn it. Our receptionist, Mrs. Brooks, must be held up again. All right..." Cooper studied Felicity until she reached Cooper's side. "You could start your charitable donations right now."

Felicity frowned. "How?"

"Reach into my left pocket and grab my keys." She jutted one dirty jean-clad hip forward.

Into her pocket? Was she for real? That seemed awfully personal. You don't just ask strangers to...and certainly not when they're wearing jeans that had quite clearly rolled around in filth recently.

Even so, Felicity's fingers tingled at the prospect of being that close to those impressive thighs. Entirely without intending to, she slid her hand slowly into the woman's pocket and clasped a metal bundle.

The heat Cooper was giving off was fierce, but that made sense if she'd just been doing physical work. Felicity imagined her in a tank top, her powerful muscles gleaming as she exerted herself in manual labor of some sort. Her arms were probably as strong and muscled as her shoulders. Because they had to be, didn't they?

"Hey, Felicity?"

"Mm?"

"For the keys to work, they have to be outside of my pocket."

Oh God! Felicity yanked them out, her whole face burning. What the hell was wrong with her?

The other woman chuckled. "Okay, it's the big key, second on the left of the ring. Thanks."

With hands shaking for reasons she had absolutely no intention of examining, Felicity managed to get the key into the lock on the first attempt and turned it until it clicked. Then she drew the door open, and Cooper pushed past her, dropping the bags just inside.

"Thanks." She wiped her forehead, which left a huge smear of dirt, then slapped the dust off her oak trees laughably called legs.

Felicity suddenly found the entire picture of dirt-smeared imperfection the most fascinating thing she'd ever seen.

"Right." Cooper straightened. She waved at the bags. "I just like to keep any food donations outside the van so they don't get stolen or spoiled by bad weather or whatever."

Felicity didn't answer. Odd how the smear loaned a rakish quality to the woman's face.

"Have I got something on my face?" Cooper asked, catching her gaze. She reached into her back pocket and pulled out a man's handkerchief to wipe it. "Gone?"

"Yes." Felicity said faintly, feeling the loss. "All gone."

"Right, then. Come on up. I can offer you tea or coffee while you wait for Harvey, our charity director. He's the one to talk to about the services we offer and how to donate."

"Or I could talk to you first. I'd like to get a feel for the whole organization. Talk to everyone. See all the facets."

Dr. Cooper shrugged, those mighty shoulders heaving up and down.

Felicity caught herself gaping and slammed her mouth shut. *Seriously inappropriate.*

"Well, it's up to you," Cooper said. "I can tell you the practical stuff about my job, sure, but I'm due to go out again soon. Rounds. Gotta feed some good boys"—she grinned—"and good girls."

Felicity peered at her, utterly lost.

"Dogs, Ms. Simmons. Among other animals. Are you a pet owner? Come on up." She led the way up some old rust-stained concrete stairs.

"I'm not," Felicity replied as she followed, studying a substantial muscled ass that should in no way be so fascinating. Except it *really* was.

"Oh? Any reason?"

Had Cooper's voice lowered a few degrees to chilly?

Suddenly Felicity didn't want the woman to think she hated animals. That wasn't it at all. "I think it would be unfair for someone in my position to own an animal. I've spent the past few years following my boss around for work. She travels all over the world checking on her business interests. For instance, I've just been living in Australia for the past ten months while she overhauled one of her magazines over there."

"Australia?" Cooper opened the double doors at the top of the stairs, pinning them back on each side with a latch. "Does that explain your un-New York accent? How weird. I thought you might be a bit English."

So English that Mrs. Allsop's entirely proper elocution lessons hadn't been in vain, then? Felicity beamed in satisfaction. "No, I'm American. I've never even been to England."

Cooper gave her an odd look, then swung the office door wide. "All right, come through. Let me just wash up. I probably look a mess. I had to play midwife to a dog that wanted to hide under a dirty building first thing. And then I was heading back to the office when I got the call about the dog food donation."

Well, that explained her clothes looking like a tramp had died in them.

Felicity studied the office. A battered wooden round table sat in the middle of the room with five mismatched chairs around it. Folders and papers spilled across it. A few desks with old-style fat computer monitors sat around it. How eighties. The largest desk had a huge phone on it and a name plate attached to the divider: Mrs. Brooks, Receptionist/Vet Tech.

In one far corner was a locked glass office. A bronze sign reading Director Harvey Clifford was stuck on the door.

Next to it was a second room, this one with enclosed walls, and a sign: Pet treatment clinic—KNOCK FIRST. A smiling cartoon dog was stuck under that.

Animal posters with motivational sayings lined the walls that didn't have windows. The ones that did looked like they were in desperate need of cleaning.

A kitchenette proved to be Cooper's destination, and Felicity tried very hard not to look as the other woman bent over a small sink and washed thoroughly with two types of soap—one smelling of disinfectant, the other of lemon. As Cooper dried her hands on a paper towel, she called over her shoulder, "Tea or coffee?" Then she slam-dunked the paper towel into a bin near her ankle.

"Neither," Felicity croaked out. "Well, not now. I'm trying to kick my excess caffeine habit. Step one, don't hit the beans too early."

"Suit yourself. Have a seat." She gestured at the round table. "I have to change. Always pays to keep a few spare sets of clothes at work in this line of business."

Felicity nodded as she slowly lowered herself to the closest chair and tried very hard not to think about the fact that changing meant…sliding pants down those impressive legs.

Maybe she *should* have had a coffee. She'd be able to focus entirely on the cup instead of the woman striding away to a room at the back of the office.

Cooper disappeared inside but didn't bother shutting the door.

A moment later came the clang of a belt buckle hitting the floor. A boot went sailing with a thud out the door, followed by, "Oops. That steer got away from me."

"Where are you from," Felicity called back, fascinated, "if you call your boots 'steers.'"

"A bit of here and a bit of there. I'm a military brat. We moved all over." Another thud, but this time the boot stayed out of sight. "What about you?

Because I'm thinking someone who sounds English but hasn't been there sounds that way on purpose. Am I right?"

There was a slap as a pair of jeans suddenly landed in a puddle within sight, and Felicity swallowed about what that meant. She wanted to shake herself. She was here to do a job—an investigation, actually, into possible embezzlement—not get distracted by an employee at the charity. *Who isn't wearing pants right now.*

"Felicity?" The vet's head poked around the corner. "Was that a touchy topic or something? Sorry if it was."

"Oh. No." *Focus.* "It's not much of a story. I had a terrible accent and took some voice lessons to sound more professional. My teacher was English, so some of her accent and sayings stuck. I've always absorbed voices, though. I'm a little surprised I don't have an Australian twang now. God forbid." She shuddered.

Cooper laughed and disappeared again. "I see." A sock suddenly went flying. "Crap."

What followed the sock were ten glorious seconds of blurred Amazon dressed only in a white T-shirt that strained across ample breasts and sinful ass-hugging black boxers chasing after it. Felicity whimpered softly.

Why in the hell did she find someone like *this* so attractive? Someone so strong? So...soft butch? Who had real meat on their bones? It was at odds with everything she knew about herself. Her head was *always* turned by lawyers. Thin, lean, compact men and women with impeccable fashion and manners and grooming who posed themselves oh so artistically. They were all fussy, neat, clever, and precise, just like her.

She definitely didn't do undulating teddy-bear-like military brats who could double as the Bank of America building. Especially not ones who crawled into dirty, creepy places to play canine midwife. There was no part of any of that description that resonated with who Felicity knew she was attracted to. And yet here she sat, unable to blot out those ten glorious blurred seconds.

Cooper gave a sheepish laugh as she leaped back into her changing room. "Sorry about that. I'm so tired that my coordination's well and truly fried right now."

Like my brain. Apparently.

"It was a long night," Cooper continued. "Well, morning. I've been going fourteen hours already. I swear I'm usually the height of professional and manage to keep my clothes on a lot of the time!"

"Fourteen hours?" Felicity gasped. She might do that regularly, but she was in upper management and had a desk job. Vets did this, too?

"Don't worry, I only have a few more hours left. Then I'll take a nap." A disembodied hand flung out and pointed.

Felicity followed it and saw a small open door she'd missed before. She could see a makeshift bed.

"Great for catching some Zs when I'm doing a double shift."

"Do you do a double shift often?" Felicity asked, curious.

"Every now and then. Pet emergencies are part of life, and my usual casual replacement is getting his gallstones out." Cooper stepped back into the main office area, knotting a bundle of dirty clothes in a bag. She shoved it under one arm, then tucked her T-shirt into her clean pair of jeans. She did up a solid silver buckle on her belt. "Much better, right?"

Felicity took in the flannel shirt, white T-shirt, and faded blue jeans. "Y-yes," she muttered, feeling her cheeks catch fire. "Very nice. Yes."

What the hell was wrong with her? She was having lustful thoughts, *on the job no less*, about someone who absolutely wasn't her type!

"Two yeses, huh?" Cooper grinned. "Lucky me." Her teeth were white and perfect, and her smile breathtaking.

Felicity wondered if the air had lost some of its oxygenation. *Oh.* So that's where that word came from. *Breathtaking.* Made sense.

"All right, let me get a coffee into me, and I'll answer any questions you like till the boss gets here." She grinned again and headed for the kitchenette.

"Right. Yes."

The woman pressed a button on a wall-mounted urn marked Boiling Water and filled a large mug. Mesmerizing.

Felicity swore at herself. She was being ridiculous. God, she'd dated Phillip for four months and had *never* been this distracted once.

"Cooper? Sorry I'm late!" came an older female voice from the bottom of the stairs accompanied by a rhythmic clacking noise.

"That's Mrs. Brooks and the world's most adorable girl," Cooper said quietly so only Felicity could hear.

"One of the kids got a stomachache, and I had to make sure she—" The voice stopped as its owner reached the top of the stairs and met Felicity's curious eyes. She was a Black woman with a round, pleasant face, midlength wavy black hair, and a strong Bronx accent. "Oh, hello." Mrs. Brooks's eyes flitted over to Cooper, who was carrying her coffee back to the table. "I didn't realize you had company."

Suddenly a knee-high caramel-colored dog burst in and rushed over to Cooper. It was an enthusiastic floppy-eared little thing, the exact kind of no-boundaries whirlwind that made Felicity take a step backward in alarm.

"Hey, girl." Cooper dropped to a crouch, giving the dog a pleased one-armed hug while holding her coffee out of harm's way. She laughed, pulling her face away as the animal tried to cover her in sloppy licks. "This is my overeager English cocker spaniel, Brittany."

Yikes. Far too much slobber. Felicity inched away in case Droolius Caesar over there got ideas of sharing the love. Instead, after a few quick sniffs in Felicity's direction, the animal seemed perfectly content to hug Cooper's side. Thank all things holy in heaven.

"And this is Felicity Simmons," Cooper said to both Mrs. Brooks and the excitable canine as she rose from her crouch. She made her way to a chair with the delighted dog doing loops in and out of her stride. "Felicity's giving us the once-over for Bartell Corporation. To see if they want to donate."

Mrs. Brooks's eyebrows lifted at the mention of Bartell Corp.

She should be impressed. It was a Fortune 500 company. *Which I'm going to be in charge of in a month.* Well, assuming she didn't screw up Elena's secret mission here.

"And this is Cassandra Brooks, who keeps our entire charity on an even keel," Cooper said, sliding her coffee onto the table and turning to Felicity. "She also sort of dog shares Brittany with me."

Dog share? Why? They weren't a couple, were they? Mrs. Brooks looked at least sixty. And Cooper was, what? Late thirties? Early forties?

Her confusion must have shown because Cooper added, "Britt's mine during the day and Mrs. B kindly keeps her on nights and weekends because her apartment allows dogs, unlike mine." She scowled. "A situation I'm trying to fix, but it'd be easier if affordable, dog-friendly buildings weren't so hard to find in New York."

Felicity nodded neutrally, having precisely zero interest in the sleeping arrangements of Brittany, the slobbery dog.

"So," Mrs. Brooks said as she put her handbag on her desk, "potential donor, you say?"

Felicity nodded.

"Excellent. You'll be wanting this, then." She rummaged through her drawers and pulled out a folder, putting it on the table in front of Felicity. "This is the charity overview we supply to all potential donors. If you have any questions, Mr. Clifford will be in soon enough."

Cooper sipped her coffee and watched them without a word.

Felicity made no move to take it. "If it's all the same to you, I'm not looking for the information handed out to other donors. I'm looking for the full picture. The *other* financial information, if you follow. The information not often shared."

The room seemed to get chillier.

"Excuse me?" Mrs. Brooks asked. Her mouth fell open. "What *are* you implying?"

Oh hell. Maybe Felicity really was bad at subtle. Before she could answer, Cooper chimed in.

"This is a *legitimate* charity! We do excellent work here!" Her eyes widened, and she placed her cup carefully on the table. "Mr. Clifford is scrupulous and ethical. He'd never do anything that wasn't aboveboard. Same goes for everyone here."

"Then that's both excellent and easy to prove," Felicity said quietly, spreading her hands to try and ease the tension. "Yes? Look, it's simple. My boss is one of the richest women in the media world, and when she makes an investment in a cause, she wants it to be to a charity above reproach. And I'm here to make sure that's the case. Surely you understand."

"Oh." Mrs. Brooks's hackles seemed to go down.

"Well, fine, but is there some reason you think we wouldn't be above reproach?" Cooper asked. "Or do you turn up and insult the integrity of every charity she's interested in? Is this part of your job description?"

Felicity's lips thinned. Her hands bunched into fists where they sat on the table. *Don't barge in like Rambo*, Elena had said. And here she was... Ramboing up a storm.

"I'm sure this is just standard procedure," Mrs. Brooks said suddenly, eyes darting to her hands, then to Cooper. Her voice was soothing.

It set Felicity's teeth on edge, as if she needed *managing*. She was making such a mess of this.

"I just want answers and that's it. I'm not accusing anyone of anything," Felicity said tightly. "But if you don't want questions about how you run things, maybe don't feature in stories about how you're about to shut down."

"Oh, that." Cooper said, and all the tension eased from her shoulders. "It's not true."

"Then why put it out there?" Felicity asked.

"Harvey does it every year. A story to get in new donors. It means nothing."

"So you don't need money?" Felicity's eyebrow shot up.

"I didn't say that." Cooper gave her a hard look. "Do you always twist people's words like that? Is that the lawyer in you? Or does working for a media empire rub off? A journalist thing?"

How imposing she looked, directing all that angry energy at Felicity, who glared back, refusing to be intimidated. "Look, this isn't hard. My boss read about you last year and loved Living Ruff's story so much she wanted to donate. Now with this latest article all about how you're three seconds from calling in the liquidators, she's worried that it's not a sound investment. So which is it?"

"Last year?" Cooper snorted. "Oh right. You mean the God's gift to charities article."

Felicity paused. "How do you know which article I mean?"

Mrs. Brooks chuckled. "There's only one that people remember."

Felicity frowned. "I'm not following."

"It went on for pages," Cooper said, jumping in. "It covered a day in the life of me doing my work. The reporter followed me around, then interviewed all the homeless people about what they thought of us, then talked to the local government people as to whether we were good, poked over our finances, interviewed other charities about us, too. It was like getting a journalistic colonoscopy." She shook her head. "I've never seen anything like it. Every other media story has always been a puff piece: three paragraphs, a few feel-good quotes, a photo of a cute dog, and that's it. This one was like the reporter was going for a Pulitzer. We had to prove we were worth their endorsement. Then when the story came out, it was"—she shook her head again—"astonishing."

Mrs. Brooks rose, walked to the table, and flipped open the folder she'd first offered Felicity. She drew out a photocopy of a newspaper article. "Want to read it? It brought us in hundreds of new donors from all over. And we also received the single biggest donation in our charity's history from it."

Elena's donation. Curious, Felicity slid the article closer, looked down… and drew in a shocked breath.

Suddenly a great many things became clear.

WHEN LOVE HAS NO HOME
By *MADDIE GREY*

She didn't even need to read it to know that of course the story would be exceptional. Because try as she might to deny it, the Australian was a phenomenal reporter; she had several international scoops and awards to her name these days. Felicity glanced at the publication date. August 29. Maddie had worked on this while she was freelancing in New York before she'd left for Vietnam on a travel-writing assignment.

Felicity scan-read it. Naturally, it was beautifully written. And touching. So *of course* Elena would have wanted to donate to a cause that was apparently so close to Maddie's heart.

Now it all became clear why Elena had been so worried. It wasn't about her missing money, was it? Well, that wouldn't be her primary motivation. No, Elena would be concerned how it would look if her reporter friend had written a multipage love letter to a charity that might turn out to be corrupt. Elena was worried about Maddie's professional reputation taking a dive. No wonder she had stressed to Felicity that she try and find *subtle* solutions.

She sagged. Why did everything come down to Maddie Grey? What did Maddie have that Felicity didn't? Why was Elena so…loyal…to her, so connected? It was a mystery Felicity was no closer to solving.

"What is it?" Cooper asked, sounding curious.

Felicity looked up. "I…know her. The writer." She waved at the story. "She used to work with me. Now she's"—*in photo frames on my boss's desk*—"a friend of my boss."

"Maddie? She's friends with Elena Bartell?"

"Yes. Good friends. So that explains why I'm here." It really did. Why couldn't Elena have just confided in her about this?

"Oh wow." Cooper's shoulders relaxed. "I get it. Right. Ah, sorry if I was a little hostile before. I didn't realize y'all were such great friends. Hey, if you speak to Maddie, could you tell her how grateful we are? Her story will keep us in the black for years."

"So the other article about your imminent closure really is a lie?"

"As I said, it's just a thing Harvey does once a year to get new donors on our list." Cooper shrugged. "Talk to him about it if you want to put your mind to rest."

"I will." She glanced at her watch. "When's he due in?"

Mrs. Brooks spoke up. "I texted him a few minutes ago to tell him you were here waiting for him, but he said he has some meetings. He suggested in his absence that you do a ride-along with Cooper to find out what we do here. He apologized that he can't see you sooner."

Felicity folded her arms. He'd heard she was here, a big potential donor, and had begged off to go to meetings? Was that likely? She decided to give him the benefit of the doubt.

Mrs. Brooks spoke again. "He thought you'd find it far more informative to see firsthand what we do with Cooper before you and he sit down."

That did make sense, but Felicity still felt a bit glad-handed. The thought of being forced to do meet and greets with the homeless and their animals hadn't exactly been high on her to-do list today. She would, of course, cope. Felicity lifted her chin. "Well, it's not as if I can do much else, is it?"

"I've never seen such enthusiasm for time in my company," Cooper drawled. She grinned, and a matching pair of dimples appeared. "Well? Are you up for it?"

It suddenly occurred to her that these meet and greets with the homeless would also come with a *lot* of Sandy Cooper. That wasn't unsettling in the least. Not at all. No siree. "Of course. I'm up for any challenge." As long as she wasn't expected to crawl under houses with the woman. She'd simply refuse that.

"You say that now," Cooper teased, "but I do go to some unsavory places."

Oh wait, *was* she expected to crawl under things? Worry snaked through her. Followed by horror. Then she remembered she didn't work for Cooper and that "no" was a full sentence. "I'm sure you do," she said neutrally.

Cooper's eyes darted to her outfit. "I'd offer to loan you something more appropriate, but I don't think we're the same size."

Felicity snorted. "An understatement."

"So you can make do with what you have on. Now, just so you know, I expect you to follow my ground rules."

"Which are?"

"I expect you to be polite to the clients—"

"The clients?"

"The homeless," Cooper clarified. "I don't want to hear any of the stuff you said earlier to me. About them being addicts. Yes, some are, obviously. Some have mental health issues. Some have PTSD. And some are just unlucky people, out of money or work, on hard times. The point is, I expect politeness and respect. Can you do that?"

"Of course." Indignation rose. She could be diplomatic. She could!

Cooper seemed to weigh up her answer for sincerity. "And I especially expect you not to comment on all the ways you'd fix their lives if it were you. That's a temptation far too many people have the first time they interact with homeless."

Felicity tilted her head. "I can…observe."

"In silence?"

"Yes." How ridiculous.

"Good." Cooper reached into her pocket and extracted a rubber band with which she corralled her shoulder-length blonde hair into a rough ponytail. "Okay, let's go." She paused and turned to the receptionist. "Mrs. B, I'll be back in a few hours." She clicked her tongue, and Brittany shot to her ankle.

Wait, the floppy excuse for a dog was coming? Felicity sighed. *Lovely.*

"See you soon," Mrs. Brooks said. "Oh, and good luck, Ms. Simmons."

Luck? Was she going to need luck here? Why did Mrs. Brooks sound amused? Felicity swallowed nervously, then followed Cooper to the stairs. And for the second time that day, she found herself in the rather pleasant position of following the shapely ass of Dr. Sandy Cooper. This time, though, her worried mind was fixed on what else lay ahead.

Well. *Mostly.*

Chapter 3
On the Road

THE FIRST THING FELICITY NOTICED about Cooper's vehicle as she strapped herself in was the smell. The van reeked of pet food and animals and something else she couldn't quite place. Decay? Her nose wrinkled.

"I suppose that's an occupational hazard," Felicity said as Cooper slid in beside her.

"What is?"

"The smell."

Cooper put on the radio…some thumpy country music that made Felicity shudder.

Brittany launched herself from the ground outside the van into Cooper's lap, then, tail wagging from side to side like a windshield wiper, squeezed between the two front seats to take position right behind them in some sort of dog hammock seat that put her at close human level.

The dog's warm breath was now against her ear. Felicity drew in a calming gulp of air. *Right.* She'd just ignore that along with the smell.

Then Brittany lay her muzzle on Felicity's shoulder.

Cooper shot her a surprised glance. "Well, that's different. Brittany doesn't warm to anyone new. And in answer to your earlier comment, I can't smell anything. I'm immune."

Felicity inched away from Hairy Houndini until the dog took the hint and flopped her muzzle on Cooper's shoulder instead.

"So fickle, girl." Cooper laughed and started the engine.

"Can you change the station, please?" Felicity asked as the music twanged through another chorus.

"Not a fan of Billy Ray Cyrus?"

"Is anyone?" Felicity asked. "Breaky isn't even a word."

Cooper smiled. "That radio station's Gabe's favorite. He's another vet who works with us. Feel free to pick something else."

Felicity leaned over and turned it off. "I choose silence."

"Tough crowd." Cooper shrugged. "So out of interest, have you ever had much to do with homeless before?"

"No. I don't think that's much of a problem where I live."

Cooper snorted. "If you live in New York, it's always a problem, no matter where you are. You just haven't noticed."

Felicity shook her head. "No, I—"

"Excuse me. Who is the expert on the subject in this vehicle?" Cooper asked. Her tone was light, but she fixed Felicity with a penetrating gaze.

"Well." Yes, quite right. "You."

"Good. Can you remember that today? And maybe remember the fact that most people are only two paychecks away from homelessness."

What a depressing thought.

Cooper's gaze raked Felicity's outfit once again. "Well, in your case, maybe ten, although that also depends on the size of your rent." She paused and added in a slightly taunting tone, "Or is it mortgage?"

Felicity didn't bite.

"So," Cooper barreled on, "while I've asked you to be quiet and listen, if you decide to ignore me, and you do seem the type"—her lips quirked—"don't ask anyone *why* they're homeless. It can happen for any number of reasons, and it's none of your business."

"I wouldn't." Felicity had no plans to talk to them anyway. "I'm not interested."

Cooper's eyes went hard. "I see."

"I just mean that I have one focus in life, and that's my career. Anything else is irrelevant. I say *they do them, I'll do me*, and we'll get on fine."

"Well, that's convenient."

"Why? You just told me not to interact with them, and now that I say I don't want to, you're pissed?"

Cooper shook her head in apparent exasperation. "I never said don't *interact* with them. I said don't judge them. Watch and listen. You can smile, make eye contact. Make them feel seen. Tell them your name."

"Why would I do any of that?" Felicity asked, baffled. "I'm not planning on making friends, just seeing what you do."

Cooper's jaw tightened. "You don't see a need to make a human connection because they're not real people to you, are they? You don't think of them as having lives and hopes and dreams just like you."

Snorting, Felicity said, "That's absurd. I don't see a need to make a connection with *anyone* unless it's career related. If that ever happens accidentally, well, it's…unexpected, I suppose, and rare. But I don't seek it out."

There was a long silence as Cooper digested that, then she laughed. "You're actually serious, aren't you?"

"Very."

"My God, how do you even get by in this world with that hands-off philosophy?"

Felicity shrugged. "It's just how I am. I don't see what the issue is. I'm truly uninterested in pretty much everyone. If I had my way, I'd never speak to anyone I'm not forced to deal with."

Cooper's brow puckered. "Are you shy? Or an introvert?"

"Neither." Felicity met her gaze. "I'm simply focused. I've been like this since I was twelve. Now, are we ever going to get underway? Charming as this view of Ode to Concrete Park is." She waved at their surroundings. "What are those weird tables for, anyway?" She squinted.

"They're for dominoes, which are popular around here with the Hispanic community. You'll see them full by the time we return." Cooper paused. "Are you… Do you have empathy for others?" she asked cautiously.

Felicity sighed. "Of course. Yes, I dislike suffering, and I even cry at funerals. But is it truly inconceivable to you that some people don't like getting into other people's business *at all*? That I'm perfectly happy as a loner? I just don't find being sociable uplifting. I truly do prefer my own company."

"I've never met anyone like that before." Cooper rested her hands on the steering wheel and looked at her. "Well, no one who's just straight out admitted it."

"Me, either," Felicity said a little mournfully. "Society expects us to all be people who need people. They even sing songs about it. Well, I don't and never have." She eyed Cooper ruefully. "You know those questions where they ask who would you take to a desert island? I'd take no one but a good book, and I'd be perfectly happy. And honestly, if the book was very good, I'd even decline a rescue."

"You know…I think I believe you." Cooper let out a small chuckle.

It was such an attractive chuckle, much like the rest of the woman, but Felicity was determined not to be derailed further by surface distractions.

"Why would I lie?" Felicity eyed her.

Cooper snorted. "Good point. All right, can we get back to what I was saying about the clients? Maybe you could please make an effort to at least fake it? A few smiles? One hello?"

"I don't fake anything," Felicity said honestly, "not unless it's absolutely essential for my job. This doesn't sound essential to me."

"Just great." Cooper grumbled as she reversed onto the street. "All right, one last thing: don't be offended if someone reacts badly to you. You don't know what their week's been like or what someone did to them just before they met you. If they're rude, just apologize, move on, and don't make a fuss."

"I promise not to be offended if they say any unfortunate things." Felicity flapped a hand. "*Now* is that it?"

"Yes." Cooper sighed. "Call me crazy, but I'm guessing you didn't volunteer for this assignment." She put her foot down on the gas pedal.

The G force, minor though it was, pinned Felicity back in her seat for a hot minute.

Brittany gave a bark of excitement.

"Do you always drive so fast?" Felicity gasped. Was the universe mocking her for bemoaning Amir's sedate driving? Surely it wasn't too much to hope for a speed between placid and space-shuttle launch.

"I'll add my driving to your list of *does-not-approves*. Along with the van's music, smell, and our clients." Cooper gave her a knowing look. "And we're going fast because I'm late. If I don't reach Webster Avenue early, my client will have been moved on."

"Moved on?"

"Some police aren't charitable about the homeless. They only see an irritation."

Felicity considered that. "And what do you see?"

"Someone whose animal needs some food, love, and a checkup." She smiled, and those dimples came out again. "I love Lucille. That's the animal I'm hoping to visit today. Her owner usually visits a free shower service that runs around this time." Cooper glanced at her watch. "I've got some concerns about a possible growth on Lucille, among other issues, so I'm looking more closely at the case."

"Growth?"

"You don't seriously want all the details?" Cooper's gaze raked her up and down.

"I'm not some delicate petal." Truly, Felicity wanted no details, but she didn't appreciate being treated like she'd crumple.

"Aren't you?" Cooper's expression was challenging. "Tell me, Ms. Simmons, how much does that outfit you have on retail for?" Her lips quirked.

Felicity glared. None of her damned business.

"That's what I thought. Look, if you're back here tomorrow, invest in a pair of jeans, some boots, and a thick long-sleeve shirt at a minimum."

"No, thank you. I'll look like a trucker. A butch lesbian trucker," Felicity sniped.

Suddenly Cooper's expression shifted from amused to frosty. "And what would be wrong with that?" She met Felicity's eye. "I had you pegged as some ivory tower liberal. But I swear, if you start quoting Bible passages or redneck shit at me, I *will* kick you out; I don't care what the net worth of your boss is."

Surprise flooded Felicity. "You'd toss away a potential large donation due to some perceived political differences?"

"Homophobia is *not* a political difference. It's a people difference." Cooper glared at her. "It's a who-you-are-at-your-core difference. So what's it going to be? Because even if you don't care that you just insulted me, I won't expose you to vulnerable clients, a not insignificant number of whom are on the street because their families found out about their sexuality."

Insulted me. As in…Cooper was a lesbian?

"I didn't realize you were…" Felicity waved her hand. Although come to think of it, she felt a bit stupid not to have at least considered the possibility immediately.

"Well, I am. So if you *are* homophobic, I can pull over right now and we can go our separate ways."

"Of course I'm not homophobic." Felicity huffed. "My God, two of my last three lovers were women. So sue me if I don't want to look like some clichéd bad-butch movie stereotype." She folded her arms. "I have standards."

Cooper braked. Hard. "So you're a butch-hating bi? That's supposed to be better?"

"Don't be ridiculous. I'm a bad-fashion-hating bi. I've seen butches in sinfully gorgeous suits, and I'll have you know they're beautiful. Or handsome. Whichever. It's the *clothes*, not the person I object to. Would it kill some people to make an actual effort? How limited *is* their imagination? Jeans, boots, tees, and flannels? Every single day?" She let her Midwest accent off the leash. "Are they off to a rodeo? Or to plow a field before climbing into their truck?"

Cooper went completely still.

Suddenly Felicity realized why. Cooper was wearing jeans, boots, a T-shirt, and a flannel shirt. That exact butch-trucker look that Felicity had just run her mouth off at. She swallowed. For some reason—and this really was quite mystifying—she truly didn't want Sandy Cooper angry at her. Especially since, despite everything Felicity had just said about that fashion combination, Cooper looked fine. *So. Fine.*

"Do I offend your eyeballs, Ms. Simmons?" Cooper asked silkily.

"No!" Felicity said quickly. "Quite the opposite."

Why had she said that? She groaned inwardly. "Can we just enter it into the record that I'm neither conservative nor homophobic nor butch hating nor whatever else you're unraveling over and get on with this?"

Cooper's eyes now held an amused glint.

Great. Felicity's unfortunate slip had not gone unnoticed, it seemed.

"You *like* my look on me? Even though I'm not…off to a rodeo? Or… plowing fields? Or climbing into my big bad truck?" She punctuated each word as though it belonged to an erotic movie title.

Did she have to do that? Felicity ground her jaw and forced herself not to picture Cooper wrestling things or climbing into trucks with that superb round ass of hers. "Can we just…*drive*?" She pounded that last word with venom.

With a chuckle, Cooper took off again, weaving in and out through traffic, once more hitting a speed Felicity found disconcerting. That wasn't the only disconcerting thought occupying her.

Felicity *wanted* Dr. Sandy Cooper. Every way there was.

What a fucking disaster.

Lucille turned out to be a cat. An old thing with tatty ears, eternally pulled-down whiskers, and wide eyes that looked utterly pathetic. And Felicity was in love.

Damn it. It was the real reason she never wanted a pet. She was mad about them. Dogs and cats and anything furry and cute, and she couldn't stop the grabby hands and ache to cuddle. It was beyond unseemly; it was appalling. And she knew what she was like, what would happen next. She'd get attached—and that would not end well.

It was bad enough riding with Brittany, being two feet away from an animal so beautiful that all she wanted was to pet it and murmur that fact into its floppy brown ears… Well, as long as it kept the slobbering to a minimum.

Cooper had left Brittany guarding the van, its window down a little, and Felicity could still see that brown nose poking out, avidly sniffing the world.

Animals were Felicity's Achilles' heel. They had so much power and made her so weak. They sucked you in, made you fall for them, and they could break your heart into bits and pieces. She wasn't about to put herself through that. Never again. No, she was a focused and professional woman who did not have time for…fluffballs. But that didn't mean she didn't still ache to hug the most pathetic-looking puss she'd ever seen in her life.

She forced herself to watch impassively as Cooper inspected the animal, which was curled in her lap, while chatting to the owner. The woman, Norma, according to the name atop Cooper's notes, was sixty-something with tired eyes, missing teeth, a thin gray frizz of hair capping off weathered dark-brown skin, and as many scars as her cat had.

Felicity's heart melted all over again when the cat stretched, offering its belly for a rub. *Christ.* Maybe she should sit on her hands. Or focus on its ugly bits. Felicity bit her lip.

"I'm worried about Lucille," Cooper told the woman. "Gastroenteritis doesn't just affect humans. It's really painful for animals. It can be life-threatening if they become dehydrated."

"I get her plenty to drink," Norma snapped. "You saying I'm neglecting her?"

"Not at all. But even with the best intentions, it's harder for animals on the street to get ideal nutrition."

Norma glowered. "We don't just eat out of trash cans, you know."

"I know." Cooper shot her a worried look. "I really wish you'd let me get her properly looked at. The vomiting could be a sign of something worse."

"And have 'em take her off me? Say I'm a bad owner? I might trust you, but not them. I hear stories."

"We have a little clinic at Living Ruff that should be all that's needed to check her out thoroughly," Cooper said kindly. "No need to involve anyone else at this stage." Her fingers drifted tentatively to the cat's belly, assessing. Lucille immediately pushed a paw against Cooper's hand, not once showing claws, but the message was clear.

Cooper immediately shifted her hand. "Lucille is lovely. I just want her around as long as we can manage it."

"I look after my girl. Not like some of those assholes around here, breeding them and fighting them for money. I'd never do that."

"I know. I can see how much you love her." Cooper smiled gently. "You know how to get in touch if you decide to go ahead with a full checkup."

"I have yer number." Norma waved at a battered iPhone poking out from a haphazard pile of supplies.

"Good. Meanwhile, I have some food for her, if you need spare."

"Like I said, we make do," Norma said, her chin stiff and proud, but her eyes darted to the bag of food next to Cooper's feet. "Not gone broke yet from mah singin'. Secret's to get a good spot, lots of people. 'Sides, soul ain't never goin' out of style."

"Can't argue with that. So"—Cooper patted the bag—"what about I leave you some? Lucille needs the best she can get right now. I've included an electrolyte solution to rehydrate her and get some nutrients back in her. It's chicken-flavored to make her drink it."

"All right, then. Thanks."

Cooper put a bulging plastic bag of pet food and liquids beside her. "Are you both okay for warmth?"

"Yes," Norma said. This time there was conviction in her eyes.

"Good." Cooper eased the cat back over to Norma, gave it a scratch behind one ear, then smiled. "You're adorable, Lucille. Right, Felicity?" She turned to look at her.

Felicity froze, not expecting to be drawn into any kind of conversation. They'd talked about this! "Ah…" Her gaze darted back to the cat with its enormous, beautiful eyes. "It's a cat. I'm sure all cats are equally valid to their owners."

What the hell kind of answer was that? Felicity's cheeks grew warm, and she leaped to her feet. "I'll, uh, be in the van."

She felt Norma's hostility as she bolted and dimly heard Cooper apologize for her.

Why am I making such a mess of this? How hard was it? "Your cat's lovely, ma'am."

Idiot! She'd negotiated multimillion-dollar deals for Bartell Corp that didn't feel this fraught. She leaned against the locked van, waiting for Cooper's return.

Shortly afterwards, the van beeped, and Cooper opened the back to return supplies to it. She removed her disposable gloves with a snap and cleaned her hands with antibacterial gel.

Felicity climbed into the passenger seat. Moments later, the rear doors slammed closed hard enough for the whole van to reverberate slightly, then the driver's door opened.

"Okay, what the hell was that?" Cooper asked as she climbed into the front seat and sat heavily.

"What was what?" Felicity asked, voice tight.

"Half the time all these people need is a bit of comfort. A kind word. I wasn't asking you to marry the cat, just say it was nice so the client would feel good. And what did you do? 'It's just a cat,'" she mocked. "'All cats are equally valid.'"

I know! Fuck, I know! Felicity inhaled. "I was caught off guard," she said instead.

"Felicity," Cooper said, sounding exasperated, "I wasn't asking you to lie or fake anything. It was not a difficult task. The cat was obviously adorable, and all you had to do was agree and offer kindness to a woman who has next to nothing. That cat is her life, and you dismissed it like it was a...*thing.*"

"I didn't mean to!" Felicity said, voice rising. "I wasn't expecting the question! I thought we'd agreed I'd not say anything."

"We agreed you wouldn't judge clients, take offense if they were angry, or ask them intrusive questions. I had no idea you thought ignoring humans extended to their *animals*! Felicity, this is nonnegotiable: if you ride with me, I expect you to be kind about people's pets, even if you can't stand to look at them. Got it?"

Felicity gave a tight nod.

"Christ." Cooper shook her head and started the van. "I just don't get people who hate animals."

"I don't hate them," Felicity whispered. A flash of a ginger cat bumping under her chin demanding cuddles flashed into mind. She pushed the memory away.

A moment later, as if sensing her misery, Brittany dropped her muzzle back onto Felicity's shoulder and gave her a hopeful look. Felicity pushed her away, too.

"Could have fooled me." Cooper stomped her foot on the pedal, and Felicity had another experience of a rocket liftoff.

She couldn't be bothered arguing. She was too busy trying to keep her breakfast down.

Felicity was coping well, she thought, with the disease and decay she kept witnessing, courtesy of Sandy Cooper. They stopped for an early lunch with Cooper ordering a meat-filled hero while Felicity opted for a whole wheat, ham, and lettuce sandwich. They ate at a wooden outdoor table so small that they kept knocking knees. Cooper's fault, of course—she had a lot of leg.

Felicity distracted herself from that thought by surreptitiously sneaking Brittany food every time Cooper looked the other way. She was helpless to refuse those huge sparkling brown eyes gazing up at her like she was the most wonderful creature in the universe. Dogs were so sneaky like that. Playing on your vanity.

Anyway, she was just getting rid of food she wouldn't eat. That's all it was. She'd never been a big eater, and the serving sizes on their sandwiches were enormous. It practically begged people to feed their hungry dogs under the table. Or other people's. Whatever.

Cooper talked a lot about the work she did, and Felicity largely listened. Not to what she said—the topic of various animal ailments was presently ranging from dull to gross—but her voice. It was deep and delighted as she ran through her cases.

"You're not even listening to me, are you?" Cooper asked, scrunching up her paper napkin. "Am I so boring?"

"What? No," Felicity said in surprise.

"What did I just say?"

Caught, Felicity offered a tight smile. "You're pleased that the dog will make a full recovery." It was a stab in the dark.

"Uh-huh. Just for that, I'm not giving you the head's up about our next case."

"Oh no," Felicity said with faint sarcasm. "How *will* I cope?"

"You'll really wish you had had advance warning on this one so you could stay in the van with Brittany. But no, I've decided you can just see for yourself."

That did sound ominous. But how bad could it possibly be? "I'm sure I'll be fine."

"Mm. Let's see what the future brings."

———◆———

The future brought with it a rather wretched smell. Daisy the rottweiler had a…back-door issue. One so foul that Cooper was double gloving up and reaching into the dog's…

Felicity's eyes went wide. No, surely she wasn't about to…

Cooper met her horrified gaze, grinned, and turned. "I suppose you'd like to know *all* about what I'm doing." She directed the comment to the dog's owner, a small man called Carl with worn sun-browned skin and dark eyes who looked older and more tired than any human being should. He reminded her of a sinewy old farmer broken from working too long in the fields.

"I've seen yer do it before," the man said.

"Ah, but Ms. Simmons here is dying to learn all about my job." Her fingers entered the danger zone.

Felicity and Carl both winced.

"Impacted anal glands are not generally life-threatening but can be very painful and difficult to treat if left too long," Cooper said conversationally. "Anal glands are two little scent glands just inside the anus."

Did she have to say anal quite so often? Devilment danced in Cooper's expression. Felicity narrowed her eyes. *Oh…* She was doing that on purpose.

"The glands release a foul, smelly discharge when the animal defecates. However, sometimes this process doesn't happen properly, and the discharge doesn't release. If it is not treated and left to build up, the glands can swell, become painful, and even infected. So I'm here to determine whether they are full or not. Daisy here has had this problem in the past."

The smell was grotesque. Felicity wished she was back in the van, but there was no way she was letting Cooper win this game.

"If full, you squeeze them. A foul content comes out, and the animal experiences immediate relief." She looked down as the smell intensified… among other things. "Like *that*."

Oh God. Felicity tried not to gag.

"If really full, I'll often suggest the animal is looked at again in a month or so, and we repeat the process." Cooper paused. "Are you okay, Ms. Simmons? You're looking rather green."

"She sure is," Carl agreed. "Like she's gonna puke."

"I am not!" Felicity protested, but even so she backed away to get downwind of certain smells.

"It's okay, love," the man called out with a cackle. "I damn near puked up ma guts the first time Cooper did this to Daisy. It's the smell, I reckon. Like rotten eggs, dontcha think?"

"Oh, for sure," Cooper said, finishing up. She snapped off her gloves and put them in the waste bag she kept with her, then put on a new set.

"Takes a strong stomach for newbies." She glanced at Felicity and grinned. "How's your stomach going?"

"You're loving this way too much," Felicity grumbled. "And for the record, that was the grossest thing I've ever seen in my life. I'm going to leave you to it." She glanced at the owner and tried to think of something positive to say. "You have a…fine animal," she announced suddenly.

It came out stilted and weird, mocking almost, and both Carl and Cooper looked at her oddly. One with suspicion, the other with surprise.

"Glad you approve," Carl said snidely, his bushy brows furrowing.

Felicity gave up, grabbed the van keys Cooper had tossed in a heap on her clipboard earlier, and left them to it.

Brittany gave an enthusiastic bark at her return, doing little circles of delight before flopping her head on Felicity's shoulder again.

"You do know you saw me less than ten minutes ago, right?"

When Cooper rejoined them, this time there was a little amusement in her eyes. "Well, you tried."

Cheeks burning up, Felicity stared out the window. "I meant what I said. Daisy is a fine animal."

"You sure you're in senior management at some international company? How is talking politely to strangers so hard for you?"

She wished she knew. Felicity could argue circles around the clones in gray suits who thought they were better than her until she proved them wrong. But that part of her life was bloodless and emotionless. In fact, there was no investment of feelings at all, unless you counted vindication when she won. All of that, everything, was about business. It was safe.

But here, now, nothing was centered on doing deals, and everywhere she turned, she was being hit by powerful emotions. Sadness, pity, anger, regret, and loss. It was horrifying. And she was only halfway through the day.

At Felicity's silence, Cooper continued. "You just don't seem to do the small-talk side of things well. I thought schmoozing was a prerequisite for those kinds of jobs."

Sighing, Felicity folded her arms. "It's insincere. I see no need to indulge in it." Well, to be accurate, Felicity could distract anyone bothering her with irrelevancies by shifting focus back to work.

"So you're out of practice?"

"I don't think I was ever in practice." Funny how she'd never stopped to wonder if that was a bad thing.

"You really aren't like anyone I know." Cooper's gaze was direct and curious. "But Brittany seems to like you, and she's an excellent judge of character."

Brittany's head lifted off Felicity's shoulder and turned to Cooper, ears twitching at the mention of her name.

"Damn, I left my notes behind." Cooper climbed out of the van again. "Try not to look too horrified if my dog licks you or something."

"I make no promises," Felicity sassed back.

Clearly deciding she'd been talked about enough without being petted, Brittany suddenly squeezed into the front seat and curled up on Felicity's lap.

"Excuse me." Felicity eyed her. "I did not give you permission to do that." She kept her hands well above the bundle of warmth in her lap and gave the dog a suspicious look. "What's next? You expecting belly rubs? Never going to happen. Do you hear me? Never."

Brittany gave an adorable little huff of happiness and closed her eyes.

Felicity's hands were still hovering in the air as if she were about to play the piano when Cooper returned.

Cooper glanced at her, then the dog, then back to Felicity again. "That'll teach you to feed her. You're stuck with her now. Brit's anyone's for a bit of ham."

She'd seen that? "Well, *I* wasn't going to eat it all," Felicity muttered. "Seemed wasteful to throw it away. Now I'm stuck with a canine parasite."

"Seems like it." Cooper's gaze was speculative. "You know, you don't have to keep her on your lap if you don't want her there. Just give her a push, and she'll go back to her seat."

"Right." Felicity did as instructed, and Brittany, remarkably, squeezed into the back. And once again, the dog lay her muzzle on Felicity's shoulder.

She sighed inwardly. "Must you?" she muttered to the animal.

"Apparently you're the chosen one now."

"Just my luck," Felicity said under her breath.

Cooper eyed her speculatively. But all she said was, "All right, let's get going." She suddenly laughed as she started the engine. "My God, your face when you realized where my hand was about to go. Priceless."

"Yes, well, for some reason I'm not immune to the sight of someone shoving their hand up a dog's backside."

"I suppose. If it makes you feel better, it's the job vets hate second worst of all."

Felicity paused. "If that's only second worst, what's the worst job?"

"Don't ask that, Felicity." Cooper's expression was grim. She thumped her foot on the gas pedal.

———◆———

The rest of their time together blurred as Felicity silently observed Cooper interacting with the homeless and their pets. She was confident, calm, and comforting, even when, as happened at least once, she got cursed at by clients who weren't in the best of states.

Felicity had a renewed respect for her, and she couldn't get what had been left unsaid out of her mind. Sometimes, some awful times, Cooper had to put animals down. *That* would be the worst thing for a vet.

Felicity doubted very much she could do that, ever. She could understand the necessity, but she was too weak herself. Just as well she didn't own a pet, then. She'd be useless at being strong when they needed her most. Why did they have to be so tempting, though? She'd probably only be able to hold out a week more, maybe two, before she completely fell for Loki, the cutest little tree defiler.

Felicity forced that disturbing thought from her head and raised something that had been bothering her.

"Can I ask you something?" Felicity began. "About Norma, the first client we saw today. She's homeless, yet she also has an iPhone. How can she be begging for money when she has a fancy phone? Is she scamming people?"

Cooper sighed. "I hate that question. Can I ask *you* something? If that phone was given to her by a loved one to keep in touch because they're worried about her, is that okay with you?"

"I—" Felicity frowned. "Yes?"

"If she got it from her last employer and was then made redundant but allowed to keep it, is *that* okay with you?"

"Yes, of course."

"So why don't you just assume that's what happened and move on?"

"Is it?"

"Why does it matter to you?"

It just did. Felicity wasn't sure why.

"You're focused on it maybe because you think homeless people shouldn't have anything nice or it means they're scamming people. She should sell her phone for food or accommodation if she's so hard up, right? Why is a phone seen as an essential to everyone except the homeless? A phone lets her talk to family for her own mental health and well-being, and it can help her get a job. This is her most precious possession, and yet so many people think she doesn't deserve it. Worse, some people think the poor should be punished for being in their situation, and owning nothing good ever is part of that view."

"I didn't say that. I don't want anyone punished for being in a bad situation."

"But they don't deserve a phone, same as everyone else? You know what society's dirtiest secret is? How close we all are to being Norma or Carl."

"I'd never let myself get into that situation." Never. The thought turned her stomach.

"You think Norma and Carl didn't think that once, too? Most homeless are homeless because they've experienced major trauma in their lives." Sadness crossed Cooper's face. "That can include unemployment, mental or physical health crises, addiction, disability, losing their home, being a victim of violence, and family breakdown." She ticked the items off rapidly as though she had reeled the list off far too many times to far too many ignorant people. "Can you stop trauma happening to you? Are you *that* impressive?"

"You think I'm impressive?" Felicity asked, surprised.

Cooper rolled her eyes. "Talk about missing the point."

Felicity bit her lip. Oh, she got the point. She just didn't see it as relevant. She'd find a way out, if it was her.

I'd never let that be me.

Besides, Cooper was wrong. The people she'd seen today weren't like her at all. They were mainly older, a few teens, often minorities, many veterans, a lot with disabilities, and basically not her in any way, shape, or form.

The thought was a profound relief.

"Last stop for the day," Cooper announced, breaking into her thoughts. "A head's up. This client, Kristie, is a bit…prickly. Try not to bite back, hmm?"

Felicity nodded as she left the van. Prickly she could handle. It wasn't like she was unfamiliar with that trait herself.

"Most of the homeless here used to be at Fordham Plaza," Cooper said conversationally as they picked their way across a park. "The Fordham Metro–North station across from the plaza was a good spot to stay out of the cold and use the restrooms. But local businesses complained about the number of homeless sleeping inside. So they padlocked it."

"Well, I suppose you wouldn't want a subway station filled up with the homeless every night," Felicity said. "How could commuters use it as it was intended?"

"That's the thing. They padlocked it to everyone and for all hours. It's just empty and stays locked now, servicing no one. It's a case of even if the homeless aren't bothering anyone or aren't in anyone's way, people don't want them around. Happens a lot. Have a look at park benches some time. Have they got dividers in the middle to prevent people stretching out? Little random bumps in weird places under freeway overpasses? They're all anti-homelessness measures. It's cruel, is what it is. Anyway," Cooper said, "here's where a lot of the homeless gather in the northwest Bronx these days. Many won't go near a shelter because they're afraid or don't want their gear stolen. So they've formed a little community. Yes, they'll fight each other sometimes, often over nothing at all, but they'll have each other's backs, too. If someone needs help, they'll be there."

They stood in a clearing filled with small tents and tarpaulins strung up from trees. Smells of cooking rose from a tiny camp stove with a man crouched over it. Scrambled eggs. Maybe.

Trash seemed to be everywhere, but Felicity soon realized it was mainly recyclables, which seemed to be the stock in trade for the homeless. At the far end, one of the newer tarpaulin constructions had been hung with what seemed to be great care. The front was open like a tepee but could easily be lashed shut at night. A battered suitcase sat open to one side, a handful of clothes spilling from it—a black and red T-shirt, torn black jeans. An old ice-cream container held a knife, fork, and spoon. Next to it sat an enamel mug and a slice of bread on the ice-cream lid. Above, strung like Christmas lights, was the owner's laundry: four pairs of battered socks, an old bra, and assorted panties.

In front, a large white and gray dog lay sprawled out, more or less guarding the figure inside. The animal seemed to be some sort of bulldog or a bullmastiff or, hell, something with bull in the name.

A woman sat cross-legged on a mat, bent over a torn, mud-spattered newspaper, pen in hand, doing a crossword puzzle. She was white, lean, midthirties, and sharp-featured.

So this was Kristie.

She glanced up, sized Felicity up, and snorted. "You're new. It shows."

"I'm not anything. I don't work with Dr. Cooper."

Kristie bent her head back down. "That's timing. A six-letter word for exacting and annoying?"

"Felicity Simmons, meet Kristie."

Kristie looked up. "I'm thinking *pedant*."

"Excuse me?" Felicity sputtered.

"I meant the crossword clue. But if the Manolo Blahnik fits..." she smirked.

Felicity blinked. How the hell had some park-dwelling woman correctly identified her shoe brand?

Cooper's eyes shot down to Felicity's feet, mouth falling open. "Oh Jesus, tell me they're not designer."

"Oh, they are." Kristie said helpfully. "That's the Listony navy blue suede pump. Thirty-mil heel. Retails for seven hundred. You know, I had a pair just like them once. Bold wearing suede out here, though, with the mud and all, but I imagine Felicity here didn't plan ahead too well for her slumming-it day." She gave her dog a playful pat and turned to Cooper. "Here for Ruby, then? She's been gassy lately."

Cooper got to work while Felicity observed, disconcerted beyond measure. Every word out of Kristie's mouth turned out to be sharp and biting, which fit, since that's how she would describe Kristie's personality.

Sharp and biting? The woman was a damned cheese.

Kristie apparently didn't mind sharing, unbidden, her story. She'd run her own business before being in a bad car accident. Unable to work, she'd lost her company. No job ended her insurance, which cost Kristie her home, spiraled her into depression, and led to a painkiller addiction. She'd driven her few remaining friends away with an asshole attitude.

Try as she might, Felicity couldn't find any part of her downfall that wasn't just pure chance, not poor decisions. Something that could happen to anyone. Well, maybe not the addiction, but Kristie had already been homeless by then. Random bad luck. That's all it was. Compounding awfulness upon awfulness. Felicity had never felt so disconcerted.

The woman's shrewd, calculating gaze never left her the whole time. That was disconcerting, too.

"Nice dog" was all Felicity said, pointing to the brute of a thing slumbering on Kristie's thigh.

"She stops me getting robbed, bashed, or raped, so yeah," Kristie said, eyes lethal as ever. "Almost lost her last year when a social worker thought she would be better off without me. I told the bitch I'd kill myself if she took her." Steady, even gaze. Her eyes were fixed on Felicity's like points. "Meant it, too. I had to threaten to take my case to the media. Bitch backed down. Benefits of being a former PR expert—I can still talk the talk."

Felicity could believe it. She didn't know what to say to that.

"Pleased to report that Ruby is happy and healthy." Cooper broke the silence, looking up. "And I for one am very glad you're still around, Kristie. Besides, I'm sure Ruby appreciates her nice warm human pillow."

"Thanks, doc," Kristie said, breaking into a rare smile. "You're good people. So that Pets in the Park open day thing still happening on Wednesday?"

"Yes."

"I'll be there. Time Ruby got the wash and pampering of her dreams."

Cooper smiled. "I think she'll enjoy that. You can get some pampering, too, if you want. We're laying on the full works. Mobile showers, haircuts, and so on."

"I won't say no."

"Excellent. I might see you both there."

Cooper rose, said farewell, and headed back to the van.

Felicity found herself frozen under Kristie's assessing gaze.

"Sucks, doesn't it?" Kristie intoned. "Knowing it's not just those *other* people who end up here. Sometimes it's people exactly like you. That must rattle your cage."

"I don't know what you mean." Felicity folded her arms.

"Oh, fuck off with the defensive crap. Sure you do. Hell, I used to *be* you. I even thought the homeless were to blame for being where they are. Karma fucking sucks, let me tell you. Be grateful you still have it all. It can go just like *that*." She snapped her fingers. "And you get that now; I know you do or you wouldn't look so fucking haunted."

"You don't know me." Felicity turned on her heel and left, heart racing.

Back in the van, as Cooper sorted things out in the back, Brittany once again crawled into her lap. Felicity stared down at the bundle of fur and her comforting warmth. She made no move to touch. No point getting attached. Brittany and Cooper would be gone soon enough, after all.

"This is getting habit-forming," Cooper noted with amusement as she climbed in beside them. "Brit. Back seat!"

Brittany obeyed with some reluctance, resuming her position behind Felicity's shoulder.

"You know, I remember when she was *my* dog," Cooper said with a hearty sigh, "not that you seem to appreciate her undying loyalty. Have you even petted her once?"

Felicity pinched her lips. "She's a slobberer. I don't want her to get the idea that my outfits and her saliva should mix."

"I…see." Cooper eyed her. "How…mercenary."

Felicity shrugged. "She'll live."

"Mm." Cooper started the van.

"Can't something be done to help Kristie?" Felicity asked. "Get her back on her feet? Has anyone tried to help her?"

"So you finally cracked."

"What do you mean?"

"The thing about this job is, you always meet someone you wish you could help more. I did wonder if Kristie might be the one."

"Why?"

"Ever heard of Bacon Branding?"

"Of course." Felicity nodded. "It was one of the hottest new publicity companies in Manhattan a few years ago."

"That used to be Kristie's company. She was ambitious, young, career focused. Had so much attitude." Cooper's eyes crinkled. "Remind you of anyone?"

"You think I only care about Kristie because she reminds me of me?"

"She doesn't remind you of you?" Cooper lifted an eyebrow.

"Okay, sure. A little." *A lot.*

"Look, it's simple: You worry that if it happened to her, it could happen to you. So the human brain goes one of two ways. Either you find ways to blame everything that happened to her on some action she did, not the randomness of the universe, so you feel less afraid. Or you rush around and try to find a way to help remove her from her situation so you can stop worrying about her."

Felicity frowned, not liking how close to the truth that felt. "It's… unsettling. None of what happened to her was her fault." At the flash of irritation on Cooper's face, Felicity added, "Not that I think anyone deserves to be homeless."

"How reassuring," Cooper drawled. "Do you know most people avoid interacting with the homeless because it's terrifying to think 'There but for the grace of God go I'? It's funny, though. You know what else is terrifying?" Cooper slapped the dashboard. "Driving. Going at speed and knowing you're relying on other motorists to obey the laws and not be too drunk or high or dangerous so you get to point B. And your chances of dying in a car crash are higher than ending up on the street. But we push *that* fear from our mind and carry on daily. It'd be nice if people would deal with their own discomfort about the homeless the same way."

Felicity mulled that over. "But dealing with cars is a necessity. You can avoid the homeless for years, if you want."

"And that's why nothing ever changes. Out of sight, out of mind. And in answer to your question, many people have tried to help Kristie. That's the problem with addiction. It gets its teeth in you, and it doesn't matter how rich and successful you were before, you're still a victim to it. She struggles reintegrating back into society because of her addiction. She doesn't trust shelters after being robbed in one. But mainly she stays on the street because of Ruby."

"Why?"

"She tried to check into rehab once but was told it was her or Ruby. They had no facility to house animals, too. She has no friends who could mind her pet. And we're not set up at Living Ruff to take in a dog for weeks and weeks while she gets clean."

"So she's just…stuck?" How awful must it feel for someone who was at the top of her game to find no other solution than staying where she was—at the bottom.

"For now. She's looking at her options. The Pets in the Park event might help. It brings a whole lot of government and charity services together to assist the homeless who have pets. She might find something that works for her."

"That's good." But Felicity still felt unsettled.

Cooper smiled. "I can hear your brain churning over. Don't you remember the first rule I gave you?"

"Politeness and respect."

"Yes, but also don't try and work out how to fix their lives for them. Kristie's not a child. She's smart and knows her own mind. It's not for you to fix anything. She's getting there slowly. The main thing is, she has Ruby. That dog has kept Kristie alive. And not just physically. Kristie's mental health is much better since Ruby came along. And I'm happy to say I was the proud matchmaker. I rescued Ruby from a bad situation and thought they'd make a good match. I was right."

"That must be a nice feeling, seeing them so bonded," Felicity observed.

"It is. It makes me very happy."

That must be nice, too, Felicity thought. Being very happy. She didn't feel that emotion often.

Cooper yawned, hiding it behind her hand. "Long day. I better get back to the office. Get a bit of a nap in before round two. The boss'll be in by now so you can check with him that we're legit when we get back." She gave a small smile. "I mean, assuming you're now satisfied we're not running our charity as a front for a secret drug operation or something."

"I don't think anyone would put their hands up dogs' bottoms as a front for anything. No one's that dedicated."

Cooper chuckled. "I'd have to agree with that."

Before long, they pulled up outside the charity's office. There was a knock on the driver's side window, which set off Brittany into an excited series of barks.

Cooper wound her window down. "Shush, Brit. Down, girl!"

Brittany did exactly that.

Ugh. How could one dog be so adorable?

A kind-looking fifty-something man, his face pink from exertion, was beaming at them. He looked like a milkman from a wholesome fifties sitcom who'd unironically say things like "shucks."

"Dr. Cooper, I just saw you pull in and thought I'd say hello to your guest." He waved at Felicity, an idiotic grin plastered to his face. "Come on upstairs and we'll properly chat. I'm Harvey Clifford, director of Living Ruff New York." He turned his attention back to Cooper. "And as for you"—he frowned—"I've seen your time sheet. Go home. Now."

"I was going to have a nap and get back to it after that."

"No. Absolutely not. You're of no use to anyone if you keel over. What is this? Your seventeenth hour?" He shook his head. "Go home, Dr. Cooper. I've already called in Dr. Mendoza to replace you for the rest of today."

"I—"

"No. No arguing. My concern is for the welfare of my team before anything else. Home."

Cooper sighed. "Fine. Let me just get my things from upstairs and give Brittany back to Mrs. B."

"Of course." He smiled again, then his gaze took in Felicity. "All right, then. Ms. Simmons, wasn't it? Mrs. Brooks says you're very excited to go through our books. So let's make that happen. Come on up." He turned and headed toward the building.

Felicity eyed him in surprise. That was entirely too welcoming.

"Guess I'm off the clock," Cooper said. "Hey, maybe you'll get to ride with Dr. Mendoza later. That'll be hell for you. The man has a *chinchilla* as a riding companion."

Felicity swallowed. "I think not." Her limit for cute animals had been exceeded for the day. She'd probably wind up snuggling the damned thing within two minutes. "Absolutely not," she said more sharply.

"Well, suit yourself." Cooper climbed out of the vehicle, and Brittany bounded out beside her. "Hey, Mitch?" she called to a man lurking in the shadows of the building.

He pulled his hoodie off his head, revealing dark brown skin, unwashed hair, and a full beard. His clothing was as filthy as his smile was wide.

"Watch the van for us for an hour? Gabe'll be here soon to take over rounds."

Mitch widened his lazy grin. "Sure, Coop."

Cooper thanked him and headed toward the office, Felicity trailing behind as Brittany scooted up ahead of them.

"Mitch is great," Cooper said conversationally. "He's the reason we have a van still standing each morning, not a shell without tires on four stacks of bricks."

"Oh." Felicity hadn't thought of that. "Well…good deal for you, I guess."

"Good deal for him, too. He can sleep in it on the nights he's watching it, if he wants, and we pay him security guard rates to boot."

Well, didn't *that* just explain the weird smell in the back. Felicity wrinkled her nose.

"You're doing it again," Cooper said. "Making a face. Which I assume is accompanied by that snooty brain of yours judging people."

Snooty! "Excuse me, it's a little hard not to judge. You let your expensive work vehicle be used as a flophouse for some random homeless man!"

"Who says he's random? Mitch is one of Mrs. B's boys. Hardly a stranger to us."

"He's Mrs. Brooks's son?" Felicity asked in surprise.

"She fosters kids. Mitch was one of hers a few years back, and he aged out of the system. He got hooked on some stuff and wound up on the street. But he still loves his former foster mom, so he's never too far away. Likes to keep an eye out for her, make sure she's okay. He's really loyal. And it's mutual. Mrs. B loves knowing he's around. She's always trying to get him into jobs and re-engaged in life. It's a sweet thing, actually."

Oh. Well, whatever worked.

When she reached the top step, Cooper turned back.

"All right, I'll leave you to my boss's charms. He's really enthusiastic about Living Ruff"—Cooper grinned—"so strap yourself in and prepare to have your ear talked off."

"Good to know. Thanks, by the way. For taking me on your rounds."

"I'd say any time, but I suspect you wouldn't think that's a good thing."

"No." Felicity shuddered. "I'd say better you than me." She glanced down to find Brittany's butt parked at her ankles. Her fingers twitched to just lean down and… "Perhaps you should call off your menacing dog, too." She gave the faintest uptick of a smile.

Cooper chuckled. "You really are something else."

And for once that didn't sound exactly like a bad thing.

Chapter 4
A Prod and a Poke

HARVEY CLIFFORD'S OFFICE WAS A little chaotic with stacks of folders everywhere, including on top of a filing cabinet, proving he didn't know or care about its function. Framed photos of him beaming next to a regal, beautiful woman and a child hung along the wall. Not just a couple of photos, either. Felicity stopped counting at ten. Proud family man, then?

On his desk sat a small, colorful crocheted dog with LIVING RUFF NY embroidered on its chest. It was the ugliest thing Felicity had seen in some time—and she'd seen all of Maddie Grey's garage band T-shirts.

"That's our mascot." Harvey smiled at her from behind his desk as he caught her gaze. "You like him?"

"Um…very…." Felicity cast around for a tactful word, remembering how Elena had cast doubts on her diplomatic skills. "…orange."

"That he is." He beamed again, and his eyes, brown and kind, shone with amusement.

"So your financials?" Felicity said, sliding into a visitor's chair opposite him. Her back instantly snapped straight. It was one of those old wooden banker's swivel chairs with a stiff green leather seat. Either Harvey Clifford liked relics, or he hadn't updated the furniture in quite a few decades.

"Right to the point, huh?" Harvey smiled again. He leaned in and spread his hands. "I was delighted when I heard from Ms. Bartell. It'd be such an honor if Bartell Corp donated to our cause. Such an honor," he repeated.

"Yes," Felicity agreed. It was.

His expression shifted to regret. "I trust you'll explain that the article she saw was just a thing I do every year to drum up new sponsors. It's a way to add subscribers' names to our newsletters and hopefully sign them up as regular donors. Ms. Bartell didn't sound entirely convinced, which is why you're here, I imagine. But I'll show you." He poked through his drawers and pulled out a battered manila folder. "See?"

He spread out before her a bunch of news articles, each with different years on them, all with headlines announcing Living Ruff was on the brink of closure. Harvey's expression turned sheepish. "I know, I know. It's a bit shameless of me to play with people's sympathies like this. When I first began, I used to shout about how well we were doing, and you know what happened? No one donated at all! All our money had to come entirely from my wife's charity luncheons. But then one year a reporter inaccurately claimed we were about to fold, and donations rushed in!" He shook his head. "It's a curiosity of people wanting to back the charity about to drown instead of one that's well-run and prospering."

Well, that certainly simplified things. If this was just a publicity stunt, Felicity could reassure Elena that her donation hadn't been tossed at a failing organization. "May I take copies of these?"

"Of course. I'll get Mrs. Brooks to run some off before you finish up with us." He looked especially eager now.

A prickling sensation crawled up Felicity's neck. It all seemed aboveboard, and yet something didn't feel quite right. Her gaze slid around the outer office. It was all so old. The computers and phones were ancient, like they had not been updated in years. Where was the evidence of Elena's donation? Harvey could have afforded to modernize everything with all that extra money. Surely no one liked antiques this much.

"Mrs. Brooks mentioned something earlier. A big article that generated lots of donations," Felicity began.

"Oh yes, that. Wonderful story, wonderful! It really helped us out. We were in shock at the results. Money poured in. We even got $1.4 million from one anonymous donor." He nodded fervently. "I wish I could thank them personally."

"That's a life-changing amount of money for a small charity. Where did you end up spending it?"

Harvey's eyes clouded, and the delight fell from his expression. "We have a new program in the works. When it's ready, it'll be in our media release. I hope your many Bartell Corp publications will report on it."

"What new program?" Felicity asked, confused by his abrupt shift in demeanor. "I mean, what type is it?"

"I don't want to discuss it yet because it's only early days." He shifted a little in his chair. "That would be like asking to see an artist's half-finished painting."

A half-finished painting? He thought of some charity program as art?

Except...he didn't, did he? Harvey's eyes darted away from hers. Elena was right. The man was a terrible liar.

"So it's a program...on an unspecified topic." Felicity allowed her skepticism to show.

Harvey gave her a smile so bland it was almost nonexistent. "All in good time. So if that's everything, I have a meeting soon." He shifted again in his seat. "You are welcome to continue to see how we do things. Dr. Gabriel Mendoza will be in shortly, and you're welcome to ride along with him when he does his rounds. He covers a different area from Dr. Cooper; goes all along the East River."

Felicity peered at him, confused as to why the other vet's route was relevant. Or was Harvey just rambling?

"Or you can always come back tomorrow. Dr. Cooper has a clinic day for walk-ins. Just does patch-up jobs in here for animals with minor matters. The more major injuries we send on to other clinics and hospitals."

Definitely rambling.

His eyes darted back to Felicity's. "Feel free to skip that, though. Clinic days can be a bit... Well, not for everyone." He brightened. "But on Wednesday there's a huge open day for homeless in the park where all the services come together to help them out. My wife and Dr. Cooper will be representing Living Ruff. You can see most of what we do then. What will it be?"

His tone of voice told her either way this meeting was over. She had no interest in riding around visiting more hard-luck cases. Doing it for three hours had been more than enough. "Tomorrow," she said. "I'll attend clinic day with Dr. Cooper."

The thought of skipping a day in Cooper's company felt strangely unsettling. She absolutely refused to analyze that feeling further.

"Your choice. Clinic opens at eight here. It's excellent that you'll see all the good we do. I hope you'll convey that back to Ms. Bartell." He rose and extended his hand for her to shake, which she did. "A pleasure meeting you."

And with that, she was practically bundled out his door.

———◆———

That night, Felicity was restless. She barely tasted her low-fat vegetable lasagna or the small glass of red wine she'd washed it down with. Even her guilty pleasures failed to amuse her: *Game of Thrones* repeats, crime shows, and her beloved wildlife documentaries.

No matter how she turned over her conversation with Harvey, thought about the basic van, and even more basic office supplies, she couldn't square it away with a charity suddenly flush with cash. She needed to talk to someone who knew Harvey Clifford, someone who could give her a bead on him. A vision of a particular towering vet filled her mind before she could stop it, and she glowered.

No, someone else. Besides, she couldn't tell Cooper that she thought the woman's charity director might be shady. She was clearly loyal.

Finally, she decided to call one person who might have some insights, even though she generally didn't like asking Maddie for anything. It was just too embarrassing to need someone who would only tease the hell out of her for it.

"Felicity?" came Maddie's perky Australian accent. "This is a surprise. I thought you'd rather have water torture than call me." She laughed.

"Yes, well," Felicity said primly, "I have business to discuss."

"Really? I'm all ears. I can't think what I could know that you don't already." She paused. "Maybe teacup hurling. Trajectories and the like."

"Don't make me regret telling you about that. God!" Felicity rolled her eyes, even though the annoying woman couldn't see her.

"I'd have thought getting promoted for it would make that a fond memory." The smile in Maddie's voice was clear.

"You'd be wrong. Now, can we stop with the small talk? I need your help."

"Go on."

"You did a story last year about a charity, Living Ruff New York. Do you remember it?"

"How could I forget?" Warmth filled her voice. "I looked at every aspect of it and met so many amazing people. And don't get me started on that gorgeous vet." She chuckled. "Wow."

Right? Felicity wanted to say. It wasn't just her who appreciated the aesthetics of Dr. Sandy Cooper, but damn if she'd admit it to a living soul. "Yes, well, I'm sure Dr. Cooper's gorgeous, but I need to ask you about Harvey Clifford."

"Who mentioned Cooper? She's not the only vet there." Amusement filled her voice. "So you noticed her, too? How interesting."

"Can we please focus? This is important. I need to know about the charity director. Is he honest? Aboveboard? How deep did you go into researching him?"

"Pretty deep," Maddie said, sounding more serious now. "He dotted his i's and crossed his t's on everything. He was really honest about anything I asked about. He's so passionate about his charity, it's not funny. And then there's his wife…" She made a faint choking noise.

Felicity frowned. "What about her?"

"She's…" Maddie paused. "Let's just say Rosalind Stone is definitely the brains of the foundation. And she's not easy to forget."

"Why not?"

Maddie laughed. "She's like Elena, if Elena were a kick-ass socialite with a sole mission to help animals."

"Oh. I see." Well, now Felicity *had* to meet her. "Back to Harvey. Did he mention being interested in starting a new program? Even just as an idea?"

"No. What sort of program?"

"He won't say. He's very tight-lipped about it."

"That's odd. He was upfront about everything with me. Maybe it's just too new to discuss?"

"Maybe." Felicity was unconvinced.

"May I ask why you're digging around some charity I wrote about once?"

Maddie didn't know? Well, if Elena had wanted her to know, she'd have told her. "It's just something on the side for work. I need to know if Living Ruff is on the level."

"They're good. Really good. The homeless adore them. The local government supports them. Other charities say they're exceptional. If you're thinking of donating or Bartell Corp is, I can't think of many better causes."

A muffled voice sounded in the distance that wasn't Maddie's. Felicity frowned. Oh. She hadn't even asked if Maddie had company. She glanced at the clock and did a quick mental calculation, then gasped. "Oh! I'm sorry I called so late, Sydney time. What was I thinking!"

"Hey, relax. I'm not in Sydney. I'm in New York this month."

"You are?" Felicity blinked. "Why?"

"Visiting an old friend." Maddie laughed. "Well, I better not call her old. Anyway, I think you might know her quite well."

"I suspect she probably does," an unmistakable voice said in the background.

Elena? Elena was with Maddie? At...ten in the evening?

"Why is Elena there?" Felicity blurted out.

"She lives here. I'm visiting her, remember? Netflix night. I wanted to see her movie pick. You'll never guess."

Oh, Felicity was quite sure she'd never guess. Elena had been a mystery to her for years. "I have no idea," she said faintly.

More murmuring sounded in the background.

"Okay, I've been instructed not to tell you to maintain Elena's mystique." Maddie laughed. "I better go. Popcorn's getting cold. Hope I helped. 'Night!"

Felicity mumbled a goodbye, then stared at her phone.

In all the time she'd known her boss, Elena had never once suggested they do anything together in their downtime. That old curl of jealousy swirled up that Maddie had somehow broken through Elena's walls, but she forced it down again. No. Elena could choose whoever she wanted for friends. Even annoying Australians whom she repeatedly fired.

With a growl, Felicity turned on her TV and tried to watch *Jeremy's World*. The man was attempting to tame a hissing Bombay cat. She rather admired the animal. Nothing like a bit of attitude.

Hours later, after tossing and turning and getting precisely no sleep, Felicity sat up in bed.

It took her a moment to focus her thoughts and realize what her brain had been picking over all night.

And don't get me started on that gorgeous vet. Wow.

Felicity had been vaguely aware that Maddie was into women. Something about a French designer's daughter kissing her months ago came to mind. But tonight Maddie had more or less confirmed it. Felicity wondered if Elena knew about Maddie's sexuality. Would it matter to her either way? Probably not. Elena's best friend, *Style International*'s art director, Perry Marks, was gayer than a *Xena* convention.

Besides, maybe it hadn't even come up. Why would Maddie ever discuss her interest in women with Elena Bartell, media god? Those two probably spent their time together analyzing geopolitics and how it influenced the news or some such thing. In between, apparently, watching Netflix together.

Suddenly Felicity wondered what movies Elena liked. Maybe something classic, like *Roman Holiday*. Thrilling romances with zippy Vespas and beautiful fashion and Italy.

Then she wondered what movies Sandy Cooper enjoyed. Probably something involving truckers or lumberjacks, given her clothing choices. Felicity's mind tumbled into a fabulous abyss. Oh yes, sweaty women lumberjacks in tight tank tops chopping down trees. Her breath caught, and suddenly it was Cooper holding an ax, sweat running down her biceps, a smear of dirt on her brow. Tank-Top Cooper turned to Felicity and asked her to wipe it off, her voice a sultry tease.

Felicity swallowed. With a strained, needy sigh, she slipped her hands into her pajama pants. Her last extremely guilty thought was that she absolutely shouldn't be doing this.

Not that that stopped her.

Chapter 5
Separation Anxiety

FELICITY WAS NOT IN AT eight the next day, although she was dressed, ready, and staring out of her apartment window with more than enough time. She'd already had breakfast, cleaned up a new mess she'd discovered under her lilly pillies—thank you, evil Loki—and informed her driver to stand by. Then stand by some more.

Felicity usually wasn't one for procrastination. She looked down on it in others. But honestly, she wasn't quite ready to be in a confined space with a woman whose image had given her two shattering orgasms the night before. Even now, just thinking about Cooper all sweaty and dirty and swinging an ax with ease as her powerful arms rippled... And *oh God.* It was humiliating and galling before you even got to how guilty she felt. Worst of all, even the reminder of her fantasies made her arousal spark again.

Over her third cup of coffee—yes, yes, Felicity was breaking all her vows—she decided enough was enough. From this moment on, she would be nothing but the height of professional with Dr. Cooper. There'd be no teasing and nonsense, no unprofessional carrying on. Felicity would see to it that Cooper was nothing more than a vet she needed to engage with in order to carry out her boss's assignment. Nothing more. And she would absolutely not picture Cooper in any compromising way that could lead her thoughts to stray into dangerous realms. She could damn well control her distracting hormones. Starting right this minute.

At nine thirty, Felicity was in the Living Ruff office, mentally prepared with a poker face that she was quite sure would win her any tournament in Vegas. She nodded briefly at Mrs. Brooks, who waved her closer.

"So you came back for more, Ms. Simmons," Mrs. Brooks said, eyebrow lifting.

"Ms. Bartell wants a thorough assessment." Felicity flicked her fingers down her pale-green blouse's sleeve, divesting it of any lint that dared cling to it. "When she wants thorough, that means more than one day."

"I see," Mrs. Brooks said. "Well, it'll be a dull day for you since Dr. Cooper usually doesn't allow visitors with her when she's dealing with clients in the clinic room. She likes to keep things as peaceful and quiet during treatments as possible. So I'm afraid you'll not be seeing much—unless you're going to be doing rounds with Dr. Mendoza?"

"No," Felicity said. "I'm interested in learning what an on-site clinic does."

"Exactly the same as what a vet surgery does but without the operations. Any seriously injured animals we send elsewhere. We have an arrangement with a local animal hospital to treat our referrals, and we split their operating costs with them as part of our charity work."

"That sounds like a good deal. And the hospital doesn't mind? It must cut into its profits, not charging the full amount."

"The hospital agrees with us that alleviating animal suffering is everyone's top goal, and that also alleviates a lot of the owners' suffering too. You see how attached they are to their pets, right?"

"Yes." Felicity nodded. "Like anyone else."

"More than anyone else. Some homeless, their animal is their only friend and only living, breathing being they'll talk to all day. They're an enormous comfort when you're alone and sad." A yawning noise came from somewhere out of sight. "Speaking of comfort…look who just woke up."

Felicity shifted and peered past Mrs. Brooks to the floor. Brittany was stretching and standing. Then she spotted Felicity.

Uh-oh.

Brittany gave a joyful bark and raced over to her, leaping up and down just in front of her but not on her.

"We had to train her not to leap on people," Mrs. Brooks said, "but can't curb some animals' enthusiasm for the *darndest of things.*"

"You mean me?" Felicity asked sweetly. She leaned away from the excited animal.

"Well, you don't seem particularly appreciative in return."

Felicity folded her arms, unwilling to explain her complicated relationship with animals with the office gatekeeper. "Where's Dr. Cooper?"

"She's in with a client now." Mrs. Brooks gestured at a closed door on the other side of the room. "If you wait, she shouldn't be long." Mrs. Brooks glanced at Brittany. "Down, girl." Then she added dryly, "She's just not that into you."

Felicity rolled her eyes. "I'm sure she'll get over me three seconds after I'm gone." She chose a chair close to the clinic room and settled in to wait.

Mrs. Brooks shook her head. "Weird thing about Brittany is, she never does this with anyone else. If she were a cat, I'd understand. They're contrary and seem to love people who are indifferent to them. But Brittany in the past has only ever gravitated toward those who adore her. She just *knows*. I suppose you're the exception." Mrs. Brooks eyed her in bafflement, then returned to work.

Felicity glared at Brittany, who had now decided the best spot in the universe she could possibly be was sitting on Felicity's feet. Or to be more specific, Felicity's Italian handmade Dear Frances forest-green cube boots. "I suppose you think my designer shoes just need a polish," she murmured to the dog.

Brittany gave a happy sigh and settled her head on her front paws.

"Emotionally blackmail me all you want, but I'm not for the turning," Felicity whispered. "I'm not a pet person. If I give in to you, what's next? Kitten calendars on my office wall? A puppy screen saver? My authority with my staff would evaporate. You just don't understand anything."

Brittany didn't seem to mind and settled in for another nap.

Fifteen minutes later, Felicity was multitasking on her phone, investigating a newspaper Elena had flagged as having potential for a buyout.

Harvey Clifford had arrived, politely nodded at her, and left her to it. A few minutes later, the other vet, Gabriel Mendoza, breezed in. He was handsome enough to grace the silver screen and seemed to know it. He offered a dazzling smile as he introduced himself, informed Felicity she was brightening the office with her "ravishing beauty," engaged in a brief chat, then collected some reports and breezed out again.

After he'd gone, Felicity caught Mrs. Brooks's eye. "Does he do that with everyone?"

"I don't think he even realizes he's in charming mode half the time. He likes you, sure, but he's harmless."

"Ah." Felicity went back to her phone. "Well, not interested."

"Oh, I think he realized that when you asked him if he had to do any impacted anal glands today."

"Yes. That was quite the expression he pulled."

"Indeed. Remind me not to mess with you, dear."

Felicity smirked and returned to researching the buyout contender for Elena.

"Hard at it, I see." A familiar voice interrupted her thoughts five minutes later.

Felicity looked up to find an amused Sandy Cooper leaning against the door frame of her now empty clinic room as a man scurried away with a... well, some sort of reptile.

At the sight of Cooper, Felicity's mind lurched straight into her erotic dreams of the previous night. Suddenly the woman in front of her was pressing Felicity against the back of a huge tree and sliding her fingers into her panties while saying, "Reach into my left pocket and grab my keys, will you?"

Then...

Two yeses, huh? Lucky me.

You like my look on me?

Felicity squirmed for half a second before fury at herself overrode everything. For fuck's sake! She forced the thoughts from her mind and focused on the memory of yesterday's miserable rottweiler getting her impacted anal glands fixed.

Well, that worked. Now she felt sick.

"You okay, Felicity?" Cooper's lips curved. "You look twitchier than a cat on a hot tin roof. And I'd know: I've rescued more than a few." She chuckled, warm and rich.

Like runny chocolate. The sort you could drip on nipples and then lick off. Arousal tickled between her legs.

Felicity's eyes flew wide open. This was beyond unacceptable. Unprofessional. "Dr. Cooper," she began, relieved at how normal her voice sounded. She could do this. *Focus.*

"So formal." Cooper smiled adorably. "Yesterday I was just Cooper. Did I fall so far in your estimation overnight? Did I do something?"

Fucked me against a tree till I screamed?

Cheeks now scorching, Felicity cleared her throat and tried to think of anything else but that. "Was that an iguana?" she croaked, pointing toward the door the client had just exited through. "I researched animal laws extensively before I began this assignment. I know there's a bunch of pets you can't keep in New York." She tapped her phone, searching for the list she'd saved days ago.

"You don't say," Cooper said evenly.

"It says right here, article 161: prohibited is any member of the family *Iguanidae*. So wasn't that man's pet an iguana?" Felicity asked.

"If I say yes, will you report the matter to the authorities?"

"Shouldn't you?" Felicity gave her a perplexed look. "Don't you have a professional obligation to call the department of health if someone is keeping an animal that's illegal?"

"Some animals are dangerous and should be immediately reported and removed. I would absolutely call that in," Cooper said. "A well-loved and safely kept iguana? Hypothetically speaking? Well, that's open to debate. Unless the pet's part of the exotic-animal trade or a threat to public safety, why would you involve authorities who'll only seize the animal? The authorities have enough to worry about without bothering pets and owners causing no harm."

Felicity digested that, uncertainty filling her. She was a lawyer. The laws actually mattered to her. There had to be a reason some of these animals were banned.

At her silence, a darker look crept into Cooper's face. "Would you like to know what happens next? If you call up the department of health and report seeing an iguana leaving here? First, we'll be issued a warning for treating illegal pets. Next, assuming they find the owner, they'll issue him a violation order demanding his pet be surrendered. He'll have only three days to ask the commissioner to be heard and make a plea to get his animal back. Most homeless don't have the high-level negotiation or legal skills to navigate that hearing, so sometimes we'll go with them. We attend the hearings, wasting hours of time that could be spent helping other animals so people like you feel good about the law being enforced. And by the way, they almost never side with the pet's owners because the law's the law. Is that you, too, Felicity? Are you so black-and-white that the law is always the law?"

Felicity bit her lip. And they were back to nuance again. Did Elena have a point? Felicity's ability to see shades of gray wasn't exactly well honed. And when put as Cooper had explained it, it did seem like a lot of time and effort for a nonproblematic animal. "So iguanas aren't dangerous?"

"If that's what it was," Cooper said, eying her closely.

"You were in with it at least fifteen minutes. If I can identify an iguana, you surely can."

"Did I?"

Oh. Cooper didn't trust her.

"I'm not sure it was an iguana *exactly*," Felicity lied.

"Good. And so you know, I treated the client's pet and warned him it would be against the law to keep an iguana as a pet…if, hypothetically, that's what it was. What happens next is up to him. Now"—she faced Felicity square on—"am I about to have the Department of Health and Mental Hygiene paying Living Ruff a visit?"

"No," Felicity finally admitted. It was unsettling having her world view challenged everywhere she turned. If someone had asked her that morning whether she'd aid and abet someone breaking the law, she'd have laughed in their face. Now she wasn't sure where she stood on so many things. At least black-and-white was simple. This was just…not.

"Felicity? What's wrong?"

"It's disconcerting finding things I thought for a fact may not be."

"Well, that would be unnerving," Cooper said with a small grin. "But remember that Maya Angelou quote about doing better when you know better?"

Felicity stared. Cooper was quoting a poet to her? *Cooper?* Her Paul Bunyonesque vet?

"Now what is it?" Cooper's eyebrows lifted.

"You surprise me."

"I'm not supposed to know Maya Angelou quotes now? Or is it my flagrant breaking of the law in front of a lawyer? Or—and this is the big one—is it you discovering you're okay with all of the above?"

"The latter." Felicity ran her hand down her sleeve. "I am not used to being in a situation of not clearly knowing my own mind."

"Maybe cut yourself some slack. Growth is only possible when you're faced with new experiences, so I wouldn't sweat it. Anyway, you chose compassion over sticking to the rules, so I think you might actually be all right, Felicity Simmons."

Compassion? Felicity sucked in a dismayed breath. That didn't sound like her at all. Were company CEOs and COOs known for being compassionate? Wasn't it weak to be compassionate?

She wished she could ask Elena, but they weren't exactly…friends. Or even really at a point where she could ask anything so vulnerable. For the first time in years, Felicity wished she had a friend to consult.

"Why do you look so shocked," Cooper asked, "like I just gave you bad news?"

"I like knowing where I stand. I'm not good at fuzzy areas in life. It gives me indigestion."

Cooper chuckled. "Ah. Well, we can't have that. Let me distract you. Ordinarily, this is a task for a vet tech"—she glanced at Mrs. Brooks, who was on the phone—"but an earlier client dropped off something I will need some spare hands to deal with. Are you free?"

Felicity rose to her feet. "How can I help?"

"I need you to hold a particularly squirmy pair of kittens I'm deworming."

"I—" *Kittens? No, no, no!* "Deworming?" Felicity pulled a dismayed face.

"You'll survive." Cooper grinned.

"Doubtful." Felicity took a step back.

"You're being ridiculous."

"Am I?" Felicity shook her head hard. "I don't want to touch kittens."

"Allergies?" Cooper asked.

"No."

"Phobias?"

Felicity scowled. "I'm not *afraid* of them." Well, not exactly.

"Then you have no excuse not to make yourself useful. Let me get them from their cage. Will you please assist? I mean if it won't wrinkle your doubtless very expensive threads." Her eyes drifted appreciatively across

Felicity's designer wardrobe of green blouse, gray pants, and matching gray blazer, the latter of which now sat on the back of her chair.

Felicity sighed. *Kittens.*

———————◆———————

"Here." Cooper plopped a ginger floofball into Felicity's left hand and a black kitten with enormous blue eyes in her right. "Stop them fleeing while I get the syringe primed."

Felicity stared at the black cat, whose eyes threatened trouble. Sure enough, it leaped from her hand, up her arm, then bounced on her shoulder and flung itself at her blonde bun.

"Gahhh!" Felicity's hand shot up to de-kitten her formerly impeccable hair.

It then leaped from her head, sailing off into the abyss. No! She reflexively jerked her hand out, which sent the second kitty flying.

Two kittens were airborne. Felicity tried desperately to catch them both but only came up with one: ginger. Which promptly tried to burrow up her loose blouse sleeve via her wrist. Now half a kitten stuck out of her sleeve, tail swishing dramatically, as Felicity spun around to look for the black kitten...only to find it in Cooper's hand.

Her expression was incredulous. "Looking for this?" she asked. "Honestly, Felicity, you had one job. Hold two kittens."

"I— They got away from me." She tugged on ginger's tail to extract it from her sleeve. Claws dug in. *Ow! Fuck, fuck, fuck.* Felicity's eyes watered.

"Do you really hate animals so much that you can't even hold two harmless little kittens for one whole minute?" Disappointment etched Cooper's face.

Harmless? Tell that to her poor abused arm. "I keep telling you, I don't *hate* them. I just don't...react well to them. And it seems to be mutual." Finally, she pulled the kitten clear from her sleeve and glowered at the squirmy thing that had left pucker marks all down her skin.

It reminded her of Loki. What *was* it with her and cute devil spawn?

"Well, I agree these kittens should be anywhere but in your custody." Cooper rubbed her thumb under the black kitten's ear, then scooped her into one arm.

That seemed a bit unfair, and Felicity deflated. *She* hadn't made the cats go ballistic. They just had.

Cooper stroked the kitty's whiskers back, eased open the jaw the tiniest amount with the same hand, and with her other injected liquid medication toward the back of its tongue. Then her holding hand closed the cat's jaw, gently stroking its chin for about three seconds. "One down." She gave the kitten a fond pat before returning it to the cage. She prepped a second syringe and looked at Felicity expectantly.

"Ginger, please?" Her eyebrow arched.

Felicity promptly deposited the animal onto the metal treatment table and backed off.

"It's not a rattlesnake," Cooper said as she repeated the process with the second kitten. Into the cage it went after a little pat. Cooper whipped off her gloves and tossed them in the trash. "Well, that's how it's done."

Felicity nodded. "You're good at this."

"I'd like to think so after all this time. But our whole team gets the credit. It's not just me keeping Living Ruff's lights on. Gabe's a whiz at handling difficult clients having mental health episodes. Harvey and his wife keep things ticking financially and the donations coming in. And then there's Mrs. Brooks." Her eyes turned fond. "That woman runs it all. Not just a vet tech or a receptionist or a PA. She looks after our day-to-day admin: accounts, spreadsheets, and finances. She has a gift for it."

"So why's she wasting it here?"

Cooper froze and turned to stare at her. "Wasting it?"

"I—" Oh, that hadn't come out right.

"Wasting. It?"

"I mean, if she's so good, she could get a job anywhere," Felicity scrambled, not liking the dark look in Cooper's eyes one bit. "Out of the charity sector. Private business. Earn her worth. Enjoy good perks."

"Has it even occurred to you that that's not what everyone wants?"

"Oh…well—"

"Ambition doesn't drive everyone. Not everyone wants the money or the perks, either. Mrs. Brooks loves helping animals. And she appreciates being close to family and others she's come to care for. Such as Mitch."

"Mitch, the van minder?"

"Yes. Among others. She has so many people who love her all over the Bronx. She'd never want to leave any of them for some extra cash or a big title."

Felicity tried to work out what that would be like: driven by friendship and affection, not ambition?

"Did I just melt your brain?" Cooper asked.

"No comment." Felicity folded her arms, scowling.

Mrs. Brooks stuck her head in the office. "Sorry to interrupt, but Daniel's here in a bit of a state."

"What's wrong?" Cooper straightened.

"He won't say. But his dog looks in a bad way."

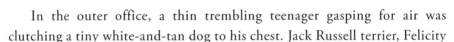

In the outer office, a thin trembling teenager gasping for air was clutching a tiny white-and-tan dog to his chest. Jack Russell terrier, Felicity identified.

"Daniel?" Cooper said softly, getting closer.

The dog growled, barked, and attempted to lunge at her but was tugged back tighter in Daniel's arms. The dog was so little that it seemed no real threat, except for some weird drool coming from its mouth.

Cooper stepped back and her voice became softer. "Daniel? Can you tell me what happened?"

Wide, terrified eyes met hers. "I ran the whole way here. Fast as I could. Fuckin' cops tried to stop me, claimed I wouldn't be running unless I'd done something bad. Crime of running while Black was what they meant." His voice rose in outrage. "I showed them Jasper to explain and said 'Yo, look at his mouth!' Then they said they had to report it and were gonna take him! My boy *doesn't* have rabies! Why'd they go and say a thing like that?"

Trembles overtook him again. "I fucked off outta there when they went to their car to call animal control." He darted a look over his shoulder. "Probably still looking for me."

"I think you've lost them. May I look at Jasper, please?" Cooper asked, holding her arms out.

Daniel hesitated, panic still clear on his face. "He doesn't have rabies," he whispered. "You won't hurt him, right?"

"I just want to examine him."

Daniel trembled again. Suddenly he looked so small in his oversized jacket and drooping pants, scuffed and muddy where they met old dirty sneakers. Was he even eighteen?

"Now then, Daniel," Mrs. Brooks cut in briskly, "I'm just gonna get you a nice cup of sweet tea."

"I don't drink tea, ma'am."

"No arguments. You need it. You sit your backside down right here and let Dr. Cooper do her business of taking care of your dog."

"I—" His wide eyes swept the room as if sizing it up for threats, then he sank into the chair in the face of Mrs. Brooks's no-nonsense maternal demand. Then Daniel handed off Jasper to Cooper.

She cradled the dog in her arms, soothing it, which seemed a miracle to Felicity because something was definitely not right with that animal.

"Can you tell me what happened to him?" Cooper asked as she studied the dog.

Daniel swallowed. "Nothing?" His voice was pitched weirdly high. "He just got sick?"

The kid should not play poker.

"Well, it's not nothing, is it?" Cooper said kindly. "Jasper's foaming. So come on, what happened? Did he get bitten by something? Eat something weird?"

Daniel trembled even more. "You won't report me? Even if I say that something bad happened?"

"I know you love Jasper, but we've gotta look out for him, don't we? He's our priority, and he's not well. So you need to tell me all of it."

"I—" Daniel sagged. "Yeah." Then he started to cry and buried his face in his hands. His small shoulders lifted up and down. He looked like a child about to lose his whole world.

"Tell me," Cooper said even more gently.

"Jasper found some weed. Ate the whole pouch before I could stop him. It wasn't a small pouch, either." His eyes went wide with fear. "Please, *please* don't tell the cops."

Weed? The idiot had dosed his dog on marijuana? Felicity inhaled sharply. Some people didn't deserve animals. That's all there was to it.

"I see." There was no judgment in Cooper's face or voice. "Okay, let's figure out how Jasper's doing. Has he been peeing a lot?"

The young man whispered, "Yeah. Lots."

"What about tremors? Hyperexcitability?" She regarded the dog's muzzle. "I can see excessive salivation."

He nodded hard. "Yeah."

Mrs. Brooks bustled up holding a huge mug of milky tea. "Here you go. Get that into you." She slid it across the table in front of Daniel. As his mouth opened, probably to argue again, Mrs. Brooks's tone became firm. "None of that, now. You need some sugar in you after all that stress. Don't need you fainting into a heap on our floor. I'll find you a granola bar, too. Or maybe some of my homemade cobbler? I brought some in today, and it's too good not to share, I can tell you. Wait here."

Daniel looked out of his depth, and the puff went out of him. His eyes signaled defeat. "Yes, ma'am. Don't much like tea, though," he muttered.

"It's not about what you like; it's about keeping your strength up." Mrs. Brooks bustled away again. "You got to live to fight another day, young man. If not for you, then for Jasper."

"I guess. Yeah." He looked at Cooper, and his voice cracked when he asked, "How is he? Is he gonna live?"

"Jasper needs an IV and some medication. We need to dilute the toxin in his body and protect his kidneys. After that, he'll be fine. But I'll need to keep him here for a few hours, and—"

Daniel shook his head. "No!" He looked panicked all over again. "I can't! If I leave him, you'll give him to the cops, and they'll say I'm not fit to have him. I need him!" Tears filled his eyes again. "Jasper's all I got after Dad kicked me out." He drew in a ragged breath, and his voice came out like a growl. "Said a faggot and his faggot dog belong together."

"Hey." Cooper's voice was reassuring. "No one's talking about you giving him up. And no one here's about to call the police." Her gaze slid to Felicity. "Right?"

Felicity pursed her lips. "No one's calling the police." Even though the kid was an idiot. She kept that blunt but accurate assessment to herself.

"O-okay." Daniel exhaled, his brown eyes still full of fear. "Okay. Just make him better."

"Absolutely," Cooper said with a smile. "You stay right there and let Mrs. Brooks fuss over you and get you fueled up again"—she waved in the direction of the older woman heading their way with a huge plate of food—"and I'll start Jasper on his treatment."

An hour later, Daniel was a lot calmer and had been stuffed full of assorted foods, including Mrs. Brooks's homemade peach cobbler. It looked sinfully good, not that Felicity would dare try it, not with her family's genetics, despite multiple offers and the suspicious glares that met her refusal. Mrs. Brooks was a hard woman to turn down, as Daniel had discovered, too.

The young man was now on the other side of the office, sitting beside Jasper in the clinic room as the dog slumbered through his treatment, an IV doing its work.

Felicity waited for Cooper at the table in the main office area as the vet finished cleaning up.

"Let's hear it," Cooper said when she finally joined her.

"Hear what?"

"You're making a face. You're judging Daniel, I think. Why?"

They were out of earshot of everyone, but Felicity darted a look around to check to be sure. "His dog got into his marijuana stash," she said, incredulity edging her voice. "I can see he loves Jasper, but maybe that's not enough. Surely the dog would be better off with someone else?"

"I see." Cooper's eyes hardened. "So we should take dogs off everyone when the dog gets into something it shouldn't against the owner's wishes."

"It was *weed*," Felicity hissed. "Mind-altering drugs! Not like Jasper chewed up a shoe."

"And you think this has never happened to anyone with a roof over their heads?" Cooper leaned in. "Before I joined Living Ruff, I was a vet in a high-end practice. Some very well-heeled Manhattan clients came in with dogs and cats suffering from far worse than weed. A lot of expensive drugs wind up inside people's pets. So why should Daniel lose Jasper when no one else loses their dog over accidents? Animals get into things. That's how they are. They're curious and don't know any better."

"He's so small, though." Felicity glanced back over at the sleeping terrier. "Weed aside, it's unsafe for Jasper being out in the elements. He needs so much better care."

"The same could be said for Daniel."

Well, that was sadly true. They were both too thin and small. When they trembled, it was hard not to have your heart go out to them. "Will they be okay?"

"I hope so. I think Mrs. B wants to adopt Daniel," Cooper joked. "If he comes around again, she'll make sure he's well-fed. She'll make sure he knows that before he leaves. And I know she'll be looking up some LGBT homeless services to see if they can help him with options."

That was something, she supposed.

Mrs. Brooks suddenly loomed over them. "Are you free for a pickup, Dr. Cooper? Those crates are ours if we want."

"Now?" Cooper glanced at Daniel and Jasper through the clinic door.

"I can mind those two. And my vet-tech credentials aren't just painted on," Mrs. Brooks said. "Go before they change their mind." She shooed Cooper. "I'll call you if there's a change here."

"All right." Cooper rose. "Thanks."

"Where are we going?" Felicity stood, too, and followed her down the stairs, with Brittany bringing up the rear.

"A local company that makes animal crates has some spares they want to donate, and they're not far from here. They told us last week they might be ours if we picked them up when they called."

"Animal crates?"

"A rare few homeless shelters allow animals to be with their owners, as long as the pets are caged at night. Being able to donate these crates to our clients is a simple way we can help them sleep off the street."

"Okay." Made sense. "Why don't all the shelters do that? Let owners keep their animals with them overnight in crates?"

"They have all sorts of excuses, mainly about cost and insurance issues, but unless the law changes, they don't have to," Cooper said. "Basically, no one's making them."

"Ah." Felicity scanned the streets as they headed for the van. Despite some lively Spanish-speaking men crowded around the tables playing dominoes with a gusto that mystified her, the park was as cold and concrete as always. "Someone should make them."

"No argument from me." Cooper's expression became defeated. "I've tried. My friends on city council have tried. There's a lot of red tape in the way of making that happen."

When Felicity slid into the passenger seat, Brittany was in her lap in two seconds.

"You're nothing if not predictable," she told the dog in exasperation.

Brittany snuffled and hunkered down.

Felicity sighed. "Well, it's not like I can stop you."

"You know damned well you can," came Cooper's voice from the rear of the van, where she was noisily making space for the crates.

Well, she had a point. "Move, dog," Felicity said sternly. "Back in your seat." She gave Brittany a half-hearted poke with her finger, then melted at how soft the dog's coat was.

She was saved from doing something hopelessly pathetic when Cooper returned and ordered, "Brit. Back seat."

The dog obeyed after a huff so disdainful and human it almost made Felicity proud. Hell, that dog was every kind of awesome.

"What I was getting at before," Felicity said as she did up her seat belt, "is that Daniel has a choice in living where he does. Jasper doesn't."

"I always love that argument"—Cooper started the van—"as if people think, 'I have all these options, but no, I really think it's the streets for me.'"

"But just because Daniel means well and has no other choices, it doesn't change the fact that Jasper's life could be much better."

"Better how?" Cooper asked as she put her foot down on the gas. "You met a dog today that is, aside from the marijuana high, healthy, fed, and well loved. He is loyal as hell to his owner. Jasper doesn't care where Daniel sleeps. He's hardy and strong. Daniel loves Jasper, and Jasper loves Daniel. Those two would die for each other. As long as that equation remains true, I'll always do my best to keep them together."

Felicity turned and gazed out the window as boarded-up shops, panhandlers, and gaudy signs flashed by. Maybe Cooper was right. It was hard to argue the logic that no one grew up wanting to live on the street.

Kristie flashed into her mind. There was a woman who might have freed herself from her addiction long ago, but she wouldn't until Ruby could be with her at the treatment center. Which might be never. That was loyalty—or love.

"So quiet. Should I be afraid?" Cooper asked, tone faintly teasing.

"Processing," Felicity murmured.

"Good," Cooper said kindly. "I appreciate your capacity to do that. Not everyone can."

Felicity turned to look at her. "How long have you been doing this? For Living Ruff?"

"Ten years."

"How aren't you burned out?" Felicity eyed her. "All the bad things you see, day in, day out?"

"I don't look at it that way. I see the best of us. I see a man who'd go hungry rather than deprive his dog because that's how much he cares. And then I see him overjoyed when I turn up and he realizes his dog won't be hungry for a while."

"Glass half full." Felicity thought about that. She closed her eyes. What a life it must be for people like Cooper, viewing the world with a whole lot less cynicism.

They drove on in silence for a few minutes. Then Cooper spoke. "Out of curiosity, how strong are you?"

"If you're about to ask for help in moving a bunch of animal cages, you'd have more luck with Brittany." Felicity opened her eyes. "My doctor says I have all the muscle tone of an earthworm. Which is a bit insulting, given how often I hit the gym in my building."

"How can you go to the gym and have no muscle?" Cooper asked, eyebrow lifting.

"Well, I don't lift weights or anything. The treadmill's an excellent place to get my thinking done. I jog. A lot."

Cooper laughed. "I'd knock my front teeth out on a treadmill—I'd never figure out the speed. I don't bother with the gym. Why pay when I get a free workout every day? I cycle to and from work."

Felicity now had a rather marvelous visual image of Sandy Cooper powering along on a bicycle. She wondered what she wore. Tight Lycra bike pants maybe? Or she just tossed a muscled leg over, jeans and all? Probably tucked the jeans into work socks poking out from her sturdy boots? She licked her lips. "How far is your place from work?"

"It's only a three-mile ride. Some of it's even scenic along the river. I'll miss it."

"Why miss it?"

"My building used to allow pets. A new owner bought it and changed that. So no Brit for me at home. I'm looking to move."

"A new owner can't just arbitrarily change the rules." Felicity frowned. "There are regulations to prevent that."

"No, he can't, and he grandfathered the rules so any existing pets could stay, but residents would be banned from having new animals. The problem is, I was listed as having a cat when I moved in. When Molly died, I adopted Brittany but never changed my status officially. I didn't think it would be an issue. Now the owner's management team says they have to treat Brittany as a new pet."

She slapped the steering wheel. "I've got a few neighbors prepared to testify that I've had Brit three years. The owner says the paperwork is all that matters and told me either I had to leave or Brit did. So great, now I'm apartment hunting. And Mrs. B's been fantastic, taking Brit home with her each day, but I really miss my girl at night. I can't even lounge around my place with her on the weekends."

"Would you like me to look at the bylaws? See if I can find a solution?" Felicity asked. "Believe it or not, I'm very good at what I do."

"Don't judge you by how you handle small talk, random pets, and moving crates, you mean?" Cooper laughed.

"Something like that. I don't mind. It'd be a nice change to use my knowledge of the law to examine something at the micro level instead of macro."

"Thanks for the offer, but I've already had a lawyer look at this, and he says the new owner is perfectly within his rights. And since the building manager lives two doors down from me, I can't just sneak Brittany in or anything." She exhaled. "It's just a pain to be looking for somewhere new, that's all." Cooper's expression turned thoughtful. "So that's what you do, then? Examine the law at a macro level? What does that even mean?"

"It means big-picture things. I've spent years negotiating with or overseeing lawyers who do deals to take over media publications. Over a hundred lawyers worldwide report to me." She paused. "Well, they *did*. In my new role, that's something I'm a step above now. I'm soon to be the one deciding which mastheads get bought out, which get stripped and sold, which employees are kept or fired. I deal in the lives of thousands of employees and turnovers of many millions."

"That's a lot of power," Cooper said quietly. "A whole lot for one person."

"I suppose it is," Felicity said slowly. "I don't think about it like that too often. In terms of power."

"Perhaps you should. Perhaps that would make you excel at what you do. Or excel *more*. I wouldn't presume to suggest you're not already excellent." Cooper's lips ticked up.

Felicity ignored the humor and everything else because Cooper had a good point.

She thought about it some more while Cooper effortlessly hauled two dozen animal crates into the back of the van, slapping dust off her jeans with mighty whacks that absolutely didn't make Felicity squirm a little in her seat. Cooper gave a smirk at Felicity's obvious uselessness as she slammed the van doors shut.

Later that night, Felicity turned over the idea again: how much power she was inheriting.

Elena wore power effortlessly. It didn't seem to trouble her much at all, but then she was used to it, wasn't she?

But Cooper was right. It was a lot for one person.

Elena was never cavalier with flexing her power, although her many former personal assistants might take a different view. Firing them so easily wasn't, for Elena, about showing off her clout. It was about having standards and her employees not measuring up.

Power—its use and reach—was a different animal entirely.

Elena had wanted to know how Felicity handled herself outside her comfort zone of boardrooms and deals. At the time, it had seemed so random. Just another curious whim in a long line of them from her unknowable boss.

Questions and doubts churned as Felicity gazed unseeing out her balcony. Then came a blinding insight: being a leader of a corporation wasn't just about allocating resources in the most efficient way, was it?

So little in life was black-and-white, rule bound, and about the letter of the law. Sometimes things like, say, illegal iguanas, didn't neatly fit. Throwing a bureaucratic mindset into a delicate situation would be a disaster. Adaptable, open minds were needed to look at the impact of decisions, not just the rules. The best managers could navigate those shades of gray effortlessly.

Felicity could see now that need for nuance, as Elena had called it. Taking into account more than just the end goal.

Which begged the question…

Do I have what it takes to do my new job?

For the first time, Felicity couldn't answer that. Not decisively the way she'd always been able to in the past.

She drew in a shaky breath. Well, that was depressing.

Either way, Cooper was right about one thing: it was a lot for one person.

Chapter 6
Pets in the Park

THE NEXT DAY, FELICITY WAS up early after a sleepless night filled with far too many doubts. Resolving to dwell on it no more under the auspices of WWED (What would Elena do?), she instead threw herself into the day ahead.

The Pets in the Park event was pretty much what she had expected. Lots of animals, lots of homeless, lots of tents all crammed into one place.

She wandered through the park, taking in the array of minibuses and stalls. She was impressed at the number of volunteer organizations that had shown up to offer services to homeless people and their pets, including mobile showers, dentists, hairdressers, and animal groomers, along with suppliers of free clothing, toiletries, food, and blankets. Tents were manned by government representatives keen to explain educational, legal, healthcare, and housing opportunities.

At least a hundred people had gathered so far. Felicity was surprised to recognize a couple of them from rounds with Cooper.

One in particular was headed her way, a trademark smirk firmly affixed.

"Look who it is," Kristie drawled. "The me I used to be."

"Really? I didn't realize you were once a lawyer for a media corporation," Felicity shot back.

"Someone woke up on the nitpicky side of bed today. I meant you remind me of my glorious type-A self back in the day."

"Well, there are lot of type-A people in New York." Felicity gave her a stubborn look.

"Whatever." Kristie snorted. "I think I almost like you. You don't fake being interested in me, suck up to me, or try to rescue me like the social workers. They want to save me from myself and get quite worked up about it because I'm too corporate white girl for them to ignore." She rolled her eyes. "They try to hide how much I rattle them—the way you're trying right now." Her look was goading.

Felicity refused to be baited, no matter how close Kristie was to the truth. "You know, you could just let them help," she said, tone dry.

Kristie folded her arms. "Why should I? It's always about them and their insecurities, not what I need. If they really wanted to help me, they'd know it's me *and* Ruby or don't bother." She nodded to the dog in question, presently up to her neck in shampoo at a grooming stall, tongue lolling. "She's saved my life twice, and I owe her everything. She's family to me, but they act as if she's disposable. They say earnest shit like, 'Kristie, dear, we need to work out who'll take your animal for you while you get clean.'" Her tone as she imitated them was saccharine. "Fuck off. They don't understand anything."

"So if there was a way to keep Ruby with you, you'd do their programs?"

"What do you think? You think I *like* this life? That my BA in marketing is best spent on working out where to sleep each day?" She glared at Felicity. "Or how it feels begging money for tampons every month but you can't say what it's for because that's too embarrassing, and people only want to buy you a meal because you apparently can't be trusted not to blow their precious five bucks on drugs? Or what it's like to always be hunting for a safe place to take a crap where sleazes don't jump you and security guards don't rough you up? Then there're the creeps in executive suits offering you food or a shower for sex, who look at you like you're a worthless piece of shit."

Anger flashed in Kristie's eyes. "I hope you never know how that feels. Worst part is that the threat is *constant*. It hangs over you twenty-four seven and never leaves. You wake up exhausted. You have so many stress conditions, it's insane. But I'd still put up with all of that for Ruby."

Felicity felt nauseous just imagining that much anxiety. She wasn't exactly physically tough to start with. Not that Kristie looked any more solid. "You're right. I had no idea."

Kristie exhaled. "I know you didn't. No one does till it's them."

A blow-dryer started up, and Felicity glanced over to see Ruby now getting A-list treatment from the groomer. "She'll never want to leave. Look at that smile."

"Right? Only reason I drag myself to these things. Everyone needs their pamper day. Ruby's owed."

"And you, too?"

Kristie shrugged. "Ruby comes first. Now and always."

They watched for a few minutes as Ruby turned into a tongue-lolling, gently dried ball of contentment.

Genuine delight crossed Kristie's face. "I'm really glad I came," she said quietly. She glanced at Felicity. "Well, thanks for treating me like a normal human being. I've missed that. Although I bet it's killing you at least a little not to do *something* to save me."

"Thought never entered my head," Felicity protested, lips quirking a little.

"Thought so." Kristie's eyes crinkled. "Look, just don't take for granted what you have."

"I don't."

"You do." Her expression turned rueful. "But that's okay. Everyone does. I did, too." Kristie collected Ruby, thanked the groomer, shot Felicity a knowing look, then the pair wandered away.

Felicity was still thinking about Kristie when she finally noticed a big handmade sign in front of one of the tents that said: Free vet care! Come on in! Living Ruff New York.

Cooper was busy cleaning a small cut on the paw of on an enormous Doberman when Felicity found her. A white-haired, toothless woman with an infectious cackle sat in a chair beside her chatting away.

"And then Blunders ran off and brought back the shoe. I have no idea to this day whose shoe it was, but I just added it to the pile. She's a real shoe thief. Wouldn't mind if she stole something in my size, but she never does." The woman threw back her head and laughed, a naughty guffaw she accompanied with a thigh slap against her thin, flowery dress and black leggings.

Felicity stood back for a while, watching the smooth, gentle way Cooper handled both animal and owner. She had such a likable energy, something

Felicity had always lacked. In so many ways, Cooper was her complete opposite. She tried to think of one thing they had in common and gave up.

Eventually, Cooper spotted her and waved her closer. "Morning. Come in, Felicity. Blunders and I are all finished, aren't we, girl?" She glanced back at the enormous brown dog and scratched under both ears.

Blunders wagged her stump of a tail in delight.

"Thank you, dear," the elderly woman said as she led her dog outside the tent. "Blessings on you."

On her way out, she passed a forty-something Black woman in a chic navy business suit who was striding in.

"Cooper!" she cried out, a smile washing her face.

The woman had a presence that Felicity instantly recognized. This was someone confident, used to having power, who wore it effortlessly.

"Deedra!" Cooper scrambled over to give her an engulfing hug. "It's been months! How have you been?"

"Oh, keeping out of trouble for the most part. You know me." Deedra smiled even wider, then caught sight of Felicity. "Hello," she said, eyes lit with curiosity. "I suspect you're not one of Dr. Cooper's regulars."

Excuse me? Felicity folded her arms. "I'm just here observing today. I'm hardly homeless."

"Just teasing," Deedra said. "I've yet to see anyone homeless wearing a fourteen-hundred-dollar coat…at least not a new one." She laughed.

Cooper's eyes went wide; she choked and turned to look at Felicity's outfit. "Felicity? You wore a fourteen-hundred-dollar coat to a homeless open day?"

"I wear fourteen-hundred-collar coats wherever I like," Felicity said defensively. "It gets cold."

Why was Felicity's face heating up now? It wasn't a crime to appreciate quality clothing, was it? And this was the warmest coat she could find on short notice before she got to her faux furs. It just so happened to be her Joseph Cenda designer cashmere coat. And it was only twelve hundred dollars, thank you very much. Never let it be said that Felicity was incapable of bargain hunting.

"Whoa, whoa." Deedra lifted her hands. "I'm sorry for starting something here. I promise, I was teasing. Please forgive me, Ms…?"

"Simmons." Felicity shot a worried look at Cooper, wondering if the expensive coat had ruined the woman's opinion of her.

Deedra's eyes darted back and forth between them. "Wait, are you two…" She swished her finger at the two of them.

"Of course not!" Felicity said, far too fast and far too loud. She cringed inwardly.

"Well, that was decisive," Deedra said impishly. "Your poor ego, Coop."

"It certainly was." Cooper's eyes and voice were cool. "Nice to be appreciated. Anyway, Felicity Simmons, meet Councilor Deedra Randall. She and her team are working on some vital legislation for the New York City Council. If it passes, it will mean homeless people can't be turned away from shelters or addiction programs if they have a pet. Not just government facilities, either. All of them. Public and private."

Felicity's head snapped up. So people like Kristie could get treated? "And will you get it passed?" she asked, leaning in.

"Through *council*, yes, I believe we have about sixty percent support there. It's hard; there are vested interests. The private facilities, profits and nonprofits especially, are putting up a fight, arguing it's too expensive to implement."

"What's the issue, then, if you have the votes to get it through council?" Felicity asked. "Is there some impediment after that?"

"Yes." Deedra gave her a measuring look. "There is a nasty roadblock."

"The mayor," Cooper inserted. "He's threatening to use his veto power when the legislation comes before him. He keeps talking about risk to staff and residents from dangerous dogs—being exposed to lawsuits and so on if one attacks. I met with Mayor Browning several times explaining how animals can be crated at night—explaining how roomy portable kennels are. You saw those crates yesterday—they're comfortable even for big dogs. And I told the mayor that Living Ruff supplies them for free to anyone who needs one. He just kept talking right over the top of me about the cost, risks, lawsuits, and how hard it would be to do."

Felicity's eyes narrowed. She hated assholes like that. Oh, she'd faced down more than a few bombastic lawyers in her time who thought speaking louder overcame logical points. It was always most satisfying to beat that type. "He sounds charming."

"You can see for yourself soon," Deedra said. "He doesn't want to look like too much of an asshole about the homeless issue and the fact he'll singlehandedly be the one preventing them getting off the street. So he'll be here today for a publicity stunt. Photos, media, waving at homeless people to show he's not so bad. Probably cuddling a homeless person's dog…after they've been through the free grooming, of course."

"I can't imagine anyone here will be pleased to see him."

"No, but it'll be about viewers at home saying, 'Oh, well, I can see he's looked at both sides.'" Deedra scowled. "It's not both sides when one group stays homeless and the other just counts their money and says, 'Sorry, can't help.'"

Felicity's eyes hardened. "Mayor Browning is up for re-election soon. That's the reason for the publicity stunt today?"

"Yes," Deedra said. "We've been stalling on finishing up writing our legislation on this until after the polls. The idea is, if he loses, maybe the next mayor will be more open to it."

"I've seen Mayor Browning's approval ratings. He's not losing." Felicity eyed them both. Surely they had a plan B.

"The race is tightening." Deedra said, apparently trying to find a positive spin.

"No, it isn't," Felicity said with certainty. "Browning has big business in his pocket. Funding. A solid message. He's not losing. I've also seen his competition. Her messaging is all over the place. Browning will be re-elected. You know I'm right."

Deedra and Cooper exchanged tense looks.

"Well, fuck," Cooper muttered. "There goes any hope for fixing this shit."

Deedra sagged. "Mm."

"Not…necessarily." Felicity's mind began to churn. This, at least, was something in her wheelhouse. "You"—she pointed to Deedra—"need to tell me everything you know about the upcoming legislation."

"I—excuse me?" Deedra peered at her. "I'm not following."

Felicity didn't care whether she followed or not. She could see quite clearly Kristie never getting off the street again, the way things were going. It wasn't rescuing if she fixed an injustice, was it? Besides, it would be helping everyone, not singling her out. It was just *correcting an issue*. And

Felicity was damned good at fixing problems, especially where the law was involved.

She went to a small fold-up table near the back of the tent, beckoning for Deedra to follow her. "How long do we have?"

"Until?"

"The mayor's arrival."

"Two hours."

Felicity glanced at her watch. "All right, then. We'll have to work fast." She pulled out her phone and began tapping furiously, then making notes. Facts were not difficult to lay her fingers on. *Google, I could kiss you.*

"What *are* you doing?" Cooper asked, looking mystified.

"Changing the mayor's mind." Felicity studied with satisfaction the results she was seeing on her screen. She punched in the number for Bartell Corp's senior accountant.

"Thomas? Felicity Simmons. I need you to drop whatever you're doing and help me crunch some numbers. Accuracy and speed are paramount. Also, I'll need someone to fact-check stats from news sources as I send them. We only have two hours." She laid the phone down, tapped in an email address, and hit send. Then she scooped it up and resumed speaking. "Can you double-check my math, too? I've sent an email on everything I need."

She listened as Thomas made keyboard clacking noises, then glanced over to Deedra, covering her phone's microphone. "What are you waiting for? Sit. Here. Now." She tapped the other side of the table. "Be part of the solution."

Thomas spoke in her ear again, regaining her attention. "Looks simple enough. I'll get back to you. And your math seems right, but I'll double-check it anyway."

"Good," Felicity said, the thrill of the hunt filling her. She glanced at the time. "One hour and fifty-five minutes, Thomas. Do not let me down."

"I'm on it, Ms. Simmons."

She ended the call and met Deedra's eyes. "Everything you know about your legislation." She reached into her handbag, pulled out a pen, and pushed it across the table, then flipped over a pile of vet-care brochures scattered on the next table that had blank backs. "Write it down now." And tapped them.

"I'm sorry, but who are you again?" Deedra looked as if she'd been hit by a speeding truck.

"I'm a lawyer who knows how to fix this."

Cooper choked, looking astonished.

"I am also the deputy chief operating officer of Bartell Corporation," Felicity finished. And this time, it finally sounded real.

Deedra, eyes wide, glanced at Cooper, then Felicity. Then she picked up the pen and began to write.

"How long have you known Cooper?" Felicity asked as she and Deedra made their way toward a makeshift stage area. According to Deedra's estimate, the mayor would be here to do his publicity stunt speech in under five minutes.

"We met years ago, one of the many times she addressed the council demanding more rights for homeless people's animals. She fought a good fight but lost on that issue."

"Does she lose often?" Felicity asked.

"Truthfully?" Deedra's lips quirked. "Quite often. She's passionate and emotive about her animals, but that doesn't sway lawmakers. She's hopelessly disorganized, jumps from topic to topic, makes a big speech, but it's all over the place. What's needed is a cool, hard head, a legal mind who can shred arguments." She eyed Felicity. "And that's you, isn't it? I looked you up while you were researching. You handle all legal issues from all over the world for Bartell Corp newspaper buyouts and mergers."

"I used to until recently." Felicity said. And for the first time in a long time, she decided not to hide how proud that made her. "My strength is in finding loopholes, hidden information, seeing what the other side is hiding. The mayor won't know what's hit him."

"I hope so. But why are you helping Living Ruff? What have they got to do with you or your corporation?"

"I'm spending a few days determining whether a donation is a good idea or not for my boss."

"You suspect it might not be?" Deedra sounded incredulous.

"I like to form conclusions based on facts I've obtained personally. Why is that surprising?"

"I thought it was common knowledge that Living Ruff is gold star. They're one of the best charities our council deals with."

"And Harvey Clifford?"

"Boring, by the book, never puts a foot wrong, as far as I know."

"Hmm." Felicity said. His cagey mention of some vague new program was still stuck in her head. "We'll see."

They neared the stage just as Mayor Browning was taking the microphone. He launched into a monologue, talking up the Pets in the Park open day initiative as if it had been his idea.

"Blowhard," Deedra murmured. "He's even worse when there're no cameras around."

"Most men in power are," Felicity noted. "Trust me. I've met them all."

"I'll bet you have." Deedra smiled. "All right. I'm going to make myself scarce."

"Where are you going?" Felicity asked in surprise.

"You forget I still have to work with that man. I'd rather he didn't know I was your co-conspirator. Good luck. Oh, and hey, don't mess with Cooper, okay? She has a soft heart."

"I—what? Excuse me?"

"I said what I said." Deedra glanced around, caution in her eyes. "Look, it isn't common knowledge and I'd like to keep it that way, but we dated a few years ago. We worked out we're better as friends. I'm naturally protective of her, and you are her type."

"What type is that?"

"She does appreciate career-driven bossy types who get shit done." Deedra winked. "No wonder she liked my bad ass. But all I'm saying is, don't be a bitch to her, okay? I mean, I'm guessing you're straight. Either way, shoot her down gently if it comes to that."

Felicity blinked. Okay, she had to process all of this later. *In detail.* Because Felicity was sure there was no way Cooper would ever look at her romantically. But right now the mayor was asking if there were any more questions from the media.

Deedra was gone by the time the man's gaze scanned the reporters huddled in front of him.

The media had already run out of questions, which wasn't surprising since they weren't looking terribly interested in the photo op. Why would they be? Following a blowhard but boring mayor around on his campaign stops had to be a special form of torture for political reporters seeking real news.

Felicity edged into the media pack and lifted her hand. "Mayor, what's the status on the legislation to allow homeless people to keep their pets when going into a shelter or an addiction-treatment facility? At the moment, isn't it a case of them having to give up their pets in most situations?"

Browning swung to look at her. "Sadly, it's a fact of life that we just don't have the money or enormous resources required to cater to every homeless person and all their animals. Something's got to give. And it's a shame, but the sums just don't work."

"So you are planning on vetoing the legislation when it crosses your desk?"

"I'm sorry, who—"

"Bills 1483 and 1484."

"—are you?"

"Felicity Simmons."

"Which media company did you say you were from?"

"I didn't." She glanced at the assembled media, who looked suddenly more awake, now that their boring assignment had taken a controversial turn. "It seems there's some interest in you answering the question."

"Those bills aren't on my desk yet, so it's just a hypothetical." His tone was glib. "And I don't engage in speculation."

"They could be on your desk tomorrow," Felicity said. "The council members are stalling because they think you'll veto it. So will you?"

"I make no apologies for doing what's right for this city." He leaned over the lectern. "Oh, it's a lovely thought: everyone keeps their animals, and into the treatment centers and shelters they go. But what if their animal caused a problem? It'd be unworkable. Any lawyer could tell you the potential risk, both physical and financial, we'd be exposed to if a dog turned out to be dangerous."

"Well, *I'm* a lawyer. And you're right, I can tell you the risk. Of the eighty thousand homeless in New York, four thousand live on the street. At any given time, up to twenty-five percent of those people keep a pet. So we're now talking about a thousand people and a thousand pets. You refer to risks from dogs. If we assume eighty percent of homeless people's pets on the street are dogs, a high estimate, by the way, then we're now down to eight hundred people and eight hundred dogs. Are you with me so far?" She offered him a glittery smile that just dared him to challenge her.

Browning snorted. "If you don't think *eight hundred* potentially dangerous dogs in shelters couldn't wreak havoc…" He gave a smug smirk. "Listen to her." He glanced at the attentive media. "She thinks just because they're homeless people's pets they'll all *magically* behave."

"I said no such thing." Felicity straightened. *Time to crush him.* "There are six hundred thousand dogs in New York. Last year there were reports of five thousand incidents of bites. Not all serious, of course, and some might be one dog biting multiple people, but for ease of simplicity, let's say that's five thousand dogs that bite. That translates to one in every one hundred twenty dogs being a danger to others. Which means for our eight hundred dogs owned by homeless people, we're talking 6.67 dogs that might be a danger." She lifted her voice. "Mayor, you want to veto *all* homeless people bringing animals into shelters or treatment clinics on the off chance that seven dogs might be an issue. *Seven.*"

The media began to titter. And it wasn't just the reporters. Homeless people and service providers had been gathering as the media conference continued.

"You know it's not that simple." The mayor tried again. "Insurance companies see risk everywhere, whether it's big or not. They'd impose steep insurance costs on shelters and clinics because they have big payouts to consider."

"Oh really?" Felicity rocked back on her heels. "Last year the average insurance payout in New York on pet injuries was"—she glanced at the figures she'd cued up on her phone—"$55,801. And they paid out on just 893 insurance claims for dog injuries, both big and minor. Extrapolating that to our eight hundred street dogs, we're talking fewer than *one case a year* that would result in an insurance payout."

The mayor's mouth fell open. Cameras started snapping wildly.

"And by the way," Felicity continued, "the legislation *already* exists saying homeless shelters can insist pet owners keep their animals in appropriately sized crates at night. Crates are provided for free by several charities here today, including Living Ruff New York. So what exposure is the city really facing here?"

"And what if it's not just dogs?" Mayor Browning blustered. "What if they want to bring their…pet weasel, or tarantula, or monkey?"

"Then the shelter would quite rightly turn them away because all three are illegal as pets in New York. Anything else?" She gave him a withering look.

Satisfyingly, the vein in his neck started to pop. "You do realize that not every homeless shelter or treatment clinic is run by the city. Private companies and charities wouldn't be happy at having to pay extra in insurance and facilities to cater to filthy, flea-ridden street animals."

A murmur of anger went through the crowd. Mayor Browning had obviously forgotten who his audience was.

"Yes, private companies such as Brightheart Services will have to make a few modifications. Remind me," Felicity said. "Doesn't Brightheart Services provide ten percent of the four hundred fifty shelters in New York? Are you worried that your sister, the director, will be unhappy about that?"

Mayor Browning's face turned white. "What are you implying? You're suggesting I won't allow homeless people to keep pets because it will affect the bottom line of my sister's company?"

"What an excellent question," Felicity mocked faintly. "Is *that* what's happening here? You'll veto these bills for family profit?"

"I never said I'd veto!" he roared.

"Oh, my mistake. So you're saying on the record that you definitely won't veto?" Felicity asked sweetly.

"Who the hell do you think you are?" The mayor's face darkened. "I'm not in the business of taking *suggestions* on how to run my city from any random lawyer who passes by. You might be some liberal homeless person's advocate, but I deal with *real business* and *real laws,* which you clearly know nothing about!" He gave her a triumphant sneer.

"So do I. I'm the deputy chief operating officer of Bartell Corporation. Perhaps you've heard of my global media company?"

He paled. "Oh… I—"

"So I have only one question, Mayor." She glanced at the media pack, which had closed in, tense with excitement. "Will you do right by homeless people who, like anyone else, don't want to lose their beloved pets just to get shelter or overcome addiction? Or do you plan to veto this law?"

The silence dragged out.

The mayor's eyes darted around the crowd.

"Don't veto!" shouted a masculine voice in the audience. "Let us keep our pets!"

"We love our animals!" shouted another. A feminine voice this time.

The crowd began to roar their support.

The mayor finally sagged, cleared his throat, and lifted his hands to quiet them. "I will back this legislation." Then his expression softened to a charming smile for the cameras. "I would *love* to find a way to help pets stay with their homeless owners when they're looking for addiction treatment and accommodation. Assuming it is legally workable, of course."

"Oh, it is," Felicity said firmly. "I've had the numbers checked by a team of experts. So thanks to your announcement, I'm sure you'll find the legislation on your desk very soon."

The crowd applauded and cheered. Several people whistled.

The mayor stalked off stage, a sour expression on his face, and media instantly swarmed Felicity.

"How do you spell your name?"

"Why are you involved?"

"How long have you been an advocate for the homeless?"

"Is this your personal view, Ms. Simmons, or a Bartell Corp position?" Felicity turned at that and recognized the questioner: the man wrote for one of Elena's shoutier populist tabloids. If he thought this issue had Elena's interest, he'd turn it into a dogged campaign. Elena never interfered with the political or policy direction of any of her papers, but more than a few toadies, like this reporter, tried to curry favor in the hopes it might earn them her attention. It never did, but they persisted anyway. That could be useful.

"While I'm making an investigation of my own into the homeless now," Felicity began, "I can say Elena Bartell is firmly in the camp that people and their pets belong together." She prayed Elena wouldn't be too annoyed about that. It was an entirely benign comment, surely.

The man met her eye and gave a slight nod. Yes, the mayor's feet would be held to the fire until the legislation was brought in.

Good.

She answered the rest of the questions, and an amused reporter commented: "Not sure if you're aware, Ms. Simmons, but we were going live for a short piece on the mayor's campaign just as you asked your questions. Everyone saw him pledge to pass the legislation. Can't wriggle out of it now."

"How convenient," Felicity said.

"That whole thing was hilarious. I thought he was about to burst something."

"Well, as long as the plight of the homeless potentially losing their pets is amusing…" she couldn't resist saying.

"I didn't say that," he sputtered.

"Didn't you?" Felicity asked innocently. "Now, if you'll excuse me. I have actual business to attend to. Business that doesn't involve mocking the less fortunate."

He shot her a disgruntled look and headed back to his cameraman.

Felicity smiled at his retreating back, enjoying it all far too much. She didn't particularly care for reporters, even if they were Bartell Corp's bread-and-butter. They could be just as smug as politicians and lawyers. Never hurt to point out when they were being assholes.

Oh, how she loved this. Winning. Crushing inferior rivals with clever words and exacting facts. She just wished Elena could have seen her. Or wait— No. She'd just invoked Elena's name in a way that would induce a reporter to write a favorable story. Probably better if her boss didn't see that.

"Well, that was certainly impressive. And entertaining for you as well, so don't bother denying it."

Felicity turned to find an immaculate slim older woman with fine-boned porcelain features eying her. Recognition hit. This was Harvey Clifford's wife, the philanthropist who'd created the Living Ruff foundation two decades ago.

Her ethereal face gave an impression of someone in her early fifties, but that was more likely a testament to the expensive beauty treatments and other interventions favored by women of her wealth and status. She wore a long emerald peacoat, wool black pants, and stylish leather boots.

So Felicity wasn't the only one wearing fourteen-hundred-dollar coats.

"Rosalind Stone," the woman supplied. "Walk with me, please." Rosalind turned on her heel and strode away, clearly used to being obeyed.

Felicity, well attuned to working for a woman exactly like this, couldn't help but admire the absolute confidence, and did as ordered.

"So," Rosalind said, when they were far enough away from the media throngs and milling crowds, "you're the Bartell Corp executive my husband's showing my charity to this week. Felicity Simmons?"

"Yes."

Rosalind's eyes raked her up and down. "I thought you'd be older, given how extensively your resume reads. Deputy COO of Bartell Corporation and you're only thirty-six?"

"You've looked me up?" Felicity asked.

"Of course. I like to know who's sniffing around my investments. *And* my husband."

Felicity's eyebrows shot up. "I can assure you I have no interest in your husband."

"Oh no, I'm well aware of that." Amusement lit her gray eyes. "I'd say you're more interested in our head vet. Would that be correct?"

How on earth could she possibly know that? Felicity gaped at her. Not that she'd ever admit her attraction for Cooper, but how could a complete stranger—

"Your astonishment is rather adorable. It might interest you to know that my husband has great recall of detail when he recounts his day over the dinner table. He doesn't always put the pieces together the way I do, though. I was rather amused at all the clues he dropped."

Felicity stared at her.

"Apparently you turned down multiple chances to do rounds with our dashing Dr. Mendoza, who is catnip to every straight single woman for miles. Instead, you opted to follow Dr. Cooper around the entire time, even to"—she paused for dramatic effect—"fetch animal crates, I believe it was?" Her eyes crinkled in laughter. "No one could possibly find old cages that interesting. However, I'm well aware our Dr. Cooper attracts her own following from ladies of a certain…inclination."

"Excuse me? I was being thorough, assessing all of Dr. Cooper's duties," Felicity argued, suddenly feeling stripped bare and hating it. "I was being professional! And that's quite some imagination your husband has."

"Oh, he doesn't have a clue, my dear. Even I wasn't sure until just a moment ago. Your panicked reaction gave you away. Anyway, that's neither here nor there. I'm not worried about my husband straying, in any case. I should say that from the outset. I have absolutely no doubt as to his loyalty. He is too focused on things that matter to him most."

"Focused?" Felicity asked.

"When he gets something in his sights, whatever that is, he tends to stick to it loyally, hopefully, tenaciously, and with utter devotion. I'm sure you can appreciate that quality. I mean, your CV says you do. Is it true you're soon to take over as Bartell Corp's acting COO as well?"

"Yes." Felicity regarded Rosalind with interest. The other woman's sources were clearly impeccable, given Felicity's next promotion wasn't yet widely known outside of the company. Rosalind was also exceptionally accomplished, financially brilliant, beautiful, and yet…she'd married slow and steady mediocre bookkeeper Harvey Clifford? "So was that what happened with you and Harvey? He set his sights on you and stayed loyal?"

Rosalind laughed. "Quite the opposite. Oh, it's a funny story how we met, and I don't mind sharing. You must understand, when you're a woman in my position with wealth and influence in charge of my entire family's considerable resources and businesses, I attract certain approaches quite regularly from men who are fortune hunting. It made it quite hard to work out who was genuinely interested in me."

"I can imagine."

"Mm. I am an animal lover, famously so. And one day at my local dog park, I was walking my beautiful Saluki, called Flynn. He's not with us anymore, poor darling. Have you ever seen a Saluki, Ms. Simmons?"

"I don't think so."

"You'd know if you had. They're a most arresting dog—tall, lean, and elegant with this dignified snout that makes them seem so intelligent. And Flynn certainly was smart. He was also *so* energetic, I needed to get him to his favorite park twice a day or he climbed the walls. And one day I'm there, and I see this man playing with a fluffy white Maltese. And by playing, I mean literally. He's down on all fours in the grass having enormous fun." She smiled. "I watched this grown man, completely indifferent to what anyone thought, giving his little dog the time of her life."

"Harvey?" Felicity couldn't quite picture the staid man she'd met doing anything of the sort.

"Harvey." Rosalind confirmed with a smile. "So I asked him about his dog, and he launched into a great enthusiastic description about her personality and how he'd come by her. He then asked about my dog, and I pointed out Flynn running around. He wanted to know everything. We ran out of time talking, and he asked when I'd next bring Flynn back to the park. He sounded so interested. So I told him when. But later that night, I grew suspicious that maybe he was only trying to get to know me in a roundabout way."

"Makes sense."

"I turned up at the appointed time without Flynn. I thought if my dog was just a ruse to get closer to me, Harvey would be just as happy to see me without him."

"What happened?" Felicity asked, drawn into the tale.

"He saw me, and his whole face lit up. Then he looked all around, behind me, everywhere, and his expression dropped as he asked where Flynn was. When I said my dog couldn't come, Harvey promptly offered to reschedule our meetup at a time when Flynn could be in attendance."

Felicity laughed. "Only your dog mattered to him? Ouch!"

"Exactly." Rosalind gave a soft chuckle. "And at that minute, I think I loved him. There wasn't anything manipulative or game-playing about him. What you see is what you get with Harvey. He is always open and honest in all things. After that, I set my sights on him romantically, deciding I greatly approved of the idea of a man in my life as in love with animals as I was. It took him at least six weeks before he realized I was actually pursuing him, not just being friendly."

Felicity laughed. "I don't suppose humble bookkeepers get chased by wealthy socialites with multimillion-dollar businesses too often."

"I see I'm not the only one who does her research." Rosalind tilted her head. "So to get to the point, Harvey is kind, decent, and honest, a loyal husband and an excellent father. He is meticulous in his detailed retelling of his day, even if he can be quite...myopic at working out what it means. I don't suffer such a blind spot." Her gaze turned sharp and assessing. "So why are you investigating my husband, Ms. Simmons?"

"What makes you think I am?"

"One doesn't need to send the second-in-command of a multinational corporation to personally investigate a charity the boss is interested in donating to. What are you really doing at Living Ruff and with Harvey?"

Felicity regarded the woman's cool gaze. She had no idea if Rosalind was in on whatever Harvey was up to or maybe even behind it—if indeed there was anything up at all. "What do you think is going on?"

"Honestly, I don't know." She looked aggrieved. "At first I wondered if you wanted to poach him for a job within your organization. Ms. Bartell is famous for head-hunting, although it's usually from within organizations she's just acquired and stripped for resources."

Felicity folded her arms. "No."

"No." Rosalind sighed. "Well, I admit my husband isn't exactly head-hunting material. What he lacks in business acumen is more than made up for with his passion for my foundation, though."

"You think he lacks business acumen? Why appoint him director, then?"

"It's not too taxing to manage a foundation like Living Ruff, and all he wanted to do was work with animals, so it seemed a good fit. It's not like we don't get independently reviewed each year, like every other charity, so I'd have heard if he had made any major errors. Clearly, he hasn't." She paused for a moment. "Maybe I'm being unfair. Living Ruff isn't just *not making errors*. It's doing well."

"I heard it brought in a donation of over a million dollars last year. That's more than doing well."

"That's very true. Maybe I've undervalued my husband's efforts." Rosalind looked thoughtful.

"Did Harvey say what he spent that big donation on?"

Rosalind nodded. "Oh, he was very keen about some new plan to help train a select few homeless people to become vet techs. Of course, such things take time to set up, so I've heard nothing more since he first raised it with me. But he kept me up a few nights with his diagrams and explanations for it." She gave an indulgent smile. "He does get so passionate about his little projects."

Training a couple of homeless people to become vet techs sounded like a worthy program. Why had Harvey been so cagey? Felicity scrutinized Rosalind's expression but could see nothing but genuineness in her eyes.

"You should talk to Dr. Cooper about it, if you're interested in how the program will work," Rosalind continued. "It was her proposal. In fact, it looks like you'll have your chance right now. Our head vet looks exceedingly pleased with you."

She smirked, her gaze drifting beyond Felicity's shoulder. "Not that I can blame her. What you did today was exceptional. It'll impact so many people, Ms. Simmons. That's the other reason I wanted to introduce myself: to say well done. Now I'll leave you both to it. Good day, Ms. Simmons." She strode away after a polite nod.

Felicity turned to find Cooper screeching to a halt a few feet away, mouth open.

"I—" Cooper began then stopped. "That was... God! You with the mayor?" She shook her head. "Felicity, that was the most incredible thing I've ever seen. You are *amazing*."

Without warning, she grabbed Felicity in a bear hug, lifted her off her feet as though she weighed nothing, gave her a quick spin, then dropped her back on her feet. "Oh, my God, woman! You're about to change *so* many lives."

Felicity, feeling a little giddy and dizzy, neither of which had anything to do with the spin, warmed with pleasure. "Oh, well, it's not hard. I know law. I used what I know. And I had Thomas and his team sending me stuff. And a lot of credit goes to Deedra. She's all over the facts on insurance payouts for dog incidents."

"Yes, Dee's great, but no one else has done what you did. Just stood up to him and demanded he explain his position, then pulled apart his BS. It was like having the Terminator on our side!" Cooper grinned. "God! I had no idea you were this good. None. I mean, it makes sense—your title and all—but all I've seen was—"

"Me unable to tell someone their dog is nice *and* sound sincere?" Felicity suggested.

"Exactly." Cooper chuckled. "You brilliant woman! Do you know how long we've all been advocating for this? The pet issue is half the reason we have so many homeless on the streets. This is a game changer!"

"Believe it or not, I was actually paying attention to all your little rants."

"Rants?" Cooper's hand thudded over her heart. "Is that how I sound to you? All...ranty?"

Felicity's lips curled.

Cooper laughed and wagged a finger at her. "I'd buy you a beer right now, if I wasn't on the clock. But tonight I'm taking you out to dinner to celebrate. No arguments; it's happening. Okay?"

Go out with an Amazon who was looking at Felicity as if she were a god? "Fine. But wine. Not beer."

"Whatever you want, my liege!" Cooper did an exaggerated bow, then laughed and headed back toward the Living Ruff tent.

Felicity watched her go, admiring the sway of her powerful ass and legs—and her mouth was dry again. Her phone beeped in her pocket.

She gulped when she read the name on the text. Elena.

Apparently I have a long-held view that pets and owners should not be parted? - E

She swallowed hard and tried to think what to say. *Sorry for using your name in vain?* No, fuck it. Deputy COOs don't apologize for taking a stance, even one using their boss's name. Instead, she wrote:

Are you saying you don't think that? :)

Okay, the smiley face might have been a little unprofessional. A lot unprofessional. She held her breath. Then wished she could retract the whole message.

No. - E

Relief coursed through her. That was not an admonishment. It wasn't anything negative. It counted as enthusiastic support, if you knew Elena Bartell. Well, today was definitely looking up. Her heart did an excited little thump. And if she was being entirely honest, it was not all to do with her boss's approval.

While Cooper went back to assessing animal health, Felicity wandered from tent to tent, seeing everything she'd missed earlier while researching how to beat the mayor.

A meowing sound attracted her attention, and she poked her head in a nearby tent.

Oh!

A harried-looking woman was attempting to write up some notes while young cats crawled all over her. It was ridiculously adorable, and Felicity had to fight her natural instinct to squeal and say "aww." Instead, she firmed her jaw hard and said, "Did you hit a cat Xerox machine? Exploded twenty copies?"

The woman looked up with a wry smile. "Almost. A client with a momma cat brought in all its kittens. She tried but can't care for them. I'm writing up a report, and they'll go to a no-kill shelter. It's hard to type with a cat trying to lick the Enter key and another leapfrogging the screen. And as you can see, the animal crate I have is full already." She waved to a cage containing a ferocious-looking mutt. "Hey, if you have a spare fifteen minutes, could you distract them for me while I finish up?"

I'd love to, Felicity almost said. But that was far too needy. "Certainly," she said instead. "I'll corral them on the floor."

"Good idea. I think that one's close to eating printer paper." She nudged a spotted black and white cat away.

Felicity scooped the kittens up and gathered them in her lap. What had happened to her that life kept hurling kitties at her lately? Was she cursed to forever encounter felines or something?

Well, whatever the reason, there were no witnesses to hold her cute-animal weakness against her so, she decided to indulge herself just this once.

She gave each cat a long scratch as she mentally named them to keep them straight in her head. Within moments, they were crawling all over her: in her hair, down her shirt, in one pocket.

Felicity was in seventh heaven. She might have even cooed. Just a little.

Fifteen minutes flew by, and Felicity found herself laughing at their antics while the harried form filler shot her occasional amused looks.

"I see I chose well," the woman murmured. "You're a natural. I'd have lost three of them by now if you hadn't stuck your head in."

"I don't mind," Felicity said, glancing at her paperwork. "I'm all about assisting people in succeeding with business."

"You're here for me, not to play with the little kitties?" She chuckled. "Right."

"Exactly," Felicity said, keeping a straight face.

Suddenly Cooper stuck her head in. "There you are—finally! I was going to ask if you wanted a ride back to the office…" She petered out as she digested the scene before her.

Felicity was on the ground, a small cat in each hand and one halfway buried down her Vera Wang blouse. And several climbing over her legs and feet.

Cooper stared in astonishment.

Felicity's cheeks felt like radiators, they were flaming so much. "I—" What could she say? It was a damning scene. "Er…"

Cooper stared some more. "You faker," she whispered in wonder. "You adore animals!"

"Don't be silly. I'm assisting this woman with her paperwork."

The woman in question shot her an amused look. "Yes, indeed," she drawled.

"And I'll pass on the ride, thank you," Felicity said stiffly. "I'll see you tonight. You can text me the details. Mrs. Brooks has my phone number."

She scrambled to her feet, shooing assorted kittens off her lap like a short, hairy waterfall.

That only left the one nose-diving into her bra. Felicity tried to pluck it out with as much dignity as she could manage—easier said than done when it applied claws in protest.

"Ow! Let go," Felicity ordered with a grimace.

Could this be any more humiliating? Finally, she extracted the sticky kitty, who emitted a disgruntled mew as it left its warm nest and was deposited hastily on the floor.

Right, then. There was no way Felicity was going to look at Cooper, so she bent her head and scampered the hell out of there before it could become any more awkward.

Cooper said not a single word as Felicity flew past.

Chapter 7
It's Not a Date

Felicity found herself strangely nervous, though she couldn't exactly pinpoint why. It wasn't as if this was a date. It was just a celebration between two professionals over dinner. Nothing to see here.

Except there was something to see. Cooper, out of her usual outfit of jeans and flannel, was sitting at a table wearing a beautiful black lapelless fitted blazer and a crisp white linen shirt. Felicity couldn't see the pants yet as she joined Cooper, but if they matched that sleek blazer, Felicity was pretty sure there'd be some internal swooning in her future. Which flew firmly in the face of her plans to tell her hormones to cease and desist.

The restaurant was called Full Moon Pizza, established 1976 in the Bronx's Little Italy. While the big, unsubtle redbrick construct didn't seem like Felicity's kind of place, she was learning lately that looks could be deceiving.

Her nose twitched in delight at the tomato and pesto smells emanating from the kitchen, and she smiled at Cooper. "Oh, that does smell good," she said as she sat. "Hi."

"Hi right back. And what were you expecting?" Cooper grinned. "I'd whisk you off to a bowling alley and feed you hot dogs?"

"Absolutely," Felicity said with feeling. "I never know what to expect from you, so that's as likely as anything."

"Hmm. I'm not sure if I was just insulted or not."

"Being unpredictable is not an insult," Felicity suggested.

"Oh, I bet it is to you. I bet you love everything ordered and at your fingertips and oh-so-carefully planned in advance." Cooper smiled wide, her white teeth dazzling against her tan skin.

Felicity was suddenly only too aware of Cooper's three open shirt buttons that promised a hint of cleavage if she were to angle herself forward even slightly. Instead, she leaned back and said, "If that were true, how do you explain the press conference I torpedoed today?"

"I'd call that all in a day's work for you—being prepared and knowing your stuff. You know, today I saw you become someone else. You reminded me of a big cat stalking in the grass, waiting for the mayor to expose his jugular. I could almost see you wiggling your butt with your tail swishing, anticipating. And then *attack*!" Her hand made a swishing, clawing motion.

"How bloodthirsty." Felicity cocked an eyebrow. "Except I didn't become someone else; that's just who I am all the time. I'm always expecting to use my skills at a moment's notice, so I'm metaphorically crouched and ready. Well—"

She stopped as a waiter appeared to fill up their water glasses and take their drink orders. After he left, Felicity continued. "Except when I'm with you. Then I'm just..." She faded out, trying to think of how to explain the extraordinary feeling of being so wrong-footed so often. When was the last time she'd ever felt like that?

"Out of your depth and wondering why you agreed to this assignment?" Cooper's eyes danced.

"Something like that. Although I'd never admit to being out of my depth. *Show no weakness* is a motto to live by." She took a sip of water.

"Sounds like a lame motto," Cooper said, sounding amused. "Everyone has weakness. It's all about facing it or, if need be, running like hell to escape it." She grinned. "That's good advice for life and rhinos, by the way."

"I'll defer to your expertise on that one." Felicity's lips quirked up.

"Today was the best day." Cooper sighed happily. "The absolute best."

"I agree." Warmth flooded Felicity as she recalled all the highlights.

"You're thinking about the kitties you got to play with, aren't you?" Cooper said with a chuckle.

"Pfft. Don't be ridiculous. I got distracted for a few minutes. I'm talking, of course, about my grand victory."

"I saw your face, you know. And even if I hadn't, I know Suzanne—the woman you were helping with her paperwork. She said you were in there for fifteen minutes and totally besotted. Why do you pretend to not like animals while secretly coveting a cleavage full of cats?"

Felicity rolled her eyes. "Gah, don't remind me. I'll be picking cat hair out of my bra for days," she muttered. "Annoying beasts."

"You *love* those beasts. Why on earth don't you have a cat? Or a dog? You clearly love them. I'm sorry I ever claimed otherwise." Genuine curiosity filled Cooper's expression.

"It's...complicated. I like your suit, by the way. Zara?"

"Whoa. You can tell that just by looking?"

"If you hang out at enough fashion weeks with a fashion-worshipping boss, you do notice labels."

"Makes sense. Nice distraction, by the way." She leaned in. "So...back to you and animals? What's the deal there?"

Felicity picked up her menu. "Shall we order?" Her eyes flicked instantly to the low-carb options. "The Caesar salad looks good."

"Okay, I can take a hint." Cooper lifted her hands in surrender.

Thank God.

"What would you like to talk about instead?" Cooper continued.

Dropping the menu, Felicity looked up. "What's your take on Rosalind Stone? She cornered me today for a chat. I felt like she was trying to tell me something, but I'm not sure what exactly."

"She does come across like that," Cooper said with a chuckle. "I've had a number of formal dinners with her as part of the charity, and she is formidable. Some might dismiss her as an empty-headed socialite, but I've seen her behind the scenes and at fundraising galas, and she can work a room like a top political operator. And then there's her financial side. Did you know she inherited everything from her rich parents under the proviso that she provide well for her siblings?"

"They either had a lot of faith in her or none in her siblings," Felicity observed.

"Both. Anyway, she did so well at her various businesses and investments that she's one of the wealthiest women in New York."

"She is?" Felicity thought she was knowledgeable about all the major movers and shakers in the US. How had Rosalind flown under the radar?

"Rosalind told me once she prefers it when people underestimate her. She calls it a sound business strategy. She tries to keep her name out of those rich lists, for instance. Don't feel too bad you couldn't read her today. Rosalind is a mystery. She is several moves ahead of everyone and plays her cards close to her chest. It's rare she'll share anything much."

Felicity blinked. "Today she gave me the entire story of how she met and fell in love with her husband."

Cooper peered at her. "Are you serious? I knew her eight years before I could worm that one out of her. What brought that on?"

"I have no idea."

"That is really unusual. What else did she talk to you about?"

"She was wondering why I was sniffing around her husband."

"You and Harvey?" Cooper laughed. "Seriously?"

"Well, I gather she didn't think I was interested in Harvey romantically, but maybe on the off-chance I was, I suppose I'm now fully briefed that he's as loyal as a man can be." Felicity turned the odd conversation over. "Actually, she mainly wanted to know what I'm doing at Living Ruff. And we talked a little about a program you'd come up with: training homeless people to be vet techs?"

"Oh that." Cooper gave a wistful look. "I pitched it to Harvey two years ago. Every now and then we meet a resourceful, bright young client who has so much wasted potential, and you just know, if only someone gave them a break, they'd soar. I suggested to Harvey that if we found someone like that who was interested and who loved animals, we could pay for the costs of their tuition, offer them the practical support of a vet-tech apprenticeship at Living Ruff, and help get them on their way. I'm not talking a big scheme. Just one candidate every few years as we find them. We could really change lives. Harvey loved it, but we didn't have the funds to try it."

"So now that you do, it's happening?" Felicity asked.

Cooper shook her head. "Why would you think that?"

"Rosalind seems to think that's what Harvey's doing with that big donation from last year."

Cooper's eyebrows shot up. "He never said."

"Why wouldn't he?"

"I guess, knowing him, he's probably still working out the pros and cons. Slow and steady. He can be a bit of a turtle." She smiled. "This is great news, if it's true." She paused. "But he still should have told me if he was going ahead with it."

"Maybe he'll get around to it soon." Felicity reached for the menu again. "I'm starving. That Caesar salad really does look good." It didn't, but what else was she going to eat that wouldn't go straight to her hips?

"The salad? We're eating in New York's best-kept secret. You have to try the specials menu. What about the meatball parmigiana?" Cooper's eyes took on a dreamy expression.

"Little fatty cheesy balls? Pass." She pursed her lips.

"Felicity, we're celebrating! Why not spoil yourself tonight?"

"And blow out like an elephant?" She waved in Cooper's general direction. "I think not."

"You mean like me? I'm an elephant?" Cooper's mouth went wide and round.

Felicity was flooded with horror. "God no!" How could magnificent Cooper, with those mighty limbs and, *mercy*, those shoulders, ever think Felicity was fat-shaming her? Didn't she understand how much Felicity deeply appreciated her body? "My comment was actually about me. I come from…sturdy stock," she confessed, plopping the menu down with a huff. "My mother and sister. Round as bowling balls." She made the shape with her hands. "And to be taken seriously, to succeed in work or life, the rule is: be sexually attractive to men. I don't have to like it, but that's the truth. All right?"

Cooper regarded her in astonishment. "You eat for…society? For… status?"

Was that so ridiculous? Half the planet did. Appearances mattered. "I'm hardly unique on that score."

"What of your father? You've only mentioned your mother and sister."

"What about him?"

"I don't mean to pry, but you had the weirdest look when you mentioned your family just now."

"If you don't want to pry, then don't." Felicity glared at her, then wished she hadn't. "Sorry. I'm ruining our nice dinner. It's an old, sort of touchy issue."

"What is?"

"My father."

"Okay, new topic, and I hope it's not touchy. too. Where are you from?" Cooper asked gently.

Felicity hesitated. She really did want to fix the mess she was making of their dinner conversation. "The Midwest. Pinckney, Michigan, specifically."

"I haven't heard of Pinckney."

"It's just next to Hell. I mean that literally. Hell's the name of our neighboring town. They trade on it. Bikers and tourists love it."

"No way. Are you pulling my leg?"

"Why would I make up being one step away from Hell?"

"Good point." Cooper laughed. "I don't think the Michigan accent's terrible, by the way. It's sweet." At Felicity's blank look, Cooper added, "The day we met you said you used to have a terrible accent."

"It's only terrible in the sense it got in the way of my promotional aspirations and me being taken seriously. So my voice teacher, Mrs. Allsop, wrenched the hick right out of me."

"Hick? You?" Cooper paused, eying her with confusion. "You thought you were a hick?"

A waiter appeared, placed their drinks in front of them, and asked what they wanted to eat. Felicity stuck with the Caesar salad, and Cooper opted for garlic bread and a Sicilian pizza that sounded both unholy and unhealthy. Felicity tried to hide her horror, which only made Cooper laugh.

"If you hang around me, Felicity, you're going to have to get used to seeing a lot of food groups."

"Yes, well," Felicity said dryly, "I expect that's true." She couldn't contain the little buzz she got from the suggestion there might be more *hanging around.*

"Hey," Cooper said, "you didn't answer the question. Were you a hick? Do you originally come from a family of hicks?"

"Okay, I might be exaggerating," Felicity said, reaching for her wine. "But we weren't polished. My mother and sister are proud of their roots. My father, however, complained often of our unimpressive status and took off for New York with a less embarrassing woman. His secretary. Tiffany was not round or of sturdy stock, nor did she speak like us. Her accent was sophisticated; so was her fashion. She was so sleek and waiflike, she always looked as if a stiff breeze could blow her away."

"She sounds like you," Cooper said quietly. "You're a bit of a flight risk in a stiff breeze, too."

"Now, maybe. If I'd stayed, I'd have ended up just like them." Felicity rolled her eyes. "I can just see it: big, sprawling old property with chickens and dogs and cats. Career aspirations that extend only as far as Ann Arbor and not a mile more. You know, my mom spends her days teaching snot-nosed children and schmoozing at fundraisers, despite once having a career in biophysics. And my sister?" Felicity lowered her voice and darted her eyes around the room. "Works at a herbology place. Her whole life is three things: that store, her hippie husband, and their perfectly plump, excitable children exactly like her." She shuddered. "I'd have sooner died."

"Are they unhappy?" Cooper's brow puckered. "What's wrong with that life?"

"What's wrong with— Haven't you been listening?"

"I have. I heard your father rejected your family—you—for what you were, so you became what you thought he liked. Thin, driven, without an accent or anything else holding you back. All that Pinckney baggage gone. I'm curious: did that baggage include having pets?" Cooper asked, looking thoughtful. "Were they something too uncool or needy to be in your life? Something not befitting the new high-flying corporate you?"

Silence fell. Felicity's nerves started to fizz, and she felt as if she'd just been slapped. She stared at Cooper in dismay as her anger rose, strong and sharp. "You have a lot of nerve."

"I—"

"You think you can just strip me down to the bones like that?" Felicity glared at Cooper, fueled by white-hot rage. "You think *that's* what I deserve? I told you things I rarely share with anyone, and you sit back and pick me apart, like it's some curious little game? You have no right!"

"No, Felicity, I—"

"You know nothing!" Felicity slapped the table so hard that the cutlery bounced and heads swiveled to stare. *Fuck them.* Hurt warred with rage. She'd never thought Cooper would be one to mock her choices or assume the worst of her.

"Felicity?" Cooper's tone was pleading, and regret clouded her eyes. "I'm sorry. I didn't mean to sound like I was judging you. Please calm down."

"I'm perfectly calm," Felicity snapped. "You know, this is not the first time I've been treated as though I'm some zoo oddity to be picked apart. People often assume the worst about me because I don't conform to how they think I should be. I'm not warm enough. I don't smile enough. I don't hold my tongue or lie or coddle to protect fragile egos. Apparently, I have 'all the maternal instincts of an alpine glacier.' Direct quote from my previous boss."

Cooper winced.

After a sigh, Felicity barreled on. "Look, I know I don't fit easily with people. I rub everyone the wrong way—and sometimes that's a choice. Either way, I've learned not to care what most people think of me. However, with you…" *God. I care.* "Well, for some mystifying reason, I lowered my guard. Congratulations on landing a few direct shots to the ribs. That doesn't happen very often, I can assure you."

Felicity's throat tightened as she realized how vulnerable she sounded. She stiffened her spine.

"I really am sorry," Cooper repeated, eyes pleading.

Their meals were delivered. Felicity waited for the waiter to leave before speaking again. "I'm excellent at my job, I'll have you know. I'm the second-highest executive in my entire international company! Me! And I did that despite coming from some backwater town in Michigan, and without any help from my *stupefyingly* unambitious mother and sister, who lower their sights at every opportunity, or from my impossible-to-please father."

She hissed out the last words, venom embedded deep, then stopped suddenly, her heart thudding at the reminder of what had happened. Packing her bags and heading to college. Then once she had her new law degree, tracking her father down to show him her "worthy" size-zero shape and perfect dress style.

Her father had taken one look at her and mocked her accent—something about not being able to take the Midwest out of the girl. Then he'd looked past her shoulder as he asked whether she needed money. He'd been all business. Perfectly polite.

Everything about Robert J. Simmons was business. He'd dismissed her and all her efforts to be worthy, to impress him, before she'd had a chance to explain she was there for him. For them. To start over.

That casual dismissal had burned and burned. Naturally, she'd taken it as a sign she wasn't enough—well, not yet.

So she'd worked harder. Felicity had made it her mission to become partner in her new law firm by age thirty. It became her mantra.

And…she'd failed. But then Elena had offered her a job as chief of staff. The oddest thing was, after working with Elena for a few months, she no longer fixated on what her father thought of her. She'd even stopped envisioning the day he'd meet her for lunch and profess pride in her accomplishments. She'd gotten over her touchiest of issues. Or so she thought.

Then she'd received a call from the waiflike Tiffany.

"He's dead," the woman said bluntly. "Your father. I thought you should know."

The words ricocheted around her body, slicing through her heart. Now she'd never know if she'd measured up. Felicity had felt sick at the thought. "How?" was all she managed to croak out. "How did he die?"

"Heart attack. While fucking his mistress."

Oh. What could she say to that?

"There's a few things of his you might want. I mean, I don't want them. I'll make up a box. Send it over."

"Was he happy?" Felicity asked. "With life?"

"He had a smile on his face when he died, if that's what you mean," Tiffany said bitterly. "By the way, I've seen the will. You're not in it. No one is. He's giving it all to some business institute. A scholarship program for up-and-coming wolves of Wall Street." Her short laugh was empty and cold. "That sly bastard. Fuck him. Sorry, Felicity." Then she hung up.

The box Tiffany sent over contained his CD collection, stubs from a couple of concerts he'd attended, and all his business certificates, awards, and degrees. A huge stack of them. That was his legacy.

As Felicity stared at it, she knew two things. She was just like him and she didn't know how to be anything else. The oddest thing about that day was wondering if she should *want* to be any different.

The memory faded, crumpling inside her like a ball of paper. She looked up at Cooper. "I'll thank you not to sneer at me for how I navigated my circumstances or make ill-founded assumptions. You have no right to do that. None."

"I know. You're right," Cooper said quietly.

Felicity wondered why even now thoughts of her father could set her off so easily. How even brushing against those memories caused so much pain. It was ridiculous the way she'd once worshipped the man. He hadn't exactly been father of the year.

Suck it up. He'd said that to her once when she was at her lowest. When she was so young.

And she had sucked it up. She'd *kept* sucking it up. No one touched her—not deep enough that they might cause real hurt. Her father had shown her how to harden her heart to stay safe from such painful distractions. Perhaps he'd been good for something after all.

"Look, I don't avoid having pets because I see them as baggage or too uncool or needy," Felicity said crossly. "That has nothing to do with anything."

"Okay." Cooper said, biting her lip. "I would appreciate it if you could explain, though. I promise not to judge or make assumptions." She sounded so sincere.

Felicity blew out a breath. "I had a cat once when I was a child. She was ginger and fearless and utterly beautiful." She played with the stem of her wineglass as her thoughts drifted to a vision of the affectionate pet. "I told her all my little secrets. We were inseparable. I adored her."

"She sounds wonderful. What was her name?"

"We called her Brave because when I was a toddler, our biggest dog accidentally knocked me over, and Brave rushed in to get between the dog and me, hissing until he bolted. But one day Brave got sick, and my parents decided she should be put to sleep." Felicity's heart started to pound.

"That's so sad. But it can be a kindness—"

"No!" Felicity's cry startled them both. "I mean, it didn't feel like a kindness to me, but I was so young." She ground her jaw. "Afterward, all I did was cry for days and days."

Suck it up.

"Oh, that's so sad."

"My father said I wasn't emotionally strong enough for a pet, given how I'd fallen apart. And I guess he was right. The problem is, I get so attached."

Cooper regarded her in silence, understanding crossing her face. She reached for Felicity's hand and squeezed it.

"I know, it's a bit silly," Felicity said, feeling embarrassed. "Me, a grown woman, too scared to take on an animal for fear of how I'll be if anything happens to them. But I vividly remember losing Brave. That was so traumatic and life changing, I'd rather not go through that again. *Ever.* At the time, I was very hard to live with, crying and carrying on for so long. I'm not surprised my father left not long after."

Cooper's eyes radiated concern. "You must know that's not why he left."

"Well, obviously, as an adult, I'm aware that while I didn't make life enjoyable for my family, the main reason Dad left was that thin, hot secretary."

Cooper's hand squeezed Felicity's again. "And now you avoid being around animals? Because they're linked to so much loss? Not just losing Brave but your dad, too?"

"I am fine with animals if they keep their distance, but as fate would have it, I've been around more of them this week than I have since I was a child. The truth is, I'm a sucker for them. All animals. Small ones, big ones, hairy ones, ugly ones. I just— God, I want to hold them all." Felicity met Cooper's eyes, then she looked away. "But I'm not strong enough to go through having a pet again. I have no clue how you do it day in, day out, befriending them left and right and then losing them. Like Lucille, that beautiful old cat who ever-so-gently pushed your hand away when you were examining her stomach? She was just too precious... I don't want her to die."

"Neither do I." Cooper drew in a breath. "I swear I want to hug you so much right now. I had no idea you'd been going through all this. Have you seen your father since he disappeared with the secretary?"

Felicity withdrew her hand, uncomfortable and embarrassed all over again. "Yes, once. I didn't measure up, despite everything." She gave a tight laugh. "Well, he's dead now, so if I ever do reach a status he'd finally consider impressive, I'll never know."

"Well, then, he's a fool not to have seen how amazing you are. You're plenty impressive to me."

Felicity lifted her head. That felt…wonderful. "I'm glad you think so." She could count on one hand the number of people whose opinions mattered to her: Elena. Her mother, despite her lifestyle choices that involved quitting academia, lady-bird hair accessories, and loving Pinckney. And now…Cooper? Felicity had known her only a few days, so what on earth was that about?

"Definitely impressive," Cooper said. "You had Councilor Deedra Randall, who is known to be a dragon when it suits her, in absolute awe of you. And you carved up our mayor today like it was nothing. You did it for people you don't even know and animals you're too afraid to even touch." Cooper's head tilted. "Would you mind if I asked if you have many close friends? Or, well, any?"

Felicity speared lettuce onto her fork with force. She always hated this question, especially since Starbucks employees apparently didn't count. "There's nothing wrong with being career focused and having no distractions. You don't *need* friends to prosper."

"That's what I thought. And the reason I asked is because I see someone who managed to conquer the universe completely alone, without any support. That's incredible."

"I have support," Felicity protested. "My boss is mentoring me. She's exceptional."

"Is she a friend, though? I mean, do you ever go out for a drink after work? Hang out at each other's places?"

Felicity heart contracted. "No. Actually, I'm not… I'm not sure why she doesn't…why…" She really didn't have the first clue to understand what she lacked that made Elena never confide in her or reach out in friendship. And yet Maddie did it effortlessly. She'd just blown in, and suddenly Elena was emailing her when Maddie was off on assignment in Vietnam five minutes later. It was so frustrating.

"Do you want friends?" Cooper asked gently.

Felicity couldn't answer. Did she want something she'd never sought out? Others seemed to think it was worthwhile. Felicity hadn't really had friends since school. "They're unnecessary distractions," she muttered with little conviction. "Emotional roller coasters are exhausting. Human or animal. This was what my father was trying to tell me back then. He told me to suck it up so I wouldn't be weak."

"Weak?" Cooper blinked. "How old were you?"

"Twelve."

"He told a *twelve-year-old* to suck it up?" Cooper eyed her. "To me you sound like a perfectly lovely, sweet child who adored her cat. You didn't need to change who you were to be good enough or worthy of him. You don't have to be this driven woman you're trying so hard to be. You're already enough, Felicity. You're there. You've made it. Okay? You can relax now."

Felicity chased some chicken around on her fork. "Hardly. I'm about to take over all of Bartell Corp. I'm far from ready to relax." She took a bite, chewed without tasting it, and swallowed. "And I'd really rather never discuss my father again. The topic gets my blood boiling."

"Okay," Cooper lifted her hands. "Sure. But hey, if you ever want to talk about demanding dads in the future, though, I'm all ears. I have one of my own. My dad's this big ole Army dude who decided I should be an Olympic athlete." She chuckled. "Even as a kid, I was so big for my age."

"I can believe it." Felicity forced herself to unknot her muscles, relieved at the conversation shift. "Which sport?"

"He didn't care. He tried me on all of them."

"And were you any good?"

Cooper shrugged. "Sure. World-beating standard, though? Not even close. Besides, my good boys and girls were calling. I just can't stay away from animals. Like Brittany—oh, she was love at first sight. She was given to me by a homeless woman just before she passed away. The woman was so scared I'd say no and Brittany would end up in a shelter. But I was smitten. Been stuck with that amazing dog ever since."

"Like gum on a shoe." Felicity said dryly. "You have that effect, too, you know."

"I'm like gum? Used, icky gum?"

"In the sense you're hard to shake," Felicity said. "Memorable." She reached for her wineglass and took a sip.

Cooper beamed. "Okay, speaking of memorable, you have to try a bite of this. It's fantastic."

Felicity was shaking her head, even as Cooper pointed a pizza slice just outside her mouth. Lord, this was so wrong. It was intimate, for a start, and she barely knew Cooper, although God knew her hormones definitely wanted more. Not to mention, hello, carbs! And cheese! But…why did it have to smell so sinful?

And *oh*. Suddenly she was tasting the food. Chewing slowly. Swallowing. It was *glorious*. Felicity sighed out appreciation, melting under the delicious spices. It had been years since she'd eaten something so flavor packed. "Heavenly."

"Why do you look so surprised? Haven't you had pizza in a while?"

"No, not in…" She stopped and thought. "Well, I haven't had carbs in any major form since I was sixteen. So twenty years."

Cooper looked horrified. "Is this all about the women in your family being round again? Because twenty years without pizza is overkill, don't you think?"

"I guess I have been on the world's longest diet." Felicity shrugged, suddenly realizing how absurd that sounded. "I don't have an eating disorder, if that's what you're wondering. I just… Well, it's a habit now. It started out as a preventative measure against my genetics, yes. Then after a while, it just became convenient to pretty much eat the same things all the time because I don't have to think about it and my clothes always fit, and that's the end of it. I'm busy, and it's easy. But I need to remind myself that a lapse every now and then is hardly a calamity, especially given this is what I'm missing. Actually, it's wonderful."

Cooper grinned. "Does that mean you'd be open to trying more things? I'd love to reintroduce you to every food there is. I'm an expert, given I love to taste *everything*." She patted her rounded stomach. "Which probably shows."

"Oh, it shows." Felicity said, then realized with alarm how that sounded. "And it suits you," she rushed on. "All of you seems so in proportion. Wide shoulders, long powerful legs, full hips, and round stomach. You're just so…substantial." She licked her lips at the thought. In fact, ever since she'd met Cooper, she couldn't imagine any body shape more impressive than hers.

"You seem to have thought a great deal about my body." Cooper's eyes sparkled.

"Oh." Felicity felt her cheeks warm up. Yes, that had sounded a bit too appreciative, hadn't it? *Christ.* "I mean, it was a purely aesthetic observation. Like how Brittany is short and brown."

"Tell me you did not just compare your date to her dog." Amusement laced Cooper's tone.

"I—" Felicity paused. "Wait. This is a date? I was under the impression it was a celebration."

"Can't it be both? I mean, I thought you were pretty brazen in your appreciation of me the first time we met. Remember when you took over two minutes to get my keys out of my pocket, like you were on the hunt for buried treasure?"

Oh God. She'd been *that* obvious?

"And just now you listed all my physical attributes in a pretty flattering way. What's a girl to think? That you merely like my aesthetics in the same way you like my dog?" Cooper's expression turned cocky.

It was annoyingly attractive.

"I don't know where you got the idea I like Brittany," Felicity sputtered, desperate for a distraction. "That's crazy talk."

"Oh yes, I can tell by the way you push her away the moment she sits in your lap." Cooper chuckled. "Is a date with me such an out-there thought? Or does it scandalize you to be dating a lowly vet from the South Bronx when you're a highflier about to take over an international media corporation?" Her expression was teasing, but there was a sharpness in her eyes.

"You're missing the point. I've always known nothing could get in the way of my career. It doesn't matter what or who the distraction is; my eyes are fixed on the prize."

"So it'd look bad if anyone found out you dated someone way, way down the ladder like me?" Cooper frowned. "Someone with no ambition other than to do exactly what I'm doing? And who's happy doing just that?"

"Could you stop putting words in my mouth?" Felicity asked in exasperation. "I'm saying that very soon I'll be famous enough that I'll be watched by the media and my industry, examined for every little thing. Will I be deemed worthy to replace Elena Bartell even in a temporary capacity? That's what they'll want to know. I'm very aware of that. That's my focus. This is a difficult, precarious time for me, navigating what's to come, wondering what sort of job I'll do, and now you want me to think about dating? Why would I complicate my life like that?"

"So I'm hearing you're a bit prickly on the idea of us having a date."

"No...I'm just prickly in general," Felicity said in frustration. "Can't you tell the difference? This isn't even about you. Not really."

Cooper nodded. "I hear you. And ordinarily I'd just say, 'Hey, I like you, and I admit I may have a thing for bossy executive types who know their own mind. That's a powerful lure to me. Let's go out.' And you'd say, 'Can't, busy empire building,' and we'd go our separate ways. But there's a small problem."

"There is?" Felicity couldn't imagine what the issue was.

"Today, after what you did to the mayor, it was like being hit by electricity. Fork in a socket, slammed into the ground, little cartoon birdies dancing around my head." Cooper grinned.

"Sounds...painful."

"Felicity, I never saw anything more astonishing in my life than when you made the mayor agree to let through those bills. For years I've been dreaming about getting them passed. I wanted to kiss you on the spot. Don't you get it? You knocked my socks off, and I'm not sure I'll be able to ever get them back on again. I might be stuck barefoot for life." She gave a lazy smile but her gaze was honest and intense.

Felicity blinked in surprise.

"So tell me," Cooper continued, "how do I walk away after meeting someone like you? You're this beautiful, clever, giant-killing lawyer queen, Felicity Simmons. You're so fucking impressive to me that I can barely remember how it felt three days ago before I knew you. Really, is it so hard to understand why I'd want this to be a date?"

Felicity swallowed. *I'm beautiful to Cooper?* Weedy, weak, rail-thin, pale, and one-stiff-breeze-away-from-tumbleweeding-down-the-street Felicity Simmons was beautiful to the powerful Sandy Cooper?

"I have always been really clear where I stand," Felicity whispered as the energy arced between them. "My career comes first. At least for now."

"I know that."

"And my career's about to take a steeper trajectory very soon."

"I know that, too."

"And I'll be in the public eye. And very busy. And working around the clock."

"All the more reason you should have someone around who might be a safe space for you to talk to. And you know, have a date with. Share food. Because even kick-ass executive women need to eat."

"I...do." Felicity had never felt more conflicted. So if in doubt, retreat. "I think we should go home now. Separately, I mean. To our respective homes. The meal was...lovely." Even if all Felicity could remember of it was a mouthful of heavenly Sicilian pizza.

"Separately, because it's not a date," Cooper said, smiling.

Why did she look so amused? Felicity suddenly realized her fingers had slid to tangle with Cooper's.

Dear God, when had that transgression occurred? She snatched her wandering hand back, mortified. "Exactly. And we are definitely not taking *this* anywhere. Okay?"

"Whatever you say." Cooper merely grinned.

◆

Their first kiss came three seconds after Cooper closed her apartment's front door behind them and pressed Felicity against it.

Cooper offered a roguish smile, then her lips crushed Felicity's.

Felicity opened her mouth with a soft groan, hands scrabbling to grab Cooper's shirt, tugging her closer. As the probing softness of Cooper's tongue teased her own, arousal exploded through her like oil in a hot pan. It was frantic and demanding and so, so hot.

"Not a date, huh?" Cooper laughed against her lips. "Not taking this anywhere, huh?"

"Oh, shut up," Felicity snarked back and reached for her again, kissing her fiercely.

The woman could kiss, she'd give Cooper that. It wasn't just what her mouth was doing, either. It was the sheer size of her, the press of her weight, the feeling of all Felicity's senses being overwhelmed.

"I'm definitely not dating you. Or anything else," she added breathlessly when she struggled to come back up for air. "It's a distraction. All of this is a distraction."

"Mm, it *sure* is," Cooper drawled. "I'm plenty distracted right now. And I'm wondering what you'd do if I just stepped back and started peeling off all my clothes. Right in front of you. Would you enjoy that, Ms. Simmons?"

Felicity swallowed. "W-what?"

Cooper grinned, took a step back, and began to do exactly what she'd promised, her gaze scorching. She tossed her jacket behind her. "You know, your eyes have been stripping me naked for the past hour."

Stupid traitorous eyes.

Even as her pulse rate leaped, Felicity struggled to get a grip on herself. Would indulging in this be…unprofessional?

Cooper's fingers plucked at the remaining unfastened buttons of her shirt, eyes fixed on Felicity. One button, then two. More skin. She paused, making sure she had Felicity's eye, then continued. Three. Now four.

Cooper drew her shirt off, smirking as she reached for her bra and unhooked it from behind.

Felicity's lower stomach clenched in delight as Cooper drew the soft white material slowly away from her skin.

Fuck. Cooper's breasts were magnificent. Pendulous, full, glorious. Felicity's mouth went dry.

"Like what you see?" Cooper teased.

Was the sky blue? Loki chaotic evil? Elena a legend?

At the reminder of her boss, Felicity forced her brain to focus. Elena had sent her in to investigate a charity, not leap the bones of its head vet. Was this a terrible mistake?

Was it?

Except Cooper wasn't in charge at Living Ruff. She was sufficiently low enough down the pecking order to have nothing to do with whatever had happened to Elena's money. And it wasn't as if Felicity was about to bounce on the sheets with Rosalind or…Harvey. She shuddered at the last thought.

Cooper drew her pants down those long, long legs. When she straightened, kicking her pants and panties away after toeing off socks and shoes, she was entirely nude.

Felicity's brain whimpered. All those muscles and undulations, curves and flesh she'd been dreaming about for days were now in front of her. Within touching distance. She'd just have to lift her hand and—

"Was this what you wanted?" Cooper's voice was low and rough.

"No." Felicity stretched up on tiptoes, grabbed Cooper's beautiful face, and pulled her in for a kiss. "God, no. But here we are anyway. Distract me."

"With pleasure." Cooper smiled. "Very definitely *yes*."

———◆———

Felicity didn't have much memory of how she came to be naked and standing in Cooper's bedroom being kissed with such care, as though she were someone special. All she knew was that her knees were getting weaker by the second and she finally had her trembling hands on the legs and ass of her dreams.

"Christ, I love your thighs," Felicity whispered reverently, mapping them. "They're huge. And I mean that in the most sincere, best sense."

Cooper grinned. "I come by them honestly. Lots of hard work and cycling. Now, I believe you asked to be distracted." Without warning, she scooped Felicity up into her arms, walked her to the queen-sized bed, and deposited her.

Even though Cooper placed her carefully, Felicity still bounced into a tangle of splayed limbs that couldn't possibly be dignified. Her cheeks heated. She contemplated diving under the sheets, but Cooper's words stopped her.

"You are ridiculously beautiful, Felicity. Your flawless skin reminds me of a porcelain doll. Except"—she gave her a small curling smirk—"I happen to know you're not fragile. You're fierce and fucking legendary. And I can't wait to lick every inch of you."

The blush migrated to Felicity's chest and neck. It was an unusual experience being both worshipped for how she looked *and* the woman beneath that. The people she slept with usually admired only her surface, and Felicity went to a great deal of effort to ensure that was so. She didn't want anyone accidentally noticing who she really was. That was none of their damned business.

The way Cooper looked at her, though—it was as if she could see every part of her and wanted it all. Felicity drew up her knees and folded her arms around them, covering her small breasts, feeling suddenly more exposed than she ever had.

Worry filled Cooper's eyes. "I'm sorry if I made you self-conscious."

"I've always found it hard being…looked at." Looked into, she meant. She hated being *too* seen. It was so much less stressful when her lovers bedded the confident Bartell Corp executive rather than a woman with personality defects who was riddled with doubts, insecurities, and daddy issues.

It was particularly unsettling that Cooper seemed to know all that about her already. Hadn't she worked it out tonight—much to Felicity's anger and chagrin? For some mystifying reason, she wanted Felicity anyway.

"You don't like being looked at?" Cooper repeated slowly.

"Well, we're not all breathtaking like Wonder Woman." Felicity waved at her. Misdirection usually worked. Better than saying, *I can't believe you know who I am and find that remotely attractive. I sure as hell don't.*

Actually, a hero was exactly how Cooper looked right now with those supremely powerful legs, broad shoulders, and impressive breasts. She even had her hands on her hips.

"I'm not complaining that you look like some gorgeous superhero, just to be clear," Felicity added. She drew in a steadying breath and then unfurled herself from the physical knot she'd tied herself into, spreading her legs and lying back on her forearms. "I mean, I'd love you to touch me."

Cooper's eyes darkened. Her sharp gaze drifted to the small, barely-there strip of blonde between Felicity's legs, now soaked by desire.

With cheeks flaming at her own neediness, Felicity added, voice demanding, "Well, hurry up. I don't like to be kept waiting."

That seemed to break the tension. Cooper laughed and pounced playfully. She covered Felicity's body with her own, supporting her weight on her arms. "Well, I do love me a bossy woman."

Cooper kissed her thoroughly and slowly, her tongue dancing with Felicity's as she rocked against her. The sensation of their breasts, hips, and thighs rubbing was thrilling.

Cooper kissed her way down Felicity's body, flicking her tongue over her small pale nipples, teasing all around Felicity's belly button, and then… *Then* her mouth was on Felicity's clit, tongue sliding all over her most sensitive flesh, the slippery sensation sublime.

Felicity cried out and reached down, pushing her fingers through Cooper's blonde hair, scraping it back up over her scalp, pulsating her hand in time with Cooper's tongue.

"Would you like me inside?" Cooper asked, her expression pure desire.

"Yes," Felicity ground out. "Hurry."

Cooper bent down, sliding a finger inside her with ridiculous ease as her mouth went back to work.

Rough against delicate. Heat and wetness. It was hard to concentrate.

"Jesus," Felicity growled, "stop holding back. Fuck me like you mean it."

A second finger slid inside her, pumping her, filling her. The gentle action became deeper, stronger. Then Cooper's talented mouth was sucking her clit, tonguing it, flicking it.

Felicity began bucking hard against her, gasping out nonsensical words. Squirming now as ecstasy started blasting through her, she hissed out, "Oh. Oh fuck!"

Her hand clamped hard on Cooper's head. With a voice rough and needy, Felicity ordered: "There. Do. *Not*. Fucking. Move."

Cooper did not.

The woman's tiny snicker against Felicity's pussy didn't go unnoticed, but she was too busy arching, crying out, and jerking against Cooper's mouth to tell her off.

God. It was just... *Fuck, shit, holy Jesus.*

She slumped, blinked, and took stock as she tumbled down from her high.

Felicity was so *wet*. If she wasn't so completely spent, she might even be embarrassed about the puddle between her legs, down her thighs, and all over Cooper's chin and sheets.

Cooper gently eased her fingers out and wiped them teasingly all the way down her still-twitching thighs. Her knowing, glinting eyes never left Felicity's.

Felicity covered her face with a hand, too spent to worry about what a mess she must look. "Hell," she whispered, "that was...exactly what I needed."

She wondered if she should thank Cooper for following orders so well. Phillip always used to go rogue at pivotal moments, and it had annoyed the ever-loving fuck out of her. She'd missed so many orgasms because he thought he knew better. Cooper, however, was remarkably good at instruction. "Truly exceptional," she muttered.

"Oh, I definitely agree," Cooper said with a Cheshire-cat smile.

"I just knew you'd be smug," Felicity said with a huff. Not that she didn't like it.

"Of course I am. I loved watching you do that," Cooper said with conviction, meeting her eye seriously.

"Orgasm?" Felicity asked, lacing her tone with an edge to hide how vulnerable she always felt after sex. "Lose control? Be helpless?"

"No." Cooper smiled. "Well, yes. That, too. I like seeing you *naked*." She trailed the backs of her fingers across Felicity's inner thigh, raising tiny goosebumps in her wake. "Not just the outside, although you *are* delicious. I mean all of you. The real you. I like seeing you giving an actual shit instead of pretending nothing bothers you. I like seeing you look ecstatic about something. And I love how you taste. Felicity, you taste amazing."

And so ended any hopes Felicity might have had that Cooper was enjoying her only on a surface level. It was uncomfortable enough that Felicity revealed more of herself than she had to anyone else before, let alone that Cooper enjoyed seeing that side of her.

Or…it should be uncomfortable. Oddly, right now, Felicity felt appreciated, not to mention properly satiated in a way that still had her clit tingling. For once in her retort-laden life, she couldn't marshal a single objection.

Cooper's fingers danced across Felicity's pussy again, teasing and light, as if just pointing out that she could. As if appreciating the access that had been granted. "Gorgeous," she murmured.

Gorgeous? Surely she meant herself. On that note, it was well past time to return the favor. She tapped Cooper's shoulder.

"On your back." Felicity used the same commanding tone Cooper had responded to before.

Sure enough, she obeyed instantly. "Yes, ma'am," she teased. But there was something in her eye that said she'd enjoyed the way Felicity had asked a whole lot.

"Spread your legs for me."

The gleam of want in Cooper's eyes magnified.

"Fondle your breasts," Felicity said, her voice now a purr. "Show me how you like them touched."

Cooper swallowed and began to pluck at the wide nipples, tugging and teasing.

It was so arousing, Felicity could have watched forever.

"Good," was all she managed, her voice strained. "Just keep doing that. I have other duties to attend to," she said crisply, as though about to chair a management meeting.

Cooper's nostrils flared at the snap of command in her tone and a desperate *want* filled her face.

Oh, Sandy Cooper, I have your number. Felicity smiled. She slid between Cooper's legs, her narrow shoulders dwarfed by them, and took in the decidedly pleasing view.

Cooper was soaked and swollen. Felicity couldn't wait to have her. But first, she had a fantasy she'd waited quite long enough for.

She reached for Cooper's legs, pushing them wide apart, then stroked and teased all over her soft inner thighs, testing the weight of them, sliding around to tease along the line of muscle. Then she tongued along the same path, loving the panting sounds as she drew nearer and nearer to the junction of Cooper's thighs.

Her unique scent was driving Felicity crazy, as was the fact that Cooper was now even wetter.

Felicity lifted her gaze to see the raw need on Cooper's face. *She'd* made Cooper look like *this*? She blew over her lover's swollen, slick flesh. She still hadn't touched her here. Not yet. She could wait.

Cooper's pussy clenched. "Felicity," she said in a gasp, "stop teasing."

"I think you want 'Boss Me' to take you. The 'giant-killing lawyer queen,' I think you called me. *That's* who you want inside you."

Cooper groaned. Her hands began to squeeze and roll her breasts harder.

"I can see you like that idea," Felicity continued as her breath teased across Cooper's slick lower lips. "I think you're dying for my touch."

Cooper whimpered. "*Please?*"

"Well," Felicity said imperiously, thrilling at the power rush of Sandy Cooper begging. "You did ask nicely." She flicked Cooper's clit with her tongue over and over and played with her folds with her fingers for long, slippery moments until Cooper started to quiver and arch.

"Ever been fucked by an executive in a kick-ass power suit? High starched collar. Four buttons undone. The smell of success." Felicity murmured against the little nub, inspiration seizing her. If Cooper liked bossy…

"Oh God!" Cooper's eyes screwed shut. "Oh God!"

"Would you like that? Me putting on my best corporate-takeover outfit and fucking you like a boss?" Felicity's tongue did a playful little swirl over her clit. "Would *that* make you come?"

Cooper's arms and legs snapped ramrod straight, her toes and back curled, and she wailed.

Guess so.

Cooper shuddered and shuddered as Felicity licked her thoroughly, dipping her tongue inside her entrance, teasing in circles around it, then sliding back up to her clit. Finally, the shudders turned to trembles, and Cooper weakly pushed her away.

Felicity wiped her mouth and sat up. "I'll do it, you know. I have just the outfit."

Cooper groaned. "How did you know that's what I'd be into? I never told anyone."

"I can see what Deedra and I have in common." She smiled. "Besides, I'm rather fond of powerful women myself." She lightly slapped Cooper's thigh. "Obviously."

"Felicity?" Cooper's voice turned serious. "I want more."

"Well, I suppose we could go another round—"

"No, I mean more than tonight. I meant what I said at dinner: I'd really like to date you. This isn't a one-and-done thing to you, is it?"

That was the question. Felicity knew dating was off the table. Even if she was good at relationships—and clearly, she wasn't—this would be the worst time to try something new.

Her whole body pouted.

On the other hand, she wasn't even close to ready to give up the earthly delights of being with Sandy Cooper.

"How about we make it a length-of-time-I'm-involved-with-Living Ruff thing?" Felicity suggested.

"Sure." Cooper exhaled in what looked like relief. "Okay. I can live with that."

"Okay," Felicity said, then rose. She looked around for her underwear.

"You're leaving?" Cooper's eyebrows lifted in surprise. "It's late. You could stay over."

"No," Felicity said immediately. "I'm not a stay-over kind of woman. I like my own space and my own bed. Especially when I'm not really dating someone. When it's just brief and casual like this."

"Oh." Cooper sat up. Her impressive breasts looked even more glorious from this angle.

Felicity's lower stomach twitched in instant approval. *Damn.*

"You know," Felicity said coolly, dropping her newly reclaimed bra back to the floor, "I may have been hasty. Perhaps the night is still young."

"You mean you'll stay?" A wide grin spread across Cooper's face.

Felicity tilted her chin up as she regarded Cooper, expression imperious. "Did I stutter?"

"Great," Cooper whispered. "Oh, fuck me dead."

"My plan precisely." Her voice was so commanding, she swore Cooper looked about to come again.

Felicity hid her smile. This fling was doing wonders for her ego. She nudged Cooper in the ribs. Sprawled out as she was, she took up a lot of space. "Come on, make room for me."

Cooper didn't speak for a moment, then said softly, "For as long as you want."

Felicity pretended not to hear because the murmured words were weighted in ways that felt like too much. Anyway, it was easy enough to forget them as her hands found firm, warm flesh once more, and Cooper's eyelids fluttered closed.

Chapter 8
Puzzling

FELICITY WOKE TO FIND COOPER'S muscled arm pressing her chest tightly against Cooper's torso. It was delicious. She wanted nothing more than to wake the woman up and begin round three. Or was it four? In the course of their evening, Felicity had discovered how much she loved pure strength. Physical, sweaty, fling-me-down-and-fuck-me-senseless strength. God, she could do this forever.

Brief and casual, she reminded herself. This was just a fling—a glorious one—for the duration she was with Living Ruff before the real world clawed her back once more. She groaned, surprised at the surge of reluctance at the reminder.

The soft sound was enough for Cooper's eyes to flutter open.

"Hello, beautiful." She smiled. "Have a good night?"

"You have no idea." Felicity sat up, trying to gauge what time it was. She reached for her phone on the bedside table. The sheet fell away from her body as she twisted, and her lover's eyes lit up. "Keep looking at me like that, and neither of us will get to work," Felicity said, dropping the phone again. "You make me want to break all my rules and call in a personal day for once."

Cooper's hand lifted, and she cupped Felicity's small breast. Her fingers absently played with the sensitive nipple. "I know the feeling. However, I'm highly motivated in my job."

Her fingers drifted down Felicity's body, almost tickling, the movement was so light. She reached Felicity's hips, pulled the sheet away, and her fingers dipped lower. It was enough to make Felicity tremble. "Unfortunately, if I don't go to work, people's animals get sicker. Or worse. So…"

All arousal fled, and Felicity glared.

Cooper snatched her hand away. "Sorry. I know, that was the worst, even if it is accurate. Come on, let's share a shower, and maybe you'll forgive me when I've pressed you against the wall while the water's crashing over us."

Felicity swallowed, picturing that visual. Speaking of displays of strength. "Oh," she said faintly.

The look in Cooper's eye told Felicity she'd worked out exactly what did it for her. Well, good. Cooper might be persuaded to show off how strong she was more often. Repeatedly, even.

They were eating breakfast forty minutes later: Cooper, a mound of toast and scrambled eggs; Felicity, a coffee and a low-carb bar. She could barely stop squirming after what had happened in the shower. Even the thought of it made her wet. *Again.*

Cooper seemed to know it, too, based on the amusement in her eye. "Care to share?" she asked politely. "Was it the bit where I tongued you while you were pinned above me against the wall?"

Felicity's cheeks burned. "I have no idea why you assume I'm thinking of that."

"What about on top of the counter when we got out? Soap, toothpaste, and towels flying everywhere?"

That, too. Felicity's nipples stiffened.

"My favorite part was when you got down on your knees in the shower, pushed my thighs apart, and ate me out. I don't know how you didn't drown."

Felicity wasn't entirely sure either. "I think we should change the subject back to sick animals," Felicity said, eyes sharp, "to help you have some focus."

Cooper's eyes sparkled. "Probably for the best."

"Mm." Felicity drew in a breath and tried to ignore the fact that she could smell Cooper's apple-scented shampoo. She'd probably forever more associate it with phenomenal sex. "I'm going to ask Harvey about the vet-tech scheme today."

"Since it's my program, he might be more forthcoming if I'm there, too. So I'll gate-crash your meeting." Cooper rose, taking her plate to the sink and washing it. As she bent over, her tight jeans accentuated her ass in ways Felicity was helpless to tear her eyes from.

"You're staring, Felicity."

"Hardly my fault," she protested. "It's your ass calling me like a siren. Think of me like a helpless sailor dashing herself into the rocks of Scylla to get to it."

Cooper turned, smiling. "I love how you say fancy stuff like that."

"It's not that fancy. Actually, I'm not fancy in the least."

"You are to me. I'm in a Billy Joel song next to you. 'Uptown Girl.'"

Felicity snorted. "More like Midwest Girl."

"You know, that's the first time you've willingly described yourself like that. Without looking like you're pulling out teeth."

Well. That was true. For some reason, around Cooper, she didn't feel as much at war with her roots. She wondered why. "Don't get used to it," was all she said.

Cooper laughed.

"I don't suppose you have any details of your vet-tech scheme here." Felicity said. "I'd like to read up on it before I see Harvey. It's good to go into a meeting knowing all the details."

"Sure. In my office." She pointed to a door beyond the kitchen that Felicity hadn't noticed before. "I'll just finish up these dishes—won't be half a minute—and I'll help you find it. I mean…if I can remember where I put it." Her expression became sheepish.

What was that about? Felicity headed to the room in question, opened the door, and gasped. Paperwork piles were stacked from floor to ceiling. There was hardly any surface not crammed with document boxes and books. *Oh. My. God.*

"Cooper?" Felicity called out. "Did you know you've been attacked by hoarders?"

A minute passed, then Cooper joined her, regarding the room as her cheeks bloomed with redness. "Yeah. About that? I seem to be missing the office-sorting gene."

Felicity stared, her fingers twitching to reorganize all of it. It'd take, what, half a day? "I could…um…assist, if you wanted." Really, how hard could it be? "One thing I'm really good at is O&M—organization and methods. I mean… God, how can you stand it?" She spun around to look at Cooper.

"Well, I guess I'm not perfect at everything." Cooper pulled a face. "I've been overwhelmed by this for ages."

"Deedra warned me you're a little scatterbrained at organizing things. But I mean…this is complete chaos!" Felicity straightened, reaching a decision. "Not to worry. I will sort this out for you. You go in to work, and I'll have it ordered and filed and alphabetized before you know it. Then I'll be in to talk to Harvey with you."

Uncertainty filled Cooper's face. "Um…seriously?"

"You think I'm prepared to leave an office space looking like this when I could just…make it right?" Felicity shook her head. "Please let me. I mean, unless you have something top secret or embarrassing you'd rather I don't know about in here."

"All my stuff that's tax-related or private or that I'm afraid of losing, like my passport, I keep locked in there." She nudged the bottom drawer of her desk with her toe. "Everything else is just…wherever, whatever. Where it lands, it stays. I don't care if you see it. But why would you want to face it? It just… It's a *lot*. And you really don't have to. We can just close the door and forget you were ever in here."

"If we're to be a thing, however short, I'm not letting chaos reside in even one room within my radius," she said firmly. "It's done. Go." She shooed her from the room. "Leave me to perform my magic. You go to work. I'll see you there when I'm done."

Cooper chuckled and shook her head. "You really are something else."

"I'm aware." Felicity tried to sound indifferent, but she felt too delighted and warm for that. "And really, it's no trouble. I'd find it harder not to do it."

"I can see why your boss thinks so highly of you," Cooper said.

"Well…" Felicity wasn't sure what to say to that. Elena had promoted her. She'd also sent her on this assignment because she had doubts that Felicity was capable of thinking outside the box. So really, Felicity wasn't entirely sure what Elena truly thought of her. She pushed that depressing thought away and repeated, "Go. I'll text you if I have any questions about what needs to go where."

Cooper grinned. "Okay. You win."

"Of course I do," Felicity said, and smiled. "It's me you're dealing with now. Remember that."

"Oh, I will." Cooper looked half dazed and a whole lot amused as she headed out the door for work.

Felicity marched into Living Ruff just before lunchtime, her mind whirring. She'd sorted out Cooper's entire life in just three hours. The woman's existing filing system was a menace but had been hugely satisfying to untangle. Felicity had texted her a few times throughout the morning, supplying photos showing the piles getting smaller and querying whether she'd intended to file a wedding invitation from 2009 under Bills.

Cooper's replies had been three smiley faces and one "Oops. That wedding was for one of my exes—probably a Freudian move filing it there."

Of more concern was the vet-tech trainee program file. Not for what was missing but for what was in it: everything. Cooper had forgotten to mention she'd apparently thrown herself into the project with enthusiasm. She'd fully costed it out, including every local college offering vet-tech qualifications, their responses to her queries about her scheme, deans ranked from "helpful" to "useless," and suggestions involving clearing out the storeroom on Living Ruff's ground floor to make temporary accommodation for the applicants in case the college insisted on them having a fixed address before applying. Duties and ideas for how to further train vet techs in a Living Ruff apprenticeship scheme were listed in exhaustive specificity. It was astonishing in detail, even if it wasn't the slightest bit organized.

The moment she went through the folder, Felicity knew that if Cooper had conveyed all her findings and research to Harvey, there was no way he'd need to spend more than few days working out whether to go ahead on the program. It was already done. It was all here. So why the delay? He'd been sitting on Elena's donation since September 2 of last year. It was now March 17. What did he need to think about when he had all this work at his fingertips and $1.4 million to fund it? That was the question.

Cooper was talking to Gabriel Mendoza, the other vet, when Felicity entered Living Ruff's office.

"Ms. Simmons," he said with a small smile. "We meet again! And this is Felix, my chinchilla."

Felix peeked at her from Dr. Mendoza's shoulder. The tiny gray creature had huge round ears and a fluffed-up tail. Adorable! Felicity hoped her aching need to stroke the little thing hadn't turned into a meeping noise or anything embarrassing. "Felix," she repeated, her voice strained. "Okay."

Cooper eyed her closely, a smile tugging at her lips. "You're dying to pet him, aren't you?"

"She is?" Dr. Mendoza asked in surprise. "She looks like she's dying to flee the room."

Felicity gave them both grim looks and folded her arms.

"You can pet Felix, if you'd like," Dr. Mendoza said kindly, "if you're gentle and slow with your movements."

"I don't think so," Felicity said. That way there be dragons. Although knowing her, she'd want to pet the dragons, too. "Can we get down to business, please?" She glanced around. "Where's your director?"

"About that…" Cooper sighed. "I told Harvey you wanted a meeting. He said he had to duck out for a little while. He apologized."

"Well, that's annoying." Felicity sighed. "When will he be back?"

"He didn't say."

Dr. Mendoza glanced at his watch. "I'm due for rounds. It is wonderful to meet a potential donor of your standing, Ms. Simmons," he said before leaving with a wave.

"He knows who I am now?" Felicity asked once he'd left.

Cooper rolled her eyes. "Your fact-finding visit is all Mrs. Brooks is talking about." She waved to the woman in question, who was just putting down the phone.

"You make me sound like a gossip hound," Mrs. Brooks said reproachfully. "Why shouldn't I let the staff know who to impress?" The edges of her eyes crinkled. "Be glad I didn't suggest Mitch roll out a red carpet for you, Ms. Simmons. He'd have dragged one out of God knows where. He's a very resourceful young man."

Cooper laughed. "He'd find one, all right. Okay, so I agree. We must show Ms. Simmons a good time." She grinned at Felicity over the double entendre.

Felicity absolutely refused to meet her eye in case she blushed.

"Not *too* good a time," Mrs. Brooks said dryly. "I'm a happily married woman. And don't act like I can't hear you dripping with innuendo." She arched an eyebrow at Cooper. "I wasn't born yesterday, you know."

"I have no idea what you're talking about," Cooper said primly.

"Sure you don't. By the way, just so you know, Dr. Mendoza treated one of your regulars in here yesterday. Norma came in to see if there was a tumor in her cat"—she paused to tap a few keys—"Lucille. It turned out to be the kidneys you noticed that felt irregular. Lucille was given blood and urine tests, which came up clean. Everything else was fine. The cat'll probably outlive us all."

"That is wonderful news," Cooper said, then turned to Felicity. "Sometimes kidneys can feel weird in animals and get mistaken for a growth. So Lucille's fine. This is great!"

Felicity gave a stiff nod to hide her enormous relief, which earned an incredulous look from Mrs. Brooks.

"You and animals," the older woman muttered, so low she probably thought Felicity wouldn't hear. "What does Brittany see in you?"

At the mention of her name, the dog lying beside Mrs. Brooks's chair picked her head up, realized who was here, and bounded over to them with a series of delighted woofs.

"I don't know why you're so excited to see me," Cooper said, giving her a thorough pat. "I went through your joy of a reunion with me three hours ago. And two hours ago. And twenty minutes ago. I swear, the life of a dog must be fantastic, getting to greet their favorite humans repeatedly, as if they haven't seen them for weeks."

Felicity smiled at that until Brittany headed her way, looking up at her with a loving expression that just begged to be met with pats. "Don't look at me like that," Felicity said, sliding her hands in her pockets out of temptation's way. "We're not friends."

Brittany sat at her feet, bumping her thigh with her head. Felicity whimpered internally.

"Unfortunately," Cooper said with a gleeful look, "your bond was sealed the moment you fed her on Monday."

"Lucky me." She sighed and stared down at Brittany, offering her most imperious stare. "I apologize for giving you false expectations with the ham. I didn't want it to go to waste."

"Do you really dislike animals so much, Ms. Simmons?" Mrs. Brooks asked askance.

Cooper laughed. "You wouldn't say that if you'd seen her yesterday at the open day. She was up to her chin in cats, looking like she was in heaven, snuggling them all."

"I am fairly sure you mistook me for someone else," Felicity protested.

"That seems more likely," Mrs. Brooks said, disbelief clear in her eyes.

"Ri-i-ight. Okay, come with me," Cooper nudged Felicity. "Let's get a coffee and discuss strategy. I'll even introduce you to more tasty carbs."

With a sigh, Felicity shook her head and said, "If you must."

Felicity soon found herself a few streets away eyeballing a bakery called Capri. Fatty, sugary cakes filled the window. "Really?" she muttered, aghast.

"Do you mind? I *have* to inhale some rainbow cookie when I can't figure things out. Helps me think." Cooper grinned.

"Rainbow cookie?"

"It's big around the Bronx. Legendary, even."

"If you say so," Felicity said in a dubious tone.

"I do. So you grab us a pair of counter seats, and I'll order."

Felicity pursed her lips and nodded.

Before long, two steaming coffees slid onto the counter in front of her along with sachets of sugar. One coffee was milky, the other dark. "Wasn't sure how sweet you liked it," Cooper said, taking the counter stool beside her, "but I was pretty sure you'd go for bitter black."

"Is that a critique of my personality?" Felicity asked, pulling the darkest cup closer. "Good guess, though."

"It's more a powerful boss-lady thing. Dee took her coffee this way, too. Y'all think it makes you look tough. It doesn't. It makes you look insane." Cooper pulled her own drink close, added three sugars, and gave it a stir. Then she tugged a plate in front of herself. The cake slice had layers of pink, yellow, and green with a lash of chocolate icing. An edible rainbow.

"How very…gay," Felicity mused.

"Or…fitting?" Cooper suggested, tone teasing. She grinned and forked a portion off. "Try some?" She offered the fork.

"No, thanks." At Cooper's pout, Felicity added, "I'm not a cake fan. This isn't about my genetics again. Cake's simply too sweet for me. I have a savory tooth."

"Fair enough." Cooper took a bite herself and sighed happily. "More for me."

Felicity smiled and sipped her coffee. "So is Harvey ducking me? Well, us?"

"Well, I'm not sure what's going on." Cooper sighed. "I told him we wanted to talk to him about the vet-tech program because Rosalind seemed to think he was going forward with it. That's when he got a bit spooked and weird, and he was gone before I knew it."

"That's really suspicious. And yet the first day I was here, Mrs. Brooks assured me everything was completely aboveboard financially. Didn't you say the office only ran at all due to her? She'd know if something was off, wouldn't she?"

"I think she'd know."

"So maybe Mrs. Brooks is in on this, too, somehow. Whatever this is."

"No." Cooper recoiled. "She's absolutely dedicated to this charity. And by the way, so's Harvey. I mean he *loves* it."

"But you agree he's hiding something? Come on, Harvey is the worst liar."

Cooper took a sip of coffee, her mood turning morose. "He's an honest man. Well, I always thought he was."

"Cooper? Has there been any sign that he's been sliding money around before? Maybe something you paused over at the time but pushed aside?"

She slowly shook her head. "No. And I'm having a hard time believing it now. It's all so…un-Harvey. It's not like he needs the money for himself."

"True. His wife's success makes embezzlement seem an odd choice. And I really think she believes her husband when he says he's setting up a vet-tech program. I saw it in her eyes."

"Well, Rosalind is no fool," Cooper mused. "Her whole family benefits from her business smarts. She set one brother up with a sporting-goods store. Her sister runs a fashion label that Rosalind funded. Her other brother's overseas, studying in Italy. Various nieces and nephews have trust funds. She's in charge of it all."

"And she gave Harvey an animal foundation to run."

"Yes. Exactly what he'd have wanted. She appointed family and friends to the board so she could keep an eye on everything. But aside from that and running the donation side of things, she's hands-off on day-to-day decisions. And Harvey's done a good job. He gets a few unorthodox ideas every now and then, like the time he thought we should have a Living Ruff toy line. That went nowhere." She shook her head. "Or when he decided we should pretend we're on the brink of folding every year."

"Well, that one backfired," Felicity said, "given I'm here investigating."

"I'm extremely glad it backfired," Cooper said, "or we'd never have met."

Felicity smiled. "There is that. Anyway, so you're saying he runs the charity well."

"He's a committed administrator, and between him and Mrs. Brooks, the place is like a well-oiled machine. There's no excessive waste. Our office isn't cutting edge. No latest tech or computers because he channels everything spare into our outreach programs."

That explained a few things but not everything—like how bizarrely the foundation's director was acting.

"He's not blowing our money," Cooper continued. "I don't know what's going on, but he's not stealing. And before you ask, he hates drugs and gambling. The man is as vanilla as a milkshake."

"Not so vanilla that he isn't hiding something," Felicity said. "Something that's enough to make him panic. Is it possible he's hiding something his wife's doing? He's covering for Rosalind? I mean, they clearly love each other. You should hear the way she talks about him."

"And Harvey worships the ground she walks on, yes. But I meant it when I said she's a brilliant businesswoman. I can't imagine she'd ever lower herself to doing something underhanded."

"Mm," Felicity said. She didn't get that vibe from Rosalind, either. Some people just radiated competence and cleverness. Her mind drifted back to Elena.

"But that's not my primary concern anymore," Cooper said.

"What is?"

"Felicity," Cooper said quietly, "I think it's time we got to it: why are you really here?"

"Excuse me?"

"Come on. No one sends someone so senior in a global media corporation to check the books of a charity that a boss might donate to. That's…insane. I know you're not here for the reason you told us. So please, can you trust me and tell me?"

Felicity sighed. It had been much easier to fob off Rosalind when she'd asked the same thing. But Cooper deserved more. Felicity considered her options. She weighed up Elena's need for secrecy and privacy against the fact she really needed Cooper's cooperation to go any further. It came down to whether she trusted her. Surely Cooper couldn't be involved in whatever her boss was up to, could she?

Those earnest, worried eyes looking back at her told her absolutely not.

"This must remain top secret," Felicity said.

"Of course."

"My boss already donated to Living Ruff. She's the donor behind that $1.4 million last year."

Cooper's eyes widened. "Holy… That was her? I always assumed it was Warren Buffet or someone like that."

"Elena makes a lot of private donations, usually to causes she thinks no one cares much about. Her red flags went up when she read that the charity she'd given the equivalent of three years of Living Ruff's entire running costs to was about to close."

"But we aren't about to close."

"Yes, but she didn't know that. She tried to speak to Harvey about it the day the story came out, and he fobbed her off so badly and with so many bad lies that she became suspicious. She sent someone she trusts"—Felicity waved to herself—"to make inquiries on the down-low."

"She could have called in the cops for a suspected fraud," Cooper said slowly. "Why didn't she?"

"Elena's a very private person, and she'd like to keep who she donates to as her business. Besides, if Living Ruff wasn't doing anything nefarious with her donations, she didn't want to cause bad press by starting a public inquiry that could hurt the charity."

"That's very considerate of her."

"It is. She's forward thinking like that. Close attention to detail."

"You admire her a lot, don't you?" Cooper said after a moment.

"She's an impressive woman."

"I've noticed before, you know, every time you say her name, you get this look of"—Cooper waved her hand—"like Elena Bartell can do no wrong."

"Oh, I've seen her do wrong." Felicity shook her head. "Her choice of husbands is abysmal. Thank God her last one's gone, and I don't have to see his smug photo on her desk anymore. Not that the replacement photo is much better. I mean, Maddie is rather insufferable." Felicity smiled at her own joke.

"Maddie is insufferable? Maddie Grey?" Cooper sounded astonished.

Oh right. She'd forgotten Cooper had met the affable Maddie. "I—no. Not really. It's just a thing I do with her. I insult her. She laughs at me. I don't really dislike her, but she must *never* know that. Do you understand? That's a state secret."

Cooper laughed.

"No, I mean it!" Felicity said, with faux dramatics. "Although I think by now she suspects my colorful vitriol is only surface deep. Look, I admit she pisses me off because she's on the world's longest lucky streak. Everything just keeps falling into place for her. It's maddening. But I'm working hard at not blaming her for the fact that she's impossible. People like her, with her genuine niceness and annoying, perfect luck, shouldn't even exist. Ugh! Don't remind me."

"Ah." Cooper smiled. "Okay, she's a little lucky and it pisses you off. Got it."

"A little? She's a freak. She modeled at Australian Fashion Week. Did she tell you that? And she's not a model, as proved by the way she grinned at the crowd like a hyena."

"I— What?" Cooper sputtered.

"Exactly! It was a weird fluke of a thing—knowing the designer who was desperate. That just doesn't happen to regular people." Felicity thought about that for a moment, then added, "But Maddie's also about the only competent reporter I've come across in the past ten Bartell Corp buyouts, and I respect her for it. She does the research, writes well, and has earned her reputation. I was enormously shocked that Elena didn't retain her services when she shut down her paper."

"She fired Maddie?"

"More than once."

"More than once!"

Felicity rolled her eyes. "It's a thing Elena does. Don't read too much into it. They're good friends now. She emailed and called when Maddie was on a travel assignment in Vietnam. Elena takes her as a plus-one for balls and introduces her around the industry as part of a deal they did when Elena wanted one of Maddie's exclusives. Fewer balls now, though, since they're both based in that antipodean armpit. I don't think Sydney has one decent international-quality event I'd cross the road for."

"Maddie's moved back to Sydney?" Cooper eyed her in surprise.

"It's her home. She was unhappy here."

"What a curious basis for a friendship. From being fired to feted by *the* Elena Bartell."

"Exactly," Felicity slapped the table lightly. "I mean, why on earth? I cannot work that out."

"You really can't?"

Felicity peered at her. "You're saying you can?"

"Maddie and I bonded over our favorite Jodie Foster movies. How she could pick *Contact* over *The Brave One* is beyond me, though." Cooper grinned. "She didn't try to hide her sexuality while she was at Living Ruff doing all her interviews, is what I'm getting at."

Felicity frowned at the conversation leap. "I— Well, yes, I believe she's gay. So?"

"Right. Good. I wasn't sure if you knew, but I gathered she's not keeping it a secret. Anyway, she kept getting all these texts from some new woman she was into. We all teased her a little about it, the way her face lit up whenever a new message arrived. I think it's wonderful when someone's head over in heels in love."

Maddie was in love? How had Felicity not known this? "Did she say who she was seeing?"

"You really can't see it?" Cooper asked, tone rising incredulously. "Your boss and Maddie?"

Felicity laughed. "That's… You couldn't be more wrong. Elena is not into the ladies, thank you very much. I've worked with her for years. I'd have seen it if she was."

"Felicity, Elena takes Maddie as her plus-one to events."

"Yes, and I already explained that. It was part of a contract Elena signed in order to publish a scoop Maddie had done. It was business for Elena. I think she'd have agreed to take Attila the Hun to events if it meant getting that exclusive."

"Okay, but Elena kept in touch with her while she was away in Vietnam. She's a busy woman. Your boss must have really missed her."

"Friends do that, too, you know. Miss each other." Felicity scowled.

"Elena's moving all the way down to Sydney to live where Maddie lives because Maddie was unhappy here."

"Because Elena has a beautiful home in Sydney! And she can edit her fashion magazines from anywhere."

"And yet she chose somewhere far from her empire's headquarters in the wrong time zone for most business deals?"

"So what? She's the boss; she can do what she likes."

"Felicity." Cooper sounded exasperated now. "She keeps Maddie's photo on her desk in the same place her ex-husband's was."

"Well, that's just circumstantial nonsense," Felicity said hotly. "You don't know Elena. And I can tell you, she is completely, utterly, thoroughly straight."

She couldn't tell Cooper the rest. How her younger self had spent an embarrassing amount of time watching her boss for any signs of romantic interest in women while telling herself it was just admiration for an impressive businesswoman.

And the verdict? *Nothing*. Elena hadn't given any of the beautiful models, photographers, or assistants that filled their world more than a cursory glance—no matter how refined, clever, or breathtaking. On the other hand, Elena had, on more than one occasion, asked Felicity to book her and her then-husband romantic weekend getaways.

And there was also no way in hell that Elena had ever had a discreet woman on the side, either. She knew her boss's packed schedule inside and out. It simply wasn't possible without Felicity seeing some signs.

Therefore she had long ago concluded that her boss was both straight and entirely unavailable—which had been such an odd thought at the time for someone who considered herself one hundred percent straight, too. She'd never prodded that weirdness too hard.

Of course, the day Felicity discovered her own bisexuality in the arms of a female colleague, a great many things had become clear.

Not that it mattered anymore. Her pathetic little crush was in the past. And as she'd just patiently explained to Cooper, Elena Bartell was utterly, thoroughly straight.

"And you wish that wasn't the case," Cooper concluded.

A chill went through her. "No."

"Felicity." Kindness laced Cooper's are-you-kidding-me tone.

"No!" She folded her arms. "You don't get it, do you? Fine, I admit I've found her attractive. *In the past.* But so what? The world's full of people we find attractive who are unattainable. All I want in life is career success, and I can't get that if I obsess about people I can't have. So I told myself I wouldn't think about Elena like that, and that's what I've done. I moved on years ago. Frankly, I'm tired of this topic."

Cooper nodded slowly. "I believe you. I do believe you think highly of her. I believe you are attracted to her. And I believe you when you say that's something you've pushed out of your mind because that would distract you from the thing you care about most. Your career, right?"

"Yes." *Finally!*

"Well, on that last point I get it. Workplace romances can be messy, even if both people *are* into each other. But one thing I'm sad about is how convinced you are that all you're good for in this world is your career. Don't you care about attaining other things beside that? Love? Family? Anything else?"

"No." Felicity shook her head firmly.

"Never?"

"No." She gave an even more adamant head shake this time.

"What if it just...happens? You fall hopelessly in love with someone? You can't control that, surely."

"Nothing's more important than career." She gave Cooper a pugnacious look. On this, no one could sway her.

"You really believe that, don't you?"

"Certainly."

"I believe you." Cooper leaned back, her expression inscrutable.

Did Felicity detect a hint of sadness?

Cooper's phone beeped, and she reached for it, opening a text. "I asked Mrs. B to tell me when Harvey came in. She reports he's back at the office, asked where you were, and only settled in at his desk when she told him you'd gone out with me. He probably thinks we're out for hours."

"Sounds like it. Once more unto the breach?"

Cooper chuckled. "Shakespeare, right? I will miss your random classical references when this is all over."

"And I'll miss the fact that you actually find them impressive."

<hr />

Harvey did not look happy to see her, Felicity noted as she slid uninvited into the visitor's chair opposite him.

"Ms. Simmons," he said with a sigh, "I really am quite busy." Harvey glanced over Felicity's shoulder, and his eyebrows lifted. "Et tu, Dr. Cooper?"

"I'm an interested observer. It's my program, after all."

Harvey shifted uncomfortably in his chair. "Really, now's not the best time. I have a meeting"—he waved to the door—"so if you'll just—"

"You only just got here," Felicity said. "You don't have a meeting."

He blinked at her through his glasses. "I'm really very sorry. I'd like you to reschedule."

Felicity stared at him for a moment, wondering which way to play this: diplomacy or Rambo? Elena wanted the former. But if Felicity was ever to be taken seriously in her own right, not just because Elena had anointed her, then she needed to show initiative. She had to know when to ignore the rules. Time to shake the tree and see what fell out.

"Where'd the money go?" Felicity asked, voice cool. "Enough evasion. There's no vet-tech program. If there was, Cooper would know about it. You'd have consulted her. And your other vets, too."

"That program is not ready to implement just yet."

"Not ready? Dr. Cooper already costed it out in exhaustive detail for you months ago. I've seen her paperwork. It was thorough. You don't need to do any further research to know whether the program's viable. So what's going on?"

"This is most inappropriate." Anger flickered into Harvey's eyes. "I don't answer to you. You have no business—"

"I do, actually. That was Elena Bartell's $1.4 million donation you vanished into thin air. She wants to know what you did with it."

Harvey's mouth dropped open. "That money was from Ms. Bartell?" he croaked.

"Yes. Before I involve the authorities, I'm now asking you one more time: where has her money gone?" She glanced around. "It's clearly not on infrastructure. I'm sure I saw you still have Windows 98 on your computers."

"Yes," Cooper confirmed.

"So it makes me wonder," Felicity said silkily, waving at a picture of Harvey standing in front of a BMW with his daughter, "if the money went somewhere closer to home."

"What?" True outrage filled his features. "You think I'd steal from my own charity?" He shot to his feet. "I love Living Ruff." His voice was shaking now. "I'm going to have to ask you to leave. And you"—he turned to Cooper—"I can't believe you'd side with her on this. Over me! You *know* me!"

"Harvey," Cooper said quietly, "if it's all aboveboard, just tell us where the money is."

"A new program," Harvey snapped. "Now leave. Both of you."

Felicity left the office, Cooper on her heels, and they came to a stuttering halt near the round table in the center of the room.

Mrs. Brooks looked up. "I heard yelling. How on earth did you get Harvey to yell? He hasn't done it in all the years I've been here."

"Mrs. Brooks," Felicity said, "I have reason to believe your boss has done something untoward with Living Ruff donations. What exactly, I have no idea. I'd like to have a thorough look at the books. I believe you can access them. I'm especially interested in seeing the Form 990 for the current financial year that's not been submitted yet." She reached into her bag and pulled out her business card. "You don't have to agree. Just send it here. No questions asked." She slid her card onto the table, pointing to her email address.

Mrs. Brooks made no move to take it, and her eyes narrowed into slits. "Mr. Clifford would never do what you're saying."

"And if he has?" Cooper asked.

"How can you possibly believe that? He would never!" Mrs. Brooks said, darting a glance to the corner office. "I would stake my life on it—he'd never steal for his own ends."

"What if he's stealing for other ends? Ends he *thinks* are good?" Cooper asked.

"He wouldn't." Mrs. Brooks folded her arms. "He'd never steal."

"Then prove it," Felicity said, tapping the card. "*You* can find the answers."

Harvey stalked to the door of his office. "I told you to leave, Ms. Simmons. Go! And Dr. Cooper, get out of my sight. Do rounds. Now." He spun on his heel, slamming the door behind him.

Mrs. Brooks gasped. "You'd better go. I'll calm him down."

"Will you look into the finances for me?" Felicity pressed.

"He's no embezzler, Ms. Simmons," she replied. "I promise you that. You've got the wrong idea about him. You can show yourselves out," she added frostily.

Outside the building a moment later, Cooper sighed. "I hate this. I feel sick to my stomach."

"Do you think Mrs. Brooks will do what I asked?"

"Maybe. She is loyal, but even she can tell Harvey's not acting himself."

"I truly don't see what he hopes to gain by shouting at me and ordering me out," Felicity said. "He must know the next step I have is calling in the fraud squad. They'll go through his records with a fine-tooth comb anyway. So why not just be honest now?" She paused. "Unless"—Felicity inhaled—"he's buying time. Scrambling for a solution, betting I won't call in the authorities immediately."

"Maybe you're right. Maybe Mrs. B's right. But can I remind you? He's rich. He doesn't need to steal a dime."

"A dime, no. But what about $1.4 million?" Felicity sighed. "Honestly, I'm not sure what to do now. I need to think about my next step." She glanced up at Cooper. "What will you do?"

"Well, I can't do rounds. Harvey was so flustered he's forgotten Gabe has the van out doing them already."

"Come home with me, then. Maybe some genius solution will present itself. We can't stand on the street for the rest of the day. I'll call for my driver." She reached for her phone.

Cooper's expression was pure surprise.

"What?" Felicity asked.

"Sometimes I forget you're who you are. Someone who has an actual fancy-pants car and driver."

"You…forgot." Felicity huffed out a breath. "Well, at least I know you like me for me, then." She punched in Amir's number and reeled off her location.

"What makes you think I *like* you?" Cooper teased once Felicity had hung up. "I might just be in this for the sarcastic commentary."

"Well, I can see the appeal of that. Sarcasm is one thing I certainly offer in abundance." Felicity pocketed her phone.

"I like to think you'll miss me, too," Cooper said with a smile, "when this is all over and you're at the top of your glass tower at Bartell Corp and I'm still…"

"Rummaging around dog bottoms?" Felicity suggested sweetly. "Well, I can't deny you are memorable. You and your ridiculous, affection-seeking dog." Suddenly a wash of sadness filled her at the thought of seeing neither again. "You know, my apartment allows pets. Would you like to bring Brittany with us, too?"

"I knew you loved her." Cooper beamed.

"Please. I'm only thinking of you. Me, I tolerate her."

Cooper snorted. "Be right back. And of course you love her."

"Delusional, too," Felicity told the woman's retreating back.

The town car pulled up. She informed Amir to expect a woman and a dog. If the news surprised him, he showed no sign. Always such a professional. She truly would miss him when he left for Sydney, despite his snail-like idea of a top speed.

Felicity turned away from him to catch the sight of a lanky Cooper striding with Brittany dancing enthusiastically at her side. It was a stunning image.

Was it pathetic she was committing the sight to memory?

No, she told herself. Do not answer that.

Chapter 9
The Last Time

FELICITY DIDN'T SPEND A GREAT deal of time thinking about her apartment. It was where she slept, ate, bathed, and worked on weekends. It was all sleek lines and polished floorboards, brushed aluminum appliances, timber and cream accessories, and top-line fittings. Essentially, it was a showroom of good taste, an ode to swanky executive dreams. The view was to die for, too, when Loki wasn't destroying her topiary.

But now, looking at it through Cooper's wide eyes, Felicity was reminded of a few things. She was wealthy, and it showed. Felicity was how the other half lived. Well, not half. She was how the top one percent lived.

Cooper, looking dazed, had barely moved from the moment she'd crossed the threshold.

Brittany adapted a great deal better, running around sniffing everything before bolting up to the glass balcony doors and barking in excitement.

That drew Cooper's eye, and she finally focused. "Um, Felicity, do you know there's a kitten in your tree?"

"No, there isn't," Felicity said firmly.

"So it's not yours?"

"That'd be out of character, don't you think? And there's nothing out there."

Cooper pointed at the bright blue eyes surrounded by white fluff peeking out of the leaves. "You don't see a Siamese kitten about eight to ten weeks old looking right at us? Cute enough to be plastered on the side of a tissue box?"

Felicity merely lifted an eyebrow.

"Is this one of those denial things of yours? If you don't see it, you won't befriend it? Or worse, *cuddle* it?"

"Don't fall for that pom-pom. She's pure devil spawn. There'll be no cuddling from me." Felicity glared at Loki. The kitten glared right back. "Ever."

Cooper smiled. Her eyes drifted back to the expansive city view. She stilled and suddenly seemed adrift.

Brittany padded back to the lounge, having lost interest in tree kitties, and selected a designer armchair. She leaped on it, stalking around it in circles before settling.

Felicity winced and prayed her nails were clipped.

It was a sign of how out of it Cooper was that she didn't order her dog off the furniture. Not that Felicity had the heart to budge Brittany, who looked so happy, her soft brown chin plopped on an armrest, watching them both.

Cooper's eyes remained fixed on the Manhattan skyline. She finally spoke. "How did you do this at your age? You're not even forty, are you? How could you have afforded all this, in New York? I'm betting you own it, too."

"I don't rent, no. And I worked hard for what I have." Felicity met Cooper's eyes evenly. "I didn't have vacations or weekends for years—you know how focused I am on my career—and that sacrifice paid off. That, and good fortune; being noticed by Elena. That was the biggest factor. And I'm definitely inching closer to forty." She drew in a breath. "Today I turned thirty-seven."

"Wait, it's your birthday?" Cooper's eyes widened. "And this is how you're spending it? Putting the fear of God up a charity director?"

"No, I'm spending it with my lover, who I've skillfully lured back to my place in the middle of the afternoon. That's already improved my birthday considerably."

"Ah, now it all becomes clear." Cooper smiled.

Felicity headed toward the open-plan kitchen. "Drink? I've got something from the Barossa Valley in South Australia." She opened the cupboard that contained her wine rack. "Maddie insisted I'd enjoy it. It was a thanks for finding her a loan dress for some awards event in Sydney last December."

"So for all your protestations, I find out you got her a dress and she got you wine. You two really do like each other, don't you?"

"It depends on what day you're asking." *Ah.* She withdrew the bottle of Rockford's Eden Valley Riesling 2015.

"*Felicity*," Cooper drawled, "this sounds perilously close to friendship, which you claim not to do."

"Fine. I admit that I like Maddie well enough—if pressed, under torture, and with the fewest witnesses possible. We're not exactly friends, but we're not *not* friends. I wouldn't take a bullet for her, but I'd stop someone shooting her, all right?" Felicity rolled her eyes. "But you know the rules: *never* quote me." She hunted for a corkscrew. "Well? Feel like trying it? I hear the Barossa makes beautiful wines."

"Love to."

Felicity brought out filled glasses a few minutes later.

Cooper, now curled up on the luxury butter-soft leather couch, accepted the glass. "I think my dog's much better at coping with all this than me."

"All this?" Felicity sat beside her.

"It's one thing you saying what you do. It's another seeing"—Cooper waved at the multi-million-dollar view—"all of this."

Brittany plopped down off the armchair, padded over to the couch, and jumped on it, squeezing herself between them. She curled up in a ball, head on her paws, looking like she was in heaven.

"Is this going to be weird?" Felicity asked, deciding to ignore the fact a dog was now on her nine-thousand-dollar designer settee. "Because it'd be unfortunate if it was. I had hoped to celebrate my birthday, after figuring out what's up with Harvey, by taking you slowly in my bed half the afternoon and all night. And trust me, my bed is every bit as impressive as this room."

Cooper's eyebrows shot up in interest. "Is that so?"

"It is." Felicity took a sip of wine, never taking her eyes off Cooper. "So are you done freaking out yet? Can we move on?"

Brittany placed her head on Felicity's thigh. Felicity gave her an absent pat and then froze. Brittany was as soft and warm as she'd imagined. Better, even. It was too tempting…and she was only human. She thrust her fingers deep into her fur, played with her ears, and scritched and scratched her back. The dog gave a happy sigh. Her heart matched it.

Cooper watched her wordlessly, lips curling, and quietly sipped her wine. "This is lovely."

"Yes, Maddie's taste in wine is exceptional. But as I say, she is on the world's longest winning streak right now, so I'd expect nothing less."

Cooper smiled. "You might be on a bit of a winning streak yourself. I mean, come on, you're nailing the career, and then there's this place... *Christ*!" Her gaze swept the room again. "My family would go nuts over this."

"Where are they from? You said 'all over' the first time I asked, and I know your father's military, but where's home for them and you?"

"I sort of call New Jersey home, even though I live in New York."

"I've never once heard you order *cawwwfee*." Felicity smiled.

Cooper laughed. "Well, I never picked up the accent. I think it's because I'd traveled too much before then, following Dad around from posting to posting." She sighed. "As a kid, I really hated it. Always a new school, leaving my friends behind. Mom hated it, too. So when I was fourteen, she left Dad and took me with her. My brothers stayed with him—they were both over eighteen by then."

"So just you and your mom? Was that when you ended up in New Jersey?"

"Yes. We stayed with Mom's mom for a few years. I got the stability I wanted, and I got to look after my nana's dogs, too. Through them, I found my calling."

"Do you see the rest of your family often?"

"Oh sure. Thanksgiving, Christmas, and so on. My brothers have families of their own now. They're over in Normal, Kentucky."

"Normal?" Felicity eyed her skeptically. "Are you for real?"

"I can't believe you of all people are asking me that when you're one step away from Hell."

Felicity threw up her hands in mute surrender.

"Yep." Cooper laughed. "Dad's still in the military—he's got a desk job at Fort Bragg these days. Mom remarried a few years ago and moved to Indiana with her husband, who sells medical devices. She helps him around the office. Nan still lives in the same old rickety house in Egg Harbor City, New Jersey, so I visit her and her latest dogs a lot."

"So when I was wringing my hands over being from the Midwest, it turns out most of your family is, too?" Felicity lifted an eyebrow.

"I might be from the same stock as you, Simmons," Cooper said with a grin, "but I think we can both agree our paths seriously diverged." She waved at the apartment. "Uptown girl."

Felicity's lips curled a little. "You know I don't really *hate* the Midwest. Parts of it are beautiful. And I don't hate that my family's from there, either. I just wish my mother and sister had more ambition than living, working, and dying in the same place. On that score, I think my father was right to leave."

"To each their own, though?" Cooper suggested. "It's their life and all that?"

Felicity sighed in frustration. "I suppose. If they *must.*"

Cooper laughed at her long-suffering expression.

"Anyway, most of my embarrassment about being from Pinckney comes from when I first started out in New York. There was all this baggage. I had to contend with ridiculous yokel assumptions and bad jokes, comments on my accent, and the belief that I wouldn't be cutthroat enough for their business."

"I'm sure no one thinks that about you now."

"Quite right"—Felicity lifted her chin—"because I went to a great deal of trouble to hide my origins and my accent so further assumptions couldn't be made. So nothing would stand in my way."

"Ambitious."

"Always. And it worked." She smiled suddenly, pleased at how absolutely it had worked.

"I can see that." Cooper's expression became thoughtful. "So as someone who's on the edge of the same stratosphere as the Rosalind Stones of this world, tell me: why would anybody rich steal $1.4 million? Does that make any sense at all?"

"It does make sense, sadly. Here's the funny thing about people: no one ever asks the powerful how much is too much or the rich when they'll stop accumulating wealth. It's just a given they'll keep doing it."

"I suppose so."

Felicity settled back deeper in the couch. "Assuming addiction issues aren't involved, there are only three reasons I can think of to steal when you're already rich: To be even richer—the motive being purely greed. To be more powerful—a side effect of having great wealth. Or to minimize or hide a loss you've taken elsewhere."

"The third one," Cooper said. "Hypothetically, let's just assume that's what's going on. Because Harvey is neither greedy nor ambitious. So is he hiding a loss he's taken elsewhere?"

"You've said he doesn't gamble or do drugs," Felicity said. "Are you sure?"

"I'd be shocked if he did. He says he sees the pain it causes our clients, and he'd never wish that on his worst enemy."

"So he might be hiding something else. I think I'm tired of waiting for answers. I'm calling Thomas, who's been looking into Living Ruff's finances." Felicity reached for her phone and selected a number.

"While you do that, can you point me to your bathroom?" Cooper rose.

Felicity pointed out the door in question as her call was picked up. "Thomas? Felicity Simmons. I can't help but recall asking for your work-up on Living Ruff to be done by Tuesday. It is now Thursday."

"Oh." The man made a faintly strangled noise. "Ms. Simmons, yes. I was going to send you something on Tuesday, but I thought it better to dig a little deeper before submitting my report."

"You found something?"

"Quite the opposite. I can see why Peter's preliminary investigation found nothing amiss. But the more I dug, the odder it was."

"Explain."

"I have never in my life seen a charity so pared down to the bones that spends so much on its practical works. I can't find expenses for much in the way of office supplies, computer upgrades, or anything you'd expect of that nature in the past ten years. It's not normal."

"Well, Living Ruff does have the oldest computers I've ever seen still working. They don't even have flat-screen monitors."

"Is that so?" Thomas paused. "That helps make sense of things. I'd thought Living Ruff might be lying on their 990 forms and hiding expenses, even though it's perfectly fine for charities to spend money to effectively run themselves."

"No, I think they really do throw their whole focus and money at the practical side. The animals."

"How novel." Thomas made some tapping noises. "Well, because it looked too good to be true, I started investigating Harvey Clifford's family to see if there were any irregularities in their various business holdings."

"And you found some?"

"Actually, no. His family has no investments that I can find, which makes sense, given they're all somewhere between working poor and middle class. They have no money to invest. On Harvey's wife's side…" More tapping. "Rosalind Stone's enterprises range from above average to excellent. Her only investment that has even a slightly less than solid turnover is a sporting goods store run by Rosalind's brother, Charles Stone. Charles's main claim to fame is selling high-quality collectibles of baseball players…and nightclubbing like a frat boy."

"How does any of this help us?"

"It doesn't really. I'm saying that no one in Harvey's life has any bad investments that need propping up, not even the party sheep in the family."

"So we've got nothing." Felicity frowned. "Everyone's squeaky-clean."

"Which in itself is a statistical anomaly, I'd like to point out," Thomas said, sounding pained. "It's surprising to find any second-generation, filthy rich American family where *no one* has gone off the rails."

Felicity laughed. "No wonder you were suspicious. So where does this leave us? A good charity run by someone with no skeletons in the closet, and we're still missing $1.4 million."

"I'm sorry to say I've done all I can. I don't know where the money went, and we won't know until the next time Living Ruff files its tax documents. Unless Harvey Clifford gets chatty in the meantime."

"That doesn't seem likely." Felicity tapped her lip. "I don't know why he won't answer any questions, if everything's aboveboard."

"Well, he won't have much choice soon. One thing I can promise you is, with a donation that big, he'll be required by state law to get an independent audit before he files his 990 this year. If he's spent all of Ms. Bartell's money on anything at all, the purchase will throw up red flags with the auditor because it exceeds the three-percent rule."

"The three-percent rule?"

"It's a rule of thumb in auditing. A guide. You look at a charity's gross revenue, and if a purchase is under three percent of that, it's seen as typical for an organization of that size and assets base. The more you spend above three percent, the more likely it will attract attention as being out of the ordinary. For Living Ruff, specifically, that means spending $21,000 or less to not attract attention. Not $1.4 million."

Felicity blinked. "Well, I can see why that would stick out like a sore thumb."

"Yes." Thomas sounded satisfied. "Harvey won't be able to hide for long from the auditors."

"That's some comfort, I guess. So otherwise you've come up empty?"

"I'm afraid so."

"All right. Thank you, Thomas."

"Good day, Ms. Simmons."

Felicity ended the call and turned to Cooper, who had just returned. "Apparently, aside from hiding $1.4 million, your boss and his charity are squeaky-clean."

"Told you," Cooper said. "Well, except for the first part. That still stumps me."

"How are we going to get access to Living Ruff's more recent financials if Mrs. Brooks won't help?"

"No clue. And don't ask me to go all *Mission Impossible* for you and try to figure out her computer data or filing system to get that information. You know I can't even figure out my own."

"Oh, I'm well aware. I've seen your home office in its natural state, remember. I'm surprised I didn't unearth an ancient burial site or something prehistoric."

"Hey, I'm not that bad."

"No? Who filed all their takeout menus from ten years ago under H? I assume for Hungry?"

"It makes perfect sense, if you're me." Cooper folded her arms.

"You couldn't just stick them on the fridge," Felicity asked, "like regular people?"

"I could…but then where would be the challenge for you?"

"You didn't know they were there, did you?" Felicity guessed—accurately, if Cooper's suddenly sheepish expression was any clue. "By the way, not a single one of those restaurants is still in business. I researched them thoroughly before tossing out the menus."

"Of course you did. You know," Cooper said in appreciation, "I think you might be one of those rarely seen *purebred* type-As."

"Could be. I like the sound of that," Felicity said with satisfaction. Her phone alerted her to a new email. Felicity's eyes widened as she scanned it. "Maybe I *do* have a bit of luck of my own." She turned her phone to Cooper.

Cooper read the words. "Sender Anony12731@gmail.com? Okay, what am I looking at?"

"Keep reading."

"Um, it says: 'In case this is useful.' There's an attachment called '990PF-LivingRuff-next-financial-year.pdf.'" Cooper looked up again. "Isn't that what you asked Mrs. Brooks to email you?"

"Yes." Felicity tapped the attachment to open it. "I wonder why she changed her mind."

"She probably wanted to prove us wrong," Cooper said. "So…does it?"

Felicity frowned at the screen. "Give me a minute." She flicked through page after page. After a few minutes, she stopped. "Okay, so it seems Harvey *did* spend Elena's money. The expenses section lists 'Merchandise, Shenzhen Industries.'" She looked up.

"Seriously?" Cooper squinted at her.

"You said when we were having coffee this morning that Harvey wanted to have a Living Ruff toy line. Tell me what happened."

Cooper frowned. "Oh, it was nothing. It's so dumb. You know that orange mascot dog on his desk? We all teased him that he might get some toys made of it to sell. And he kept saying he might do that. I thought he was kidding."

"But the dog's so ugly!" Felicity gasped.

"Right?" Cooper rolled her eyes. "I mean *that* was the joke. It's a good thing he never went through with it or we'd have boxes of ugly unsellable toys." She froze. "Tell me he did not order over a million bucks worth of ugly dogs."

Felicity inhaled. "I don't know. Maybe?"

"Shit." Cooper winced.

Felicity scowled at the expenses line on her screen, willing it to make sense. "And if he did, where are they?" None of this seemed to line up with a man that Thomas pointed out was so frugal with charity money it was suspicious in itself. "Harvey's naturally cautious, isn't he? I mean, normally, right?"

"Yes." Cooper regarded her. "Very."

"So this big order looks out of character. Sudden?"

"Well, maybe not, if he really has been thinking about his mascot dog idea all these years. But he's usually cautious, absolutely."

"Hmm." Felicity tapped her screen and began following a squirrelly thought.

"I wish we knew exactly what he ordered," Cooper said. "Pity that secret's between him and a factory all the way over in China."

"Not…necessarily," Felicity said with satisfaction as that squirrelly thought paid dividends. "I'm guessing Harvey's brother-in-law, Charles, knows *exactly* what Harvey ordered."

"What? Why?"

Felicity turned her phone screen back around to face Cooper.

The webpage on it read:

Welcome to Shenzhen Industries, makers of world-class, high-quality collectibles. We create accurate-looking sports stars, celebrities, TV and movie characters, and other items to order, all customized to your corporate needs.

"I don't follow," Cooper said.

"What is a tiny charity like Living Ruff doing connecting with a top-range, high-class collectibles factory in China in the first place? How on earth would those two organizations have found each other? You'd have expected Living Ruff to get their bulk merchandise cheap from Alibaba like everyone else."

"I'll take your word for that. I'm clueless as to where anyone shops around for their made-in-China merch."

"Trust me, it's weird. Thomas just told me that Charles Stone runs a sporting goods store, and he's known for high-quality collectibles of baseball players."

"You think he buys his stuff from Shenzhen Industries, too?"

"I do. Think about it: Harvey's a cautious, conservative guy with a vague dream to do merchandising for Living Ruff. Suddenly, thanks to Elena's donation, he has the means to go for it. So who would he turn to for advice? The person he knows already selling collectibles. I'm betting Charles is who connected Harvey with Shenzhen Industries. Probably helped him place his order, too."

"Makes sense."

"I'll pay Charles a visit tomorrow and see if I'm right."

"That might be interesting. I've met him. He's quite the character."

"How so?" Felicity asked.

"He's as memorable as his sister but in a very different way. He's got this whole laid-back, charming rogue thing going on. He loves hanging out at fancy clubs and making a splash. Like one New Year's Eve, he bought drinks for five hundred women—who had to kiss him on the cheek to get their drink. It was so out there, it made the papers."

"So he's a player. And also, ew." Felicity scrunched up her face.

"Right? His charms were wasted on me, of course, but he gave it a crack at one office party."

"Arrogance like that turns me right off," Felicity said with feeling. "I think it's an occupational hazard—being around cocky lawyers too often makes me dislike overconfident men in my downtime. Especially ones who try to talk all over me or, worse, talk down to me."

"I can see how that'd end badly." Cooper grinned.

"Oh yes. Very much so." Felicity's expression turned evil at the reminder. "Now, can you send Mrs. Brooks a thank you while I order us in lunch?" She gave Brittany a quick scratch, then gently pushed her aside to rise.

She made her way to the fridge and the assorted menus clinging to its face. "What are you in the mood for?" she called out.

"Don't care. Not that hungry right now." Cooper's phone made a whooshing noise—probably her thank-you message being sent.

"Would you like to skip lunch, then? Go for the next item on the agenda instead?" She poked her head out of the kitchen to gauge Cooper's reaction.

"Are you tempting me with sex?" Cooper arched an eyebrow as her phone beeped. She glanced down and suddenly went still. "Mrs. Brooks said she didn't send you anything and wants to know what we're smoking over here."

"Then who did?" Felicity stared in astonishment. "What's going on?"

"No clue."

"Well," Felicity said, "I seriously don't know what's happening, even more than before. That disconcerts me. Someone leaking exactly what I need to help my investigation exactly when I need it is weird enough. But how many people would have access to that document I just received?"

Cooper opened her mouth.

"And before you begin listing the board members from Rosalind down plus the independent accountant and some random IT guy, of those people, how many know my direct email address, which, I should point out, I rarely share?"

"Not a clue."

"I can already tell you how many." Felicity barreled on. "One: Mrs. Brooks, who is the only person at Living Ruff I've given my card to. Even you don't have my email address."

"But Mrs. Brooks says she didn't do this."

"Right. So…" Felicity gave Cooper a baffled look. "I'm really out of my depth here."

"I can see that." Cooper rose from the couch and came to stand in front of her. "I see an intervention is in order. Figuring out this mystery can wait."

"What did you have in mind instead?"

"You were right. Let's move to the next item on the agenda and take our mind off things. Then maybe the answer will come to us. Besides, given you're only going to be around for a short time, I don't want to waste a second."

She kissed Felicity, her powerful arms wrapping around her.

When they came up for air, a dazed Felicity said, "Right. Yes. Next item on the agenda it is."

━━━◆━━━

Sex wasn't something Felicity had had an enormous amount of in her life, but what she'd experienced she'd categorize as ranging from acceptable to good—especially since she'd added women to her repertoire. She still liked men well enough; it wasn't a competition. But there was something to be said for how well a woman knew a body so much like her own.

That was a fleeting thought as she hunted through her wardrobe for her most kick-ass power suit. She was determined to make this the best fucking sex of her life, or at least the most memorable, given her lover was right. Time was running out.

Ten minutes later, Felicity assumed her bossiest pose and gave Cooper— stark naked on the bed—her most withering look. "I have thousands of employees," she declared. She dramatically wrenched off her jacket, tossing it behind her. "Thousands of people all across the world who answer to me." She snapped the suspenders that tramlined up her breasts that were covered only in a starched white high-collar shirt, then winced. *Oh fuck. OW!*

Cooper snorted with laughter.

Not quite the reaction she was going for. She pressed on. "I'm allowing you this. I trust you appreciate having what my employees never get to see."

With a small smile, Cooper said, "Um, hey, Felicity, I love this, I really do, especially how much thought you've put into it. But I don't care about the size of your staff. It's the size of your sass that gets my motor purring."

Felicity deflated. "My…*sass*." What the hell did that mean?

"Yeah. How you own every room you enter."

She did? Felicity's ego reinflated.

"And the way you give people these pitying looks when they say something stupid."

Felicity puffed up a little more.

"I loved how you owned the mayor. And your bossy side when you ordered Dee around? Christ, that made me *so* wet because Dee's a powerful fucking force in her own right."

Well. Felicity could work with that. She straightened. "Spread your legs, then. And don't keep me waiting."

Cooper scrambled to obey.

Felicity was rather impressed at how quickly the woman could move when she wanted to.

"I believe you wanted to be taken by a bossy woman in a power suit." Felicity loomed over her, allowing a trace of teasing in her tone. "It was your fantasy, I believe you said."

"Y-yes." Cooper's voice was a croak.

"Hmm." Felicity leaned over her and dropped her hand, assessing how wet she was with the tips of her fingers. Her own body gave a clench of approval at what she found. "I'd say you're more than a little interested."

"I am," Cooper said with feeling.

"You like powerful women," Felicity said conversationally, fingers still tracing Cooper's slick lips. "Soon I'm about to have more power than almost anyone outside of politics in this country. People will line up, wanting me for my connections, for my power," she whispered, leaning even closer. Her wandering fingertips paused at Cooper's entrance. "But all I want is *you*." She thrust.

Cooper moaned and her eyelids fluttered, then closed.

Felicity thrust deep and hard, setting up a rhythm. She lowered her body until the crispness of her starched shirt teased Cooper's straining nipples. Her lips touched Cooper's ear. "Touch yourself," she said breathlessly. "Show me you getting yourself off."

Groaning, Cooper pushed a hand to her clit, rubbing it with the side of her thumb, as Felicity took her time, sliding in and out, enjoying the rush from her favorite sight: a beautiful woman coming slowly apart. This was even better, though. Because seeing someone so physically strong letting go, opening up to her, was the most astonishing aphrodisiac.

She withdrew her hand, leaned in, and licked Cooper's fingers, still rubbing her own clit. She tangled her tongue over delicate flesh and the long digits, playing with both textures.

Cooper stiffened, her hand freezing. She pulled it away and gasped. "Oh fuck." Her back curled, and she arched, thighs locked and quivering.

Felicity tongued the resulting flood of wetness, spreading it over soft curls and tucks of flesh until Cooper weakly groaned "Oh hell. Fuck. Please! Time out!"

Felicity unfurled herself back up off the bed like a stretching cat. What a delightful sight she was leaving. Cooper spread before her in postcoital disarray? It felt like she'd just debauched an Amazon of Themiscyra—in the best possible sense.

Once standing, Felicity stepped back and placed her hands on her hips once more.

Cooper's eyes, once they were focused, drank in the sight of her. "You look so powerful standing there like that; so self-satisfied." Her smile became amused. "Be a nice overlord and take off your shirt for me?"

Felicity decided only Cooper could get away with teasing her about her authority. She shot her a withering look, then undid her shirt buttons before wrenching down the suspenders until they dangled at her side in flattened hoops. Finally, she pulled off the shirt, held it up for a moment, then let it fall to the ground.

"Would you touch your nipples for me? Stroke them? Show me how you like being touched?"

"I suppose," Felicity said, aiming for haughty. It was more breathy. Admittedly, she was as wet as she'd ever been.

She reached for her own breasts. Felicity was usually self-conscious about them. They were so small, so insubstantial next to most women's. But under Cooper's admiring gaze, they seemed perfect as she plucked at her aching, erect nipples. Felicity rubbed and rolled them, gaze locked with her lover's, the burn between her legs growing sharper.

"You're so beautiful, Felicity," Cooper said. "I love your breasts. I'm going to taste them soon. I'm going to taste all of you."

Felicity swallowed. Strong Cooper running her lips all over her body, sucking and licking her until she squirmed…

"But right now, wouldn't you rather have your fingers stroking yourself, too?" Cooper's voice was almost a purr, and her eyes were raking her.

Yes, actually, Felicity would damn well *love* to be stroking herself right now. She briefly pictured denying herself just for sheer contrariness over being told what to do. That idiocy lasted two seconds. Instead, she unbuttoned her tailored pants, slid them to the floor along with her lacy La Perla thong, and left them in a puddle at her ankles.

Felicity was obscenely wet now. She wondered what Cooper thought of her naked body. Phillip had once called her a ballet dancer without the muscles. He'd meant it as a compliment, but all Felicity had heard was brittle. Weak. Breakable. Compared to solid, sturdy Cooper, Felicity was downright insubstantial.

"Touch yourself." Cooper's hand drifted between her own legs. "I'll do it, too. Hell, I can't not. You're so beautiful."

Felicity slid her fingers down and began to finger herself in front of Cooper's appreciative gaze. Suddenly her doubts fled. It felt…so naughty. Both of them fucking themselves, gazes locked on each other. The sounds of slippery strokes of flesh filled the room.

"Fuck. Oh." Cooper's mouth fell open as her breaths turned into short, fast gasps. She opened her thighs wide, and she came—again.

Felicity's front-row seat of her lover orgasming was highly motivating. Beneath her frantic, furious fingers, her clit tightened and tingled.

"That's it," Cooper encouraged as she combed her fingers through her own drenched curls. "Watch me." And then she slid one finger inside herself.

Felicity's brain turned liquid—like the rest of her. She twitched and spasmed, crying out as she came hard. She sank onto the end of the bed, legs weak.

"Fuck," she said, when her breathing returned to normal. "Can't say I've ever done that before." She shot Cooper a faintly embarrassed look. "Put on a show."

"And what a spectacular show it was. You do so many things to me." Cooper patted the bed beside her. "Come up here. It'd be a shame to waste all this nakedness. We've got plenty of time for a snuggle before our fun ends."

Felicity paused. She wasn't one for snuggling. But then all of this *was* just temporary, wasn't it? A long fuck hello and goodbye, to put it crudely?

An exceptionally magnificent one at that, though, her brain supplied merrily.

"Well," Felicity said, slithering up beside Cooper, "I suppose if I have to snuggle for the first time, at least it'll be with someone worthwhile."

"The first time?" Cooper eyed her in surprise.

"I don't generally stick around to find out who's a snuggler and who isn't."

"Then I'm honored. And why do I suspect calling me worthwhile is the world's best compliment, coming from you?"

"You wouldn't be wrong." Hesitating, Felicity slowly slid an arm around Cooper's waist and squeezed in closer next to her.

"You really haven't snuggled before?" Cooper asked gently.

"Are we going to talk about it all day or…"

"Right, right." Cooper chuckled and pulled Felicity in properly. "Never thought I'd be the little spoon."

"There are spoons?" Felicity asked.

Cooper chuckled.

Naked skin on naked skin fizzed Felicity's brain again until she forgot the question. And oh… Why did it feel so good? Different from sex, despite all the slickness and warmth, because, well, there was always a goal with sex, wasn't there? Felicity was always motivated when goals were involved. This was just…closeness.

"I like this. It's acceptable," Felicity admitted before she could stop herself.

"Acceptable, huh?" Cooper burst out laughing. "You might be a big deal, Felicity Simmons—hell, the biggest I'll likely ever meet." Her fingers trailed along Felicity's bare arm. Goosebumps rose in their wake "But you're going to miss this, aren't you? You might even miss me."

Felicity didn't reply immediately.

"Well, I'm really going to miss you," Cooper said quietly, all traces of laughter gone. "You're like no one I've ever met in my little world. You're special." She leaned in. "You do know that, right?"

Special. No one had ever called her that—not in a good way at least. Well, maybe Elena, though not in so many words. She'd showed her that by offering her a job. But actually hearing it? That felt so…gentle. Like a compliment wrapped in tissue paper.

Tears pricked Felicity's eyes, and she blinked them away. No time to get maudlin. "I'm glad you think so."

"I do. Look, I know you're good at solving things, even weird mysteries like ours, so your time with Living Ruff might be over real soon. So if this is the last time we ever do this… Or hell, if the next time I see you you're on TV explaining how you just took over the world's biggest newspaper corporation, I'll remember *this* you. The one who cries when she's snuggled."

"I do not!" Felicity protested, alarmed that Cooper had noticed.

"The you who cuddles kittens."

"I never… That's a complete twisting of—"

"The you who rocked up on day one with all these completely wrong-assed opinions about the homeless—"

"Wrong-assed! But—"

"—and yet were prepared to ask questions and change your views when given better information—something most people move heaven and earth to avoid."

"Well…" That one at least was true. Felicity sputtered to a stop.

"And the you who loves my dog so much you can't even bear to pet her in case you get attached. Until this afternoon, when you cracked because you couldn't stand not doing it a second longer. All of these sweet and quirky and decent yous who you hide when you're playing God at work? They're the Felicity I know."

Sweet? Quirky? Decent?! Felicity was quite sure no one else on earth would ever assign those descriptors to her. She drew in a breath, not sure what to say. In any event, rebuttal wasn't what she was in the mood for. "Just be quiet and snuggle me some more," Felicity muttered. "And don't be smug about it."

"Never." Cooper chuckled, then added in a quiet voice, "Hell, woman, I really will miss you."

Me, too, Felicity thought with a faint stab of regret. *Me, too.*

Chapter 10
Mint Condition

CHARLES STONE LOOKED LIKE ONE of those swaggering ex-high school football stars who hadn't realized he'd gone to seed. His handsome face, framed by thinning blond hair, was flecked with faint red blood vessels—a sure sign his party-boy image was well earned. Broad shoulders gave way to a beer gut that puckered the buttons on his expensive-looking blue-and-gray business shirt.

With a smile he no doubt thought was charming, Charles rocked back in a black leather chair that was too big for his office at Charles Stone Sporting Goods. Some ego, naming a store after yourself when it was your sister who'd bought it for you to run.

His office was lined with shelves of collectibles. Baseball wasn't Felicity's thing, but she knew enough from her sister to recognize a few famous players. Heather had displayed posters of her favorite players in her room for years before discovering new-age men with earrings, VW buses, and weed.

Charles followed her eye. "You like baseball?" he asked, looking enthused.

"No." Felicity folded her arms.

He didn't seem to know how to answer that. After a moment, he eyed her up and down. "So my secretary tells me you're a fancy lawyer high up the greasy pole at Bartell Corp. Darlene left out the bit where you look like a movie star. Is that something you do on the side? Make movies?" He smiled and leaned over his desk toward her, as subtle as a rutting bull.

Felicity forced herself not to move an inch. "I have no time to do anything on the side when I'm so busy taking over newspapers and magazines with my boss and stripping them for assets. Think of me like a legal vulture, Mr. Stone, tearing flesh from bone." She gave him a cold hard smile to sell her bullshit. "Occasionally, I even let some companies keep their entrails."

The man's shudder was almost visceral. "I...see." Charles cautiously leaned back again and cupped his hands over his lap. "So what can I do for you?"

Felicity drew in a breath. "I've been talking to your brother-in-law, Harvey Clifford."

"Okay." He looked puzzled. "And?"

"And I know about Harvey's extensive merchandise orders with Shenzhen Industries. The same company you use for your collectibles, I understand. You even recommended them to him."

"Sure I did. Why wouldn't I? They do some great merchandise."

Guess confirmed. A thrill shot through Felicity.

Charles's expression was shuttered. "And your interest in his merchandising is...?"

"I'm investigating what happened to a sizable donation made to Living Ruff—$1.4 million."

His eyebrows lifted. "Harvey mentioned an investment that size came in last year. So that came from your company?"

"I never said that."

"Why would you be investigating it otherwise?"

Well, he had her there. "Fine. Yes, it was my boss's money, but she'd rather it wasn't commonly known."

"All right." Charles gestured her to go on.

"And since her donation apparently ended up in China with nothing I can see to show for it, I'd like to know more. I'm talking to you because Shenzhen Industries is the company that you convinced Harvey to use."

Charles regarded her for a long moment, then said dryly, "Harvey doesn't know you're here, does he?"

"What makes you say that?"

"Well, for a start, he'd have explained what happened. He might have, oh, I don't know, mentioned the landslide that wiped out half of Shenzhen

Industries' infrastructure causing a huge backlog on jobs while the factory is being repaired."

"A…landslide." Felicity eyed him in astonishment.

"A big one. Four lives lost along with plenty of homes and thousands of jobs washed away in mud and rock overnight." Charles rummaged around in his desk, drew out a folder marked SHENZHEN, and flipped through it. Pausing, he withdrew a news article written in Chinese and placed it in front of Felicity. The photo showed what looked like half a hill had landed on a factory.

He prodded the picture. "Shenzhen Industries had a major setback, no denying it, but the manager told me orders will resume once rebuilding is finished. In fact, Harvey placed a few more orders to help kick things along. The rebuild's ahead of schedule. All the goods ordered, including mine, will start arriving soon, and Harvey is well aware of all this. My question is, if you've been talking to Harvey, why don't *you* know all this?"

"You're saying my boss's donation is financing part of Shenzhen Industries' reconstruction? She didn't sign up for that."

"No, Ms. Bartell made a donation to a charitable foundation." Charles looked unfazed by the steel in her tone. "And that donation was invested in products that *will* yield a return for Living Ruff when they arrive. Didn't Harvey tell you any of this?"

"Actually, he's been cagey. That arouses suspicion, so here I am, trying to understand what went on."

"Ah. Okay. I get it now." Charles supplied a confident smile. He leaned even farther back in his chair. "That's just Harvey being Harvey. He's probably worried you'd tell his staff about his grand plans, and they'd make fun of him again about ugly toy animals."

"You mean the orange dog on his desk?"

"That's the one. He can be quite sensitive."

"Please tell me he didn't order thousands of those."

"What?" Charles burst into laughter. "Oh God, no. Shenzhen makes *quality* merchandise, not crap. You want to see what he *did* order? I have some of the prototypes around here somewhere. They came in bundled with one of my orders to save shipping costs. Harvey didn't take all his samples."

Charles rose and led Felicity through the back of the shop into a storeroom. He stopped in front of a shelf that held a small cardboard box. He opened the flaps. "Okay, remember these are just prototypes. The finished ones will be branded with Living Ruff, but you get the concept."

He plunged his hand into the box. "The idea is, he sells them at all sorts of fundraisers, charity events, schools, you name it, and it's a constant source of income for the charity. Between me and you, old Harvey's a little self-conscious about the fact that almost all his donations tend to come from my sister's fancy fundraising parties."

Charles dumped a pile of plastic shapes in front of her. "He'd like to be more self-sufficient than relying on his wife. It's a dream for him, fulfilling this project. Harvey has plans when the shipment lands to get the media involved, too."

Felicity studied the cartoon-shaped plastic dogs, cats, and fish in front of her. The quality was extremely good, and the animals were certainly eye-catching enough to work as fundraising items. "Will he ever be able to sell enough of these to get Living Ruff's money back?"

"That's where I come in. Merchandising is something I specialize in. I'm already set up for it, which is why he came to me in the first place for advice. And until that landslide, Shenzhen was rock-solid reliable with fantastic quality. I speak from personal experience."

He moved to a different box, this one huge with crisp, clean flaps. "See?" Inside were more figurines of baseball players. He pulled a couple out. "This was my last order from Shenzhen six months ago. I'm almost sold out—can barely keep these babies in stock."

Up close, she could see that the attention to detail on the players' faces was intricate and lifelike.

"The quality isn't something those cheap cowboy collectible manufacturers can reproduce." His thumb ran lovingly over one of the figures. "And any time some major league player comes in, I get him to sign a couple in his likeness, auction them off, and donate funds to a junior sporting charity. It's a really good system."

"Sounds like it."

"Harvey has seen me do this for years and wanted to know how to get into merchandising, too. When he asked me for advice the first time a few years ago, I tried to talk him out of it. You really only make a mint when you can do a vast production run. That means Harvey would buy his animals for a dime each and sell them for ten bucks. You need the capital to do economies of scale, and he didn't have it. He dropped it after that."

"But isn't he rich?" Felicity asked.

"His wife is." Charles chuckled. "But he's hardly going to ask my sister for money when the whole point of the exercise was proving he could make money on his own. Harvey's got too much pride for that. He wants to show her and everyone else that he's good at this. Worthy. She got him the director job. Did you know that?"

Felicity nodded.

"Well, so he's got stuff to prove to people." Charles waved to the box. "Unfortunately, the factory was about to send his first bulk order when the landslide wiped out the lot. Well, not just Harvey's; mine, everyone's. We're all in limbo, waiting."

"I see." Felicity wondered how he could be so calm in the face of disaster. Then again, calm wasn't exactly her strength. She did everything at a furious speed, including worrying.

"Now, most people would take that as a sign and decide it's not meant to be," Charles went on. "Lotta clients canceled their orders and asked for refunds. Not Harvey. He's got the bit between his teeth now, and he wants to see his project through."

"Charles, how many of these things did he buy?" Felicity pointed at the animals. "I mean, paying over a million dollars for bits of plastic? That doesn't add up. These are…*toys.*"

"Collectibles," Charles corrected. "And no, of course he didn't spend a million on the merchandise. Some of that money is factory setup costs for his production run. They have to retool their equipment for every new product line, and they lost a lot in the disaster. There's the computer programming, the machine-design costs. Plus there's the mold-making, which is between two hundred and a thousand dollars per animal, logo printing to add Living Ruff's name, artists and engineers to make the mold, not to mention shipping, taxes, import duties, and so on."

Charles drew in a breath and barreled on. "The thing is, he got his prototypes, loved them, then almost immediately the landslide hit. And that's when he decided to double down and go for it. And I mean he really went for it, expanding his order a whole lot. Now the range he wants is pretty extensive."

"How so?"

"It's not just *one* generic cat, fish, and dog, like you see here." Charles waved at the prototypes. "After some consideration, he decided to shoot for the rafters. He figures people who love particular breeds will want to buy that one exactly. Say a Great Dane. Or a poodle. Or a Persian cat. A clownfish. You follow? He's ordered 134 different types of animals."

"Oh God." *This* was where Elena's money had gone? It'd be faster to just toss it into the Hudson. Felicity felt a headache coming on. "That's so over-the-top, I have no words. It's ridiculous."

"Tell that to someone passionate about their animal breed. It may be no different from a Yankee fan who wants their particular favorite player. Well, Harvey decided that, no matter what the breed, he'd have the product to sell. He's really enthusiastic about that decision."

"Do you agree with that approach?" Felicity asked skeptically. "As an expert in merchandising, don't you have some reservations?"

Charles sighed. "I know, I know. Yes, obviously it's a gamble. I honestly don't know if it'll work. My business is sports, specifically baseball, specializing in the Yankees. You can put a pretty big markup on these products and get your money back, if you've picked the right players. Will a bulldog sell as well as a beagle? Your guess is as good as mine. This is his area of expertise, not mine." He paused. "But maybe he'll start a collectible trend."

"I've only ever seen these sorts of things used as fundraising *fillers*," Felicity said. "A quick way to make a couple of bucks, nothing more."

"And that's where the other part of the gamble comes in. Will people pay ten or twenty bucks for quality animal collectibles?" He shrugged. "Guess we'll find out soon."

"Harvey seems so cautious normally," Felicity said. "I don't understand his sudden appetite for such a risky gamble."

"He's a man charged up about a grand plan who wants to prove himself to his way more successful wife, and who are we to say his dream won't fly? And maybe there *is* a huge untapped demand for high-quality figurines of all the popular pet breeds. It could even become a collecting craze, if he markets it right. He could use the celebrity angle."

"How?"

"I suggested he get some A-list animal lovers to sign his pieces and auction them off to draw attention to the product. I could probably provide a few New York Yankees, too—some of those guys really worship their dogs. So getting someone popular to post photos on social media holding an animal collectible? Maybe Harvey's right and his collection could take off. Stranger things have happened."

That was true. The things people turned into fads had little logic to her. Also no denying that people loved their pets. Felicity could tell the cartoon creatures were cute enough to catch on. "So when does the first shipment arrive after the plant retooling?"

"Not sure. The factory hasn't confirmed the new schedule yet, but we'll know more in about three months. Gotta tell you, the waiting is giving me heartburn. I've already run out of Babe Ruths and Willie Randolphs entirely, and I hate not having any. People love 'em." He straightened. "Let's go back to my office. The storeroom makes me sneeze."

Felicity paused. "Would you mind if I had one of the prototypes? Something to show my boss about where her money's invested?"

"Sure. Which one do you want, cat, fish, or dog?"

"Cat."

"Really? It looks a little snooty." He grinned and handed over the white cat with its nose stuck in the air.

"The best kind." Felicity smiled. Besides, with its white fur, it looked a bit like her destructive lilly pilly kitten. Which she absolutely did not find cute in the least, she reminded herself.

Charles shook his head. "Can't say I'm much of one for animals. Can't stand them, to be honest, dropping fur everywhere, chewing up your best shoes." He led her out of the room. "It's about the only thing Harvey and I don't agree on. He's nuts over animals."

Felicity followed him wordlessly.

"Hey, can I just confirm one last time my brother-in-law's not crazy?" Charles continued. "Harvey only needs *one* influencer to put a pic of one of these collectibles on Twitter, and who knows? It could wind up an income stream for Living Ruff for years to come."

"Possibly," Felicity said as they entered Charles's office. "I'd consider offering to help connect him with a media influencer if he'd actually be upfront with me about any of this."

"Don't mind him. He's still a bit gun-shy about being made fun of, and he wants the goods right in front of him before he announces his new collectibles program. On that note"—Charles put a stilling hand briefly on her forearm—"can you remember this is *his* big project? Don't spread what I've told you around the office or outside until Harvey's ready for his reveal."

"My boss will want to know where her money went."

"Oh, of course. Tell her, by all means. I just meant everyone else. This is for Harvey to announce to the world when the day comes. Hell, he's so focused on it being a big, exciting surprise, I'm not even sure he's told my sister yet."

No, he certainly hadn't, given that Rosalind thought Harvey's new program was about vet techs. Had he lied to his wife? Or had she just assumed?

Well, he'd lied to Felicity about that vet-tech scheme at the very least, hadn't he? Saying it was on hold and—

It suddenly occurred to her that not once had Harvey claimed Elena's donation was earmarked for Cooper's scheme. She and Cooper had assumed it was because of Rosalind's belief it was.

But when confronted, all Harvey had said was that Cooper's program was not ready to be implemented yet. Then Felicity had instantly jumped down his throat, arguing it *should* be ready as Cooper had fully costed it out.

Harvey had just sat there. He hadn't corrected them, and he hadn't lied, either. He'd said only that he was working on a *new program*. Of course Harvey hadn't also explained, "Oh, that vet-tech scheme isn't going ahead. No, I threw Elena's money into a risky, stupidly expensive high-quality collectibles venture that I'm not going to talk about yet in case everyone rains on my parade or mocks me."

What an unbelievably foolish approach. He'd rather be accused of embezzlement than admit what he'd really done and possibly be embarrassed?

Men truly did fear being laughed at most of all, didn't they? Margaret Atwood was onto something.

Honestly, she didn't understand that mindset and never would. Did Harvey truly not grasp he almost had a *police investigation* land in his lap along with terrible publicity because of his secretiveness? It was just a dumb merchandise order, for God's sake!

"Ms. Simmons?"

She looked up.

"I said do you have everything you need?" Charles asked.

"Oh. Right." Felicity shouldered her bag. "You've been very helpful. Thank you for your time." Her hand formed a fist around the little white cat. She glanced down at it. "It's been...informative."

"You're most welcome." He followed her eye to the cat. "They did do a good job, don't you think? Look, I know Harvey's gambling big. I'm not sure even I'd have the balls to do what he's doing. But at least it's not cheap crap they're making for him."

"One thing we agree on," Felicity said as she pocketed the cat, "is that nothing about this exercise has been cheap."

Felicity slid into the back seat of her car. "Living Ruff, thanks," she told Amir, then tapped out an email to her chief of staff.

Scott, find someone local in one of our newspaper bureaus in China to confirm a landslide hit a factory in Shenzhen within the past six months. Shenzhen Industries. Send me details ASAP.

Of course, Charles's news article showing devastating photos of the landslide seemed convincing enough, but it never hurt to check. She didn't read Chinese, after all.

Are you free? Felicity texted Cooper next. *I have an update.*

She had a brief flicker of doubt that maybe Charles was right and it wasn't her place to spread Harvey's secret purchases all over his office before he was ready to share. Maybe she should hold off telling Cooper. Even if her lover was discreet, it really wasn't Cooper's business to know, was it?

It'll have to wait till end of day. Miles behind on clinic hours after being kicked out of office ystdy. Have dogs cats and gerbils wall 2 wall

Gerbils? Felicity shuddered.

Later, Felicity agreed in reply, relieved the decision was out of her hands. *Btw is Harvey in?*

No. Offsite all day. Tomorrow he's in again.

Thanks.

Felicity glanced at her driver. "Change of plans. Take me home, please, Amir."

"Yes, Ms. Simmons." He gently applied pressure to the gas pedal and meandered them off in a new direction at his usual tortoise speed.

She had a brief fantasy of stretching over and stomping the gas for him.

Felicity's phone rang, and she glanced down, seeing her boss's name. "Elena?" she answered.

"Felicity, did you contact Jocelyn Mathers yet about transitioning her to the Bartell Corp masthead of her choosing?"

"No, I've been busy with Living Ruff. If it's urgent, I'd be happy to—"

"Not necessary. I'd like to be the one to do it. I just wanted to see if you'd approached her yet. She'll be a valuable asset."

"Okay," Felicity said. "I'll take contacting her off my to-do list."

"Yes. How's it going? Do you have the case solved yet?"

"I think I'm close," Felicity said. "I've made good progress. I just talked to Harvey Clifford's brother-in-law today, and he was a lot more forthcoming than Harvey." She dug her hand in her pocket, and it bumped against the white cat. "It should be case closed, except that one thing doesn't add up. I was supplied a document that helped me in my investigation, and I can't work out who sent it. Or how they managed it. Or why."

"The plot thickens," Elena said in a droll tone.

"Yes, well, if by *thickens* you mean *frustrates*, then it does." Felicity pursed her lips. "So although I have a lot of answers, I keep feeling there's more going on and it's right in front of me, but I can't quite see it."

"Trust your gut and take the time you need," Elena said confidently. "You *will* crack this. Especially given it's something you care about."

"I—" *What?* "What gives you that idea?"

"Felicity, I saw the TV clip of you attacking the mayor over homeless people's rights to have pets in shelters and addiction facilities. I've only ever seen that look in your eye when your blood's up. Like the time ten or so years ago when we were on opposing teams, and you were desperately trying to save that heritage paper in Connecticut. Did you know I only kept the paper operating as a going concern because of you? You made some valid points about its historic value to the community that your boss had completely missed. I didn't even know newspapers still existed that were older than the formation of the United States until you pointed it out."

Felicity blinked. *Wait, she kept that paper going because of me?*

"My point is, I knew the moment I saw you launching into the mayor in exactly the same way that this was important to you."

"Important? Well, no, it was more that it was annoying me the way he was dragging his feet. It was of no consequence to me and—"

"*Felicity,*" Elena said, her voice dripping with sarcasm. "Remember who you're talking to. Would you kindly not spin me bull?"

"Well," Felicity said, sucking in a breath, "fine. I suppose I care. A *little.*"

"Good."

Felicity could hear a smile in her boss's voice this time, and she decided not to try and figure out why. The woman was perpetually mystifying.

"Do you need me for anything else?" Felicity asked. Her thumb in her pocket traced the plastic cat's tail curled under its feet. Her nail dug into the bottom of the figurine, feeling something under it. A sticker?

"No, your replacement as chief of staff is somewhat adequate. It'd be nice if Scott stopped smiling all the time, though. His enthusiasm is usually far too much too early in the day. He reminds me of Mad—" She stopped dead.

"Madeleine Grey?" Felicity asked sweetly. She pulled the cat out and turned it upside down.

"Never mind," Elena punched out far too quickly. "Anyway, I have to go. I'll sort out Jocelyn Mathers; you sort out that charity. We'll talk early next week."

Felicity examined a small disc-shaped sticker, its color matching the cat. How odd. Everything else about the cat was so perfectly designed. Why would they shove something on it? She nudged the sticker with her thumbnail. It peeled up entirely, revealing three words. Her heart sank at what she was looking at. "Elena, before you go...how bad would it be if this does become a police matter?"

A long silence fell, then, "I trust you wouldn't do that prematurely. I trust *you*. Remember my edict."

"Um, if at first you don't succeed, get out of my office?" Felicity suggested dryly.

"You do realize I said that as a joke." The smirk in Elena's voice was clear.

"Oh right, you mean along with 'Be grateful I don't know who you are.'" Felicity was capable of teasing her boss, too. Even if this was exactly the second time she'd ever done it in her life, and it was now twice in one minute.

A genuine laugh came down the phone, filling Felicity with delight.

"I never *actually* said that, did I?" Elena grumbled teasingly.

"I have a source who claims otherwise." Maddie, of course, and they both knew it.

"She would." Elena's tone turned thoughtful. "Back to what I meant to say. I need you to be thorough and exacting in your investigation, but then I want you to do whatever you have to. Don't second-guess yourself, Felicity. Don't worry about what I'll think. Just work out what has to happen, then do it."

Now that was excellent advice. A weight lifted off her. "Thanks, Elena. I will."

"Good. I have to go." The phone went dead.

Felicity didn't mind the abrupt departure. Elena was Elena. She put her phone away and stared at the words under the sticker etched into the cat's feet: MADE IN USA.

Chapter 11
Clear as Mud

THAT EVENING, OVER AN UNSATISFACTORY bowl of ramen noodles, Felicity discovered Shenzhen Industries did not have a single muddy footing in its entire perfectly sound infrastructure.

She'd received a message from the Beijing bureau chief for the *Asian-American Journal*, one of Bartell Corp's elite news mastheads. The email included an English translation of a couple of local news stories from the day of the landslide a little over two months ago, which was apparently as bad as it looked in the photo. The problem was, the pictured factory Charles had shown her was *not* Shenzhen Industries.

She'd been lied to. The question was: who'd constructed the lie?

Had Charles, and by extension Harvey, been duped by the manufacturing company, which was wringing money out of gullible international creditors? Sending them articles in Chinese inventing a hard-luck story on the back of a real tragedy while sticking their hand out for more orders? She shot a query back to the bureau chief.

Is Shenzhen Industries a reputable company, or is it capable of running a con?

The journalist replied almost immediately. *The former. They're gold star.*

Okay, but no company was perfect. All it took was one bad apple in a management team up to no good lining their own pockets.

So were Charles and Harvey being conned?

Charles struck Felicity as having a closed, adamant mind about what he knew to be true. People like that were ripe for scams because, once they committed to something, they just kept doubling down even when alarm bells went off because they couldn't believe what was happening to them.

As far as gullible personality types went, Harvey seemed to be far worse. After a lifetime of caution, he'd committed to his new venture, boots and all. He'd had a bad outcome with the initial order, then rather than negotiate a settlement and walk, he'd slid every one of his chips across the table and gone all in. What on earth was he thinking? The gamble itself was huge and risky, and it was all predicated on some nebulous dream of starting a collecting craze. Who starts a new project for the first time from the position of assuming they'll hit a home run?

Felicity set aside theory A, the Chinese con, and moved to theory B, the Harvey and Charles con.

The two men could be working together to fleece money from Living Ruff. All they needed was an inside man in Shenzhen, and it was simple: when ordering, you either over-ordered or overpaid on purpose, and the refund would somehow make its way to a different account and into their own pockets. It was not unlike a basic money-laundering scheme.

She phoned Saul, Elena's private investigator who found things out for a steep price. She didn't ask how he did what he did, and he never told.

Saul answered with a grunt. "Didn't expect to hear from you people again so soon. Thought your boss had her answers on her husband."

"She does. This is new. Charles Stone, brother of socialite Rosalind Stone. Can you find out for me if he's had a sudden windfall or any signs of it? Flashy new purchases, investments out of the blue, more money to burn in clubs, that sort of thing?"

"How flashy we talking?"

"One point four million dollars' worth. While you're at it, do the same for Rosalind's husband, Harvey Clifford."

"How soon do you need to know?"

"Today would be preferred."

He whistled. "I'll charge double. I have the contacts in those circles, but it's already evening."

"I'll pay triple if I have that information within two hours. Just be accurate."

"Always." He hung up.

Felicity leaned back and wondered if considering the worst of the two men wasn't a bit far-fetched. For either or both of them to be embezzling, there had to be motive.

She tapped her lip. The obvious gain was wealth. But while Harvey didn't have money in his own right, Cooper had said he wasn't motivated by greed. Besides, the man wouldn't hurt his charity. Everyone said how much Harvey loved it. That didn't explain how guilty and strange he'd been acting.

That left Charles. Was he masterminding a con on Harvey? Exciting him with all the lovely merchandise he could sell and spark a fad with? He could be working with someone at Shenzhen Industries to fleece him. But then there was motive. Charles didn't need money. Thomas had found no irregularities beyond the fact that his sporting goods store was the least successful of all Rosalind's enterprises. But that didn't mean it was unsuccessful; on the contrary, his store made a good profit every year.

What could Charles gain from a scam? Was he greedy? After power? Hiding a loss? Even if it was all three, why would he risk scamming his brother-in-law, given it would destroy his relationship with his family when it all came out? And it *would* come out the moment Living Ruff's external auditor went over their finances in preparation for filing their 990. Finding well over a million dollars had been listed as spent on merchandising with no proof to back it up would raise red flags everywhere, and the truth would be quickly revealed. Getting caught would be inevitable, so why bother?

Nothing fit. What was theory C?

Rosalind Stone? She'd already misdirected Felicity's investigation with her suggestion that a vet-tech scheme was in play. Except Felicity couldn't imagine a less likely embezzler. It was clear the woman was dedicated to the charity she'd set up, and she had more wealth than she knew what to do with.

For the hundredth time that evening, Felicity wished Cooper were here. It had been so nice last night, batting around theories, followed by sex, snuggles, more sex…then doing it all again the next morning. It was addictive, and not just because of the tingly way Cooper made her body feel.

Felicity had always thought she didn't need companionship from her lovers. Or even companionship from her acquaintances, come to think of it. But maybe that was because people usually bored her. They tested her patience with witless prattle on the mundane, like what inanity their child had performed or what they'd bought, driven, or eaten.

Not Cooper. She talked about life. Homelessness. Purpose. What mattered, what didn't. They might not always agree, but she was never boring or short of a compelling topic.

Felicity was itching to call her, but Cooper had texted an hour ago to say she was exhausted and heading straight for bed.

That was probably for the best, given Felicity's current neediness. It would be so much harder to walk away later if she kept dragging Cooper into her world every time she missed her.

Besides, if Living Ruff or its director were up to something shady, Felicity should protect Cooper by keeping her out of everything related to this con.

One way or another, a con was certainly on. That also meant, one way or another, Elena's money was gone. Where, though? That was the question.

Felicity wracked her brain some more but came up only with a few curious tendrils she couldn't quite make sense of.

The dishwasher was purring in the background, and Felicity was curled up on the couch watching *Animal Planet* when her phone rang with an unfamiliar number. She glanced at the time. An hour and fifty-eight minutes had passed.

She answered with a guess. "Saul, I presume? And with two minutes to spare, no less."

"Ms. Simmons. I like to hit my deadlines, especially with a lot of zeroes on the line."

"What have you found?"

"First, Harvey Clifford. That guy's cleaner than a nun's bedroom. His spending habits are about the same, too. He's got little wealth of his own, doesn't spend his wife's dough, or seem interested in money at all either way."

"I see." Felicity wasn't entirely shocked. "And Charles?"

"Hate to ruin a good conspiracy theory, but he's clean, too. He's not had any sudden cash windfalls. No new cars, investments, trips, party girls.

His club habits for the past six months are the same. Business is doing okay. And do not ask me how I know this, but his bank account says the same."

"You've seen his bank balance?" Felicity asked in shock.

"Not me. Hell, I'm not interested in prison time, thanks. But I know people who know people who can ask dodgy people to do certain things for certain high fees that I'm claiming I know nothing about and would never say out loud, even on an encrypted line."

Well, that explained the unknown number.

"Bottom line," Saul said, "his bank balance is not even one grand richer, let alone a million. He's not your guy."

"Damn it." Felicity frowned. "Out of curiosity, is there any way to hide that kind of money from someone like you?"

"No," Saul said with certainty, "there isn't. But if you find out he's managed it somehow, let me know. Because I'd be fuckin' impressed."

"Okay. Thanks for the quick response. Bill me. I'll take care of it next week when I'm back at work."

"Right you are, Ms. Simmons." He hung up.

Not Charles. Not Harvey. Not Rosalind. Not Shenzhen Industries. Felicity stared at the rustling lilly pilly. "How about you, Loki? Did you mastermind a scam to steal my boss's money?"

"Mreooww."

"Well, it's a working theory. No need to get offended. And get out of my damned tree!" She made a shooing gesture, which was promptly ignored. *Naturally.*

She could have sworn Loki had laughed at her.

"With that much haughtiness, you could star in a forties film," Felicity told the kitten. "You could be like Turner or Dietrich. All attitude and imperiousness."

Felicity went still as she was reminded of a book she'd read once years ago about the golden age of Hollywood and how certain subtle games were played.

Oh. All those little threads her subconscious had been trying to make sense of came into focus. And just like that, the suspect list shortened dramatically.

Grabbing her phone, Felicity tapped a text message to Saul, asking for an address.

Theoretically, this could wait till the morning. But spooked people in stressful situations sometimes ran. And…if she was lucky, sometimes they talked, if they felt safe and had the home-team advantage.

That just left one more question. *Do I call the police, too?*

Everything in her gut told her she'd get answers if she just went in softly, softly instead of employing jackboots.

She almost laughed. God. Wasn't this how Elena had laid out the assignment? Asking her to dig deep within and find some subtlety?

Be careful what you wish for, Elena.

Chapter 12
The Unnecessary Lie

FELICITY LEANED ON THE DOOR buzzer at the front gates of an impressive loft mansion in Tribeca.

Harvey Clifford's voice came through the little box. "Yes?"

"It's Felicity Simmons. I just have—"

"No. Go away."

The voice unit went silent. She stared at it, then raised her voice to neighbor-hearing range. "Mr. Clifford, I have important information about a *scam* involving your char—"

"QUIET!" His bark was ferocious.

Huh. Felicity didn't know he had it in him.

There was a clunk, and the gates opened.

Felicity followed the beautiful travertine-paved path to the front door, which opened to an enraged-looking charity director.

In his buttoned-up navy cardigan with a pale blue collar peeking above it, corduroy pants, and loafers, the man looked like a rumpled literature professor. His expression, however, could have flayed her alive. "Ms. Simmons, do not shout my business to the street."

"I apologize," she said with little sincerity. "Perhaps we should talk inside." She made to enter, but he didn't move aside.

"This couldn't wait till tomorrow?" he asked in exasperation. "It's almost ten!"

"I don't think so, no."

Harvey's eyes darted over her shoulder as if assessing whether eavesdropping neighbors were lurking. "All right. Come in."

He led her to a small book-lined room with a leather couch facing floor-to-ceiling windows. "My library. Sit," Harvey instructed.

Felicity duly sat and waited curiously as Harvey paced a nervous circuit of the room, then finally sat on the other end of the same couch.

"What was so urgent?" he finally asked.

"I know."

"You know what?"

"About the scam. How you were sucked in." Of all the games and all the possible plays, Harvey being scammed fit best. He barely spent anything on his charity that wasn't essential. The man only wanted what was best for Living Ruff. So he'd spent Elena's money with that outcome in mind, gambled it all, and lost. It might be foolish but it wasn't criminal, even if he was probably in hell about it. That would explain his erratic and furtive behavior.

She really hoped she'd worked this out right.

Harvey stared at her.

"I don't blame you," Felicity pressed on. "When I came to Living Ruff looking for answers, I wasn't expecting to find what I did. But I don't blame you. I believe you meant well."

He sagged. "You know," he repeated.

"I do." Felicity waited, praying he'd fill in the blanks for her. Reaching into her pocket, she placed the little white cat on the coffee table. "Look familiar?"

"The prototype," he murmured.

"For the Living Ruff merchandise you ordered. Yes. All the way from Shenzhen Industries, China."

He looked at her uncertainly.

"Well, officially," Felicity continued. "Unofficially"—she leaned in and flipped it over, exposing the etched MADE IN USA—"not so much."

Harvey exhaled heavily and nodded. Remorse, anger, and regret filled his face. "Christ. You know it took me *months* to notice that? To turn it over, see the sticker, and wonder why it was there. When I realized, I felt such a fool."

"You are not a fool." Felicity said, injecting every ounce of sincerity she could manage into her voice. She leaned in, meeting his eye. "I'm paid to pick things over. I look for the tiniest irregularities like this every day in my job. You're a bookkeeper who runs a charity you love. Unlike me, you are not always on the hunt for the lies, the loopholes, the con. That does not make you a fool."

"Thank you," he said quietly. Tears pricked his eyes, and he brushed them away angrily. "I've been in agony over this. The stress is killing me. I feel sick all the time. I can't eat. I can't sleep. I just… I couldn't talk about it to anyone."

"Not even Rosalind?"

"Rosalind still thinks my new program is the vet-tech scheme. It was going to be that. When Ms. Bartell's donation came in, I told my wife that's how I'd spend it. It was going to be so wonderful to help some of the clients who could embrace this opportunity and really get back on their feet."

"So what happened?"

He suddenly froze. "Don't you know? I thought you knew. You said you did!"

"I do." Felicity prayed her poker face would hold. "I'd like to hear your version, though. Charles's version is so…self-serving."

Another educated guess. He was the best fit in all this as the con master, even if he had somehow managed to hide his stolen donation well enough to evade even Saul.

On the balcony earlier, she'd remembered reading *The Girls* by Diana McLellan, an intriguing book documenting Hollywood's sapphic sewing circle—closeted lesbian and bisexual stars from the early days of movies who socialized together. One line had always stuck with her: *look for the unnecessary lie.*

In one case involving Marlene Dietrich and Greta Garbo, the actresses repeatedly and stoutly claimed to have never met, despite proof that they had. Why the lie? Pull the string, find the truth. McLellan had deduced the lie was to hide that they had been secret lovers.

In Charles's case, he'd told her two unnecessary lies. He'd said he was all out of Babe Ruth collectibles. She'd seen four on shelves in his office. He'd claimed his box of collectibles in the storeroom was six months old, but it didn't have a lick of dust on it. And it wasn't as if he habitually dusted his boxes; he'd also told her the room always made him sneeze.

Why the lies? What was the point? She had no idea, and it didn't even matter. The fact that he'd lied about minor things made it likely he'd lied about everything.

It was such a rookie error. Con artists tended to embellish stories to sell their lies, and the devil was in the detail. Lawyers did it, too. You could always spot them making up BS by the sheer layers of intricacy their arguments contained. Felicity had a lot of practice spotting liars.

"I know this is Charles's con," Felicity said with more conviction when Harvey didn't correct her earlier statement. "He set you up. And again, I don't blame you. The incredible story he told me today about how you came to be so committed to your merchandise range was a masterful performance. Throwing in a real-life landslide to explain why you had no goods to show for it was a particularly clever touch. I was ready to take that back to my boss and walk away. He's a very compelling man, Charles Stone."

"He is," Harvey said in a monotone. "So why didn't you tell your boss his story was what happened? Your case would be closed, and you could go back to your regular life."

"Because I had loose ends. Because he lied to me. He's not out of stock on the collectibles he says he is. He's had recent, fresh shipments. And I found out the landslide didn't affect Shenzhen Industries at all. It was enough to reevaluate everything he said. So yes, while Charles was convincing and I'd like to wrap this up, he wasn't convincing enough."

Harvey's fingers traced the stitching on the sofa. "I suppose you think me very foolish not to see I was being conned before it was too late. You worked it out in a week. It took me six months and Charles's secretary, Darlene, putting the dots so close together that even I could get a clue."

"I think scam artists can be very clever," Felicity said, filing away the secretary comment for later. "One person I admire a great deal has been taken in by people she trusted implicitly."

Felicity still wasn't over the fact that *Elena* of all people had been duped for so long by those in her inner circle, including her now ex-husband.

Maybe it was the sincerity of Felicity's words or maybe he was just tired of hiding, but the next moment Harvey buried his head in his hands and—

Oh God. Was he…*crying*?

Alarm shot through her. What the hell was she supposed to do with that? There was no crying in business! You just…did not…*do* that.

To give him his privacy while he collected himself, she shifted her gaze out the windows into a copse of tall up-lit elm trees lining the property border.

The sniffling eventually ceased, and Felicity turned to see where Harvey's breakdown had progressed to.

"Sorry," he muttered, fumbling around in his pocket and withdrawing a handkerchief. "I'm even more stressed than I thought. The lack of sleep is so bad. And Charles threatening me didn't help."

"He…threatened you?" Felicity asked. "What with?"

Harvey looked traumatized all over again. "Everything," he croaked out. "Look, I suppose you'll need the whole story. For the police. That's—well, that's fine. I knew this was coming one way or another. I'm glad it was sooner. I don't know if my mental health would have coped waiting for the independent audit. Those things can take forever."

"You know that's coming?"

"Of course. It's standard. In fact, the only thing that gave me a smile in this sorry affair was that Charles doesn't know that. He's never bothered to find out how charities are run, despite our family having a few. There are checks and balances in place to prevent people doing exactly what he's done. He too clueless to know he could never get away with it and will be caught eventually."

"Does that make you feel any better? Knowing he's not getting away with it?"

"Some. But not really. It doesn't remove all the ways I feel so terrible. All the ways I should have seen what was happening and didn't." He shook his head.

"How did it start? Did you tell him of your dream to have a merchandise line for Living Ruff?"

"God, this wasn't my idea. None of it was." He sighed. "Three years ago, a homeless woman gave me a little orange dog she'd made. It was a bit…" He hesitated. "It wasn't attractive, but it had been made from the heart, so I put it on my desk. You know—it was polite. Besides, Harriet is a delightful woman with a wonderful sense of humor. Truly, she'd overcome so much, and her dog had just died despite our every effort…" He sniffled again.

"Go on," Felicity prodded.

"Before long, people started calling it my mascot, and I went along with it. Why not? Ugly dogs, beautiful dogs—they're all creatures who need our love. In a way, it's poignant that Living Ruff should have an ugly mascot. We deal with things other people turn away from."

That was a surprisingly beautiful way of looking at it.

"Anyway, last year Charles came to see me at work one day for something or other and asked about the dog, so I explained about it being our mascot. He scoffed and said he knew how Living Ruff could have something much nicer. Even better, we could sell them and make money for Living Ruff. I thought he meant a little toy dog and a cat, maybe a pen, too. A fridge magnet, even." Harvey shrugged. "That sounded okay, right? Not too expensive."

"Right," Felicity said.

"Later that day he brought in some of the sports collectibles he sells in his store to show me what's possible in the world of collectibles. The quality was amazing. The more Charles talked, the more I got swept up in his idea of having a dozen animal collectibles we could sell. His idea of getting celebrities to sign some and get them auctioned off, well, that sounded great, too. I could see getting a lot of money for them."

"Had Elena donated her $1.4 million at this point?" Felicity asked.

"She had, a week before. And the previous night, talk of the donation had come up at a family dinner Charles was at." He gave her a wry look.

"The previous night? What a coincidence," Felicity said dryly.

"Exactly," he said. "I'm an idiot, of course, not noticing his sudden need to talk to me the day after I mention us coming into money. But it never entered my mind not to trust family. Especially when he has money."

"I understand," Felicity said. "So ordering some merchandise from Shenzhen Industries was raised next? Charles volunteered to be your go-between, I'm guessing."

"Yes. The first quote he got for me was great. One dog, one cat, one fish, five thousand units of each. It was very affordable. And Charles was just so enthusiastic. He offered to handle everything. He'd deal with a foreign company so I wouldn't feel out of my depth. He said it made sense since he had to negotiate with them anyway. He even suggested we combine shipping costs to save a bundle."

"And you liked this idea."

Harvey's expression was rueful. "I can't overstate how impossible it was not to get swept up in his ideas. He was there every time I turned around. So I did it. I paid for an initial shipment. Immediately, Charles suggested I not tell the staff; let it be a surprise. Since they made jokes about my mascot, he told me I didn't need to hear any negativity about my new project."

"Staff would ask too many questions," Felicity deduced. "Raise doubts about how you were spending the donation?"

"I think so. I shrugged and went with it. I also managed all my transactions in a way Mrs. Brooks wouldn't notice, at least for a while."

"How could you hide all this from her?"

"Mrs. Brooks might be a decent self-taught office manager, but I'm an experienced bookkeeper and know more than a few tricks. Tricks such as shifting office payments around in ways that aren't immediately obvious to the untrained eye. I did that to maintain the surprise." He rolled his eyes. "I *do* know how this sounds, by the way. I feel so stupid."

Felicity gave him a sympathetic look. "Go on."

"Then Charles talked me into ordering a few more animals. And a few more. Then it was, 'Have you thought of trying to start a collectible craze? People passionate about a breed would love to have *exactly* that animal.' He reminded me often he was a merchandising expert. He was so convincing. And any time I had concerns, he'd take me to lunch." Harvey's face fell.

"What is it?"

"I came to hate those lunches. By the third drink, he'd remind me who my wife was. How successful. How sought after. How lucky I was she'd even looked in my direction. Me, a lowly man of no social standing and limited worth. He chipped away at my self-confidence for months until I started to really wonder what Rosalind sees in me at all." He slumped. "You have to understand, I used to wonder that in the first place before I realized it didn't matter. But Charles pulled me back into that dark place and had me really dwell on my doubts."

"Why?" Felicity asked, aghast.

"Because he's rat cunning." Harvey's eyes were wet with tears. "My Rosalind is incredible. Beautiful and smart, and she always tells these clever little jokes she tailors just for me. She brings my dog into bed with us if she senses I'm feeling down. On top of that, she gave me our beautiful daughter. I used to think I was the luckiest man alive to have her. Thanks to Charles, I started to feel like the unworthiest man alive."

Harvey wrung his hands. "I *know* the way people look at me when they find out who Rosalind married. The surprise, the amusement. They can't work it out. And I feel so ashamed I'm not *more* for her."

"What an awful feeling that must be," Felicity murmured, appalled.

"It's horrible." His reddened eyes met hers. "These past two months, Charles has been reminding me constantly that he's very close to his sister and knows what impresses her. He made me feel desperate to prove I could be worthy of her. He made me believe that if I created a huge fundraising hit for Living Ruff, she'd be impressed. I just wanted her to look at me with pride."

"What makes you believe she doesn't already?" Felicity asked. "Harvey, I've heard Rosalind talk about you. She loves you completely."

"A man sees only his reflection," Harvey mused, and gave her a long, sad look. "In other words, we see what we expect to."

Felicity nodded. Very true.

"So after the landslide happened and Charles was in my ear about ordering big to get Shenzhen back up and running sooner, I thought this was it. I'd make a grand play and pray it paid off. Charles said I wouldn't regret it." His shoulders sank. "I did almost immediately. It just felt...not smart, but I also kept trying to push aside my doubts."

"And so by then, Charles had gotten all of Elena's money."

Harvey's head snapped up. "Oh, Charles didn't get a cent. I'm not a complete idiot, although I do feel it. When I did my first transfer, I had my bank confirm that the financial account details Charles gave me really were for Shenzhen Industries."

"Then how did Charles benefit?" Felicity asked, lost. "Does he have someone working for him over there? Someone to funnel the money back to him?"

"No." Harvey sighed. "He didn't need to. The scam never involved him getting money. His bank balance would be the same today as it was six months ago."

Score one for Saul. "I don't understand."

"I didn't either at first. I'm not sure how long it would have taken me to work out what he was up to if it weren't for Darlene. We talk whenever I'm in Charles's store. She's great." His eyes glazed over in blissful wonder for a moment before he said, "I think I'm in love with her Pembroke Welsh corgi. It's the most adorable thing. Darlene puts Sammy in shows. He's won ribbons. Corgis are so overlooked—"

"Can we please focus?" Felicity cut in, sensing he was warming up for a long, meaningless story.

"Oh. Yes. Sorry. I was bemoaning to Darlene about the landslide and wondering how long we'd have to wait to get our orders. She gave me the blankest look and said, 'What do you mean, wait? What delays?'"

"Uh-oh."

"Exactly. Long story short, she took me into the storeroom, and it was lined with boxes from Shenzhen. She pointed out one batch. 'Last month.' Another batch. 'Two months ago.' And… 'Yesterday.'"

"And the con was exposed just like that."

"You'd think so." He gave her a look of dismay. "But my confused brain couldn't put the pieces together immediately because I kept rejecting the idea that a man I trusted—family—would betray me."

"When did you realize?"

"That night I pulled out the handful of prototypes he'd given me. I found the stickers, pulled one off, and realized I'd been had. The next day, on a hunch, I went into the toy store closest to where Charles works. I found shelves of animals made by Hasbro that matched my prototypes. They were characters from some obscure children's show I'd never heard of. I stood there holding these chunks of plastic and realized I'd been conned out of $1.4 million using props totaling the grand sum of three bucks sixty."

Oh, hell. "What did you do?" Felicity asked quietly.

"I bought a couple of them from the store and marched right around to see him. I showed him the receipt, threw the toys at him, and demanded he explain."

"What did he do?"

"First he laughed and told me it took me long enough. That's when he gloated about what he'd been doing. I'd give my orders to Charles, and I'd pay Shenzhen Industries direct. He would then email his business contact at Shenzhen to say his new associate was sending them some money and to put it toward his current orders. So every time I paid for my orders, I was actually paying for baseball collectibles or whatever else he wanted for his store."

"He was using you for store credit. Well, factory credit." No wonder his bottom line at the bank was unchanged.

"Yes. I threatened him with going to the police."

"How did he take that?"

"He pointed out how there was not one thing linking anything he's done back to him. Just once he handed me a piece of paper with Shenzhen's banking details, and his name wasn't anywhere on it. Every deal we did was talked out over those lunches, and he'd make notes about what I wanted. At the end of the meal, he'd show me his list and have me confirm my order. I don't have so much as an email from him asking for a dime. Whenever I was ready to pay for a new order, Charles always took me to lunch and gave me a piece of paper that had an invoice number and an amount payable on it, nothing else."

"Even without evidence, you could make a complaint. Tell everyone what he's done."

"I threatened to make a noise. Smooth as honey, like it was nothing, he said if I reported the scam or named him at the center of it to a single person, he'd take away the thing I loved most."

"What's that?"

"Not what. Who. My Rosalind."

"How could he possibly do that?" Felicity asked in surprise.

"He said he knew exactly what to whisper in her ear to make her doubt her husband's integrity in the same way he'd made me doubt my own worth. He'd gradually over months make Rosalind believe I'd married her for money because that's her biggest fear in dealing with people: gold diggers. And after that, when Rosalind saw me for the monster Charles had painted me as, she'd get the best lawyer in town, divorce me, and take my daughter, too." Harvey looked sick to his stomach.

"But she's *your wife*, Harvey," Felicity said, incredulously. "She loves you. Surely she knows you well enough not to believe some campaign of lies, no matter who's doing it."

"You have no idea how much I want to believe that," Harvey said, his voice rising uncertainly. "I desperately do. But by that time, I had all these doubts. Charles has been reminding me for six months that I'm *nothing*. And he's right. Rosalind Stone, brilliant businesswoman, and Harvey Nothing Clifford."

He shook his head. "Her family initially opposed us marrying, you know, for exactly that reason. It wouldn't take much for them to take Charles's side if he ramped up his campaign against me. I truly hope she'd stand by me, but my worst fears now hound me all the damned time. Even if she doesn't buy the gold digger lie, what if she sees Charles is right about the rest? What if she realizes I'm just so blindingly average?"

"She chose *you* in the first place, remember? She went after you."

Harvey gave her a pensive look. "I know. But I'm still struggling with this. I wish I didn't have doubts. I felt I couldn't take the risk. Charles is *so* persuasive. He can charm the wings off bees. I imagined everyone would believe his version. He'd make them think I'm the thief. So that day I was sitting there, blood boiling as I stared at Charles, imagining my life without Rosalind and my girl, and it was torture, Ms. Simmons."

Felicity could feel his pain radiating from him. That was the thing about fear—you couldn't logic or reason it away. There was no cure for it. You had to be brave, or you would fall. And Harvey, poor man, wasn't even close to the brave type.

"And that man who I'd thought of as a brother sat and smirked back at me," Harvey said, his hands clenching into fists. "He *knew*. He's always known this was my greatest fear, which was how he played me so well. It was chilling, the moment I realized there was nothing I could do. Any way that this scam got out, it could only have come from me. Then he'd hurt me. So he had me in a corner."

Harvey's voice broke. "It's the most evil choice. I love my charity, but I love my family more. I was stuck...until you came along."

"Excuse me? How do I factor into this?"

"I thought the stress would kill me waiting for the independent audit to be carried out, knowing already the Shenzhen orders would get flagged.

It's a long process, and it'd be many months away. Then you show up investigating every little thing, demanding answers, and I was so relieved. I thought if you worked it out, at least then when it all comes out, Charles would assume it was your doing, not mine, so he wouldn't retaliate."

"You could have just whispered it into my ear. I'd have been discreet."

"I couldn't trust you not to tell Charles how you knew. I didn't even know you. No, you had to go on the hunt, look puzzled and frustrated so Charles would know this wasn't my doing." Harvey gave a tiny smile. "I'm sorry I put you through a merry chase, but I needed you to be suspicious enough to keep digging."

Felicity froze as she realized what he'd done. "*You* were the anonymous emailer! You sent me Living Ruff's next 990 form. It gave me a link between Living Ruff and Charles's store."

"Yes. Of course. Well, it was only a draft of the 990 I dashed off for you, but yes, I hoped you'd get the idea."

"How did you get my email address?"

"You left your business card on the desk. Mrs. Brooks never took it. I heard what you asked her to do. I thought about it. I hoped you'd be smart enough to put it all together if I gave you a little nudge. And I did my best to look guilty every time we spoke to make you wonder what I was hiding. Not answering questions. Not confirming or denying things. Throwing you out of the office." He gave her a sheepish look. "Sorry about that. I found it quite traumatizing, raising my voice."

"I did wonder what you were up to." Felicity said in a dry tone.

"I do apologize. I knew you'd be seeing Charles sooner or later after that. So my biggest fear became that you'd accept at face value whatever story he told you. I worried he'd schmooze you completely and send you on your way with a neat, easily digestible tale for your boss. He's so good. He can invent the most elaborate tales on the spot like it's nothing."

"Very true. The level of detail he gave me about your passion for merchandising was extensive."

"I can only imagine."

"Luckily, even Charles leaves loose ends: odd little lies, those made-in-America prototypes, and a destroyed factory I was able to fact-check with locals that was anything but."

Harvey's expression was bittersweet. "I'm glad you're a determined, resourceful woman, Ms. Simmons. I was right in thinking you'd find the truth. But I also know that the moment you leave here tonight, police will be called, and I'll lose my charity. I don't deserve it anyway, being conned like that, but at least I'll have my wife. Hell, I might even get a good night's sleep tonight."

"You're aware my calling the police will likely destroy Living Ruff? Charities linked to scandal rarely come back from it, even if it wasn't their fault."

"Yes, I'm aware. Much as I wish it weren't the case, I know you need to see that Charles faces justice. I'm at peace with what's about to happen. And please, please tell your boss I'm so very sorry I didn't look after her donation as it deserved. I would do anything to turn back time."

"Harvey," Felicity said in exasperation, "what I don't get is why didn't you simply go to your wife and tell her you were being blackmailed by her brother? Surely if you talked to her first, all of this could be avoided."

"That's what *I'd* like to know," came a low feminine voice behind them.

Harvey started, his head whipping around to face the door.

Felicity turned to see Rosalind leaning against the door's frame, expression grim.

"H-how much did you hear?" Harvey asked, face paling.

"All of it." Rosalind's lips were a tight, angry line. "I came to listen in because I thought I might finally get some answers. Such as why you've been losing hair and weight, barely sleeping, and looking ten years older these days. Most of all, I needed to know why you'd stopped talking to me about anything personal."

"I—" Harvey petered out.

"No." She gave her husband a brisk, assessing look. "Being taken in by a scam thanks to my scheming brother is one thing. Not trusting me? Doubting my love for you? That is quite another."

Harvey crumpled under her words, his shoulders sagging, his eyes tearing up.

Felicity retreated over to the tall windows to give them privacy. In the reflection, though, she could see the two clearly.

Rosalind's face softened, her eyes darting toward Felicity's back as if to check that no witnesses existed. Then she cupped Harvey's cheek in her hand and said so softly that Felicity almost couldn't hear. "You silly, beautiful man." She leaned in and kissed him lightly on the lips. "When will you ever believe me when I tell you no one has ever turned my head the way you do?"

Rosalind drew her fingertips down his cheek. "The fact that you were scammed by Charles only reinforces my belief that you're too good for this world. You see only the best in everyone. You trust without reservation. Everywhere I turn, I see manipulators. They want my power, my money, my endorsement. I accept that this is my life, that it's filled with people who only take. No one ever talks about the coldness that comes with having vast wealth. And then I come home to you."

Harvey's head lifted.

"That's where I feel only warmth," Rosalind continued in that soft, gentle voice. "And all you ever do is give."

She leaned her forehead into his. "Yesterday I called and told you I'd had a terrible day. I came home to find the most beautiful smells from my favorite meal in the oven. The music I love most was playing, even though I know Vivaldi makes you groan. You asked if I'd prefer a foot or a back massage—as if the option of neither hadn't even entered your head. Darling, I feel your love in every look and touch. I feel so much warmth. *You* are the reason I rush home early from all those charity balls and galas. *You* are my home. Don't ever doubt that again. We will talk about this properly later, but right now I need a private word with Ms. Simmons."

Harvey nodded, his hands reaching for his wife's, which he squeezed for a long moment. Their gazes were locked. Then he croaked out: "Love, I really am so very sorry."

"I know." Her smile was sad. "I know you are."

Felicity waited until she heard the door snick before turning. Rosalind had her back to her, still staring after her husband.

As long as she lived, Felicity would never forget what she'd just seen. It hadn't ever occurred to her that a powerful, imposing woman might need a Harvey in her life. He seemed to recharge her emotional reserves. That's why Rosalind loved her mild-mannered bookkeeper. Among other things, he kept her going when she was drained by a demanding world.

All the times Felicity had heard love described over the years, a concept she couldn't really relate to, it had been in terms of shallow, unrealistic ideals. True loves. Wild passion. Rainbows and roses. Not…this.

Intensity. Warmth. Intimacy. Support. Finding ways to provide what the other lacks. A partnership. A…balance.

It was confusing, actually. She couldn't quite wrap her head around it.

"Ms. Simmons," Rosalind said, her voice cool and pointed as if she hadn't just bared her soul to her husband. The tone contained a warning, too, as if daring her to even suggest she'd heard a word of that intensely private conversation.

Felicity would sooner die than admit it.

Rosalind sauntered into the middle of the library. "Thank you for solving a mystery that has been plaguing me for half a year: where my happy husband went." She settled onto the couch cushion Harvey had just vacated.

Felicity joined her at the opposite end of the couch and waited.

"So now we have a problem to solve, wouldn't you say?"

"I'd have thought it has a pretty simple solution," Felicity said. "I call the police. Harvey testifies against Charles as the victim in the scam. He also resigns from Living Ruff for his incompetence. Your brother goes to prison. The Living Ruff board appoints a new director. And Bartell Corp pursues Charles through the civil courts to get my boss's donation back."

Rosalind eyed her serenely. "I'm wondering if you're open to other options."

"Ones that won't embarrass your family, you mean? Or involve police?" Felicity asked, tone flat and cool. "Let me guess: you'll have a check written for $1.4 million in exchange for my silence?"

"That's certainly one approach. And given the…inconvenience you've experienced, I will make sure that that's on the table no matter what. It's the least I can do." Rosalind folded her arms. "But right now I'm seeking an option that won't negatively impact Living Ruff. As you mentioned to Harvey, it's obvious how a scandal will play out. My foundation will be destroyed. The homeless and their animals will suffer. We both know Living Ruff does a lot of good. So can we reach an alternative, mutually beneficial agreement?"

"That depends. Will Charles face justice? Will Harvey stay on at Living Ruff?"

"Yes and unfortunately no, in that order." Rosalind's gaze trailed Felicity's face. "Ms. Simmons, I have a proposal. But I think before I explain its merits, I'm aware you'll be naturally skeptical as to my motives. I can see you believe my only interest here is in protecting my family and sweeping this under a rug. Therefore, it's only natural you'll push back against anything I suggest. With that in mind, first I'd like to offer proof of my intentions."

Rosalind pulled a phone from her stylish navy jacket pocket and tapped a number. It rang a long time before connecting.

"Charles? Rosalind. I need you here now for an urgent meeting." She paused, pursing her lips. "I don't care. Pay her and put her in a cab. I said *now*. No arguments." She waited for agreement, then hung up.

"You're having it out with Charles?"

"Well, that implies too much leeway from his end. I'm giving him the brief chance to wheedle, beg, and explain himself, then I'm pronouncing sentence. If you feel my punishment is adequate, then we'll talk about not calling the police and how else we can move forward."

"I'm not sure why you think I'd agree to anything that doesn't see Charles in handcuffs for his scam. It doesn't get much lower than stealing from the homeless."

"I understand why you'd feel that way," Rosalind said, and suddenly smiled a teasing, slow-curling smile. "The thing about men like my brother is, you have to know where to hit them. Charles's softest parts aren't nearly as impacted by being charged with a crime he can get out of with that slick tongue of his and an expensive lawyer. What I have in mind will hit him harder and have longer repercussions."

"What would hurt him more than being publicly humiliated as a scammer in court?" Felicity asked incredulously.

"Patience." Rosalind rose from the couch and wandered over to a buffet containing bottles of spirits, wine, and glasses. "Would you like a drink while we wait for him?"

"No, thanks, I'm fine." Felicity had the strong impression she'd need to be on her toes for what lay ahead.

"All right." Rosalind poured herself what looked to be a gin. "I have a few calls to make to ensure I have my brother's back sufficiently to the wall for what I'm planning. Then we will resolve this matter entirely." She took a sip of her drink, then reached for her phone.

Chapter 13
Deal Done

CHARLES BURST INTO THE LIBRARY, his fury a counterpoint to the apologetic expression on the face of the elderly servant who closed the door behind him.

"Jesus Christ, Rosalind," he snapped. "Where's the damned fire? I was *entertaining*." His untucked, misbuttoned shirt suggested the nature of the entertaining.

"She can wait." Rosalind had positioned herself precisely in a red-velvet wingback armchair with brocade embedded in the seams. Her arms rested along the armrests, her legs perfectly crossed at the ankles; she could pass as a deportment book's cover model. Her elegant swan-like neck was angled to face the door and her brother. "And the fire, Charles, is right here." She waved to where Felicity sat on the facing couch.

Charles turned, and his face transformed. Charm spread across it briefly, then disappeared as hesitation, and finally suspicion replaced it. "Ms. Simmons, we meet again. I'm surprised it's so soon."

"Charles." Felicity used his first name deliberately. "I've just been discussing with your sister the conclusion of my investigation into Living Ruff."

"Oh?" he said cautiously, then slowly walked over to stand in front of her. He was a big man, solid and imposing, but his natural cockiness was missing. "And?"

Felicity gave a small wave in Rosalind's direction. "I'll let your sister explain what I found."

Charles pivoted back to face his sister, jaw tight.

"Ms. Simmons has deduced that you're involved in a million-dollar scam." Rosalind's eyes flashed in irritation.

"She's been misinformed." He snapped his head back and forth between the two. "I'd *never* turn on family."

"Who mentioned family?" Rosalind arched an eyebrow. "And I notice you haven't said, 'Goodness, what scam?'"

"I was getting to it," he growled.

"Don't bother." Rosalind's manicured fingernails tapped the red velvet. "Here's what's going to happen. You have five minutes to explain yourself. For every lie you tell, I will make your punishment worse. Do bear that in mind before you launch into your usual creative tall tales."

"You're not even going to give me the benefit of the doubt? I'm just guilty?" Charles glowered.

"There's little room for doubt. I've heard Ms. Simmons's evidence. It's been gathered from multiple sources."

"I'll bet it has. Well, Harvey's lying. He's a little man out of his depth trying to impress his wife with grand plans—and he fucked up. He's trying to shift the blame from his own bad decision-making. Hell, he's actually trying to prop up a factory wiped out by a landslide using donor money just to get the shit he ordered!"

"Who mentioned Harvey? You really are dreadful at this, Charles." Rosalind's restless, drumming fingertips paused. "Now, we'll call that lie number one, even though you bundled several atrocious untruths together. For the record, Ms. Simmons has been in contact with a journalist in China who informed her that Shenzhen Industries was unaffected by the landslide you mention. Not so much as a mud spatter."

"You're just taking her word for that? Over mine?"

"No. Not ten minutes ago I spoke to your secretary, who confirmed you've received many new shipments from Shenzhen in recent months. Tell me, how is that possible for a factory you just said was 'wiped out by a landslide'?" Rosalind repeated his quote mockingly.

Charles's jaw worked.

"Now, here's an interesting thing. Imagine my surprise when Darlene tells me you haven't paid for any collectibles for seven months. And yet… still they come, every one or two months. Apparently, you've received orders worth hundreds of thousands of dollars lately. Would you care to explain how you paid for that?"

Charles was silent.

"No clever little tales?"

More silence.

"Well, I have a theory," Rosalind said. "You know that I'm well acquainted with Rake's manager." She turned to Felicity. "That's an exclusive nightclub my little brother enjoys splashing his cash at to impress the ladies."

Rosalind turned back to Charles. "The club manager told me last year that you were having difficulty preventing your membership from being suspended due to exceeding their line of credit. You owed them $27,000 in August. I called him tonight to see whether you'd ever settled that debt. Sure enough, the manager said you paid the club in full last September. At the same time, in a rather interesting coincidence, you were also due to pay roughly that amount on your next round of sporting collectibles."

Charles's mouth fell slightly open.

"And yet, as Darlene tells me, Charles Stone Sporting Goods didn't pay for its goods. In fact, it hasn't paid one dime toward any of its shipments since the middle of last year. Here's where things get really interesting, though. In the same month that you paid off your club debt and missed your payment for Shenzhen, Living Ruff made its first investment in animal collectibles. Although it might have been an inadvertent investment in baseball collectibles, come to think of it. Am I wrong?"

Charles's mouth opened.

"Remember, for every lie, I make it hurt more."

His mouth closed.

"You'll notice I've left Harvey out of this. My trusting husband seems to be under some odd delusion that *you* have the power to make me dislike him. And he seems to think, again thanks to you, that he deserves it. I can forgive you many things, Charles, but not making the gentlest soul alive doubt his worth to me and to himself." Rosalind rose to her feet and stalked over to him. Although he was taller than her by a good foot, Charles shrank away in the face of her cold fury. "That. Is. Unforgivable."

He winced.

"What should I do with you?" Rosalind snapped. "For scamming my husband, bringing my charity into disrepute, putting me in a position that will force me to fire the man I love from the job that means everything to him! Not to mention, he's now decided he is unworthy of me after you've been gaslighting him for over six months."

"I meant to pay it back," Charles muttered. "Fuck it, it got out of hand. I swear I didn't intend this."

"Pay what back?"

"Harvey's credit. Come on, you know how much I love Rake's. I didn't mean the line of credit to get so high and then they were going to suspend me. And I was supposed to be paying my next Shenzhen collectibles bill then, too. But suddenly there's Harvey telling us he's rolling in cash, and I thought maybe I could just get him to pay for my collectibles without knowing. I'd pay Rake's, then my new collectibles would come in, and as soon as I made a profit from them, I'd tell Harvey they canceled his order and issued him a refund. I'd see he got his money back."

Rosalind's lips were in a thin line. "I'd possibly believe you, if you'd made any effort to pay Harvey back. You didn't. And I might have believed you if you had stopped at the first order. Instead, you were in Harvey's ear for six months until you had all of the $1.4 million donation. That's not a desperate unplanned act; it's a dedicated, well-plotted campaign of conning."

"No, I swear, it snowballed. Once Harvey got started, I couldn't stop him from trying to order more and more without letting on it wasn't real."

"Lie number two. It would never enter Harvey's head to order 134 varieties of collectible animals. He'd listen to an expert, be talked into it, but bless his heart, he's not a big, bold thinker who'd dare like that without someone pushing him. He's small picture, careful and conservative in scale. On the other hand, it sounds exactly like the BS you spin." Rosalind met his eye. "Do not *dare* to pretend to know my husband better than I do."

Charles bared his teeth but didn't reply.

Rosalind's eyes were hard. "So you're a conniving con artist who played Harvey like a fiddle for six months till you'd wrung every spare cent out of him. My God, our parents would be rolling around in their graves. No wonder they gave me the inheritance to manage."

"And that's the problem!" Charles spat out. "You lord their money over our family like *you're* our mother. How do you think it feels to have my sister dictate and oversee every dollar I spend at work? You treat me like a trained puppy begging for favors. You condescend to me from on high like you have all the answers."

"So let me get this straight," Rosalind said, stalking back to sit in her armchair. "All your scheming and conning and appalling attitude is apparently my fault." Her heated stare was so laserlike, Felicity was surprised he didn't have a pair of holes bored through him.

Charles shook his head in annoyance. "I'm saying none of this would have happened if our fucking parents hadn't given it all to you to manage. Why the fuck did they do that, anyway?"

"Because I wouldn't snort it or smoke it or drink it away; I wouldn't spend it on horses or hookers."

Charles's shoulders bunched up. "I don't do half of that."

"You did enough of it to have them worried you'd blow it all. I have no doubt you'd have been indulging yourself in destructive ways even sooner if not for me." Rosalind slapped her chair's armrest. "If you wanted to be out from under my rules so badly, no one would have stopped you striking out on you own, making a name for yourself without family money. But no. You just ruined a charity, shattered a decent man, and tried to sabotage your own sister's marriage. And all for *money*."

Charles shot her a filthy look. "It's easy to sneer at something when *you* have plenty of it."

"You'd be well off, too, if you'd stopped blowing your generous salary on showing off around clubs to women, especially those who charge by the hour." She straightened. "All right, enough. Time's up. Let's move on."

"What are you going to do?" A hint of worry crept into Charles's voice.

"It's more what *you* are going to do if you want to avoid a criminal record. First, you will apologize to Ms. Simmons for stealing her boss's donation. Next, you will apologize to Harvey for scamming him and for taking advantage of his trust in you. Third, you will email Shenzhen Industries, cc'ing me, tell them what you did, and explain that any orders outstanding should be canceled and any credit remaining put back into Living Ruff's account. Fourth, I'm taking your store off you."

His eyes widened. "No! You can't!" His voice rose a notch to panicked. "Come on, everyone knows me. That's mine. It's got my name on it!"

"Names can be changed. The store will be sold. Next, I will be informing our family of what you did. They need to know whom they *can't* trust. I won't have any of them put at risk if you ever try another stunt like this again."

"I would never hurt our family!" Charles said, fear now plain in his eyes.

"Need I remind you, *Harvey* is family, even if you don't like him. Since you've already scammed family once, claiming you never would makes lie number three." Rosalind's fingers traced a pattern in red velvet. "Our cousin Aaron has been running a halfway house for five years. Spencer House? Did you know about that?"

Charles looked mystified as to where this was going. "Yes. Bunch of grumpy old bastards live there, don't they?"

"It's a place for unmarried men who have struggled with alcohol and substance abuse, men who've just gotten out of prison after long sentences and who lack the social skills to integrate directly into society. Aaron's having some difficulty keeping managers because sometimes the clients get verbally or physically abusive. They need someone big and strong"—her eyes slid over Charles's bulk—"who won't take any nonsense to live and work there and straighten things out if they get violent."

Charles's mouth dropped open. "For fuck's sake. How long?"

"It was going to be a year. Your three lies make it a year and nine months. If you keep your nose clean, I'll try very hard to ignore what you did to Harvey. I won't forgive because I meant it when I said it was unforgivable, but I will not mention it again. Additionally, you'll be paying me back the funds you took. I'll be reimbursing Living Ruff in the short-term. You can expect an amount to be garnished from the wages Aaron pays you each week. Lastly, you won't be allowed back into Rake until your year and nine months of community service is finished. I know the manager, as I said, and he'll make it happen. I'll make it worth his while financially to keep you out."

"I can just go to another club." He lifted his chin.

"You can. But you just finished telling us that you love that one."

Charles stared at her murderously. "And if I say no to all this?"

"Then I will do the following: Call the police. Support Harvey in being a witness at your trial. Comment extensively in Ms. Simmons's many, many newspapers about how bitterly disappointed I am to have a brother letting down the family name in such a way. I will fund civil actions to have you repay the money owed. And I will never back your enterprises in any way again. Actually, that last one is a given, regardless. But on top of that, you'll be dead to the whole family by the time I'm done."

Charles stared at her, his hands bunching and unbunching. "I fucking hate you anyway, so no loss there."

Rosalind looked unconcerned. "I understand. So what's your decision? Community service or prison?"

He ground his jaw. "The first one."

"All right. I'll let Aaron know. You can start Monday. Now I think there's something you had to say to Ms. Simmons."

Charles glared at his sister and turned.

"Make it convincing," Rosalind drawled. "That's a condition, too."

He sighed, stared at his shoes, then looked up. "I'm sorry I took your boss's money. She did a good thing. I didn't."

"All right?" Rosalind glanced at Felicity.

"Yes." Felicity was hardly going to prolong this by pointing out his apology had all the sincerity of a politician around babies.

Rosalind turned back to Charles. "Good. Now leave. On your way out, find Harvey and apologize to him, too. While you're at it, maybe remember to mention you *won't* try to destroy his marriage." Her eyes were glittering with anger now.

"Okay," he said, sounding defeated. "Sure." He left.

"Well," Rosalind said, returning to her previous position in the chair. Pristine and perfect. Her mask had returned, and it was as if not a cross word had ever been spoken in this room. "It's done."

Felicity stared at her in wonder. "Yes."

"Nasty business but necessary. Now then, shall *we* talk terms, too?" She leaned toward Felicity. "The price to be paid to avoid you turning Living Ruff's finances into a police matter. I trust you've now seen I'm a woman of good faith."

Felicity nodded. "Proceed."

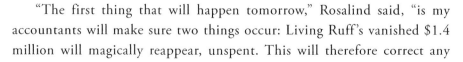

"The first thing that will happen tomorrow," Rosalind said, "is my accountants will make sure two things occur: Living Ruff's vanished $1.4 million will magically reappear, unspent. This will therefore correct any anomalies on the books come audit time, so everything will be clean. The next thing that will happen is, I will see to it that an additional $1.4 million is returned to Ms. Bartell with a full apology for any stress or inconvenience caused by what happened to her donation. It's unconscionable that she had to send her second-in-command to sort this out for her, and I'm sure having her money back safe and sound will settle the matter for good."

"I believe it would," Felicity said.

"This leads me to what happens to Living Ruff. Obviously, Harvey cannot remain as director. The board is comprised of my family and friends. The entire charity is connected to me through fundraisers I run to get donations. I need to future proof my foundation in case the scam ever leaks. No one can remain working with Living Ruff who is linked to me or Harvey; otherwise the charity will be tainted the moment the story breaks. To survive, it needs an entirely clean break from us."

"Okay…" Felicity wondered where she was going with this.

"Ms. Simmons, how would Bartell Corporation like to acquire a good, gold-star foundation that's in need of quality overseeing? And how would you like to choose its new director?"

Shock shot through Felicity. "You're joking."

"I'm deadly serious. I have deep love and concern for Living Ruff. I think, though, it would be in good hands if you took it off mine."

"Bartell Corp is a *media* empire. It has no interest in overseeing homeless people's pets."

"Why not? Things change. I read that your boss is planning to build a skyscraper. Real estate now? That's not very media oriented, is it?"

"There's a big difference between owning a building and owning a charity."

"Ah, that's the thing: charities aren't like businesses in the sense that no one *owns* them. Think of Living Ruff as a boat I built. I finished it, set everything in motion, put the board members on deck as crew, then cast it out to sea. It's now owned by no one. It just needs steering every now and then to keep it off the rocks. It's technically not mine anymore, but I do keep a fond eye on it to make sure it's fine. And I help it pay its bills."

"Well, the bills aren't something my company would be interested in taking on, thanks. Especially if you're not going to be doing fundraisers anymore," Felicity said firmly.

"I understand your concerns, but I'll see to it that my friends keep running fundraising lunches to keep it in the black, even though I'll be hands-off myself in future. So all Living Ruff needs is someone excellent to take on the cause in some showy way—so everyone gets the message it's not mine and Harvey's anymore. The current board will acquiesce if I ask them to vote in new members and let Bartell Corp people take their places. And it will need a new director of your choosing, of course."

"Are you sure you can't just replace Harvey?" Felicity asked. "That's the easiest solution."

"I'm afraid not. I know how it would look if I replaced my own husband—a man well-known to adore his charity. Everyone would immediately suspect he'd done something and ask questions. Because despite what he apparently thinks, I love him dearly and would never take something he loved away from him. Alternatively, people would think he was deathly ill, but when he failed to show signs of dying, they'd go back to assuming he'd done something bad. He's also too young to retire. So you see? I'm snookered. It has to be the clean broom coming in, replacing everyone, including the director, so it doesn't look like anything's amiss."

"And if I say no to this?"

"I'll have no choice but to close the charity."

"You could divest it to someone else."

"And I'd be obliged to disclose to them what happened: the scam, the missing donation. The more people who know, the more it becomes a potential problem that puts Living Ruff's future at risk. Really, Ms. Simmons, is this so onerous to take on? It's one little charity. It will run itself independently of your media empire; their debts and credits are theirs to worry about. Not to mention it's good publicity for your company and a great public service opportunity for those you invite to be board members. Volunteering goes down just as well with the corporate set as the wider public."

"My boss might not share your enthusiasm."

"If she didn't, she'd never have invested $1.4 million in it. You already know she's in favor. Now it's your vote. I'd like to know now, though, if you're seriously considering it."

This was too fast. "I'll need the full details of accounts—"

"I can get some of my clever people to supply that to you easily. However, Living Ruff's filed 990 forms are highly accurate, and I suspect you've already looked them up, have been through them line by line, and know the health of my foundation better than most of our board. Now you're just stalling. Are you interested in going forward with this, or am I closing down Living Ruff? If so, tell me now so I can start going into damage-control mode. Either way, your boss still gets her $1.4 million check."

"I could still call the cops, you know. Charles deserves it."

"Yes, he does." Rosalind eyed her. "Although I know my punishment will hurt him far more and far longer than the criminal justice system and impact my charity far less. Of course, we both know you could be a wrecking ball if you so desired. So will it be war or diplomacy tonight?"

The irony was that Felicity's choices had distilled down to what Elena had outlined: Rampaging Rambo or softly, softly.

Rosalind was right. The charity could be isolated financially from Bartell Corp. Publicity would also be positive. But…a homeless pet charity? She turned that over for a few minutes as Rosalind watched her silently.

Felicity made a decision.

"Put in writing Charles's punishment, outlining everything he is required to do to make amends," Felicity said. "I'll have our own clever people see that he upholds his end. If not, I will not hesitate to go to the police and reveal everything. And I'll do that even if Bartell Corp has committed to help run Living Ruff."

Rosalind tilted her head in a respectful nod. "Done. And I will include a nondisclosure agreement in that paperwork, which will become void if we breach our side and Charles doesn't do what is listed."

"Acceptable. All right, I can confirm Bartell Corp's interest in taking Living Ruff off your plate, subject to all the legalities being sorted out regarding Charles's community service and NDA."

"Well. It's been interesting doing business with you, Ms. Simmons. I had wondered if you were going to ask Ms. Bartell for permission for all this. I see now that you are the one running things over there."

Felicity froze. She hadn't seriously thought to check in with Elena. Mainly because Rosalind was right: it was clear that Elena supported Living

Ruff. But also because of what her boss had said earlier about Felicity doing whatever she had to without worrying what Elena thought.

That's exactly what Felicity had done. That's what a boss would do. Pride bloomed through her. "I'm the one running things," Felicity agreed quietly.

That felt right saying it. She rose to take her leave. "Don't be too hard on your husband. He's clearly a man terrified of losing you to the point he's not thinking straight. I've heard love does that. Makes you do the most ill-thought-out things." She smiled.

Rosalind fell silent for a moment. "Harvey will be reminded as to why I chose him. He is very special. It's rare to find someone who isn't interested in my status, money, or power, let alone doesn't see it as something to covet. All these things so many people crave just don't occur to him to think about." She leaned in. "If you ever find someone like my Harvey, Ms. Simmons, I recommend hanging onto him"—she paused and her smile grew cheeky—"or her."

With that, she rose and showed Felicity out.

Chapter 14
Ambition

IT WAS GOOD TO BE back in the office, Felicity decided. She might have only been gone a week, but she felt changed in so many ways. It wasn't just what she'd accomplished but how her eyes had been opened to things far beyond her elite bubble of entrepreneurs, lawyers, and wealth.

Today might be a Saturday, but there was too much to do before Elena left for Sydney for Felicity not to be hard at work in Bartell Corporation's round, towering headquarters.

Felicity was on the penthouse floor today—home to Elena's office, a hi-tech boardroom, and a few luxury amenities. She actually preferred her own office one floor down. Less wall-to-wall glass everywhere she turned, less ostentation, and a constant white noise of human activity, not just the sound of one lone voice on the phone in the background. Up here was too large. Too still. It made her too self-conscious.

Felicity unkinked her back. She was borrowing the boardroom today, which allowed her to spread her work out and remain close while she waited for Elena to finish up a long overseas call. Grabbing her cell, Felicity texted Cooper to suggest a date night. She had so much to tell her.

Speaking of news, Felicity still had to tell her boss about the deal she'd made. She was proud to have solved the Living Ruff case in a way that meant no bad publicity and the charity remaining business as usual.

As of half an hour ago, Felicity had a copy of Rosalind's bank deposit receipt for $1.4 million credited back to Elena. And she had a bunch of paperwork from Rosalind about Charles's community service contract and a nondisclosure agreement.

All the papers needed was Elena's signature.

"Felicity." Her name was called out almost simultaneously with a distant phone thudding into its receiver.

She grabbed the paperwork and followed the voice into Elena's office.

As Felicity sat in the visitor's chair, Elena gave her a sharp look.

"Apparently, I have acquired a charity. Would you care to explain?" She held up a faxed page that had Rosalind Stone's letterhead on it. "Ms. Stone, the chair of Living Ruff's board, sent me over some details to facilitate your agreement. She is anxious to finalize things quickly."

"Ah." Felicity had wanted to be the one to break the news. "Yes, Bartell Corp will have a hand in looking out for Living Ruff New York in a loose sense. It will run itself, though. We're just the…um…benevolent shepherds."

Elena rubbed her temple. "I sent you there to see where my money went, not make them cough up an entire charity."

"You can't exactly own a charity," Felicity began. "Think of it like a boat…" She faded out at Elena's incredulous do-*not*-continue look. "Erm, okay, forget that." Felicity then launched into a succinct explanation of it all—Harvey being scammed, Charles's blackmail, and Rosalind's deal.

"So let me get this straight. Your choices were: One, going to the police, sparking a public mess. Two, us acquiring a charity and I get my money back. Or three, the charity closing down to avoid a scandal but I still get my money back…minus the headache of homeless animals, filling boards, and related paperwork to worry about?"

"Yes, Elena."

"And you chose option two. We get stuck with a charity." Elena's eyes were sharp. "Is that what I'm hearing?"

"Yes." Felicity stared right back at her. "Hundreds of people and their pets would be affected if Living Ruff was shut down. And you wouldn't have donated if you didn't think they were a worthy charity. Now it's *your* worthy charity. I can list all the tax benefits, too, if you like."

Elena held up her hand. "That won't be necessary." She exhaled. "Well, you don't do things by half, do you?"

"Elena?"

"Did it occur to you to ask me before you made this rather monumental decision?"

"No." Felicity bit her lip. "You left it to me. You asked for nuance. You told me to be thorough and then decide without worrying about what you might think. This is the right decision. I know it is. But if I'm wrong, so what? We can hand it off to someone else later, if you don't like how it's working out. Or let it carry on unassisted entirely."

Elena leaned back in her chair. "Did it not occur to you how much work this might entail for us, a profit-based organization taking on a nonprofit? Whether it would impact the bottom line if the charity takes a loss and so on?"

"I did look into it. And there's no real work for us at all. They're separate entities. They'd file their own taxes. Their debt stays theirs. Their gains are theirs, too. It's entirely hands-off for Bartell Corp. At most we find them a new board and leave them to it. Check in on them every now and then; give them occasional donations perhaps, if you're feeling generous," Felicity suggested with a small smile. "But really, this isn't like taking over a business at all."

Elena's lips twitched. "Yes. Apparently, that's what Bartell Corp's chairman concluded, too, after he sat down in a panic this morning with the accounts team. Although it took them a lot longer than fifteen seconds to nutshell why."

That felt a lot like a compliment, but Felicity pursed her lips, wondering where this was going. "So what's the problem?"

"I'm not sure I said there was a problem. I was just curious how much thought you had put into this before saddling us with a fringe charity."

"Saddling us? Fringe charity?" Felicity eyed her curiously. "Elena, it's a charity you put $1.4 million of your own money into. If you didn't like it, you wouldn't have. I factored that into my calculations, too. Approval from Bartell Corp's chief operating officer."

"Did you now," Elena said, voice silky. "Well, it seems you've thought of everything."

Had she? Felicity thought she had, but doubts tumbled in. She ran through the variables again quickly in her head before reaching the same conclusion. "I have. Yes." She slid the NDA and Charles's community service papers onto Elena's desk. "And if I've erred, just tell Rosalind Stone you can't sign these papers and back out now."

Elena templed her fingers. "That won't be necessary." She tilted her head slightly. "Do you know why I gave you this assignment, Felicity?"

"You wanted to know where your money went." Hadn't that been what she'd said? "And you were testing me. You had questions about my ability to be subtle and nuanced and about how I handled myself while out of my comfort zone."

"Yes." Elena said thoughtfully. "But that's not all there is to it. I had one more reason. A more important one."

"Oh. Right. Yes." Felicity nodded. "I wasn't going to mention it, but I know it was a news story Maddie wrote that inspired you to donate. If she'd endorsed a charity that was corrupt, it would make her look bad. And she's your…friend." Felicity still had to swallow on that word. "So there's that."

"You really thought this was about protecting Madeleine's career?" Elena asked in surprise. "She's an award-winning reporter. She won the scoop of the decade. Her career is in no danger. Besides, if an organization she's written about does something bad later, it's hardly the reporter's fault."

"But I thought"—Felicity licked her lips anxiously—"you might worry she'd get heat for it. Mocked or something."

"Never entered my mind." Elena regarded her. "No, that's not why I sent you to look into my donation."

"Then why?"

"I had rather hoped with that fine mind of yours you might have figured it out by now." Elena smiled her most cryptic smile. "When you do work it out, come talk to me. I'm quite serious about this. I suspect that will be quite the discussion."

What does that even mean?

Felicity stared at her.

"Okay." Elena picked up a pen. "Living Ruff. Who do you have in mind as director? Rosalind made it very clear in her communications it has to be us to choose, not her. Fresh faces and so forth. You've worked with their people. It's your call. Or should Living Ruff advertise externally?"

Felicity thought for a moment. The charity needed someone good, intelligent, who understood both animals and the homeless, and would fight hard for Living Ruff. "I know the perfect choice: their head vet—

Sandy Cooper. She's been there longest and is very passionate about the clients and animals and has a track record of fighting for their rights against the mayor. She'd be an excellent spokeswoman and ideal to step up."

"A vet? Running the whole thing? Are you sure?" Elena frowned. "There's so much admin involved in being a charity director. Not much time for looking at animals."

"She can outsource what she doesn't want to handle to their receptionist, who is already excellent at that side of things. Dr. Cooper can make time to look at animals whenever she wants. Bottom line is, she's smart, dedicated, competent, and decent. Dr. Cooper deserves the promotion. She's really… excellent." Felicity felt her cheeks warm up at that.

Elena regarded her for a moment. "She seems to have made quite an impression."

Felicity folded her arms. "Yes."

"Well, all right, then. Inform the woman of her promotion, get our publicity department to prep a press release about our newest charitable venture to go out once your vet has agreed, and let's get this finalized."

"You'll have to sign the paperwork," Felicity said.

"No, this is your baby"—Elena pushed a pen and the papers over the desk—"so you get to sign off on it. Congratulations on your first completed deal as acting COO of Bartell Corp."

Oh, that felt nice. Felicity sat up taller. "Thank you."

Elena smiled. "I see you're also better at taking a compliment. Progress at last?"

Felicity had no clue what to say to that. Which was probably just as well.

At her silence, her utterly mystifying boss just laughed.

❖

Felicity straightened the champagne bottle in the ice bucket and then fluffed a Parisian cushion on her couch. She couldn't wait to share the promotion news. Cooper had just been buzzed in from downstairs, so she'd be here any second.

It had been frantic all day at work since the paperwork had been signed. Felicity had also spent half a day with the publicity department coming up with creative quotes explaining why a media company was suddenly involved in animal welfare. Then there was Felicity's ongoing confusion trying to figure out Elena's other reason for having sent her to Living Ruff.

She pushed aside that and all the rest of the day's stress. Tonight was a celebration.

Felicity straightened the collar on her Isabel Marant blouse and checked her hair was still perfect. It fell in long blonde cascades to just above her shoulder blades. It was so rare she didn't have it pinned up. But this was a special occasion, and she trusted there would be a lot of opportunity very soon for an appreciative Cooper to run her fingers through it.

At a knock on the door, Felicity ran to answer it before feeling a bit ridiculous. She slowed to a power walk, then opened the door.

What a welcome sight. Her entire body seemed to exhale in delight.

Cooper's broad shoulders were encased in a tight black T-shirt under a black leather jacket and snug-fitting pale blue jeans. Then there was the cheeky grin.

Oh yes.

Cooper leaned in to drop a roguish peck on Felicity's cheek that promised a lot more, then strode past, her tight jeans impressive against her ample thighs and ass. Words were rapidly failing Felicity.

"Hey, uptown girl," Cooper teased. "This is a nice surprise. I was about to spend a pathetic Saturday night all by my lonesome. Normally I'd chill with my nan, but she's having an early night. And my friends are busy. So… what's a poor girl to do?"

Felicity smiled, then waved her to the couch. "Have a seat. Let's see if I can make you feel a little less lonely."

Cooper's grin was even wider. "Mm. Yes, please."

Okay, this was going well. Felicity's body announced an upgrade from delighted to aroused.

"I have news," she said, closing the door and following Cooper to the couch. Felicity chose the cushion beside her and was pleased when Cooper's hand casually shifted to rest on her thigh.

"I hope this *isn't* where you tell me you've wrapped up the investigation and we're now done," Cooper said slowly. "What's your news?"

"Well, about that. Yes, my investigation is done. But our working relationship has been extended. Indefinitely."

Cooper's eyebrows shot up. "What?"

"Rosalind Stone has decided to part ways with her charity and take everyone with her that she appointed to the Living Ruff board. She asked me if Bartell Corp would be involved in the charity in her place. We worked out the details today. Bartell Corp will be supplying any board assistance necessary for the charity, and we're tossing in free tech support, too. So you can expect some state-of-the-art computers at Living Ruff come next week." She beamed.

"I think I'm going to need to sit down."

"You already are," Felicity pointed out.

"Oh." Cooper blinked. "Wait. A few days ago, you said we could be together only for as long as you were involved with Living Ruff. Sounds like you'll be involved for a long, long time."

Felicity hadn't thought of that. But what an idea…

"So does this mean you might be open to extending things?" Cooper gave Felicity a teasing poke in the thigh. "Hell, I've heard of some sneaky ways to get a girl to date you, but this takes the cake."

Felicity's mouth fell open. "Wait. I didn't acquire Rosalind's foundation just so we could start dating."

"I was kidding. But I mean…would you be interested in more?" Hope shot across Cooper's face.

"You'd like that? Us as a regular thing?" Now that she was thinking about it, Felicity's body gave a pleased little hum.

"I'd like us to not be a *thing* at all," Cooper said adamantly. "I want us to be a couple." Her expression became earnest. "I know I haven't known you long, so I don't know if you prefer casual relationships. But I don't usually go for that. I like to take my time to really get to know a woman and then see if it's a relationship with legs."

"I don't usually do relationships at all. No time. And my last one where I really thought maybe—" She pressed her lips together. "Phillip said I wasn't worth it." Felicity folded her arms. "It's hard for me at the best of times and then to find out I'm just not… The worst part was, I thought we were so compatible. We had so much in common."

"And then there's us?" Cooper asked gently. "Is that what you mean? Look, I know we're opposite in many ways, but the heart doesn't care about that. I really missed you when I didn't see you for a day. You say these ridiculous, over-the-top things that make me laugh."

"I *do* mean most of those ridiculous things, you know." Felicity's lips twitched. "Or some of them. All right, it mainly depends on whether I want someone to go away and stop bothering me or not."

Cooper burst into laughter. "See? You're hilarious."

"Truly, that usually isn't my aim." Felicity smiled. "But I'm glad you think so."

"I do. Phillip was an idiot. See, you're pretty impressive to me. I know my weaknesses. I can dither on things. I take forever to organize my stuff and work out what I want to do. I love how you just focus on your goals and go for it. I love how you casually loaded up a heat-seeking missile at the mayor and did it with ease. Because you were on a mission."

Felicity smiled. "That was a good day, wasn't it?"

"It really was. You know those bills are now on the mayor's desk? They landed there yesterday morning."

"Oh?" Felicity straightened. "What did the mayor do?"

"He didn't veto, Felicity." Cooper's eyes were bright. "He didn't veto, and you did that!" She leaned over and kissed her soundly. "So how about it? You and me, giving this relationship idea a shake?"

"I—" Felicity's heart thudded. Her hands were sweaty and… Good lord, did she have a medical condition?

Cooper's face fell. "Or not."

"No! I was just not expecting this. I had other things to talk to you about and… Well, my hands are sweating. They never sweat!" She gave Cooper a startled look. "*You* did this to me! And"—she gave her a fake outraged look—"you keep making me miss you!"

Cooper laughed. "Poor you. What next? Wanting me in your bed all the time?"

Well, didn't that sound delicious? Felicity smiled. "That has merits, you know. But my other concerns, the one I raised when we were out to dinner at that pizza place, aren't frivolous. I'm about to have a highly visible job. I'll be watched to see if I'm worthy of replacing Elena."

"And may I repeat the gist of what I said that night: even highly visible, driven boss ladies need a safe space. Someone to talk to. Someone who makes life less stressful."

A less stressful life sounded like a win. "That sounds good."

With a grin, Cooper said, "So can we make a go of this? I promise I'll bring Brittany over for cuddles if you say yes."

"Really?" Enthusiasm infused Felicity's voice before she could stop it. "Oh, I mean—"

"Save it. You're such a faker." Cooper laughed.

Felicity chuckled. "Fine. Yes. I'd love that. And I can safely say you will be like no one I've ever dated before."

"Oh, I bet. Only fancy lovers for you, right? Classy types who know what all the forks are for at dinner parties?" She smirked.

"More like…" Felicity ran a finger down Cooper's face, loving the broad planes of it, so strong and smooth. "I only date lawyers. Of a regular size and with regular hobbies. Not sun-blotting Amazons who look after homeless people's animals."

Her hand dropped to Cooper's shoulder, and she ran it down the lapels of her leather jacket over the swell of her bust until it rested on her rounded stomach. "I appreciate so many things about you that are the polar opposite of everything I thought I liked. You rewrote my rules. You made me forget every slick, sharp-tongued lawyer I've ever laid a finger on. All I seem to want is to have you toss me into bed. Or hell, toss me anywhere."

"I've noticed you like that." Cooper grinned again. "Well, I do have the shoulders for it."

"You really do." Felicity lifted her hand to trace the broad expanse in question. "But before we get carried away, I have to tell you the rest of the news. Why Bartell Corp's now permanently involved with your charity in the first place."

"Oh right." Cooper sat up. "Yes. God, I can't believe I forgot to ask. Why'd Rosalind throw in the towel? Has she decided to retire?"

"No. She feels she has no choice but to distance herself. She's had to fire Harvey. That missing money of Elena's was scammed out of him by Charles in a fake merchandising deal."

"Oh, my God." Cooper's eyes widened.

"To save the charity, Rosalind's removing him, herself, and anyone else directly linked to her at Living Ruff in case the scandal ever comes out. Since I already know the truth, she thought it would be the least problematic path for Bartell Corp to be part of the solution. And it helps that Elena already likes what Living Ruff stands for."

"Poor Harvey. He loved our charity." Cooper slumped. "And fuck Charles for that. I hope he rots in prison."

"He's not going to prison."

Cooper's eyes flashed. "Tell me he's not getting away with this!"

"Not at all. The bottom line is, he's lost his sporting goods store and is about to be very miserable for the next year and nine months managing a halfway house. Please be aware an NDA applies and you can't tell anyone this."

"There's an NDA?" Cooper frowned. "Why tell me at all, then?"

"Because as Living Ruff's new director, where and why Harvey disappeared is information pertinent to your job." Felicity waited, trying to suppress the smile she couldn't wait to let out.

"I— What?" Cooper stared at Felicity for a moment. "Director?" Then her gaze roamed until it finally landed on the bottle on ice. "You bought champagne?"

"To toast your promotion. I was asked to choose the new director for Living Ruff. The new board will sign off on whomever I choose." She looked pointedly at Cooper.

"*Me?*" she squeaked.

"Of course *you*! I wanted someone I know and trust and who has the best interests of Living Ruff at heart. It's now yours. And by the way, Elena is happy to reinvest $1.4 million with you. She thinks your vet tech scheme sounds excellent. You can finally do it. Your program can go ahead!"

Cooper's expression fell. Her hand slid off Felicity's thigh.

"Why aren't you happy?" Felicity asked in dismay.

"I thought you knew me better than this. Haven't we talked about this? What on earth gave you the idea I'd be a good director? I can't even organize my own home office! And you know that from personal experience."

"Yes, I'm fully aware, but you have Mrs. Brooks. Didn't you say she did all that for Harvey? That the office only ran thanks to her doing the books and organizing everything for him? So let her keep doing that. You can do everything else, right?"

"The job should go to someone who doesn't have to outsource it to someone more capable. It should go to someone *already* good at it! Like Mrs. Brooks! Did it never even enter your head how brilliant she'd be as a director? She already knows the charity, has the practical knowledge as a trained vet tech, does the books, takes no crap from people, and is loved by everyone locally. Why wasn't *she* the logical choice? Did you overlook her because you see her as just some middle-aged Black lady working the phones? Invisible and forgettable, right?"

Felicity's eyes widened. "Don't you dare!"

"Well, then, why?"

"Because *she's* not who I've been working with!" Felicity said in exasperation. "It's you I've been watching up close, and I've seen all the ways you fight for your clients. I've heard from Deedra how you tried often to take on the mayor and fought injustice. You'd make such a good spokeswoman. You're also decent and smart, and I admire your passion and work ethic, so *of course* I thought of you first. Why are you trying so hard to get me to give away your promotion? It isn't a dirty word!"

"I thought you understood," Cooper said in frustration. "Now I wonder if you've listened to anything I've said about my job. I love what I do! I love our clients and their animals."

"I know that," Felicity said in confusion.

"And I don't want to be promoted and forced to do anything other than what I'm doing. I'd go stark raving mad doing some boring desk job, even if I shoved the paperwork onto Mrs. Brooks. That's not me."

"You're forgetting that as the boss *you* get to decide what you do," Felicity said. "That's the reason I suggested you. I knew you could work into your schedule doing rounds or clinic days. You could choose your mix of vet work and director work exactly the way you like it best."

"I don't want to *work in* anything or *mix* anything. I love my job exactly as it is."

"But with the promotion you'd have the power to bring in any programs you want." Felicity's voice was rising in panic. This was going so horribly wrong. "How is that a bad thing?"

"Power? Me? I don't need power. I don't need a fancy title. I'm not you, Felicity. I don't need to rule the world. Don't you get that about me yet? Being a vet and only that makes me happy. If you don't understand that not everyone wants what *you* want in life, then you're not the woman for me."

"Cooper," Felicity ground out. *Why am I shaking?* "I did this for you. I thought this would give you the best of both worlds. It wasn't about me or what I aspire to; it's about giving you all these options."

"And I keep telling you that I'm happy with the options I have. I'm proud of what I do and who I am exactly as I am. And I'm sorry you can't see that. The fact that I have to keep saying this means you don't know me at all."

"No!" Felicity couldn't bear this. There was a roaring in her ears, her blood rushing through her body, frustration and pain dueling for attention. "I'm proud of what you do, too. I just wanted you to have more. That's all."

"I don't want more." Cooper blew out a frustrated breath. "You're so proud of me, you're trying to change me. Why? Is it really because you thought I'd want to be able to bring in new programs? Or was it because you'd relate to me more if I was a manager, too? I'd be more acceptable in your circles if we were dating?"

Felicity felt as if she'd been struck. "Of course not," she protested. "I chose you for director before you even brought up the idea of us having a relationship."

"So it's because you'd understand and relate to me more as a manager than a vet."

Gah. Felicity was so bad at this. It wasn't just lack of practice. She never could argue well with someone she was intimate with. It was as though she knew deep down she couldn't withstand the power they had to really hurt her. So she retreated.

Felicity felt so tired when she said, "It's not that, either. It's not about me. I keep saying, I got you the promotion for *you*. It was all about you."

"Maybe you believe that." Cooper's expression was closed. "But I remember what you said about your mother and sister. I thought you were just trying to be funny and dramatic at the time. You said, 'My stupefyingly unambitious mother and sister lower their sights at every opportunity.' Felicity, you're someone who needs people to be ambitious or you don't respect them. And I hate to say this, I'm not that and never will be."

"You don't understand. With my family, I want them to be their best selves. They could do so much more. They've thrown away their intelligence and skills to chase these random side ventures. But even so, I do respect them as people."

"Do you?"

"Yes!"

"As people. But not for choosing happiness over career. You don't respect that," Cooper concluded quietly. "You judge the hell out of them for that."

Well. She couldn't lie and say she thought their choices were in any way smart, so she stared mulishly instead.

"Felicity?" Cooper's voice became kind. "I think you truly don't understand what it's like to be someone without ambition. It's so alien to you that you *need* people that you like to be ambitious or you can't relate to them, and it hurts your brain. Ambition is what drives you, what feeds you. It's the air you breathe."

"There's nothing wrong with that," Felicity said defensively. "I'm not hurting anyone being like this."

"No?" Cooper's gaze was so sad as it scraped all over her. "What about yourself?"

For God's sake, I'm not hurting myself. And she didn't like that look one bit. Felicity sank lower in her couch. She could feel the corners of herself pulling in, wrapping her up, trying to protect her. Cooper was going to leave her now. Felicity braced herself but didn't feel ready. Ironic. You'd think she'd be better at this with all the practice she'd had in being left. And it wasn't as if she and Cooper were ever really together. They barely knew each other. A week was nothing.

It's just… It felt like they were so much more. Down deep where Felicity sometimes let herself explore, even though that seemed dangerous and risky, she could feel the connection she had with Cooper tugging at her.

Anyway, it was over now. She waited. Idly, from somewhere far away, she wondered if Cooper understood what she'd done. How she'd achieved the rather astonishing feat of making Felicity care. She forced her expression to bland and still as Cooper fixed a gaze upon her.

"I think you try to emulate your boss," Cooper said. "You think Elena is ice-cold and focused and into her career only, so you try to be exactly the same."

The last thing Felicity had expected was Cooper bringing her boss into this.

Cooper continued, "Yet Elena's given up the biggest title in the business world to accept a smaller one in a city that's not her own. Ask yourself why."

"Don't mention Maddie again," Felicity grumbled. "That's just not a thing."

"Maddie or not, she's clearly chasing her happiness. She's thrown everything away for her fashion magazines. Isn't that what you told me? She'll just be editing five *Style International* magazines out of her whole media empire. Why? Because she's decided those five magazines give her everything she's seeking, and the trade-off, the loss of power and position, are worth it for her."

Felicity stilled.

"You don't understand her decision, do you? It's another random side venture to you, like your mother's and sister's choices: baffling."

Accurate.

"Because you don't understand people making the unambitious choice. Not even people you emulate, like Elena Bartell."

Felicity surreptitiously wiped her hands down her pants, uncomfortable beyond measure.

"And then there's you," Cooper said, tone gentle. "Even with your beloved mentor's example right under your nose, what are you doing? Chasing ambition. *Only* ambition. Even if it harms your relationships." Cooper shook her head. "I can see we're incompatible."

She leaned in and kissed Felicity's cheek. It felt like a mocking parody of the sweet kiss she'd received when Cooper arrived.

"I'm going now," Cooper said.

Of course she is. Everyone leaves.

Cooper rose. "It's probably better this way, working out we'd be a train wreck together before we begin," Cooper said, eyes dark. "But call me if you discover there's more to life than your career." She turned to go, then paused. "Oh, and appoint Mrs. Brooks director as she deserves. It'll save us all a lot of trouble."

She straightened and was gone before Felicity had even registered her words.

Long after Cooper had closed the door with a soft click, Felicity stared at the bottle of champagne and wondered how everything had gone so very wrong.

Chapter 15
Alone

FELICITY DIDN'T NEED ANYONE, THANK you very much. Her fulfilling career was all she needed to be content, and she was quite sure to remind herself of that fact as the days slowly bled into weeks.

Elena finished training Felicity and completed her own transition work ahead of permanently shifting to Australia. She told Felicity she would be staying on in New York for a few more weeks to finalize things, but her office duties were over. This was her last day at work.

Elena called Felicity into her office and gave her a slow, warm smile.

"It's all yours now," she said. "Bartell Corp. I'd like to hang on to my office for whenever I'm back in town, though. If you're okay staying in your own office?"

Oh, thank God. "Yes, of course."

Elena smiled and patted the armrest on her designer executive chair. "I will, however, bequeath you my favorite chair. I'd thought about having it sent over to Sydney, but then I decided, why deprive you of the pleasure of enjoying one of the perks of your new position?"

"That's very thoughtful," Felicity said. She tried to muster a smile.

Elena frowned. "What is it? I thought this was the culmination of all your hopes and dreams. Shouldn't you be giddy with glee or whatever the Felicity Simmons version of that looks like?"

Felicity attempted to improve on her smile. She probably looked constipated.

"Okay, what is it? Really." Elena leaned in. "Is there some problem with the business somewhere?"

"No!" Felicity was dismayed that Elena would even ask. As if she'd allow that on her watch without addressing it immediately.

"Some new acquisition giving you heartburn? Or perhaps some lawyer being especially obnoxious? You have my full permission to terminate or accelerate any deal you like if they're being bastards." Elena sounded sincere.

"Nothing like that," Felicity said quickly, although she warmed at the confidence Elena had in her.

"Is it…personal, then?" Elena asked delicately. One eyebrow slid up… slowly…as if she wasn't quite sure whether this was a question she wanted to ask.

To Felicity's horror, her cheeks reddened. "I— Not anymore."

"Are you still pining for that Sydney lawyer? What was his name? Phillip?"

"You knew about him?"

"Haven't you worked out by now that I have truly excellent hearing? There is little that I miss in the office."

Felicity slumped. "He dumped me when he found out I was moving permanently back to New York. I don't…miss him."

"Ah." Elena glanced down at her fingers and her mouth opened, but no words came out, as if she wasn't sure whether to say something.

"I'm fine, really," Felicity rushed in. "Give it no more thought. I promise I'll never let my personal emotions interfere with business."

Elena's head snapped up. "Well, that's a very disturbing thought. I want your head to rule most of the time. But listen to your heart, too, on occasion. I don't want an unfeeling automaton running Bartell Corp."

"I— No, of course not. That is…" Felicity had no clue what to say. She and Elena had never had the sort of relationship that involved sharing things. She paused. And *that's* why she'd never been close to her, not in the way Maddie was. Maddie, who just blurted out things and shared her emotions with an open heart.

That was it, wasn't it? Sharing anything, especially vulnerabilities that could be used against you later, was a foreign concept to Felicity. You had to keep up your walls or people could find your weaknesses. Except…Elena wasn't looking for her weaknesses. In her own reserved, walls-up way, she was trying to help.

Felicity hesitated and then admitted, "I made a mistake."

"Go on."

"The vet I wanted to make director of Living Ruff didn't want the promotion."

Elena frowned. "Yes, I did wonder if that might be an issue. Vets tend to want to stay hands on, unless they're particularly ambitious. But you don't join a charity if you're in any way ambitious, so…"

Well, that was a good point. Felicity sighed. "I thought she'd be pleased. Instead, she was very angry when I didn't understand why she didn't want the promotion. She wants nothing more to do with me, either." Felicity looked away, cheeks flaming hot, beyond embarrassed by how pathetic she must look to someone she idolized.

The confusion on Elena's face suddenly cleared, replaced with surprise. Then understanding. "Felicity," she said carefully, "by any chance were you…romantically involved with this vet?"

"No… Well… Involved might be too strong a word." Felicity could rent herself out as a space heater at this rate. "We were intimate, though. A few times." She couldn't bring herself to look up.

"And she…matters to you, this woman? I mean compared to Phillip, the lawyer you don't miss."

"She…" Felicity stopped again as she tried to process her thoughts. "She matters."

God. The admission felt so baring. Felicity wanted to curl up in a tight ball and never look at her boss again. What must Elena think of her? How wretched must she sound? But it was a relief in a way, too. She had no friends to turn to who could help her make sense of this mess.

"Felicity." Elena's voice was low and kind.

She looked up. "Yes?"

"It's okay."

It was? How did she figure? Wait. *What* was okay?

"It's okay to let someone in if they matter to you. And it's not the end of the world if they don't share your ambition. Differences can be the spice of life." She smiled then.

Suddenly it struck her how different Elena looked. Felicity had been trying to put her finger on it for weeks, but it was right there. Elena had such a lightness to her now. Gone were the constant stress lines and down-turned corners of her mouth as she flayed incompetent employees. Elena had always had a bit of darkness to her. It was a little compelling, a little frightening. But now she seemed…*settled?*

"What's happened to you?" Felicity blurted.

"You really don't know?" Elena asked, surprise in her eyes.

No denial. Felicity stared at her, completely perplexed.

"Well, how interesting. I can see that you don't." A ghost of a smile danced across her lips. "I'll let you work it out for yourself. Anyway, right now I think it's best if we focus on you. Listen to someone who once only ever cared about showing *CQ* magazine that they'd made a terrible mistake not appointing me its editor. Everything I built"—she waved around the office—"was to that end. I made sure nothing stood in my way. Not even my own weaknesses."

Weaknesses? Elena had no discernible weaknesses that Felicity could see. Unless you counted her appalling taste in men. She shot her a baffled look.

"I can see you debating whether to tell me I have no weaknesses." Amusement danced in Elena's eyes. "Of course I do, even if I don't advertise them. Why do you think I named myself COO, not CEO, when I set up Bartell Corp?"

Felicity blinked. She'd heard Elena's standard answer on this many times. "You like to focus on what inspires you and outsource the rest. So you structured your company so that the CEO would handle all the financials, day-to-day running, paperwork, and minor boardroom matters, freeing you up for the hands-on work, takeovers, and policy direction."

"That's the official line. But it's not *entirely* true." Elena gave a small, rueful smile. "Felicity, I went from an editorial job on a fashion magazine to having my own corporation in mere months. I had only a rudimentary knowledge about running a business in those days. My knowledge gaps were vast. So everything I did, including setting aside my ego to appoint someone else CEO—someone experienced and skilled where I wasn't—was about ensuring my victory. I was determined to prove *CQ* wrong about overlooking me, no matter the cost."

"And you sure showed them," Felicity said with a grim nod. "Good. They deserved to have their stupid noses rubbed in it."

Elena's eyes sparkled. "Your enthusiastic support is appreciated. And yes, for a long time, I felt they deserved the constant reminder of their foolishness. But one day, not too long ago, I realized something: they don't think of me at all. All of my empire building has been to prove something to people who've long since moved on. Well, except *CQ's* editor, of course. Lecoq does deserve a little nose-rubbing; she's still so obnoxious about having the job I should have had."

"She really is," Felicity agreed with an adamant nod.

Elena laughed again, and Felicity was struck by how rarely she'd been privy to this side of her. *She laughs more.*

"I feel like in some ways I've let you down," Elena said, expression becoming serious. "I haven't been modeling a very well-rounded boss for you to learn from all these years. But I hope in recent weeks you've come to understand that being a leader is more than just carrying on like an ice-breathing dragon waving your power around. I hope you see now that it's about nuance, too. In fact, it's almost all nuance, if you really look at what good leadership is."

Felicity nodded. "I'm beginning to see that."

"Which brings me back to your vet. She means something to you. Tell me, is it just pride that prevents you from being with her now?"

"She thinks all I'm interested in is ambition."

"And are you?"

"No!" Felicity shot back instantly. She gasped. "No," she repeated, realizing that actually felt true. Since when? Half an hour ago she'd been convincing herself of the opposite.

"Then it seems to me you have a choice. Show her she's wrong about you. Or do absolutely nothing. Those are your options. But understand that if you want to know what your life will be like in ten years, change nothing now."

In ten years, Felicity could see herself still as acting COO. Hell, maybe even actual COO, if Elena was feeling benevolent and formalized the position. And...and— What else? Lonely nights watching Netflix, night after night, remembering a time when an amazing woman had been in her arms.

"Think about it. But remember, the only person you have to impress here is you," Elena said. "I'm already impressed, Felicity. You understand that, don't you? I would never have given you the keys to my empire otherwise. But now it's up to you to find your own path. Sometimes that means admitting your weaknesses and deciphering what makes you better. Because it's not just about winning. Anyone can win if they care about little else. It's about determining what makes you happiest...then pursuing it."

Felicity nodded slowly, even as part of her brain recoiled from the unexpected compliment. She'd pick it apart later. "I can do that."

"Can you? You know, it took me a long time to even recognize what happiness looked like. And then..." She stopped, giving Felicity an appraising look. "Well, a story for another day. As for now, I have to go. Madeleine has decided I need to see some artsy new Jean-Claude Badour movie without which my life will be incomplete."

"Seriously?"

"Yes. *Eight Little Pieces*. It sounds positively dreary, but I can't have an incomplete life now, can I? Perish the thought. All right." Elena rose, pivoting her now-vacated executive chair Felicity's way. "This and everything it stands for is now yours. Use it wisely. And remember, every now and then, listen to your heart as well as your head. You might be surprised at what you find. All right?"

"Yes."

"Good." With eyes twinkling, Elena added, "We're done."

Chapter 16
What Lies Below

FELICITY WAS AT A LOSS after Elena left the office. It felt upside down to be told happiness was the answer, not ambition, after a lifetime of following the latter. But one truth she knew was that Elena tended to be right on most things. That only made this feeling even more unsettling.

She picked over their conversation later that night as she cradled Loki in her lap, stroking beautiful white fur. She told herself she'd simply borrowed the kitten, much as one would a library book. The animal would be returned shortly, but for now the therapeutic purring was doing wonders for her seesawing mental state.

Felicity apparently had her boss's approval now. That felt…incredible. Her gaze drifted to her apartment's impressive view. Maybe she'd had the approval for a long time and never noticed. She had never made partner in her law firm, her first ambition. But she'd made it to the very top of the world's premier media corporation. What was left to do? Who was she trying to impress now, if not her father, herself, or Elena? What ambition came next?

Obviously, her immediate goal was to keep Bartell Corp running smoothly, but Elena had set so many systems and processes in place to ensure that would happen with or without her presence that all Felicity was really doing was resting her hand on the tiller.

It was revelatory to hear Elena admit she'd only built up her corporation out of spite. That sense of "I'll show you." Felicity related to that a little too well. She could admit her lawyer dreams had only been to prove to her father she was worthy. When his indifference threatened to overwhelm her, she'd gone all in, working even harder to impress him. And then the bastard had died on her before he'd uttered a single "well done."

So she'd just kept on doing what she always had—climbing ever higher, pushing away anyone and anything impeding her progress. But now even Elena Bartell had sat her down and told her that she'd already been where Felicity was, had looked around from the top of the world, and discovered there was more to life. *Below.*

That was why Elena had made the astonishing decision to walk away from her vast empire and seek out her first love. True happiness for Elena had always been editing fashion. Now she'd thrown down the gauntlet to Felicity with a challenge to find her own contentment.

Felicity looked at Loki and wondered. *What is happiness to me? Do I even know?*

Obviously it was something *below*, too, because Felicity was already at the top, and she didn't feel even remotely happy.

She tried to think back over all the times she'd ever been truly happy.

Her first day at Bartell Corp was one. But that had more been pride in her own achievements.

Her sister, Heather, who worked in a small herbology place in Ann Arbor, was the picture of happiness. With her hippie husband and three exuberant children exactly like her, Heather's smile rarely wavered.

Heather often told Felicity to relax more. Felicity had also heard that often enough growing up from her mother, Louise.

Louise was a biophysicist who'd left her esteemed university professorship to manage the Leslie Science & Nature Center. As far as Felicity could tell, the organization oversaw programs to introduce snotty schoolchildren to animals and plants to encourage them to love nature and get involved in STEM subjects.

Last she'd heard, her mother was plotting ways for local businesses to adopt owls and lease reptiles for parties. Or was it the other way around? Leasing owls and adopting reptiles? Either way, it was an absurd waste of her mother's brilliant brain, a fact she reminded her of on a regular basis.

How could either her mother or sister actually be happy about their careers? Heather had soundly beaten Felicity in school on all subjects, and yet she was prodding plant leaves for a living. Which brought Felicity back to Cooper. Imagine being given the choice of running her own charity any way she saw fit and choosing the hand-up-dog-backside option.

Felicity shuddered. And yet…Cooper, too, claimed to be happy with her choice. A choice that had no power over the direction her job took, over the programs that were implemented, and where money was spent. It made no sense wanting that. Felicity needed something so incomprehensible explained in detail. She grabbed her phone, navigated to her favorited contacts, and she tapped the first icon.

"Darling!" came her mother's voice. "I was just saying to Heather how you never call and that you dodged my birthday call last month, too. But look!"

"Hi, Mom." Felicity rolled her eyes. She called plenty. First of the month without fail. And birthdays were overrated. "Have I phoned at a bad time?"

"Not at all. Just finalizing some sponsorship packs for a new corporation coming on board next week with donations. They've asked for the rocket kits for some team bonding exercise. Fastest team to launch it or some such thing. I hope they post the video. I'll be able to use it in marketing."

"Rockets?" Felicity frowned. "I thought you were all about the animals. Or trees?"

"We do all sorts of science projects. Don't you ever pay attention to the newsletters I send out?"

"No," Felicity said truthfully.

"That figures. Too busy helping your boss empire building? Does she own the whole media world yet?" Her mother sounded amused, at least.

"Almost," Felicity said amiably. "In a way, that's why I'm calling. I'm now acting chief operating officer of Bartell Corporation."

"Darling! How nice for you."

Felicity recognized that tone. Her mother had used it when Felicity had gotten a gold star on her artwork as a kid. It was as though her mother didn't see why it was important but knew it mattered to her. "It's a *huge* deal, Mom. Bartell Corp is now a billion-dollar corporation. I'm running it. My boss is moving to Sydney to run a side division there."

"Sydney? Oh, I've always wanted to go. The diversity of flora and fauna in Australia is quite something. You know, I really should have visited while you were there—"

"Mom!" Felicity said in frustration. "I'm trying to talk to you about something."

"Yes. I hear you. What's next, darling? CEO?"

"God, no!" Felicity shuddered at the thought. "I mean, COO is where the power is at my company."

"I see. Which means you've finally done it." Her mother's tone was more speculative now. "You've summited Everest. Is it everything you wished for?"

Well, that was the question, wasn't it? Felicity brooded on that silently for a moment.

"Ah. I see."

Felicity didn't like the sound of that. "It's great, *obviously*." That came out weird.

"Yes, it sounds *so* great," her mother said dryly. "All right, darling. What's wrong?"

"I'm trying to work out what makes me happy," Felicity admitted.

"That's a good question for you," her mother said earnestly, "and I'm glad you're finally asking it. I worried about you so much as a child. You were always so determined about everything. You weren't interested in having fun or getting into mischief or staying out late like other children. No, you were all about finding your focus and studying. And when your sister did better than you in school, you spent all your vacation time hitting the books to beat her."

"I did," Felicity said with satisfaction.

"And do you remember what happened then?"

Felicity paused. "No."

"You asked me for better books. For older reading ages. You wanted the next challenge, then the next, and the next."

"Right." She vaguely remembered that. It did explain how a ninth grader had a disturbingly high knowledge of biophysics for a while. Her mother's textbooks had been a distraction until the next challenge came along. "But it wasn't enough."

"No, darling. I discovered with you that nothing was ever enough. There has never been a more driven child on God's green earth, I'm quite sure."

"I suppose not. What's wrong with being driven?"

"Nothing at all, if it gets you what you want and that makes you happy. Which I suspect is why you're calling. You've finally climbed as high as you could. Hit the heavens and still aren't happy. And you want your mom to tell you why?"

"Okay. Why?" Felicity whispered.

"Because succeeding is nothing without people to share it with. Because the thing you don't have in your life is another person to be happy for you, too."

"Not everyone needs people. Hell, you're still single. And Dad was awful and left you." *Us,* she silently amended.

"You think me being without a romantic partner means I'm without people in my life? My staff are wonderful. My friends are such a blessed tonic to anything that ails me. Heather and her family are better pick-me-ups than any pills. I have my darling animals to warm my bed. I'm as content and happy as I can be right now. But if I did find someone new, that would be beautiful, too. Although it's a bit hard to meet a match at my age with the hours I work and being as round as a bowling ball." She cackled.

Felicity winced. Even though her mother was the one making the joke, one Felicity had repeated over the years, it no longer felt funny. Why would it? Felicity loved the softness, weight, and beauty of Cooper's body, how it felt to trace her curving stomach around to her thick thighs and feel that power and substantialness. Yet Felicity had spent her whole life side-eying people who didn't fit some arbitrary thin ideal. And she'd done it for such a ludicrous reason: because her *father* judged people for their weight.

Secondhand biases had to be the stupidest of them all. They were so thoughtless, so empty. They weren't even their owner's *own* considered, stupid opinion.

How pathetic. Felicity couldn't believe she'd never seen her sarcastic little commentary on her family for what it was before. "I'm sorry," she said.

"I dread to think what has prompted your first apology in twenty years." Amusement was clear in her mother's voice.

"I used to think I was *so* funny telling people I was escaping my genetics by being on a constant diet. I loved quoting your bowling-ball line as hilarious proof. Add to that the fact I've been trying to pretend for so long that I'm not from our family or our town, along with a whole host of other self-loathing drivel, and the truth is—I am."

"You are what, darling?" Her mother's voice was kind.

"I *am* your daughter. I *am* from Pinckney. And I *do* love you, and I truly don't want to be that shallow person who obsesses over what my family looks like. And, Mom, you look *fine*! You're a total catch."

Her mother laughed softly. "You do realize I don't care what anyone thinks about my looks. I'm me. People can take me or leave me, love me or not. I'm just who I am."

Whoa. Felicity's breath caught in wonder. Why couldn't she be more like her mother? She paused at that out-of-character thought.

"That's admirable, Mom. I wish the world was more like you. Right now I'm so tired of being embarrassed or afraid I'll be judged for my roots. I've been such an ass." She drew in a sharp breath. "An ashamed, cowardly ass. I promise I'll do better in the future."

"I appreciate the sentiment. Is this about your father?" her mother asked gently. "Every time you bring up our family genetics, career goals, or hometown, it always somehow comes back to him."

"It's always about Dad. Everything is. *And* it's about me. He left us, Mom," Felicity said flatly. "He left, and I was crushed, and until really recently I've always thought *we* were why. I believed our family was too embarrassing for him when he had perfect Tiffany to race after. Now I've started to wonder why I think that. Where did I come up with that idea? Or maybe I'm having a midlife crisis at thirty-seven!"

"Darling, I love that you're asking questions at long last. I often wished you would, but you always pushed the topic away."

"It hurt too much."

"And now?"

"Now the answers about what Dad did matter far more than any old wounds."

"I have my own thoughts, of course, but the scientist in me is most intrigued to hear if you've reached any conclusions."

"Okay." Felicity thought hard. "Now I think Dad leaving wasn't about us. He was just a cheating asshole who probably didn't even need an excuse to leave."

"Quite the hypothesis." Her mother drew in a breath. "And that's why you're re-evaluating all your old views about us?"

"Yes. So I'm sorry for all my criticism of you and for distancing myself from you and Heather. I do respect you both personally."

"Just personally?" Her mother's amused tone was back.

"It's the professionally I'm still struggling with. I just don't get it. That's why I wanted to call. For you to explain."

"It's one of those things people either understand or don't," her mother said. "Your father didn't get it either when I left my college job for one he perceived to be of less importance. I explained that I wanted to get to kids earlier, girls especially, and get them fired up and embracing STEM subjects. But he was scathing of my decision."

"Is…that why he left you?" Felicity held her breath. "He thought less of you?"

"Oh, sweetheart. You really think anyone would leave their whole family just because their spouse took a slightly less prestigious job?"

Felicity didn't know how to answer that. "I truly have no idea. Did he?"

"I see." Her mother sounded disappointed but not surprised.

Felicity said nothing, sensing there was more.

"Well, I think it's time you knew the truth," her mother finally said. "Your father didn't leave me. I told him to go. I'm sorry, darling. I know you adored him and I know you wanted him to stay, but I couldn't have that sort of influence raising our children."

Shock flooded her. "You made him leave? Why?" All this time she'd feared they weren't good enough, and it wasn't even his choice?

"Your beautiful little cat, Brave, needed an operation to get well—an expensive one. We had enough money. Oh, it would have been a little tight but not terrible. We'd have managed. Your father refused to *waste the money*, he called it. Worse, he went behind my back and had her put down to ensure I didn't use any of our savings on the operation. That's when I understood I hadn't married a compassionate man. I can't even look at someone who doesn't see a pet as a family member. I'd married a man who cared more about the cost of treatment than how it would break his little girl's heart."

"Oh." Felicity blinked back tears. "God, really?"

"Yes. Now do you see? I knew you looked up to him, so I never wanted your image of him shattered. But I can see now you've been re-examining some things. It seemed time."

"Right." Felicity wiped away her tears. "Yes."

"Are you okay?"

"Of course." She buried her fingers in Loki's fur. "I'm stronger these days. And as I said, he's still an asshole, just worse, now that I know. He was so indifferent when I met up with him in New York. I tried to show him everything I'd done, and he didn't care. And we were all cut out of the will. So my new highly scientific hypothesis is: once an asshole, always an asshole."

Her mother chuckled. "Well, far be it for me to disagree with science. So would you care to share why you're reassessing your life now, darling?" Alarm flooded her voice. "Has something happened? Please tell me you're not ill."

"What? Oh no. God, no. I'm just…work. I recently spent a week with the homeless and their animals, and you get to see what matters. You know, I met a woman just like me, and she's living on the street. All it came down to was bad luck, nothing else. I know I'm lucky. More than that, I'm privileged. You'd think with all my advantages, I'd be better than just merely managing at life."

"Which is where we came in. You asked what would make you happy. And I said you needed someone to share life with."

Felicity bit her lip. "What if…I had someone…someone who maybe would be happy to be with me and who might care about me… But what if…she doesn't have any ambition at all? Wouldn't that be too different a thing to deal with? Someone so far from who I am?"

"Did you say she?" Her mother's voice wasn't exactly surprised. "I wondered when you'd realize your childhood fascination with actresses might mean something else. How many posters did you have up of that Borg lady and Captain Janeway anyway?"

"Mom!" Felicity's cheeks grew warm. "Can we please focus?"

"Oh right. Of course. Sorry. And you know, whoever you date or love, it doesn't matter to me. I'd just be delighted to hear you're connecting with anyone. I admit I've been afraid you'd end up some lonely, bitter executive that everyone calls awful names."

Why did everyone assume that about her? Her neighbor had done the same thing! "Well, I'm not bitter," Felicity said with a small laugh. "The rest of it might be true. I don't know what they call me, but I suspect it's something rude."

Her mother chuckled. "All right, then. So in answer to your question, compatibility isn't about what people do for a living or seek in life. I can see you think it is. But it's about ethics. Do you connect morally and on the same basis with your social views? Do you respect each other and each other's choices? And for you that means, can you respect her even if she is only a…" Her mother paused. "You never said what your unambitious lady does."

"She's a veterinarian."

"Felicity!" Her mother's gasp was outraged. "You were judging someone who spent years of their life studying to help animals? Do you have any idea how hard it is to complete a vet course? How few places there are in the US? It's so competitive! How on earth can you claim she has no ambition? I'd guarantee she works harder at her hospital or clinic than most people. Oh…and the fact that she works with *animals*? How wonderful! I must meet her. We'd have so much to discuss. Where does she work?"

Great. Her mother had way more in common with Cooper than Felicity did. "She's head vet at a charity called Living Ruff New York. They work with the homeless and their pets."

Silence fell.

Then her mother drew in a sharp, low breath. "Felicity Helena Simmons, if you don't marry her, I will."

"What?" Felicity sputtered.

"That's one of the most impressive things you can do, work with the people and animals everyone ignores. She must be a compassionate, impressive woman."

"She is."

"And…is that why you think you're a poor match? It's not her lack of interest in doing a job you consider more respected but you think you're not compassionate enough for her?"

Felicity's heart was in her throat. Was *that* true? And if it was, what did that say about her? And what did it say about her for her mother to even ask the question? "You think I lack compassion?"

Silence greeted her.

"Mom?" Felicity asked in a small voice. "*Is* that what you think, too?"

"Darling, no. I remember how brokenhearted you were when Brave died. I do know you have compassion. You cried for months. You wouldn't even look at animals after that, you were so terrified your heart would be broken again. And I'm afraid, so very afraid that you've been too cautious about opening yourself up ever since. I've worried you'd never trust your heart to anyone after losing Brave and then your father in quick succession."

Felicity couldn't deny it. "It's been easier to get ahead having no attachments," she said quietly. "It's not all bad."

"I'm sure. But maybe it's time for you to consider that being attached to something or someone you love won't always end in pain. And maybe you don't need to find excuses to push away someone you might have a real connection with."

Was that what she'd done? Felicity frowned. Well. It was true she'd known Cooper loved being a vet and wanted to do nothing more with her life. She'd said so. And even knowing that, Felicity had up and decided she would push her into a promotion that dealt largely with the one thing she did badly: office work.

Was that her subconscious desperately putting a stop to things before they started? Or was she just being a bit blinkered, forgetting that not everyone wanted to climb ever higher in their jobs the way she did? Or a bit of both?

"I'm not sure how things blew up in my face," Felicity admitted. "I just hate that they did."

"Well, then, how about this: when you think of your woman, how does she make you feel?"

A smile stretched Felicity's lips. Then heat filled her. And delight at the thought of seeing her again. And curiosity about whatever cases she had seen. Anticipation of telling her about her day. "Good," she said. "Really good." Then came a twinge of pain that that was all over.

"So then what's the problem?"

"She's mad at me."

Her mother laughed. "I'm so very shocked that my abrasive daughter who says the bluntest nonsense to people has somehow offended a woman she fancies."

"Hey!" Felicity, however, couldn't stop the smile.

There was the sound of voices in the background, one Felicity recognized as her mother's assistant.

"Darling, I have to go in a second. Those rocket kits won't pack themselves. But let me just cut to the chase: congratulations on making it to the top of your little mountain. Sorry," her mother said before Felicity could object, "*enormous* mountain. And now you're there, you've discovered that all your happiness isn't just sitting there like a pot of gold. You're feeling empty because you have no one to share your success with. So go, find the woman who makes you feel 'good, really good,' make up to her for whatever idiocy you no doubt spouted that made her mad in the first place—"

"Wait. How do you know it was my fault?"

"Well, even if it wasn't, which is worse: being alone but right forever, or together and briefly wrong until you forget all about this?"

"Oh."

"But it *was* your fault because you think vets lack ambition. And frankly, that's ludicrous."

"Mom—"

"No, I won't hear another word about that. The woman's amazing and driven, end of story. Now then, my last advice, and this is most important…"

Felicity leaned in, listening intently.

"Invite her to Christmas. I just know I'll love her."

"Christmas! We haven't even known each other a month."

"So what? Anyone who can get you admitting you like them and they make you feel good has to be really special. You never said a word about how Phillip made you feel. It's telling. All right? 'Bye, darling! Love you!"

The phone went dead.

Well, then. Felicity sat back, feeling a little dazed. It seemed the two mentors she most respected in life, Elena and her mom, were in agreement.

There was also Rosalind Stone's parting bit of wisdom about hanging on to those rare people who don't crave money, power, or status, but who liked you for you. Her tally shifted to three votes.

Her mission was clear: she had to win back Dr. Sandy Cooper.

Felicity suddenly felt a burn of anticipation. She always was good when given a clear mission. And as it happened…hostile takeovers were her specialty.

Chapter 17
Wooing Sandy Cooper

FELICITY APPROACHED *THE WOOING OF Sandy Cooper* (an actual to-do list title in her planner) with all the care and diligence she would any other workplace mission.

She started by writing a letter. It was short and to the point, but she trusted it got her meaning across.

Dear Cooper,

I'm very sorry about our disagreement. I was wrong to impose my view of career success on you—even unintentionally—when it's clear you're happy where you are, doing what you're doing. I respect you and your vocation. I understand you had to be very dedicated to become a vet, and that is admirable.

I trust Mrs. Brooks has been filling her new role as director adequately. The promotion was unanimously approved by our board, which I'm sure you'll be pleased about.

I'll be in touch shortly on the topic of the former matter—our unfortunate disagreement—and making reparations in regards to that situation.

Yours sincerely,
Felicity Simmons

So sue her; Felicity would never win any prizes for romantic essays. She could picture her mother laughing and saying "'On the topic of the former matter' doesn't exactly scream 'I want to date you; you make me feel *good, really good*.'" But it was just an opening salvo. Declaring her objectives. Or in boardroom parlance, a notice of intention before setting down the agenda.

She waited a few days to ensure the letter had arrived and then enacted her next step.

Flowers. She'd caught enough feel-good movies in her time to know these were a prerequisite for a burgeoning romance. She called in her new personal assistant, Beatrice, and instructed her to buy a bunch of flowers and send them to Cooper's workplace.

"Um, Ms. Simmons, what kind?"

"Expensive ones," Felicity said. "Or…rare ones? Which means they'll be expensive anyway, I suppose."

"Yes, but…um, roses or…like, what color? What sentiment? Flowers have meanings, you see and I— Well, it'd help."

As if she were about to share her sentiment with an assistant the temp agency had produced at a moment's notice when Elena had fired the previous "inadequate" assistant on her way out the door.

"I can't be required to think of everything," Felicity said, caught off guard. "Use your initiative." She stopped and thought about Cooper. "The sentiment is appreciation. Er…well, affection. And I absolutely want them at Living Ruff within the hour."

The young woman scurried out with a slightly baffled but determined look on her face.

That done, Felicity decided wooing also needed some food. That's what people did, right? All the times she'd dated, men would pick her up and take her to restaurants. Eating commenced. Flirting was had. The deal was sealed.

But what was Cooper's favorite restaurant? Felicity had only dined out with her once—that pizza place—as well as ordering in meals a couple times. Her tastes were more than a little eclectic.

Before she could contemplate that in earnest, Felicity's phone rang, and she had to deal with Denver on a contract that should have been closed by now.

Five hours and one signed contract later, she rubbed her eyes and sighed. Okay. Back to her primary mission. She looked up a number and called.

"Oh! Ms. Simmons!" Mrs. Brooks said. "I didn't expect to hear from you. Thank you for my promotion! I couldn't believe it when I got that official letter. Cooper said it was all your doing."

"Did she, now." Trust Cooper to give away the credit.

"What a surprise, you being our boss of sorts. I didn't expect that!"

Boss? Explaining how Bartell Corp wasn't really involved directly and everything was independent was getting tedious. "Well, actually—"

Mrs. Brooks barreled on: "Now, don't worry. I'm all organized. And I've green-lit the development plan Dr. Cooper came up with for training suitable clients into being vet techs."

"Well, that's good." Felicity answered. She wondered how to raise the more pressing issue. "On the topic of Cooper, what does she eat?"

Silence fell.

Oh, okay that sounded weird. Food, she eats food, obviously. "I mean, preferred dining choices. As in restaurants."

"I—" Mrs. Brooks sounded perplexed. "Why?"

"I'm planning to take her out." Felicity saw no reason to lie. If they were to become a couple, the truth would be known soon enough. "Romantically speaking."

"I see." There was a strangled sound as if she was trying not to laugh.

Felicity frowned. Why was her choosing to date Cooper hilarious?

"By any chance, are you responsible for that rather large bunch of flowers Cooper received earlier today?"

Felicity brightened. Oh good, she'd gotten them. "Yes."

"Oh, honey."

Okay, that did not sound good. "What?" Felicity asked waspishly.

"It was the most enormous bunch I've ever seen. Must have cost a packet." Mrs. Brooks seemed impressed. "I know my flowers, I can tell you that. I used to love arranging them as a girl, and I'd tell my mother—"

"Mrs. Brooks, could you please get to the point?"

"Oh yes. Right. So there was a big bunch of fluffy yellow tansies, white snapdragons, and yellow carnations."

White and yellow? Well, that didn't sound too terrible. "So why—"

"Let's just say that not even one of them has positive connotations. And all three together? It is not a good message."

Felicity gasped. "What do they mean?"

"Look at it this way: if you wanted three more damning plants, you'd be hard-pressed to find 'em. One of them actually means disdain!" She chortled.

"Oh, my God. Does Cooper know that?"

"Of course. I volunteered the meanings when she asked about such a curious-looking collection. She never said who they were from, though. I think maybe you should have a word with whoever hates you enough to do that to you. 'Cause, hon, the message sure wasn't subtle."

"But…I wanted to say appreciation!" Felicity said, aghast. "Affection!"

"Well, that didn't work out so well, did it?" Mrs. Brooks snorted.

"What did Cooper say?" Felicity asked, almost afraid to hear the answer.

"Nothing at all. I imagine she's mighty confused right about now."

Christ, this was worse than that time some evil person had sent Elena an awful plant used for exorcisms. But that had been someone trying to tell their boss that they hated her. Felicity was doing the opposite, for God's sake! What a disaster!

"You should call her," Mrs. Brooks finished.

"And have her hang up on me before I can explain? That is *not* strategically sound. No, I will turn up and whisk her away to some eating establishment she loves and explain everything when she's relaxed. Any suggestions?"

"Not a one. I've never been out to dinner with Dr. Cooper or any of the staff. I have a big family to take care of, and that keeps me plenty busy. You might try asking Mitch. Those two talk a lot. He always knows what she's up to. She sometimes borrows the van for an evening out."

"Mitch. Yes. Okay." Good, a clear path forward on her mission. "Do you have his phone number?"

"Can I remind you that the man's homeless? He doesn't have a phone."

"Well, *some* homeless have a phone," Felicity protested.

"True. Not Mitch. I got him a nice one once, but he was robbed a few years back. Said he'd never take another phone from me again. Shame, too. He's lost jobs over not being easily contactable."

"I see." Well, that was frustrating. "Can you get him for me? Put him on?"

"Ms. Simmons, I'm an old woman with one bad knee and a hip replacement. I can't be running up and down stairs so you can chat to

Mitch about your romantic business. If this was a work matter, I'd do my best, but it's not. You'll have to work this out for yourself. Now, I have to go. I'm director of a charity, and I have a lot of work to do tonight before I go home."

"Oh." Felicity could hardly argue that the woman should do PA work when she wasn't a personal assistant. That'd be mighty hypocritical. She respected Mrs. Brooks for setting those boundaries. "Yes. Fine. Good night."

The other woman hung up.

Felicity leaned back in her chair and glowered over the fact that her gift of flowers had backfired. Of course, she only had Mrs. Brooks's say-so as to what the flower varieties meant. What if she was wrong? Felicity didn't get to where she was in her career by trusting only one source. So in the interest of accuracy, she made a call that she was not looking forward to.

"Felicity? Felicity!" came a screech down the phone. Her sister, Heather, older by one year, was a joyful mother to a brood of ankle biters whose names Felicity absolutely refused to learn in case Heather took it as encouragement that she liked them.

On the plus side, Heather was all about herbs, plants, dried flowers, roots, and whatever other natural oddities her little store sold.

"Hi, Heather," Felicity said, wincing at the volume of her sister's greeting.

"It's a miracle! I usually only hear from you on birthdays and funerals. Or Christmas, when you're not working."

"Yes, well, I just had a question pertaining to your area of expertise."

"Raising happy kids? Why, of course! Are you and Phillip expecting?"

Felicity rolled her eyes. "He and I are no longer together. He refused to make a transpacific relationship work." She sniffed to highlight her indifference.

"That's no small thing, though. Oh, I'm so sorry."

"Don't be. He said I wasn't worth it. Well. He proved his inadequacies. Anyway, I have a question: if someone gave you a bunch of yellow tansies, white snapdragons, and yellow carnations, what would you think?"

Heather hissed in a breath. "Has someone put a hit on you?"

Oh crap. "That bad?"

"Worse. Seriously, does someone hate you that much? A tansy says 'I declare war on you,' the snapdragon means *deception*, and the yellow carnation is *disdain*." Concern filled her sister's voice, and Felicity warmed a little that she actually cared.

God knew Felicity wasn't the best of sisters. It had always been so hard to understand Heather and the life she'd chosen. They had nothing in common, either. Then again, having met Cooper, who seemed to share Heather's views on happiness trumping career, it seemed maybe…just maybe…Felicity was the one with the problem.

"I didn't receive them. I may have sent them to someone else," Felicity replied. "Someone I like. It was an accident. The meanings, I had no idea."

"Google *is* a thing you know. Wait—*someone you like*? Did my clueless little sis by any chance *outsource* the sending of flowers to one of her petrified minions, who got it wrong? Or worse, the minion has it in for you?"

Felicity scowled. "I'm a busy woman. I can't be expected to do everything."

"Whatever. So what's your next step?"

Felicity rather wished she knew. She couldn't exactly hire a Times Square billboard addressed to Cooper and plaster the words MISTAKES WERE MADE. She paused. Could she?

No…no, she was pretty sure that wouldn't fly.

"Felicity, are you planning to do something even more boneheaded to make up for the flowers, by any chance?"

"Well, what would you do?" Felicity asked in exasperation.

"Grovel. I'm sure he's a reasonable guy. He might even laugh."

"*She.*"

Heather squealed again.

Felicity winced. Welcome to the upside and downside of having a leftie hippie liberal for a sister. One's coming out is both welcomed and leads to premature deafness.

"That's SO cool."

Was it? Felicity failed to see the difference in who she dated.

"You *must* tell Mom."

"She knows. We talked."

"What'd she say?"

"She's in love with the fact that I'm dating a veterinarian who works for a charity helping homeless people's animals." Felicity stopped in surprise at what she'd said so easily. "Well, not *dating* dating. We haven't actually—"

She wondered if the pizzeria night counted as a date. Did they ever decide that?

"She's sounds wonderful," Heather said firmly. "So tell me about her. Sum her up for me in one word."

Felicity frowned. She filtered through a dozen words that sprang to mind about who Cooper was. Beautiful, strong, big, compassionate, thoughtful, amusing, smart… "Kind."

Silence fell. "You have never dated someone kind before," Heather said quietly. "At least not someone so kind that you see it as their number one thing. You're always about the career-climbing lawyers. So she's a keeper, okay? You need someone kind in your life. You've had so much cold, you need warm."

Felicity wanted to protest that. She hadn't always dated cold people. Wait—had she?

"Hell, even your boss is chillier than a snowdrift, and you worship her." Heather laughed.

"She isn't," Felicity said, tone grumpy. She was so over the way everyone judged Elena. "She's just acutely aware that people expect her to be her reputation and plays it up for maximum effect. I've seen another side to her, and while she's not kind, she's…"

Felicity stopped. Wait. She remembered plenty of times she'd caught her boss out in random acts of kindness. She'd dismissed them as aberrant because they flew in the face of Elena's ferocious Tiger Shark reputation. But what if those acts were a part of who she was? All this time she'd only ever focused on her icy-boss side—which was hard to miss—and ignored the other side.

So…Elena could be kind.

Apparently, it was just Felicity who was out of step here, the one everyone thought had few redeeming qualities. That probably explained why Elena had made no move to offer her friendship despite all the years they'd worked together. How depressing. "I'm apparently lacking a few things required to be good friendship or dating material," Felicity said acidly. She sagged. "No wonder Cooper gave me the flick. I'm sure the evil flowers were just the last nail in the coffin."

"No, Felicity. One bad gift isn't the end. If you want this woman, you've gotta show her you have more self-awareness than a drunk duck and win her back."

"How?" Felicity asked. "I was planning to turn up when Cooper finished work and take her to her favorite restaurant. Although I can't very well do that since I don't know where she likes to eat yet."

"You were going to turn up and take her?" Heather asked. "Felicity, knowing how you do things, was your idea to roll up in your fancy car, pop the door, and suggest she get in?"

"I—yes?" That did sound rather suave, didn't it?

"I'm not sure if you think you're James Bond or prepping a kidnapping, but that's not how you woo someone! People are tired when they finish work. They want to go home, get changed, freshen up, have a choice in whether they're eating out, all that."

"And how would I know?" Felicity asked in exasperation. "I've never been the wooer before!"

"All right, so the wooing with food idea is sound. But what if instead of dragging her into the car off the street—"

"I wouldn't—"

"Close enough. Find out what she likes to eat and bring it to her at work."

"I still don't know her favorite food."

"Who does?"

"Apparently, Mitch. The homeless guy who guards the charity van at night. Well, sleeps in it…guards…same thing."

"So just ask him."

"He doesn't have a phone number."

"I swear, Felicity, I don't get how you can be such a brilliant lawyer and not see the obvious. Go and talk to him. *In person.* Like you should have gone and selected the flowers *in person.*"

"I'll take your suggestions under advisement."

"Don't be afraid to grovel. Kind people are also forgiving people."

There was that. "I'm sure they are, but I'm not the groveling type."

"No? You sound like the desperate-to-be-with-this-Cooper-person type, though."

"I'm not desperate!" Felicity scowled. "And I'm just strategizing my next move. That's all."

"Well, go strategize it with the words 'I'm sorry I couldn't perform a simple Google search while sending you floral tributes, but I was lazy and decided to outsource. Also you're gorgeous and I want you *desperately* for lesbilicious good times.'"

Felicity glared at her phone. "Are you quite done?"

"I think so." Heather sounded far too amused.

Inhaling, Felicity forced out her next words. "How're things at home? How's everyone?"

"All excellent. I'd tell you all about them, but I know you have no interest." She sounded extra amused now. "But invite me to the wedding, and I'll bring the whole brood so you can catch up."

"There'll be no wedding!" Felicity said in astonishment. "I haven't even worked out how to date her yet. Or even if Cooper wants anything more to do with me!"

That made her heart clench just a little bit in ways Felicity detested.

"Ha." Heather laughed. "Better get right onto that then. I'm sure you'll work it out. Remember, it's the personal touch she's after. Gotta go. Love you!"

Felicity said something along the lines of "you, too" and the phone went dead. Well. That was illuminating. She glanced to her outer office. Now then… To find the snake in the grass. "Beatrice!"

The assistant scurried in, looking her usual cross between hapless and terrified. "Yes, Ms. Simmons?"

"I heard my flowers arrived," she said silkily.

"Oh, that's great." Beatrice's face brightened. "I insisted they get there fast. The man in the store was pretty rude saying it couldn't be done, not for rare and exotic blooms, but don't worry, I *insisted* and told him who you were and how important it was and that he had to drop everything to create your order."

"I see." Now it was all becoming clear. "Why do I get the feeling he suddenly agreed and hung up?"

Beatrice's eyes went very wide. "How did you know?"

"Just a hunch." She gave a cold smile. "Blacklist the company. His work was subpar."

"Oh, I had no idea. I'm so sorry."

"Next, call Amir. I need to go to the South Bronx right away."

"Um…now?" Beatrice glanced out at the darkening sky. Her voice dropped to a warning whisper. "There? At *night?*"

"Yes. I need to see a man who guards a company van after dark, so I can't very well turn up in the daytime."

"You do?" Beatrice ran a hand nervously along her starched skirt suit. "Maybe someone else could— I mean the South Bronx is just— It has a reputation."

Was this how Felicity had sounded when Elena had first announced her assignment, too? Probably. No wonder Elena had looked so amused. In reality, Felicity hadn't felt unsafe even once while she'd been embedded at Living Ruff. That probably had something to do with the fact that she'd had a sky-scraping Amazon at her side, but still. Fear hadn't even entered her mind.

She stared at Beatrice pointedly.

Finally, the woman got a clue. "I'll call Amir right away."

"You do that. And tell Scott to put the report for Bowen Press at the top of the pile. I want to go over it ASAP."

"Yes, Ms. Simmons."

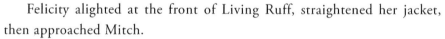

Felicity alighted at the front of Living Ruff, straightened her jacket, then approached Mitch.

He was leaning against the van having a smoke, hunched into his hoodie. She could see his lips drawing deeply on his cigarette beneath his thick black beard. Mitch eyed her approach with suspicion at first, then recognition.

"Well, hello," he said. "Look who it is. Lady who comes wit' her own driver." He glanced over Felicity's shoulder and squinted. "What year is she anyway?"

"What year is who?" Felicity asked.

"Your Merc E-class sedan, right?" He whistled low, impressed. "Fuck, I'd love me some fancy wheels like that."

"Mitch." Felicity drew his attention back to her.

His eyes focused on her again. "Coop's not upstairs, if you're looking for her."

"What makes you think I was?"

"I've seen you followin' her around a few weeks back, y'know. You kinda stick out 'round here." He laughed. "Anyway, she's gone home. 'Bout an hour ago."

"Well, fine, but it's you I'm after."

"Me?" He eyed her in confusion. Then his eyes flicked back to the car. "This where you make some weird rich-lady sex proposition?"

"Excuse me?" Felicity's eyes widened.

"I've heard 'em all. Fancy ladies lookin' for some rough trade like the street boys never say no. Fuckin' insultin' is what it is—"

"Mitch!" Felicity said in exasperation. "I'm only in the business of recruiting an ally. Nothing...*else*." She drew her mouth into a firm line.

"That so?" He studied her for a moment. "Okay then. What're ya pitchin'?"

"Mrs. Brooks suggested you'd know Cooper's tastes in eating out. As in you know where she goes and favorite foods and so on."

"More than know." He puffed up. "Sometimes I drive her when she knows she wants to have a few drinks. She trusts me with the van." He gave the vehicle a proud thump. "And I know all the ways to avoid traffic. Fastest shortcuts. Bein' a local helps."

"Excellent." Now they were getting somewhere. "So where does Cooper like to eat?"

"A whole bunch of places. Like German and Indian and Irish. Sometimes I-talian." He pointed in various directions as he spoke.

"And her favorite?"

His brow puckered as he considered that. "Why do you want to know? And why not ask her yourself?"

"I'm planning to bring her a meal as a surprise."

Mitch eyed her up and down. "And does Coop *want* to be gettin' this surprise?" He tossed his cigarette butt to the concrete and ground it under a dirty boot. "I don't want Coop getting herself some stalker."

"A *stalker*!" Felicity glared at him. "You think *I* look like a stalker?"

"What? You think just 'cause you're some rich blonde white chick you can't horndog after someone who doesn't want it? 'Sides, Coop's had some trouble in the past with people hangin' around her in a way she didn't like. Sometimes people just don't have it all connected right upstairs." He tapped his head. "Coop's mah friend, and I keep an eye out for her. That includes not assumin' she wants *anyone* poundin' on her door that she doesn't know's coming."

Felicity had to appreciate the man's loyalty. "I assure you she would like this surprise from me." She injected every ounce of confidence she had and gave Mitch an imperious look to sell it.

"Tell ya what. I'll ask Coop tomorrow if there's anyone she'd want surprisin' her with dinner, and we'll take it from there."

"Fine." Felicity ground out. "I'll give you my card. When she says yes, you can text me the details of her dining choices."

"Text?" He snorted. "How do you reckon I'd be doin' that without a phone?"

Oh right. Good question.

Which was how, an hour later, Felicity was heading back into work, having bought Mitch a new phone and an ample amount of credit. She'd already received a text from him.

This phone is lit. Got all sortz of shit on it. Mrs B says I can recharge it @ her office. Also she told me to tell u ur all right. - Mitch-man

She smiled at his sign-off name. A tendril of warmth curled in her belly. If the phone helped him get a job, even better. She tried not to notice how good it felt to make someone happy so easily. Even if Felicity didn't have the first clue as to attaining it herself.

A text arrived from Mitch at seven thirty the next morning. Felicity was just logging on at work when it landed.

Yo, spoke to Coop. She say she cant think of any one shed want to hav dinnr with

Oh. Well, that hurt.

Then she say but if food just appeard 2day she wuldnt say no to it coz she doing a 16 hr shift coz doc gabe is off sik

Sixteen hours? That was disgraceful. Surely there were other options than making one person work a double shift. She'd have to talk to Mrs. Brooks about— No. It wasn't her place to meddle.

Her phone pinged again.

Said she mite look favarbly on persn who made it happn

Favorably? A slow smile curled Felicity's lips. Well now, that sounded promising. She texted him back.

Submit all her favorite restaurants now please, Mitch.

Over the next five minutes, a list of a dozen names tumbled into her phone, some with questionable spelling that required decoding. Felicity set up a spreadsheet, consulted opening times and menus, and examined her options. Sixteen hours was indeed a long shift—what time had Cooper started? That being the case, she should break the period up with more than one arrival of food to ensure Cooper was well-fed.

But which restaurant? Mitch had proved useless at telling her what Cooper's absolute favorite was, but he did know some of her favorite dishes. In the end, she did what anyone overwhelmed by too much choice and not enough information would do: she chose them all.

Nine of the restaurants offered deliveries, so she staggered those throughout the sixteen hours. The three that did not, she phoned in and paid for orders at set times, then enlisted Mitch to pick up the dishes and bring them into the office. So no matter the time, from ten in the morning today onwards, there would be plenty of food options for the overworked Cooper to choose from.

With that sorted to her satisfaction, Felicity tossed her phone into her drawer and headed into her next round of meetings involving Bowen Press, a small press with seven community newspapers that offered remote regional advertising monopolies.

———◆———

By nine that evening, she'd finally finished every last scrap of paperwork and had sealed a deal with Bowen Press.

Her stomach grumbled, reminding her that she hadn't eaten anything since the boardroom lunch tray of sandwiches. She hadn't had a chance to learn of Cooper's approval over the movable feast she'd sent her way, either.

Felicity turned on her phone. The screen was filled with missed calls and messages. Alarm flooded her. A lot were texts from Mitch. One call from Cooper. And a number of messages left by Mrs. Brooks. The general theme seemed to be ENOUGH ALREADY.

Uh-oh.

With hands shaking, she called Cooper. "Um, hi, it's…"

"Ah yes." Cooper's voice was dry. "My generous food provider. I know you think I eat a lot, but that was insane. Do you know I had to abandon my work today to handle the piles of food that kept coming and coming? We ended up running an impromptu soup kitchen from Living Ruff's front steps to get rid of all the food. That took ages. We had hangers-on who wanted to chat, and then there was the clean-up. You're on Mrs. B's shit list. Which you probably know by now, if you've listened to her messages."

"Oh, my God." Felicity cringed. "I'm so sorry."

"If you'd listened to what I asked for, you'd have heard me request a—singular—meal. But you don't seem to listen to my wishes, do you?"

"I just couldn't decide what to get you, and so I—"

"More money than sense? Is that what this is?" Cooper sighed.

"I'm trying here." Felicity scowled.

"Then stop. Please." Cooper paused. "It was obvious from your apology letter that you really have no clue how to do this. And I'm not sure I want to be caught in the next avalanche as you try to figure it all out. So…please. We're too different. We shouldn't be dating."

"You don't know that."

"Come on. I've said it all along: you're the uptown girl. How long before you get tired of dating a lowly vet who doesn't fit in your world and leave anyway? So why not do us both a favor and walk away now?"

"Because you're *kind*!" Felicity hadn't meant to say that. But in for a penny— "I mean, I don't date kind. I never have. You're the first. I only ever date lawyers who are just like me."

Like Phillip. The fact that she'd once thought he might be the one was galling now. She pushed on. "And now that I've had a taste of how it feels to be around someone like you, that's what I want."

Felicity suddenly thought of Harvey and Rosalind, how his gentleness and warmth was a perfect foil for all the demands everyone put on her. He energized her. But it was more than that. Felicity just hadn't fully understood what she was seeing that day.

Hell, Cooper had already given her the answer twice now, spelled it out for her, and still Felicity hadn't seen. Kind people were safe places to relax into. They were…home. And Felicity hadn't had kindness or a sense of home for so long that she didn't know how much they mattered. Cooper had shown her that they did. Now it was all she could think about.

"I love your kindness," Felicity went on. "And your compassion. Being with you for even a week made me see the world with new eyes."

"I shouldn't have to be your white knight, Felicity," Cooper said, sounding tired. "The savior dragging you around so you open your eyes to the world."

"Too late. You already did that. You've already changed me. I'm different."

"I think you're probably right. You are." Cooper inhaled. "But maybe *I* need kindness, too? Thoughtfulness? You think problems can be solved with money being flung at them—enormous feasts and bunches of flowers. A big generic grand gesture. You could have given that to anyone."

"What?" Felicity gasped. "Anyone who knows all your favorite foods!"

"I didn't mean that side. I'm not unappreciative. It was a nice idea, and the homeless around here loved it, but *everyone eats*. Your gift wasn't about me specifically—who I am and what I want. So I'll tell you what: do one thing for me that's all you—not an assistant, not Mitch, just *you*. Something that shows you understand who I am and what matters to me. Something you can't spend one dime on. And if you do that, I'll date you. Otherwise, I like you; you're smart and beautiful and you're probably going to rule the world someday, but you're not who belongs with me. Goodbye, Felicity."

The phone went dead. Felicity stared at it in disbelief.

Well. It wasn't unreasonable what Cooper had asked for. She pursed her lips. A challenge had been thrown down.

Something that shows you understand who I am and what matters to me. Something you can't spend one dime on.

As far as Felicity could tell, what mattered to Cooper most were animals.

And that was the moment Felicity had a most genius idea—if she did say so herself.

Chapter 18
A Most Genius Idea

ONE THING FELICITY COULD ALWAYS be counted on for was to find loopholes in any legal matter. It's what had made her such an effective chief of staff for Elena. Lawyers from all over the world sent in various paperwork, and Felicity checked that all was in order. She'd caught shoddy work, illegal clauses, and most especially, glaring loopholes.

Which was how she now found herself on a Saturday morning just over a week later at Cooper's door, holding a piece of paper she hoped would change everything. The paper hadn't cost her a cent. But she hoped Cooper would appreciate how much effort she had made—personally—to make it happen.

She'd texted first, explaining she had what Cooper had asked for. And Cooper's reply of "We'll see" was a bit ominous.

But now, as she stood with her hand poised before Cooper's door, doubts drowned her. Wooing someone with a legal agreement wasn't exactly romantic, was it?

No. She was all in now. Felicity rapped sharply.

Cooper opened the door dressed in faded blue jeans worn at the knees with hints of a tear starting—and Felicity was pretty sure that was a genuinely acquired rip, not the preshredded variety. A mustard-colored sweater with the hint of a white shirt collar peeping up completed the picture.

"So, Ms. Simmons," Cooper said with her eyebrow tilting up, "here to woo me?" Her gaze slid over her. "Well, come in. I'm amazed you kept your designer outfit down to just the belt and shoes."

Felicity wasn't about to admit it was *all* designer. "I can do low-key," she suggested.

Cooper laughed. "Sure you can. Drink?"

"No, thanks." Felicity glanced around, then swallowed nervously. "I just want to give you a gift from me to you. No money changed hands, it's not generic, and I worked on it all myself. It's something you want and can't get for yourself. I—" Her nerve failed her as she handed over the document. "I hope you like it."

Cooper's eyebrows shot up in surprise as she accepted the piece of paper and unfolded it.

Felicity's doubts swam circles in her stomach as she watched her read.

Then Cooper sat heavily on the couch and read some more. "Wait. Is this what I think it is?"

"Your building's owner, Lawrence Tubman, letting you keep Brittany with you? Yes."

Felicity had spent over a week on this, digging until she found out that Tubman had used one particular man for all his property deals: a lawyer known in certain circles for particular legal irregularities in property valuations.

Long story short, the lawyer was rumored to be bribing or schmoozing city officials to get his wealthy clients a rarely used tax abatement—namely 421a—applied to their property deals, which slashed many thousands of dollars off how much they owed the city in fees. It *was* curious how 421a only ever seemed to be applied to the mega-rich's apartment sales but no one else's properties, and usually only when *one* particular lawyer was on the job.

Felicity had paid Mr. Tubman a visit and pointed this out while explaining how much she loved solving mysteries and puzzles. She mentioned in passing how one or two of Bartell Corp's thousands of reporters might be interested in investigating 421a exemptions—particularly why the sneaky rule was used just for the ultrawealthy. Just a general story, of course. No names. But senior city officials might decide to then investigate past deals of all 421a valued properties.

Mr. Tubman, being a rather smart individual, had asked what it would take for Felicity to be less interested in solving certain puzzles and mysteries.

Felicity had then mentioned how much owners loved having their pets with them in their apartments.

Now, as of nine this morning, all of Mr. Tubman's three residential buildings were pet-friendly. What a coincidence.

"I can bring Brittany here?" Cooper's voice broke, hope leaking from her voice. "She can stay home with me for good?"

Felicity nodded and pulled out her phone. She walked back to the door, sending a quick text: *Now.*

Moments later, a honey-brown blur scampered down the hallway. As Felicity widened the door, Brittany burst into Cooper's apartment, following her nose to her old home and adored owner.

"Brit!" Cooper squealed. She crouched and flung her arms around her dog, who enthusiastically barreled Cooper over, flattening her onto her back.

Brittany then set about licking a layer of skin off Cooper, who kept laughing and crying out "down, girl" and "arghh" between gasping laughs.

Felicity glanced at Amir, who was smiling from ear to ear, a plump tear running down his cheek as he placed all the dog toys and Brittany's little bed just inside the apartment door.

"Thanks," Felicity told her driver with a smile.

"My pleasure, Ms. Simmons." Amir lingered a moment, his brown eyes warm as he soaked in the sprawled-out woman laughing helplessly, pinned down by a bouncing, gleeful dog whose tail was swishing back and forth. "That's a sight to see," he said softly. Amir wiped his eye discreetly before turning and leaving, closing the door behind him.

Felicity looked back at the joyful Cooper-Brittany swirl. Her heart contracted at the sheer delight of them both. "I could come back, if you like. Let you two get used to Brittany being home again?"

Cooper's eyes were shining with tears. "She'll calm down in a minute. And don't go. I just... I'm overwhelmed. How?"

"I keep telling you I'm very good at what I do." Felicity smiled confidently. "Sooner or later you might believe me."

Cooper sat up. "I believe." She said it so earnestly. "Truly. You're a goddess."

Felicity laughed. "Well, you're officially good for my ego." She lowered herself to the floor beside Cooper and Brittany. "Just so you know, when

I got Mr. Tubman to make this change, I convinced him to do it for all residents in all his buildings. I didn't want you singled out for attention, and I thought you'd feel weird getting special treatment that others couldn't have. So…here we are. Pets for everyone." She grinned.

After burying her face in Brittany's fur for a long hug, Cooper looked up. "You really are something else, Felicity Simmons."

Oh no. Was Cooper *crying*?

Felicity panicked, glancing around furiously, unsure what to do. Were there tissues anywhere? Was she supposed to pat her on the back and say "there, there"? That'd be condescending, though, wouldn't it? She agonized for another moment and then went with what she most wanted to do. She slid an arm around Cooper and whispered, "Are you okay?"

"Yeah," Cooper said between sniffles. "I really am. I really, *really* am. A bit embarrassed to be making such a fool of myself, but hey, it's not every day something like this happens."

Brittany licked her salty cheek, which caused Cooper to laugh again.

"So," Felicity said carefully to double-check that she hadn't misread the room, "I did okay on my assignment?"

Cooper burst into tears. Proper ones this time, which Felicity regarded with even more alarm.

"Sorry. Christ, what you must think of me. I just hadn't realized how much I've been aching for Brittany to be home with me. And yes, Felicity, my God, you did more than okay. You gave *family* back to me. This is the greatest gift anyone could have given me. So you proved me wrong." She met Felicity's eyes, tears streaming down her cheeks. "You really do get me, don't you? You knew what I most wanted."

Felicity tightened her arm around her. "I hoped I did. And I'm hoping I'll have an opportunity to get to know you a lot better. So if you could stop saying ridiculous things like 'I'll dump you as soon as I get bored with you being a lowly vet as I climb higher' or whatever, that'd be good. Because for a start, I'm already at the top now; and second, where on earth am I going to find anyone kinder or more decent than you in my cutthroat world of corporate media?"

"Flatterer." Cooper smiled through her tears.

Felicity gently wiped them away with her finger. She met Cooper's eyes. "I'm serious, Sandy," she said, using her first name with great care. "I want to be with you. I also have no intention of going anywhere, in case you're afraid you'd be left behind and I'll be jet-setting the globe. I know that, thanks to your childhood, you aren't interested in moving around. So FYI, aside from occasional travel for work, I have this wicked power called delegation."

"You're really not going anywhere?" The question was laced with something painful.

Felicity understood the question wasn't just about geography. It went a lot deeper. "I'd really like to hang around and get to know you properly. Please say that's what you want, too. More of us together."

Cooper looked down at the legal agreement Felicity had given her, the typing now splotched with tears, then looked back up.

"Well, I can't have Brittany moping around without you. I swear all this past month she kept looking for you behind me every day I arrived at work."

"Well, yes, quite right. We can't let your dog down." Felicity leaned over and gave Brittany a blissful scratch behind those floppy ears.

In return, Brittany's soft eyes gave her an adoring look that melted her heart into a puddle.

Oh lord, Felicity was in trouble now between these two. *Don't break my heart, please.*

Cooper smiled. "Hey, I have a confession."

"Yes?"

"It's not just Brittany who's been missing you."

"No?"

"I admit I might have been so frustrated with those evil flowers and so much damned food that the office still smells like a food market. But it was impossible to forget you. You made everything interesting. I can't stop thinking of this powerful, impossible woman who blew into my life and seemed to think nothing of upending my world."

"To be fair," Felicity protested, "I didn't think *nothing* of it when I did it."

"Christ, we're really doing this, aren't we?" Cooper said, leaning in close inside Felicity's personal space. "You and me? What do we even have in common? Aside from a shared desire to snuggle Brittany?" Her hand buried deep into her dog's fur.

"A shared desire to snuggle each other?"

"Aside from that?" Cooper asked.

Felicity thought about it seriously. "A shared desire for a fairer world?"

"All right," Cooper said. "That I'll take."

Brittany suddenly barked, jumped up, and ran over to a window and stared at the skies.

Felicity turned, curious.

"Brit's a passionate bird spotter. Where she's sitting is her favorite view of the pigeons that land on the neighbor's window ledge."

Felicity couldn't see any pigeons.

Cooper's fingers slid under her chin, turning Felicity to face her. "Forget the birds," she said, lips curling, "because for someone who claimed to be in the business of wooing me, you seem pretty slow on the uptake. I've had my lips next to yours for a good minute now."

"Please, it's called foreplay," Felicity said archly, secretly appalled she'd missed an obvious invitation. "I've looked into it. It's apparently good for increasing sexual tension."

"Is that so?"

"It is." Felicity leaned in, kissed her quickly, and pulled away. Her plans of teasing Cooper more flew out the window when the other woman tugged their heads together and kissed Felicity properly. Her limbs went limp and useless, and arousal flared sharp in her lower stomach. *Oh God.*

Cooper smiled against her mouth. "I missed that, too. You're a superb kisser. Because you go from hard-ass to melty in ten seconds."

"Okay, first, I don't do melty, so enough of that," Felicity said, trying not to sound too out of breath. "And second, foreplay is over."

Chuckling, Cooper said, "Yes, I can see it is."

◆

Felicity woke up the next day, naked and sore—in the best possible sense—with Cooper's fingers stroking her most intimate area. "More?" Felicity said with a mutter. "Insatiable."

"More," Cooper confirmed. "I have plans. You have the prettiest little clit that I'd hate to neglect. It's so cute the way it peeks out. I think it's smiling at me."

"Oh, my God." Felicity's cheeks flooded with heat. "You can't just say that out loud."

"No?" Cooper smiled. "What about 'I have a strap-on'? Would you like me to fuck you hard and fast and just mmph—"

Felicity silenced her by hauling her down for a crushing kiss. She then pulled back slightly to make room to growl, "Enough talking. Start doing."

***

The next time Felicity woke up, just as naked and a little sorer—in an even more pleasant sense—Cooper looked smug.

Felicity closed her barely open eye and rolled over onto her stomach. "Lord, I swear, if you're up for round five or whatever this is, I'm going to need a raincheck."

"Nope." Cooper beamed. "I'm just appreciating you." Her fingertips ran along Felicity's spine to where the sheet bunched. "I love your ass. It's gorgeous. And the way you were up on all fours a few hours ago letting me take you from behind was the hottest damn thing."

Felicity groaned as her pussy clenched at the reminder. "Don't get me all worked up again. I'm just a humble lawyer, not a powerhouse vet with energy reserves up the yin-yang."

Cooper laughed. "You? A *humble* lawyer?"

"Whatever," Felicity muttered into her pillow. "Compared to you, I feel like a weakling. I *am* a weakling! The way you flung me around and had your way with me? I think you might well have literally fucked me senseless at one point." Arousal sparked again at the reminder. "Oh God. I can't go again, even though the mind is willing. It's so-o-o willing."

"Relax, weakling," Cooper teased. Her fingers did a little twirl across the small of Felicity's back. "While you've been sleeping away the day, I've fed and walked Brittany, explained to her in-depth how she lives with me now once more and that's not changing, but pine and pout as much as she likes, she still doesn't have bedroom access."

"Good. No dogs in beds," Felicity mumbled. "Fur. Shedding. Bad."

"So articulate. It's astonishing this is the same woman who sweet-talked my building owner into new rules."

"Well, sweet-talked, terrified. Tomahtoes, tomaytoes."

"I did wonder." Cooper's smile was evident even with Felicity's eyes shut. "I don't think I thanked you properly for what you did. I told you once when I tried to walk away from you that *I* needed kindness, too. I'm sorry I didn't understand that you already are kind. You do have compassion, and I didn't see it because you hide it so well behind your enormous walls. Sorry I misjudged you. But I guess that's why you got your promotion, hmm?"

"What?" Felicity cracked an eyelid again. "I was promoted because you misjudged me?" She rolled over onto her back, enjoying the appreciation lighting Cooper's face at her boobs sliding into view. "That makes no sense."

"No, Felicity. Your boss had to have known you were compassionate. We agree she's seeking happiness over career these days, right? So no one like that would put someone who's only career hungry in her place to run her corporation. She'd put someone like herself, right? So she had to know."

Felicity sat up. "Oh fuck."

"What is it?"

"That's what she was trying to say! That's the answer!"

"Who? What?"

"I need to see Elena."

"What, now? It's a Sunday!"

"She's flying out to Sydney tomorrow." Felicity slid out of bed, then paused. "But I'll be back in time for a celebratory lunch."

"What are we celebrating?" Cooper asked, her voice both rough and filled with warmth.

"Us. Together. The future. Our relationship." Felicity blew out a breath and suddenly realized she was standing naked in front of a woman whose eyes were roaming her avidly.

She straightened, put her hands on her hips, and let Cooper look her fill. It was a mirror of the first time she'd done this, when she'd been so caught up in self-consciousness, wondering what her new lover would see. "Something to remember me by"—she smirked—"until our lunch."

"I love the view. Fuck, I really do." Cooper swallowed. Her eyes were appreciative. "Hurry back," she whispered hoarsely. "After lunch, there will be more flinging."

Anticipation filled Felicity as she raced from the room.

Chapter 19
The Girl from Pinckney

FELICITY HAD NEVER BEEN TO Elena's place socially before. Hell, she'd barely visited for work. Usually it was to drop off or pick up something or to collect Elena on their way to an event. But here she stood, about to knock on the door of Elena's New York apartment and…discuss things.

Elena answered after a few minutes.

Her surprise at Felicity's unexpected visit couldn't possibly trump Felicity's surprise at Elena's appearance.

The media mogul was in jeans. Tatty, worn, paint-spattered jeans. They were loose, looked lived in and comfortable, and went with the sinfully tight white shirt a little too well.

"S-sorry," Felicity said. Her gaze met dozens of boxes behind Elena. "I should have called. Well, I mean I tried, but your phone's not answering."

Elena widened the door. "Come in. Yes, sorry, my battery died and I'm still trying to work out where I put the charger in this mess." She followed Felicity's gaze to all the boxes. "I'm having a last-minute frenzy of working out what I want to send on by container ship, things I won't need immediately. I suspect my late uncle's tailor's dummy collection will be taking the sea voyage." Her eyes narrowed. "However, there's no way I'm allowing my family heirlooms to be packed by graceless oafs. Hence the DIY work."

"Oh." Some days it was hard thinking of Elena Bartell…well, Bartlewski, really…having family at all, let alone one gifting her heirlooms. She just seemed to have been hatched fully formed, a media mogul to be reckoned with. "I could come back at another time, if you'd prefer."

"No, it's fine. Come into the kitchen. I believe there's still a couple of chairs left. I'll make us tea."

Felicity hated tea, but she'd never actually gotten around to telling Elena that. No time like the present. "You don't have coffee, do you?"

"Of course."

Huh. How easy had that been? Felicity perched on a bar stool at the granite kitchen counter and watched as her boss busied herself finding a pair of mugs, then digging out tea and coffee and milk. "I didn't know you drank coffee. It's always tea at work. How do you take it?"

"Black. Just black."

Elena nodded and made no further comment until she slid the mug over and took the bar stool opposite Felicity. She took a sip of her tea and smiled. "Well, I don't have to ask why you're here."

"You don't?"

"If it was work, you'd have launched straight into it at the doorstep. You've figured it out, then? Why I sent you to that charity?"

"I think so." Felicity bit her lip. "You weren't sure I had enough compassion. You were afraid the person running your corporation might be someone lacking in empathy, and you needed to know. Or maybe you thought I had *zero* compassion, and you hoped I might acquire some while surrounded by people less fortunate." She really hoped it wasn't that more damning one. "And by me choosing to save Living Ruff, I proved I was compassionate. Because I realized later you never once said what you thought about me making the charity Bartell Corp's concern."

Elena's eyes crinkled. She tilted her mug toward her in silent salute. "I always said you were smart."

Felicity inhaled. "Why did you even hire me in the first place if you were afraid I was heartless?"

"That's just it. I thought quite the opposite."

Felicity's mouth fell open. "You did?" She'd tried so hard to show the world how tough she was, and Elena hadn't seen that at all.

"Remember the first time we met? Or well, the first several times?"

"Across boardrooms. My law firm was defending the interests of newspapers you were taking over."

"Yes. I noticed you right away. The serious woman with the Midwest accent and sharp mind who everyone ignored. I'd see things firing in your eyes whenever you realized your boss had erred; it was written all across your face. And you would scribble him frantic notes that he barely even looked at. I wondered about you. How you'd gotten into that negotiating team in the first place. Where you planned on going."

Felicity remembered those meetings all too well. Her boss had been useless. "You told me once my team would have won a deal if I'd been running the meeting."

"You would have." Elena's eyes became half-lidded. "We kept bumping into each other. And every time we did, you looked older, sadder, and your accent was less Pinckney, Michigan, more 17 Cherry Tree Lane, London."

"Where?"

"Don't you read the classics, Felicity?" Elena's eyes brightened. "Mary Poppins lived there with the Banks family." She steepled her fingers. "But I made a mistake. I offered you the chief of staff job based on a wrong assumption."

Alarm prickled through Felicity. "You did?"

"I thought a woman from Pinckney, Michigan, would be more well-rounded than all my other lawyers put together. You'd have seen more of America, have more empathy and connection with people. I assumed you might have a few down-to-earth Midwest sensibilities lurking under your fierce persona. That's necessary because we live such a privileged existence."

"We do." Felicity had come of late to see just how much that was true.

"I'm aware every day that I'm a far cry from being a poor Polish-American girl who mended other people's clothing to help her family make ends meet. I know crushing poverty; I know the smell of it, the taste of it, the burning need to flee it. And it shaped my ambition. I might have talked myself into an editorial job I had no qualifications for, changed my name, and made sure I never looked back. Even so, I never forgot where I came from. And I thought a Pinckney, Michigan, girl probably understood that, too. I could see you reshaping yourself every time we met, changing your look from long hair to tight bun, your accent, your attitude until no one dismissed you. I saw aspects of me in you. But I was wrong."

Felicity swallowed. "Wrong?"

"I used to wish, when I was younger, that I could obliterate my past. I saw it as embarrassing. Some people, like my charming rival Emmanuelle Lecoq, occasionally liked to remind me of it. She was a bully who loved to bring up my past and tell me it belonged in the gutter along with me. Younger me would have done anything to have wiped it away like a stain. Older me wishes no such thing. I'm aware it made me who I am. But that's me. I don't know how you achieved such a feat of wiping your past from every part of you, but it seems you succeeded."

Felicity stared. Was that how it seemed?

"The longer you worked for me, the more I noticed: You connected less with people than anyone I'd ever met. You displayed no interest in understanding their lives, interests, or anything unrelated to your job. You were incapable of small talk. Your focus was absolute. In fact, the first few years you were in my employ, I used to watch you in frank astonishment at the way you interacted with people. Because you only had two settings: brutal or awkward."

Ouch. Felicity's shoulders sank.

"I know I make the occasional cutting comment, but it's generally done to remind people I'm not to be messed with. I like to think it's never cruel—it's either honest, or it has a purpose. But you?" Elena gave her a look of deep concern.

"Felicity, do you remember when we were based at the *Hudson Metro News* and an employee's son fell ill? She wanted to go home to be with him. You told Madeleine the woman should have thought of that before she procreated. That parents play the parent card too often."

Oh. That. She was only being flippant. She wasn't even entirely sure she'd meant it. Trust Elena to have overheard that.

"That gave me pause, Felicity. The unnerving truth is, it made me seriously afraid of what sort of a person you were. Despite your skills and expertise, I did not want a Lecoq running my company."

Felicity was nothing like that evil snake. She opened her mouth to say as much.

Elena put up a hand to stop her. "I'm aware it might have been your idea of a joke, but at the time I wasn't sure. You are a fine lawyer, Felicity, an excellent manager with an eye for detail, and as clever as anyone I've met. But while these are important facets needed to run a corporation, I had to be sure I had someone in charge of my business who doesn't *only* put the bottom line first."

"Cue Living Ruff," Felicity said.

"Yes. I thought if I sent you to meet people who don't take anything for granted, you might come away with a bit of personal growth. Or at the very least, some self-awareness that we exist in a bubble filled with experiences so entitled that they have little bearing on the real world. I wanted you to have a wake-up call and return with a bit more appreciation of what you have. Most of all, I needed to see whether those glib lines you toss out that make you sound so uncaring were just a front."

Elena suddenly looked uneasy. "And in one moment of clarity, it also occurred to me that you might have been trying to mimic me. What if you'd concluded that being cold and harsh was what I wanted from you?"

Shock ran through Felicity. Elena's personal opinion of her was far lower than she'd even imagined. Did Elena truly think she didn't care about anyone? Was *that* how the world saw her, too?

"I'm truly sorry, Felicity, if you've been assuming my occasional pointed jabs are what I want to see from my managers," Elena went on. "And I'm well aware I may come across as indifferent to most things, but it's a deliberate choice I play to keep people on their toes. But with you, I truly couldn't tell whether it was a game you played or who you really were. So I had to know for sure. Did you have it in you to empathize with others? Could you make the occasional decision with your heart, not your head? That was the plan. And it seems you overshot even my ambitions." Elena shook her head incredulously. "You came back *owning* the charity."

Well, not exactly, Felicity wanted to say. But for some reason no one ever wanted to hear the boat analogy.

"*And* I got my donation back, which you've no doubt seen I've reinvested back in the charity. Further, you ensured Charles Stone would be punished and would make amends. It's remarkable. You really stepped up. Most of all, you impressed me, Felicity. I'm now in no doubt that Bartell Corp is in fine hands."

Felicity stopped panicking, and a weight lifted from her shoulders. She'd done right. Still she shifted uncomfortably. Compliments tended to make her break out in hives because she always had to pick them over for their deeper meaning. "Well, it was the logical choice to get the charity and your money back. Double win."

"The Felicity *I* knew before all this would have let the charity fold because you'd have decided it was one less headache for Bartell Corp. Or you might have gone to the police to punish Charles for daring to take even a dime from me." Elena cocked an eyebrow. "Am I wrong? If I had asked you this as a hypothetical before you visited Living Ruff, what would you have decided was the best course?"

"Fold the charity," Felicity admitted with a rueful smile, "and go to the police anyway, but only after I'd received that refund for your donation."

"And you know what? That would have still been a sound business option," Elena mused. "But I would have been disappointed." She smiled suddenly. "Would you like to stay for lunch? I think we're going to the place around the corner. It has a lovely salad range, so you'll be safe."

Was Elena actually teasing her about her famous diet preferences? And wait— "We?"

"Oh, Madeleine's around here somewhere." Elena waved carelessly behind her, indicating the rest of the apartment. "She volunteered to help me pack since she had nothing else going on. I mean, if you can stand lunching with the 'annoying Australian,' too?" Elena's lips twitched up.

The woman really did have exceptional hearing if she'd heard Felicity call Maddie that. "I'm sure I'll find ways to amuse myself." Felicity smiled back. "I haven't politely reminded Maddie about her being from a feral dingo-bred clan for at least a year. For some reason, she seems to find that hilarious."

"Well, then, by all means. Lunch." Elena's eyes sparkled.

And that was the moment Felicity felt it. The first tendrils of friendship. Actual, real, not just business-related friendship.

Instinctively, she understood that this was the first time she'd ever properly seen the real Elena—someone who teased her as an equal, shared stories about her own past, and actually explained in full her business decisions.

It felt momentous, in a way: intensely private Elena offering her this gift.

Felicity wasn't even sure if she'd be worthy of it. She wasn't great at friendship, obviously. But this offer wasn't a ticking time bomb. It was something rare and precious. She'd treat it accordingly.

"Oh damn!" Felicity said, startling them both. "Oh gosh, sorry, but I can't. Cooper—the vet from Living Ruff that I…that I'm seeing"—her eyes darted worriedly to Elena—"we're supposed to have lunch today."

"And you promised her first," Elena mused. "That's quite all right. My offer was impromptu. I'm not asking you to choose."

"Oh…er…right." Felicity fidgeted. *Thank God.*

"I'm also pleased to hear that you've worked out what matters in life." Elena leaned back, her eyes twinkling. "And I won't ask you to bring your vet to lunch today, either, because judging by your impressive blush and conflicted expression, it was considerably more than lunch that was promised to her."

Felicity was pretty sure she was about to die of embarrassment. She rubbed her flaming cheeks. "God," she squeaked.

"It's fine. I understand—your girlfriend comes first. But next time you're in Sydney—for the Australasian Legends of Publishing Ball, I believe—I'll expect a raincheck on lunch. All right?" Elena's eyebrow lifted. "I'm sure I can convince Madeleine to make an appearance, too. For old times' sake."

"Yes. Definitely." Felicity exhaled. "I'd like that a lot. Really."

Elena's answering smile was one of her rare genuine ones that reached her eyes.

It was curious how Elena seemed to understand these things so well. Had she always been this astute about relationships? Felicity didn't think so. But maybe Felicity really didn't know her boss nearly as well as she thought. Maybe one day she would.

That thought filled her with warmth and satisfaction.

———◆———

That night, Felicity snuggled up in bed with Cooper and a certain dog, because Brittany had apparently found out her mistress could, in fact, be manipulated through pining and pouting.

Felicity found she didn't mind sharing her bed as she told Cooper about her conversation with her boss.

With her absent-minded fingers roaming Brittany's beautiful fur, Felicity said, "Elena wondered if I was too heartless. Too lacking in compassion to run her empire." She gave Cooper a worried look. "She feared for me. She's one of the most fearless people in business today. And she was afraid *I* was too hard."

"From what you've told me, she isn't as hard as everyone thinks, not when you drill down. I'm wondering if all this time you've been projecting onto her your idea of what a successful COO looks like."

"Perhaps," Felicity conceded. "She was afraid she'd been a bad mentor, making me think I have to act a certain way. But her reputation *is* well-founded. I've seen her do some brutal but necessary things that cost communities their old newspapers because she could see no way to make a profit. She'd try a few options to see if she could save them, but the numbers weren't there. So she asset stripped them, keeping only the best staff, which she put to work on her other mastheads. She does that, you know."

Felicity was suddenly anxious Cooper would only see Elena as a ruthless corporate asshole. "She talent spots. That matters to her most: finding the right people for the right jobs, making all the pieces fit. It's not just a bulldoze-everything deal."

"Felicity, why do you care what I think of Elena? She's going back to Sydney tomorrow. You'll only see her a few times a year after this."

"Because she's one of a tiny handful of people in my life I deeply respect, and I want you to like her."

Cooper regarded her with interest. "I've only ever heard you talk about Elena as worthy of this lofty praise. Who else do you respect?"

"Aside from you? My mom." She frowned. "That…took a while. I kept seeing her through my father's judgmental eyes, which shaded how I viewed her. And I honestly couldn't understand her taking a lesser position than the one she had as a college professor. But I see now that she stepped down to take a charity job where she could shape young minds at an earlier age, really get kids into STEM, especially girls."

"That's admirable. So wait, your mom works for a charity, too? Which one?"

"She's the executive director of Leslie Science & Nature Center at Ann Arbor."

Silence fell.

"What?" Felicity asked.

"That's a seriously well-respected organization. They do amazing work. But, Felicity, how the hell did you turn out to be a hard-assed lawyer and come from a mother up to her armpits in frogs and owls and trees?"

"Well, I leaned toward Dad, the lawyer. Heather, my sister, leaned toward Mom. She's got such a fixation on plants and herbs. Her husband is totally into essential oils. So they're all about feeding people's souls."

Cooper's eyes brightened. "Your family sounds incredible. You must be so proud."

A glib retort lurked on the edge of her tongue, but Felicity stopped it. She really thought about her family dispassionately without the lens of her father's snobbery.

Heather was kind and warm and welcoming to everyone. She never said a bad word about anyone, not even their father after he'd left. And her mother had such a calm, clever countenance that Felicity had for so long overlooked for jokes about round Midwestern women who kept chickens and cats and dogs. Why? Because Felicity was a complete jerk, obviously. Eternally focused on the wrong things. Her family *was* wonderful.

"Yes," she told Cooper earnestly. "I am proud. I should warn you, though: my family does come with Heather's loud and enthusiastic rug rats." Felicity winced at the reminder.

"You don't like her kids?"

"Try any kids. Small, evil knee-cap assassins? No, I do not. Don't get me wrong: I'd jump in front of a train for Heather's pint-sized shriekers. Hell, I'd give them my kidney, if they needed it. But I don't have to like the happy little monsters."

"Aw, they sound like a wonderful handful. That's okay, I'm awesome with kids; they love me. Wait'll they get a load of Auntie Cooper. How many kids does she have?"

"Oh, who can keep count? Two or three?" Felicity threw up her hands. "Maybe four?"

Cooper stared at her in astonishment.

"What?"

"Good thing you're cute. That's all I'm saying. Look, I'm calling bullshit on you this time. I know you think pretending you don't care about people or their lives is a way to show how career focused you are or whatever. But this is me. And it's your family. Stop pretending you don't give a shit and just tell me."

"Three," Felicity admitted, followed by a sheepish look. "And yes, fair point. I've been reassessing lately a lot of things I do without thinking. I should probably add this to my list." She exhaled. "You know, Elena told me that in the office I pretty much only say brutal or awkward things."

Cooper laughed. "Wow. You must be fun to work with."

Felicity gave a tiny head shake. "She's not entirely wrong, but I swear there's a reason. It's not *just* me disliking people. When I first started out in law, my firm was a bit less evolved than companies are now regarding women. They wanted to give me all the family cases. The soft stuff. I declined. They asked often about when I'd get married and were children in my future. They definitely saw women as weaker and assumed most weren't serious or in it for the long haul. Me being from the Midwest made the assumptions even worse."

"That's unfair."

"Right? So I decided I'd make them rethink all that. Any situation where a soft, warm comment would be expected from the woman in the room, I started coming up with the edgiest, hardest thing I could think of. It became a habit to stop people thinking of me as weak. I do it automatically now—reflexively saying cold things without thinking. It's almost a skill to be this awful, you know." Felicity prayed her honesty was at least... charming?

Cooper's lips twitched. "And the awkwardness?"

"That's just me being a total write-off at social skills. I got so focused on career so young that I haven't had much practice connecting with people for the sake of it. And it never seemed important because there was always someone else ready to jump in and schmooze in my place. I never really got the knack of it."

"I sort of got a clue about that when you struggled to say nice things about our clients' pets." Cooper leaned in and added conspiratorially, "I worried you were a sociopath." She laughed.

Felicity winced. The remark reminded her of Elena's face when she revealed that she didn't know whether Felicity had a heart. There had been definite fear in her eyes. It stung.

All this time she'd thought she'd been impressing her boss with her laserlike focus on business. Instead, she'd made Elena fret that she might be a cruel bully like Lecoq. Clearly Felicity had messed up without even realizing it. *How* hadn't she realized this?

The longer she was with Cooper, the more she started to see how far she'd taken things. Maybe it wasn't too late to stop being *quite* so brutal. She'd probably always be somewhat abrasive; that's just who she was. But Cooper was also right: Felicity pretending she didn't know how many nieces and nephews she had hardly announced to the world she was serious about her career. It announced she was unfeeling. No wonder Elena had been worried.

I've been an idiot.

Well, thank God Cooper saw through her BS and liked her anyway.

"All right, so it's settled," Cooper suddenly announced.

"What is?"

"We're going to meet your family, including Heather and all three of her rug rats, at the earliest possible opportunity. Oh, and you're going to meet my nana. She'll love you. Of course, she'll take one look at you and decide you need fattening up, which is seriously her favorite thing in life." Cooper patted her rounded belly. "I can attest to that."

"You want to meet my family?" Felicity hesitated. "You know, it's bold to voluntarily go on a trip to Pinckney. There's not much there."

"Didn't you say Pinckney was near Hell?"

"Yes."

"Then we're definitely going. I've never been to Hell and back." Cooper's laugh was full and booming, and her belly bobbed up and down so hard that Brittany gave a long-suffering sigh and lifted her head off it.

"Sorry, Brit, hon," Cooper said, giving the dog an affectionate pat. "Just making some life plans with my girl here. You understand."

Felicity smiled and couldn't stop. That's what they were doing, weren't they? Family meetups? *Life plans.* She'd never so much as done a meet-the-parents with Phillip. These plans augured well, Felicity thought with satisfaction.

Maybe they'd last as a couple; maybe not. Maybe Cooper would take one look at Felicity's touchy-feely, liberal-leftie family and run screaming into the night. Somehow, though, as she pictured Cooper slurping Heather's homemade ginger beer and her mother discussing the finer points of reptiles and rockets, she didn't think so.

"What has you grinning like that?" Cooper poked her playfully on the shoulder.

"Us." Felicity slipped her hand over Cooper's waist and held her tight. She actually had a life now, full and filled with promise, and it was one she was proud of. "But just a head's up, Dr. Cooper: I've formulated a new plan, thought it over in great detail, and implemented it."

"Oh?"

"I'm *never* letting you go."

"I see," Cooper replied seriously. "Good to know." She offered a wide and dazzling smile. "Well, I'm sure as hell not foolish enough to get between Felicity Simmons and her grand plans. So that's a big ole 'roger that' from me."

Felicity could not stop the smile that flooded her face. "Well, then," she said, laughing, "that's that."

Epilogue

The Australasian Legends of Publishing Ball was one of those essential work events that Felicity was expected to attend, even though it involved traveling half a world away to Sydney. It didn't help her mood that it separated her from Cooper for far too long. Although in this case, too long only meant a few hours because Cooper was back at their hotel enjoying the minibar and cable movies and waiting for her return.

Cooper had taken news of Felicity's trip to Sydney with delight, deciding it should be used as a joint vacation. She'd never been to Australia and had already informed Felicity of the list of animals she intended to visit, starting with and not confined to koalas, kangaroos, emus, platypuses... or was that platypi? She'd have to ask Cooper later.

"Are you even listening to me?" Perry Marks, *Style International*'s global art director, looked extra dashing tonight in his black tux and white shirt that contrasted with his dark skin and gleaming bald pate.

"Not really, no," Felicity admitted. "Were you saying something gossipy or informative? Or just informatively gossipy?"

"I'm wounded!" he announced in his most dramatic tone. "But right on the money. I was telling you about a new designer who's rumored to have knocked up one of the hottest models in the world... And they've decided she'll just model his outfits, expanding belly and all, as if nothing's changed."

"How"—Felicity sought the right word—"fashion-y of them. Making a splash with the ridiculous." She looked around. "Elena here yet?"

"Not that I've seen. I did get to dress them both, though, so it'll be grand entrance when they arrive."

"Them both?" Felicity frowned and looked at him. "Who are you talking about? Don't tell me Elena's dating someone new. Is there another gentleman we're all supposed to smile at and pretend he isn't beneath her in so many ways?"

They headed into a corridor within the heritage-listed hotel.

"For a smart woman," Perry said, "you can be exceptionally dense at times."

"What on earth do you mean? Are you saying I know this man she's with?"

"I'm saying that even with the clues rammed close together, you can't seem to see the bigger picture. Shall I recount for you? Elena suddenly taking a massive interest in the weather and travel hot spots around Vietnam at the exact time Maddie Grey was there."

"Maddie? That old chestnut? You can't be serious. I know that woman has been lucky at everything lately, what with all those career scoops. She's probably got the longest winning streak on record," Felicity said, still a bit annoyed that one woman could live such a charmed life. "But I can assure you she's not *getting lucky* with Elena. Besides, Elena's straight as an arrow."

"She's about as straight as I pretended to be at school. You're like one of those historians who dig up passionate love letters between a same-sex couple and argue that was just the florid language of the day between two *very good friends*."

"Oh please. Elena's never dated any women! You might think you know her because you're her best friend. But I'm the one who actually knows her best. I organized her work diaries. I knew her schedules. And I organized her secret little getaways with her husband. You have no proof except a sudden interest in her friend's well-being when off the beaten track in Vietnam."

"The photo on her desk," Perry continued, ticking off his fingers as though Felicity had never spoken. "The fact that, while you were doing your hand-over month with Elena, the whole time—all of it—Maddie was staying with her."

She was? "Well, friends do that." Not that Felicity had a deep well of understanding on the topic.

"A month? I bet you couldn't spend a week with a friend before wanting her gone."

True. Except Cooper, but that was different. Felicity couldn't get enough of her girlfriend these days, and it had been a *whole* lot longer than a month. Not to mention her mother had, as predicted, loved her; her sister kept making wedding jokes; and Felicity's nieces and nephews had tried to sneak into the car to come home with them when they were leaving.

And then there'd been Nana Cooper. Felicity adored Cooper's grandmother. The woman kept exclaiming that Felicity was a refined young woman Cooper could learn a lot from. Frankly, it was hilarious and surprising that Cooper hadn't sprained her eyeballs from rolling them so hard. So really— Wait. What were they discussing?

"You're doing it again," Perry said. "Drifting off into the haze of new love. Is it a he or a she this time? Don't think I didn't work out that you and Larissa Andino had a fling. She wasn't exactly subtle the way she was sniffing around you at that LA white ball."

Felicity stared. How on earth had he noticed that? Even Felicity hadn't noticed that!

"Never mind. Surprise me later with your mystery paramour," Perry barreled on. "In the meantime, look: love's absolutely everywhere."

She followed his gaze.

Elena was at the end of the corridor, head bent, talking to Maddie softly. The media mogul suddenly stepped right inside Maddie's personal space and reached for her hand, intertwining their fingers.

Oh. My. God.

Maddie turned at Felicity and Perry's approach, a smile washing across her face. "Hey! How are…" she began before fading out at Felicity's doubtlessly startled expression.

Perry gave them a smug snort and a friendly wave.

Speechless, Felicity couldn't tear her eyes away from those interlocked fingers, even after Perry nudged her in the ribs.

Elena and Maddie?

After a few murmured words and a tiny smile, Elena tugged Maddie into her arms and kissed her thoroughly. *Extremely* thoroughly.

So endeth any merry delusion they were just good friends.

Perry clasped his hands to his chest and looked about to weep with delight.

Felicity slumped against a nearby pillar. "Oh! Of bloody *course*! Longest winning streak ever!"

Cooper would be impossible after this. Perry, too. She pushed that out of her mind and regarded the couple with fresh eyes.

So much love. That's definitely what it was. It was clear to anyone looking that Elena only had eyes for one person in the universe—and it was mutual.

"Come on," Felicity said to Perry. "Let's go get some booze into me so I can review how blind I've been under the forgiving haze of alcohol."

"Well, I wouldn't say no to that." Perry chuckled and left with her.

***

By the end of the evening, Felicity was tired. She'd done some imbibing with Perry, sat through a sweet, self-deprecating speech from Maddie as the youngest winner of the Coleman Prize for Journalism that had earned enthusiastic applause, and decided it was now or never. Time to hunt down her boss.

She found Elena leaning into Maddie, whispering in her ear in a quiet corner, a small smile playing around her lips. It could have been about any topic, but now that Felicity knew the truth, it looked that much more intimate.

Approaching loudly—lest she interrupted anything that would traumatize her—she caught Elena's eye first.

"You could have told me." Felicity said, folding her arms.

"What, and ruin the moment you figured it out? Oh, I'd never deprive you," Elena said, eyes bright with amusement.

"And you!" Felicity turned on Maddie. "Well, of course you won the queen."

Maddie's cheeks reddened, but she didn't deny it. "Yeah. I did."

"Hmm." Felicity eyed them both and then relented. Maybe falling for Cooper had melted her defenses because she found herself saying seriously, "I'm really very happy for you both. I mean it."

Maddie grinned and flung herself into a hug, which Felicity sighed and endured while Elena leaned back and just laughed.

Once they parted, Felicity gave Elena an aggrieved look. "All right, I'm going to borrow your—" She stopped and wondered what the right word was for their relationship. *Girlfriend? Lover?* She almost shuddered at the mental images. "—*Australian* for a few minutes."

Maddie chuckled. "Sure."

Elena gave a soft huff. "I'm quite certain you could come up with a better term than that."

"Ex-assistant then?" Felicity asked mischievously. Then she paused and eyeballed Elena worriedly. "Oh God, please tell me you two weren't going at it when you were Maddie's boss? Were you defiling the desk whenever my back was turned?"

"Don't be absurd, Felicity. Besides, desks are for work only." Elena straightened. "I'll leave you two to catch up. I have to talk to Perry about the fall lineups. Make sure he doesn't get his head turned by fuchsia again. Once was enough." She drifted away.

"So…" Felicity eyed Maddie. "Vietnam, then? You two were on then? That's why she was tracking you all over the country, emailing and calling every time I turned around?"

Maddie's eyes became distant at some fond memory. "Yep. But it started a bit before that, around Australian Fashion Week, back when I started freelancing."

"How on earth did I miss that?"

"I have no idea. Elena's changed so much that I think it should be obvious to everyone. I mean, she's still cool and controlled, of course. But she's so much lighter."

She was. Felicity nodded slowly. "Well. Yes. I'm glad she is. After the horrors that evil ex Richard put her through, she deserves to be happy."

"So do you," Maddie said kindly. She leaned in and added in a low voice, "Elena tells me you've fallen for a veterinarian. She didn't say who, but I'm guessing since you met some vets at Living Ruff, that narrows it down a whole lot. And if it had been studly flirt-boy Gabe Mendoza, she'd have just told me. Which means"—she grinned—"you and Cooper, huh?"

Felicity's cheeks burned red hot almost instantly, and she rued the day she'd inherited such pale skin. She briefly considered denying it, then couldn't bring herself to. Finally, she just huffed and said, "Yes."

"Oh, mate, I'm so, *so* pleased for you." Maddie flung herself into another hug, this one even more affectionate than the last. "She's funny and friendly. I liked her a lot. She's bloody terrific. You snagged a good one."

With a weary sigh of defeat, Felicity went along with the whole body-mashing thing and hugged her back. They broke apart. "She is. And you should talk."

Maddie chuckled. "I know. Elena's a goddess, and I'm the luckiest woman alive. Well, this calls for shots! Let's get smashed like a bobtail lizard on the M1."

"Ew. Does Elena know you think roadkill's hilarious?" Felicity arched an amused eyebrow.

"Oh, she knows. She likes me anyway." Maddie's happiness was addictive. She linked her arm through Felicity's and hauled her toward the bar. "Isn't that the best thing about being in love? When our partners know all our worst shit and super weird baggage but think it's endearing?" She laughed.

"That is a definite bonus," Felicity agreed, "especially when one has as much weird baggage as me." She muttered the last part half to herself, then waved the bartender over and ordered them both drinks.

"You know, you're not that weird, Felicity," Maddie said after the man had left. "Actually, I always thought you were hilarious. So full of bullshit and fake dramatics. You were the funniest part about working at *Hudson Metro News*. I think you're an acquired taste. And good on Cooper for seeing that."

Warmth filled Felicity at the words. Okay, *fine*, she really did like Maddie Grey. Felicity drew in a breath and admitted something that was doubtlessly fueled by a considerable amount of alcohol. "If Elena had to fall in love with anyone, I'm glad it was you. She's brilliant, and you're kind."

She hoped Maddie wouldn't be offended by that distinction, but Elena was brilliant in a way few people were. And Maddie was kind in a way few people were as well. Women with icy fronts needed kind partners, Felicity had recently concluded. That's all there was to it.

Maddie shot her a surprised look, then elbowed her. "Heh. I knew you liked me. And before you deny it, it's mutual. Not that surprising, though, since I'm fond of all my friends."

The bartender returned with their drinks and retreated.

Felicity was still focused on one important word. *Friends?*

"Well." Felicity couldn't think of anything else to say. She smiled. "Okay, then."

Maddie laughed and raised a glass, clinking it against Felicity's. "To the goddesses who chose to love us…for some mystifying reason."

Felicity's smile was wide. "To the goddesses who chose us."

Cooper was enjoying the delights of the penthouse suite's impressive jacuzzi when Felicity returned.

The woman looked utterly delicious. Naked, slippery, smooth, muscled, and curvy all at once. Cooper's eyes were sparkling and beautiful.

Wow. I love her.

Felicity's tension fell away, and she slumped against the wall. "I'd have rushed here sooner if I'd known this brazen scene awaited."

Cooper merely leaned back farther, pushing her bare breasts above the water's surface.

"Vixen." Felicity kicked off her heels and slowly peeled off her hose, realizing she had her lover's rapt attention.

Although that was good for her ego, it wasn't a striptease; Felicity was dead tired. All these meet-and-greet networking things were exhausting. Not to mention Elena's amusement every time she met Felicity's eye. That had been a bit much.

"If you take any longer," Cooper called out, "the water will be cold."

"Sorry," Felicity said, shaking herself. "I was just thinking about tonight. Certain things came to light." She shed her dress and then hung it in the closet. "I'm still processing. And I'd have been back sooner, but Amir's driving is just so…*ugh*…sedate. He's always so careful, plodding all through Sydney's back streets. I miss my own driver back home. He'd have lapped Amir."

"It was nice of you to hire Mitch. I know how much he loves driving flashy cars. He's in heaven."

"Niceness had nothing to do with it," Felicity said. "Mitch knows New York like the back of his hand, every shortcut, and understands when I say 'step on it.' I mean it. It's like being in a turbocharged rocket."

"Seriously?"

Felicity grinned, then pulled off her bra and panties and headed for the tub. She slipped herself between Cooper's powerful thighs and pressed her back against those tempting, pillowy breasts. She sighed. This felt like home.

"You're such a softie," Cooper murmured in her ear. "And I'm going to have words with Mitch about keeping you alive."

"He's not *that* bad. And you should talk, the speed you drive," Felicity murmured, closing her eyes. "Anyway, don't you think he looks sharp in that uniform? He's so proud of it."

"He is. You pretend you're not being kind, but I heard from Mrs. Brooks about your other new hire. A certain receptionist?"

"Ah."

"I know Bartell Corp said it would pay the new receptionist's wages as part of its charitable contributions to Living Ruff, but it was wrong not to consult Mrs. B first on who you chose. She was ready to give you one of her old-fashioned paint-peeling dressing-downs before I explained why you did it."

"My hire has excellent credentials. In fact, she's overqualified."

"Felicity," Cooper said with a tut, "Kristie is a prescription-pill abuser who has been homeless for three years and doesn't play well with others. Her insistence she has to have her dog with her at all times is the only thing Mrs. B approves of because Mrs. B completely adores Ruby. And Ruby adores her as well. But we both know Kristie was not the first choice or even the hundredth choice for that position."

"I know that. But her job has conditions. Staying clean. Attending her support group."

"Why did you do it, though?"

"What happened to Kristie could happen to anyone. I couldn't forget her. She could have been me. Hell, she already *sounds* like me."

"Oh, I've noticed. We all have. When you call Living Ruff now, Kristie answers with exactly your brand of disdainful, bored tone. It's a miracle we still get any donations after they've been through her."

Felicity couldn't contain her laugh. "I know, I know. Sorry. Okay, I'll talk to Mrs. Brooks and apologize for meddling in her domain. I have plans for Kristie in one of our marketing divisions that desperately needs an injection of originality. But first she has to feel comfortable in a workplace again. I talked to her about it, and starting small is the key. Don't worry. I'll explain to your boss that it's only temporary."

"Mrs. B will be most relieved to hear that," Cooper said. "She was going to call you anyway and tell you our good news. Daniel's our first successful candidate for the vet-tech course."

"That skinny scared kid with the weed dog?" Felicity's eyebrows shot up.

"It's not a weed dog!" Cooper sputtered and splashed her. "But yes. Daniel passed all our initial assessments, got high marks on the academic side, and we're moving him to the next stage. He's very excited. Mrs. B's momma-bear instincts are in overdrive too. She's talking about letting him stay with her for a little bit till he finds his own place."

"Well, good." Felicity smiled. "And it's a great scheme. I hope it pans out for him."

"Me, too." Cooper's arms drifted around her, sending tingles through Felicity's body. "By the way, you came in tonight talking about certain things coming to light and then got side-tracked. What things?"

"Ah. That." Felicity opened her eyes. "Turns out Elena is in love with Maddie after all. I saw them kissing."

"Oh, the shock," Cooper drawled. "However will I cope? Fuck, Felicity, her *photo* was on her *desk*. You said they watched movies together! She was with Elena every time you turned around. She was helping Elena pack to move to Maddie's hometown!"

"Yes, well, it turns out I missed it all. Or rather I'd based my conclusions on out-of-date research." Felicity closed her eyes briefly again and sighed. "There was a time I'd have been so jealous. A long time ago, I hasten to add."

"I know." Cooper began lathering up Felicity's arms with soapy bubbles. "It was pretty obvious, your crush."

"Really?"

"Mm. The admiring way you talked about your boss."

"Do you think Elena knew?" Felicity shot her a worried look.

"Yes." Cooper's voice contained amusement. "And that's why I never worried. If she'd wanted you, my love, she'd have plucked you from under her nose years ago and had her fun." She teased Felicity's arm. "The fact that she didn't meant she wasn't interested. Probably because her type runs to sweet, laid-back reporter-type Australians, not kick-ass, powerful women in executive suits. Fortunately, my type *is* kick-ass, powerful women in executive suits."

"Good to know," Felicity said languidly, "although I appear to be out of my executive suit right now. Would you like me to get out and put it on?" She pretended to rise.

Cooper's powerful arm tightened around her. God, Felicity loved feeling how strong she was. Cooper's arm relaxed. "Don't go getting any crazy ideas. I love you right where you are." She leaned in and nuzzled Felicity's ear. "Matter of fact, I love you."

Warmth filled Felicity's chest. "It's so weird."

"God, don't call my first ever declaration of love weird," Cooper groaned.

Felicity playfully slapped her arm. "It's so weird because when I came in tonight and saw you looking gorgeous and pleased with yourself, I thought, 'I love her.' I hadn't even gotten one heel off, and that was all I could think. You're mighty alluring."

"Ah. Well, that's good to know. To think you worried we'd have nothing in common. And there's the fact we both love each other." The smile in her voice was clear.

"Actually, it was *you* who worried that. Don't forget we both love Brittany, too."

"Who has probably forgotten us, given Mrs. B's looking after her. She spoils my girl so."

Felicity snuggled back deeper against Cooper's wet, bare skin. "Know what other girl needs spoiling? I'll give you a hint. She loves you more than legal loopholes, winning deals, and Bartell Corp." She turned in the tub to face Cooper, careful to avoid a mini tsunami.

"Any more hints?" Cooper asked, her voice low and husky.

"Just one." Felicity leaned in and kissed her, savoring the slippery, wet sensation.

Cooper grinned. "Hey, I think I know." She kissed her back, lingering and affectionate. "It's my uptown girl."

"Hmm," Felicity murmured into her skin. "Uptown girl? Yes and no." She dropped briefly into her native accent. "I confess there's also a lot more Midwest girl in me than I let on."

Cooper's eyebrows lifted in surprise at the admission.

"But as to being yours?" Felicity met her lover's eyes and gave her a fond look. "Oh yes. Most definitely. Yours." She smiled, her fingers tracing Cooper's strong jaw. "You know, I believe I may have made a mistake earlier this evening."

"You did?"

"Mm." Felicity locked eyes with the most beautiful woman she'd ever known. Someone kind. Someone she loved and who loved her back. "It's so obvious, now that I think about it. I think maybe *I'm* the lucky one. And right now?" She leaned in and whispered sincerely into her lover's ear as her fingers slid down to fondle a delicious breast: "Longest. Winning streak. Ever."

Other Books from Ylva Publishing

www.ylva-publishing.com

The Brutal Truth
Lee Winter

ISBN: 978-3-95533-898-5
Length: 339 pages (108,000 words)

Aussie crime reporter Maddie Grey is out of her depth in New York and secretly drawn to her twice-married, powerful media mogul boss, Elena Bartell, who eats failing newspapers for breakfast. As work takes them to Australia, Maddie is goaded into a brief bet—that they will say only the truth to each other. It backfires catastrophically.

A lesbian romance about the lies we tell ourselves.

A Roll in the Hay
Lola Keeley

ISBN: 978-3-96324-355-4
Length: 185 pages (66,000 words)

Veterinarian Tess has quit the city and her cheating girlfriend for a new life in a Scottish village. On day one, she has a run-in with stuck-up Lady Karlson who tries to boss Tess around as if she owns the whole town… which she sort of does. But could there be something more to the constant, rising tension between the warring pair?

An enemies-to-lovers lesbian romance about making your own path.

Not the Marrying Kind
Jae

ISBN: 978-3-96324-194-9
Length: 314 pages (113,000 words)

Small-town florist Ashley loves creating wedding bouquets. Her own love life is far from blossoming since she's stuck in the closet.

Sasha isn't faring much better. Her bakery keeps her too busy for romance anyway.

When the town's first lesbian wedding forces them to work together, Sasha is soon tempting more than just Ash's sweet tooth.

What else is on the menu in this delicious lesbian romance?

Epiphany
Paulette Callen

ISBN: 978-3-95533-364-5
Length: 148 pages (32,000 words)

Animals, wild and domestic, and the people who love them enliven Callen's writings. Ranging in style and tone from mystical to personal, from funny vignettes to unsentimental explorations of why we together form the fabric of life, each selection provides a deeper sense of our interconnectedness in this fragile Earth tapestry. We needn't look to the stars to know we are not alone in the cosmos.

About Lee Winter

Lee Winter is an award-winning veteran newspaper journalist who has lived in almost every Australian state, covering courts, crime, news, features, and humour writing. Now a full-time author and part-time editor, Lee is also a 2015 and 2016 Lambda Literary Award finalist and has won several Golden Crown Literary Awards. She lives in Western Australia with her long-time girlfriend, where she spends much time ruminating on her garden, US politics, and shiny, new gadgets.

CONNECT WITH LEE WINTER
Website: www.leewinterauthor.com

The Awkward Truth
© 2021 by Lee Winter

ISBN: 978-3-96324-583-1

Available in e-book and paperback formats.

Published by Ylva Publishing, legal entity of Ylva Verlag, e.Kfr.

Ylva Verlag, e.Kfr.
Owner: Astrid Ohletz
Am Kirschgarten 2
65830 Kriftel
Germany

www.ylva-publishing.com

First edition: 2021

No part of this book may be reproduced, scanned, or distributed in any printed or electronic form without permission. Please do not participate in or encourage piracy of copyrighted materials in violation of the author's rights. Thank you for respecting the hard work of this author.

This is a work of fiction. Names, characters, places, and incidents either are a product of the author's imagination or are used fictitiously, and any resemblance to locales, events, business establishments, or actual persons—living or dead—is entirely coincidental.

Credits
Edited by Alissa McGowan and Julie Klein
Cover Design and Print Layout by Streetlight Graphics